Lives of Courage

Canadä

*The Publishers acknowledge the financial assistance of the
Government of Canada through the Book Publishing Industry Development
Program (BPIDP) for our publishing activities.*

National Library of Canada Cataloguing in Publication Data

Smallwood, Bill, 1932-
Lives of courage, 1912-1932 / Bill Smallwood.

(Abuse of power: Canadian historical adventure series ; 7)
ISBN 978-0-88887-360-6

1. Atlantic Provinces--History--20th century--Fiction.
I. Title. II. Series: Smallwood, Bill, 1932- . Abuse of power:
Canadian historical adventure series ; 7

PS8587.M354L59 2008   C813'.6   C2008-903349-3

Cover art by Eugene Kral.
Cover design by Bull's Eye Design, Ottawa
Printed and bound in Canada on acid free paper.

Lives of Courage
1912-1932

Bill Smallwood

Borealis Press
Ottawa, Canada
2008

---※---

Special thanks to classmates of mine from the
Royal Military College of Canada
for their interest and help

3108 Arthur Beemer
3164 Paul Ruck

Apology to a dear friend who asked that his name
(Doctor Timothy Parker)
not be mentioned on this dedication page.
Go to www.abuseofpower.ca
and www.billsmallwood.ca
to see some of Tim's work.

---※---

ENJOY CANADIAN HISTORY
by reading other books written by Bill Smallwood

ISBN 0-88887-198-8   ***The Acadians*** (1749 – 1757)

You are witness to a truly great love story. There is action: Indian raids and massacres, a Royal Navy amphibious assault against a hostile shore, and sea battles. Don't miss it!

The Acadians (narrated by the author) is available on CD and MP3

ISBN 0-88887217-8   ***The Colonials and the Acadians***
                                                (1757 – 1761)

The military campaigns against Louisbourg and Quebec are woven into the family stories with great attention to the actual events.

ISBN 0-88887290-9   ***Crooked Paths*** (1755 – 1862)

A New England girl and a Nova Scotia boy are lost to their families. They find each other through a tale of bloody battles, shipwrecks and courtroom dramas.

ISBN 0-88887-281-X   ***The Planters*** (1761 – 1921)

William Brewster leads the Mayflower Pilgrims to North America (1620). Subsequent generations of Brewsters continue to seek their vision of religious freedom in Nova Scotia.

ISBN 0-88887-328-X   ***Expulsion and Survival***
                                                (1758 – 1902)

Following the capture of Fortress Louisbourg, the British order the expulsion of Acadians from what was to become known as Prince Edward Island. Most of the Acadians were gathered up and expelled; some attempted to stay on the island where survival would be difficult.

Lives of Courage

ISBN 0-88887-338-5   *Rebels, Royalists and Railroaders*
(1841 – 1910)

For generations the family had dedicated itself to serving King and Country; that faith had been shattered by the family member who raised a regiment to fight the English King during the American Revolution. Then the family found a new cause: Canada's Intercolonial Railroad.

The Series: each book is a complete story unto itself and was written to be read independently of all the other books but, when taken together, they make a series.

CONTENTS

Chapter One
The Russian

November 1912
Halifax, Nova Scotia

The young man paused in front of Carleton House, intrigued by the heavy brass doorknocker. He had extended his hand to touch it when a uniformed hotel employee opened the door from the inside.

"Good afternoon, sir. I do hope you have a reservation."

The young man removed his gloves and opened his cloak as he passed through the open door into the foyer.

When the gentleman didn't respond, the doorman continued, "During the month of November, the Halifax Merchants Association comes here every Monday for dinner."

Joe Smallwood looked around for someone to take his hat and cane. "Yes, good afternoon." He began to shrug himself out of his cloak.

A bellman appeared from nowhere to give assistance, but the doorman stopped him with a raised hand while continuing to address the stranger.

"Sir, we are fairly well booked and I can save you the trouble of disrobing if . . ."

"I am with the H.H. Marshall party." Joe waited for the doorman to lower his hand before giving his cane and hat to the bellman. "I'm Joe Smallwood, part owner of Mister Marshall's southend store."

"Excuse me, Mister Smallwood. I'll be sure to recognize you on your next visit." With a very different face he spoke severely to the bellman. "Mister Smallwood is a member of the H.H. Marshall table." With the new client now properly inducted and categorized, the doorman turned his attention to other clients who were arriving. "Ah! Messieurs Schwartz! Am I to expect your father? No? Your regular table awaits you,

1

gentlemen. Of course our manager, Mister Pass, will see to your requirements right away."

Meanwhile, Joe's cloak, cane, hat, and gloves had been taken and he was being nicely fussed over as he was seated at an empty table set for six. He watched as the other two gentlemen entered the room and were ushered by the hotel manager to a smaller table in front of a huge fireplace. Joe knew them by sight; the very German-looking one was William, the eldest son of W.H. Schwartz and Sons—tea, coffee, and spices—who selected the chair with the best view of the room and closest to the fire. The chair creaked as he pushed it back enough from the table so he could stretch his feet out before the fire. "Ah! Have them bring coffee, Mister Pass!"

"Of course, Mister Schwartz," the hotel manager responded cheerily as he beckoned for a waiter.

The slight, handsome Fredrich Schwartz wagged his finger that he didn't want coffee. "Tea, if you please," he said to the approaching waiter.

"As you wish, Mister Schwartz." The manager moved toward the back of the room, adjusting a knife, straightening a napkin, his head half-turned in the direction of the Schwartz brothers keeping an eye out in case they should have any unspoken need. He noticed when the stranger at the H.H. Marshall table rose to welcome Mister Marshall. Seeing the older gentleman's broad smile, Mister Pass correctly assumed that it was proper for the young man to be at that particular table. As he left the dining room, Mister Pass also noted that the greeting was effusive.

"Joe! Good to see you, my boy! How was your trip?"

"Bagged a couple."

Mister Pass continued on toward the pantry wondering what would have been "bagged." *Probably some business reference . . . these young people torture the English language,* he thought, *with their smart talk. Acquired several new clients, perhaps?* On his way back with two servers—one for the coffee and the second with the tea—he overheard more and was a bit startled.

"Cut 'em off at the knees and packed 'em in ice."[1]

Oh dear, the intrigued Mister Pass thought, *I shall never know what that is all about . . . but at least Mister Marshall doesn't seem perturbed.* He continued supervising the delivery of the drinks for the Schwartz brothers, who were discussing membership in the Waegwoltic, the newly created country club for the town's elite. Mister Pass was aware that membership in the Waegwoltic, a hot topic in the town, was a prize to be sought after. Mister William had been making the point that even a senior army officer of the Halifax Garrison should come from a socially prominent family to be considered for membership and when he paused—perhaps to take a breath— Mister Pass looked to the other Schwartz brother expectantly for a comment. Mister Fredrich, with his blue eyes seeming to gaze far beyond the walls, was slow to respond. Just as Mister Pass was considering moving off to be closer to the Marshall table, Fredrich said, "You forgot to mention non-Catholic and non-Semitic, brother."

Ah, ha! The manager thought, *this might be interesting.* He lingered, fussing with the positioning of an empty chair at the next table.

"They can join their own clubs. The Wag belongs to people with the proper social credentials, Freddie."

There was no comment from the brother.

William persisted, prodding Fredrich for a response. "I know you don't like it, Freddie, but that's a fact of Halifax life."[2]

"Mister Pass!" H.H. Marshall beckoned.

The manager sighed as he promptly positioned himself next to Mister Marshall and bowed his head to Marshall's level so that any message could be spoken without being broadcast to the room. "Yes, Mister Marshall?"

"Do you have anyone on your staff who can speak Russian?"

"I don't know, sir. Everyone speaks English to me . . . although there are several who are definitely not native sons." *Would this have something to do with the "cutting off at the knees"*

*and "packing them in ice"? Shipping something to Russia? You
never knew with H.H* . . . Mister Pass raised his head and stood
upright. "There might be a person like that in the scullery." He
paused and then added, "I could enquire, sir." He waited, hoping he would be given more information, but was disappointed.

"Thank you."

"I will get right back to you," he said as he left for the
kitchen.

Marshall turned his attention to Joe Smallwood. "Tell me
more, m'boy. Why do you need a Russian interpreter?"

"Roy Curry of the Brunswick Street Church told me he
knew of a strong, healthy man looking for work. I told him
that I could always use a hard worker."[3]

H.H. Marshall, always the direct get-to-the-point type of
man, asked, "So, where does the Russian language come in?"

"He's Russian. When I said that I could use the man,
Curry told me he would get him released from jail."

H.H. almost choked on his cigar. "We don't want a jail-
bird working for us!" In a cloud of smoke he leaned forward,
red-faced and, while jabbing his finger in the general direction
of Joe's heart, said; "You have better judgement than that, Joe!
Why commit us to the church . . . to hire a . . . a . . ."

Joe made calming motions with his hands. "There is no
commitment to the church, H.H., believe me. Curry will be
going into training to become a minister but, right now, he
does some altar-boy kinds of things around the church. He's
not a cleric."

A gleam came into the older man's eyes. "Now, that's better. That's the Joe Smallwood who is making tons of money
for us at the southend store." Marshall expertly flicked the
cigar ash into the tray. "So this choir boy knows of a hardworking foreigner . . ."

"Yes. If I guarantee his employment, the authorities
will let him out of jail. Since I want to know more about the
man . . ."

"And he speaks only Russian?"

"Yes, he only speaks Russian."

Marshall watched as several more men came through the front door and were relieved of their outer apparel. "Here are the rest of the boys." In a musing voice, Marshall said, quietly, "Why is Joe Smallwood hanging around a choir boy?"

Joe knew better than to mislead his boss. "I want to become a member of the Waegwoltic."

"*I'm* not a member of the Wag."

"I know it's hard for an outsider to . . ."

"It's impossible!"

"Well, the Currys are a well-established Halifax family. I thought if I made Roy look good in the eyes of the church, the senior Curry might recommend me to the Wag membership committee."

"Humph!"

"I've already bought the boat—the finest motor launch on the North West Arm."[4]

H.H. Marshall shook his head, saying nothing.

"As soon as I'm a member in good standing, I'll be sure to recommend you, H.H.," Joe said with a twinkle in his eyes. He looked over H.H.'s shoulder at the approaching Mister Pass. "Looks like . . ."

Mister Pass stopped at the Marshall table. He cleared his throat. "Ahem. I'm sorry but we don't have . . ."

Joe could see discomfort written large on the manager's face. Joe thought, *probably the very first time Mister Pass has ever let his most influential customer down.* "That's just fine, Mister Pass. We thank you for trying." Joe put on his widest smile as he said, "Do you know how many moose it takes to make a moose-leg table?"

"Wha . . . a moose . . . what?

"How many moose would I have to bag to make a moose-leg table?"

Ah ha! He said he had bagged a couple! Mister Pass smiled back. "A couple?"

"Mister Pass, you are a man of many parts! That's right! Only the forelegs are straight enough to use as table legs." Joe's deep brown eyes sought out the manager's. "Not one man in a hundred would know that, Mister Pass."

The Next Day
Halifax Prison

The next day those eyes were closely examining Vladik Sopotov as he told his story to the interpreter provided by the Immigration Department. Joe concluded that the prisoner didn't look much like a Russian but he certainly was a handsome little fellow . . . not much more than five foot two . . . if that . . . blond hair, blue eyes (certainly nothing like the big, burly sailors from the Russian ships), broad shoulders, well-muscled arms and chest, a flat belly, and expressive hands which he let drop as he finished speaking to the interpreter. His eyes now downcast, Vladik seemed to grow smaller—as if he were shrinking into himself—while he heard the three strangers talk about him in a language he didn't understand.

The interpreter, a Mister Garner, who had responded to the Curry family's request to assist their son, said, "I knew right away he was Russian. You can usually tell by their garb but this prisoner's clothing is in tatters." He sucked on his pipe as he continued speaking, "Unrecognizable by his clothes . . . (puff) but . . . (puff) I still was able to speak to him . . . (puff) first off . . . (puff) in his own tongue."

"Yes, you did," the Curry family heir piped up in an encouraging tone of voice. Believing that Joe Smallwood was a plain businessman with no real sense of grace, Roy Curry wanted the interpreter to get on with it—get on with it or Joe Smallwood might lose interest. "Yes, you certainly did. Tell us about him." Roy Curry was relieved to see the interpreter put the pipe aside and turn his attention to Joe Smallwood.

"Not having his garb to go by, Mister Smallwood, I picked out his language by his national features. My informed guess? He's from near Minsk because he's fair-skinned, blue eyes and small . . . like a horseman. They are Orthodox Churchmen, maybe even Greek Orthodox." Mister Garner turned his head to ask the young man something, "Yes, Eastern Church, he says. Catholic, he says." Garner shrugged. "No matter. He came to Montreal last spring because he had heard that Canada was a land of plenty."

Joe interrupted, "How could he get work if he doesn't speak the language?"

"Sent along with a bunch of other immigrants to work for a contractor in Ottawa. He did just fine, it seems, because, by freeze-up time, he had saved forty-five dollars. With winter approaching he thought it would be milder near the ocean . . . besides, he might find work all winter long loading and unloading ships here at Halifax."

"I guess that's true enough." Joe scratched his chin, "But what got him put in jail?"

The interpreter sighed and reached for his pipe. "Unlike Montreal, we've no employment agency delivering gangs of men into the hands of contractors." He looked around for something and then, not finding an ashtray, knocked his pipe out on the heel of his shoe.

Roy Curry cast a worried glance at the door. He leaned toward the interpreter and spoke in a near-whisper. "I have been a prison visitor for the last ten months and they don't put ashtrays in these rooms because the authorities don't want the prisoners to have access to matches."

"No smoking, is it?" Garner scraped the ashes and unburned tobacco around with the toe of his boot, at the end placing his foot squarely on the mess. He went on with the story. "It was a kind-hearted judge who gave him three months of hard labour in city prison so he could keep warm over the winter."

Joe shook his head from side to side in disbelief. "He got three months of hard labour and he didn't do anything wrong? What happened to his money? His forty-five dollars?"

"Stolen from his rooming house while he was out looking for work. He hasn't heard anyone speak his language since he left Montreal."

Joe rubbed his chin saying, thoughtfully, "No one to explain things . . . why he was in jail, how long he'd be there . . . ."

Roy Curry explained. "The jailors say he's been so morose that everyone believes him to be a bit cuckoo."

Joe looked at Curry. "It will be of some benefit to you at the church if I give him work?"

Curry beamed but, almost immediately, cast his eyes down. "It isn't for me, Joe. It is the Christian thing to do that we help this poor soul in distress." He folded his hands in his lap, keeping his eyes downcast.

"Yes. All right, Roy." Joe spoke to the interpreter. "Will he work for me? Tell him it'll be hard work, moving stores and loading and unloading wagons." As Garner talked to the little man, Joe could see despair and hopelessness in the man's eyes. "Tell him he will get paid for his work. I'll give him a fair wage."

Vladik Sopokov slid off his chair and fell to his knees in front of Joe. He took Joe's hands and kissed first one and then the other. The man was crying, saying the same words over and over.[5]

Startled, Joe cried out, "What the hell did you tell him, Garner?"

"I said he would be leaving the jail and going to work. When I told him you would pay him a fair wage, that's when he slid off the chair."

Joe stood and grasped the man's hands, pulling him upright, patting his shoulder. "Tell him he can work as long as he likes . . . What the hell is he saying?"

"He says you are a saint."

"Well, I'm not that."

"He says he will always work for you." Mister Garner told the little Russian to sit down; that Mister Smallwood would be along to take him to his place of work on the morrow. "He says thank you and bless you, Mister Smallwood."

The three Canadians got up to leave the interview room.

"Tell him I will be back, for sure."

"Yes, I will. And I will put him in touch with the Russian Consulate so he can resume contact with his family in Russia." Mister Garner spoke to Vladik, who immediately jumped up and shook hands with the three of them. Garner spoke in a firm voice and pointed at the chair. The Russian immediately sat down but didn't take his blue eyes off Joe's face.

Joe shook his head. "They must be worried sick about him."

"He says he has a wife and children, but you never know about foreigners." The interpreter opened the door. "They quite often tell you what you want to hear." He held the door as Joe and Ray stepped outside. "Young Mister Curry, you will tell your father that I have helped . . ."

Roy Curry nodded. "And the church is grateful for your good intentions, I'm sure."

Behind them, the Russian listened for their voices as long as he could while the guard led him away to the cells.

Endnotes

1, "Cut 'em off at the knees and packed 'em in ice." Joe Smallwood was referring to the two moose his father (Duke Smallwood) and he shot to make a moose leg table.

2. " . . . country clubs like the Waegwoltic organized in 1908 and open to both men and women of appropriate social standing and religion. The careful ordering of Halifax society into Catholic and Protestant, black and white, Semite and non-Semite to say nothing of class and gender was usually reflected in sports clubs." *Halifax: The first 250 years*, by Judith Fingard.

3. Curry: I have changed the name of the family.

4. Joe Smallwood bought a well-equipped powerboat that he placed on the North West Arm. Joe believed he would have no difficulty becoming a member of the Waegwoltic and would require a proper boat.

5. Vladik Sopokov: this name is fiction. The incident of putting an immigrant in jail "for his own good" is true according to newspaper accounts of the time. Joe Smallwood did hire a Russian but I do not know where he found him.

Chapter Two
Lady Betty

March 1914
Halifax
South End

It had snowed, rained, and then snowed again making it very difficult to clean off the sidewalk and steps in front of Joe's store—not unusual for the time of year but always unpleasant. The morning air was sharp, the sky dark and gloomy. White puffs of Vladik's breath hung in the still air as he struggled with the ice and snow. He had taken his heavy lumberman's jacket off and had draped it over the upright shovel handle as he used a pickaxe on the stubborn parts.

"Son of a dog!" was what Joe heard as he came up behind the little man who was sending chips of ice flying in all directions.

"Son of a bitch, Vladik," Joe said with a smile when the perspiring Russian stopped work to let his employer go by. "Son of a dog, nyet. Son of a bitch, da."

"Son of a . . ."

"Bitch."

"Beech."

"Close enough, Vladik."

"Priest in . . ." Vladik pointed at the store. "I . . ." he motioned the turning of a key and opening the door.

"You let Mister Curry into the shop."

"Da. Mister Curry in shop."

"And he isn't a priest yet, Vladik. He's going to school to learn . . ." When Joe saw the quizzical look on Vladik's face he smiled. "Not priest yet. Maybe soon." Joe waved his arm around. "Come in when you are finished. Get some of that new coffee I'm trying out. At Schwartz's they said that after a second cup I'd be able to outrun a locomotive." He went into

11

the shop. "I'm looking forward to that," he said as the door closed.

Vladik smiled. He understood "coffee." He was soon finished and inside the store, where Roy and Joe were having a serious discussion. Vladik could see that his favourite Canadian wasn't very happy. He helped himself to a coffee.

"You told me . . ."

Roy Curry interrupted. "Yes, I know, Joe. I told you that my father would approach the membership committee. I didn't guarantee you a membership card." Seeing the dark shadows behind Joe's eyes, Curry hurried on. "What you did was a fine, Christian act that has its own rewards." There was still no response from the stern-faced Joe Smallwood. "God knows that you were the only man in this city to succour this poor soul." Curry had pointed at Vladik, who immediately put his coffee down and stood almost at attention.

"Yessir," the little man said.

Roy Curry dismissed the Russian with a wave of his hand.

In a muted voice, Joe said, "This isn't the time to discuss him. He understands a lot of English now."

"You brought the subject up, Joe."

"I brought up the Waegwoltic, Roy." He put his coffee cup down. Joe had made up his mind about something. He gave the other two men a broad smile. "We did the right thing, Roy. You improved your chances for a clerical collar," he paused while he stepped over to where Vladik was standing and, putting his arm around the little man, gave him a scrunch—which was as affectionate as Joe Smallwood could be with another man. "Yes, you got your chance to be a cleric and I got a new friend." He turned Vladik around and pointed him toward the door. "The usual breakfast, Vladik."

Vladik went over to the till, punched up "no sale," and removed twenty cents. "Breakfast for Mister Smallwood: milk and toast. Breakfast for Vladik: liver, bacon, fried potatoes and coffee." He grinned, bobbed his head at the soon-to-be priest, and went out the door, carefully closing it behind him so that the shop wouldn't lose much heat.

Both men could hear him whistling as he went up the hill.

"And I got to thank you for that, Roy." Joe extended his hand. Roy took it. They gave one shake and then Joe withdrew his hand.

"I didn't think, Roy . . . would you like some breakfast? I can catch him up."

"No, thank you, Joe. I have to go to the manse this morning and help the . . ."

"Well then, thanks for dropping by with the news. I know you did the best you could for me."

"Yes. Well . . . ." Curry pulled his black overcoat close to his chin and stepped out into the cold. He carefully closed the door. He adjusted his black felt hat against the brisk sea breeze that had sprung up. Pulling on his black leather gloves, he marched up the street, unconsciously whistling "Onward Christian Soldiers."

June 6, 1914
Halifax

When he heard the tinkle of the little brass bell over the front door, Joe called out from the back storeroom, "Is that you, Vladik?"

"Yes, Mister Smallwood."

Joe wiped his hands on his apron. Then he dug into the deep front pocket searching for a cigarette. "*The Herald* is on the counter. Pick a headline from the front page and start reading." Joe found the cigarette package but it was empty. He shoved it back and went to the front of the shop to get some more.

"Lady Be . . . Bet . . . Betty missing." There was a pause as Vladik looked up as Joe entered the shop. He continued, "Was Lady Betty fr . . . forced . . ." He stopped with his finger pointed at a word.

"Just a sec, Vladik." Joe looked over his assistant's shoulder. "Forced victim . . . go on, Vladik." Joe ducked down and checked but there were no cartons of Black Cat under the counter. He would have to get one from the display in the front window.

"Was Lady Betty forced victim of a . . ."

Joe smiled when he thought of the last time that Vladik had heard the word "elopement"; *Roy Curry's sister had taken off with one of the telegraphers from the dockyard. Now, <u>that</u> was a big fuss. I wonder who this Lady Betty is?* "Vladik, you saw that word when Miss Curry . . ."

"Yes-s-s." Vladik read the entire headline. "Was Lady Betty forced victim of an elopement."

Joe reached around the Black Cat display, reading the advertising text as he stretched to snag a carton. "In every packet of Black Cat cigarettes you will find one profit-sharing coupon and a booklet describing our splendid gifts and how to get them." Joe smiled; *that ad campaign was sure selling a lot of cigarettes.* He looked up at the large image of a handsome cat positioned just above the text. *Too bad cats aren't really that nice.* He slit the seal with his thumb, retrieving the coupon. *Forty of these coupons will entitle me to three Durham, duplex, hollow ground and double-edged blades for my razor.* He remembered the blurb from the top of the Durham box: *you can safely shave with your eyes shut or in the dark.* Joe smirked at the thought. *Not likely.* He stood up and turned around in response to the tinkle of the doorbell.

"Good morning, Joe, Vladik." Standing in the door was the almost-reverend Roy Curry. Although Mister Curry had started his clerical training and there were good reports across the town as to how he was getting along, he wasn't yet a cleric. Joe would probably always think of him as "almost reverend."

Vladik put the newspaper back in the stack and, with a tip of his head in acknowledgement of the presence of the other man, picked up an apron from the back counter. "I go work," he said. In a moment he was gone, the door to the back storeroom closed, the two men alone in the shop.

"I hope you have been well, Joe."

"Just fine, Roy. Happy for your sister."

Roy Curry blushed. "They have gone to Montreal to visit an aunt."

Gone to Montreal to have the baby is more likely. "When are they coming back?"

"Mama didn't say."

"Weeks or months," Joe maliciously persisted.

Roy Curry opened his mouth several times. "Nice of you to ask," he finally said. "You heard about Lady Betty?"

"Yes, I saw the headlines this morning. Who is . . .?"

"The owner? Eric Oland is her owner."

Her owner? Joe reached for the *Herald*. He quickly scanned the article to find out who Lady Betty was. He smiled, amused at the contents. "They seem to be poking fun at Mister Oland."

"Yes. Totally unnecessary. That pipsqueak of a reporter is holding the Waegwoltic up to ridicule."

Joe chuckled as he read further. "It says here,

> ' . . . by strange coincidence, five years ago a youngster of criminal tendencies, made off with a pleasure boat on the North West Arm. He was pursued and apprehended by the police. After serving a term in the re-formatory, he was given his liberty. A short while ago, the lad was con- victed of theft. Last Saturday night, the lad became tired of hotel life at Rockhead City Prison and made a bold bid to obtain his freedom. He was successful and made an almost miraculous escape from durance vile. The next morning the Lady Betty was gone. Was she led astray by her youthful suitor? Could . . .' "

"Oh, I say! That's enough of that drivel! A proper gentleman like Eric Oland moors his boat at the Waegwoltic and a juvenile escapes jail. The two situations are connected only in the twisted mind of that writer. I bet if Father checked the rejected applica- tions for Waegwoltic membership, he would find that very same *Herald* reporter . . . perhaps even his editor."[1]

"I can imagine that."

If Roy was listening he wasn't hearing. "On second thought, it couldn't be the editor because his father-in-law is a member."

Joe looked up from the paper. "*Lady Betty* is a boat?"

"Yes. She's a very fine yacht belonging to the Oland family." Pointing at *The Herald*, Roy shook his pouty little jowls as he pronounced, "We must find the *Lady Betty*, or evidence of her destruction, as soon as possible to shut up this despicable . . ."

It dawned on Joe. "You want to use my cutter."

"Yes, Joe. You have the biggest motor launch on the Arm with the best endurance. Using your boat, we can make a sweep of the entire area in one day and find her before this . . ." Roy picked up *The Herald* and shook it, " . . .goes any further."

"I don't even know Mister Oland."

"Ah, but Eric knows your boat. You moor it just north of the Waegwoltic moorings."

"But not *at* the Waegwoltic," Joe said, meaningfully.

"And Eric knows me and I told him you were a friend of mine." Roy Curry put on an innocent look that his mother must have thought was particularly cute on her little boy. "I thought you might help me in this, Joe."

Joe sighed. He was suffering a bad case of sour grapes about not getting a Wag membership. *And, H.H. and the boys tease me about it. Perhaps . . .* "Who will be on the search party?"

"Eric, of course, and Will Schwartz . . . probably the Cumberlands, father and son. Not a large party. They will bring the lunch baskets."

"Fine. When do you propose going out?"

"There was an early gathering at the Wag this morning and I told them that you would be ready in two hours." Roy pulled on the gold chain draped across his vest, revealing a rich-looking gold watch. He snapped it open and examined it while he said, "I suppose that means you should be at the club in forty minutes if you don't mean to keep the gentlemen waiting."

"Oh, I won't keep the gentlemen waiting, Roy," Joe said with a growing sense that he was being drawn into a situation he would soon regret.

"I would have been here earlier but I had to stop at the manse."

Joe refrained from any comment as he removed the receiver from the wall telephone and jiggled the hook. "Hello, Central. Give me Lorne 57, please." Joe waited a moment and then said, "No, operator, there will be someone there by now . . . that's H.H. Marshall's midtown store."

"You know, Reverend Tait held a morning breakfast service for all the apprentice clerics. It was necessary I go there first." Curry twisted his interlocked fingers forward and back. "His homily was longer than usual."

The first pangs of regret were welling up in Joe's chest but he carried on. "Frank! This is Joe Smallwood. Is Hank there? Good. Send him down to me . . . tell him he will be here for the day. Where will I be? Where will I be . . .?" A deep breath. "I'll be out on the water looking for *Lady Betty*." Joe scowled. "No, I won't be charging Oland a fee . . ."

"That's nice, Joe." Roy picked a piece of lint from his wool suit coat. "Eric is a man of substance but he will appreciate your gentlemanly gesture."

Joe spoke through gritted teeth. "Frank, put Hank in a cab, right now. Tell him to hold the driver at my front door because I'll need the ride to the Waegwoltic." After a moment of listening, Joe's face turned dark, his brown eyes flashing lightning as he growled into the mouthpiece, "All I want from you, Frank Dodge, is your co-operation. I don't need your observations." He smashed the receiver down on the hook. Slipping off his apron, Joe reached for his suit coat.

"You should be wearing your sailing whites, Joe, but I suppose you don't keep them nearby."

"I'm going out to wait at the curb, Roy. You explain to Vladik what is going on." With that Joe wrenched the door open and stormed out into the fine, early morning of a beautiful Nova Scotia spring day.

* * *

At the Waegwoltic's floating dock, Joe could see that someone had towed his powerboat, *Carolyn*, from her mooring further up the North West Arm to the Wag. A group of men were standing around, killing time, and obviously awaiting his arrival.[2]

A tall, thin man with distinguished-looking greying hair stepped forward. "Ah, Mister Smallman, I presume. Let me introduce the members of the search party." One of the party leaned forward and said something to him.

"Oh, my dear, dear fellow. I am told I have your name wrong. Small-wood, Mister Small-wood, I do hope you can forgive me my transgression. After all, it's not as if we have been properly introduced. We'll just have to start all over again, won't we? I am Eric Oland." He didn't extend his hand but gestured at two of the men, who possessed remarkably similar features and builds. "Messieurs Cumberland, father and son. Last, but not least, is Mister Schwartz of *W.H. Schwartz and Sons*, he being one of the 'and Sons.'"

Mister Schwartz tipped his yachting cap to Joe, who noticed, for the first time, that the thin Schwartz brother was blind . . . or nearly so. *A blind man on a search?* Joe nodded back and felt a little silly since the Schwartz fellow probably couldn't see him. Flustered, Joe glanced at the three other men, who were carrying picnic baskets and two large canvas bags.

Mister Oland gestured in the direction of the men. "They're Wag employees."

The men were bare-headed but touched their forelocks just as if they were pressed men from the old days of the Royal Navy.

"With your permission, Mister Small-wood, they will come along to assist in the retrieval of *Lady Betty* if we should find her . . . or handle the grappling hooks if we should believe her to have foundered." He clapped his hands like a school-marm and raised his voice. "Tempus fugit! Let us move along with the expedition. If you have brought your keys, Mister Small-wood, please be so kind as to open the cabin and do the things you powerboat people do."

The members of the search party, decked out in their white trousers, canvas sailing shoes, blue jackets (the club crest on the breast pocket), and peaked sailing caps—the Cumberlands with telescopes tucked neatly under their arms—helped each other into *Carolyn's* cockpit.

The working party, dressed in sweaters, shirts, and brown pants, waited until the *Carolyn's* captain, in his brown business suit, had boarded and had begun getting *Carolyn* ready to sail. Then the workers passed the victuals and equipment over the gunnels and hopped aboard.

With a bit of prime to the engine, Joe was gratified to hear *Carolyn's* muffled growl. When he throttled back, he almost shut her down, when one Cumberland said to the other, "Smelly things." Joe remembered his Aunt Mary Anne and one of her sayings: *in for a penny, in for a pound.* He forced a smile to his lips and ordered, "Cast off, fore and aft."

The gentlemen watched as Joe and the Wag employees handled *Carolyn's* departure.

* * *

By midday every conceivable place where *Lady Betty* could have drifted, given the wind and the tide of the previous evening, had been carefully searched.

Joe throttled back. After turning the craft into the wind, he handed over the wheel to the nearest Wag employee and, with the help of the one named Mark, broke out the anchor. In a moment, the anchor was rigged and a small splash announced its trip to the bottom, where it quickly set.

Joe was sensitive and alert to any more yachtsmen's comments about noisy or smelly powerboats, but there were none.

Mark had found the deck chairs that were stored in the cabin. He brought them out.

Joe took one of the chairs. "We'll set them up in the cockpit, Mark."

Mister Oland suggested that the chairs could be set up on the forward deck, leaving the benches in the cockpit for the use of the work party. Mark was very quick to follow the suggestion, carrying all of the chairs forward.

Mister Schwartz remained seated on the bench. "I will be much more comfortable here, if you please." He sat, both hands on his cane, leaning forward. "You don't mind, do you, Eric?"

"Not at all, Fredrick. The boys will see to you."

Oland and the two Cumberlands sat down on the foredeck and were quickly engrossed in each other.

Mister Schwartz spoke. "Mister Smallwood, Schwartz's has found you to be a very good customer."

Joe smiled and sat down next to him. "I like your products. I like the way they're packaged and they are very easy to sell."

"That's nice to hear."

Joe held up a plate. "I am holding up a plate with ham sandwiches to the left and what seems to be egg salad to the right . . . my left and right . . . I'm sorry. I'm not very good at this."

"You don't have to be good at it to keep me happy, thank you, Mister Smallwood." Schwartz chose an egg salad.

There were several moments of silence between the two. The Wag men were very quiet while the buzz of voices from the foredeck indicated that the other group was getting along well.

"I suppose you wondered why I came along today." Schwartz had a piece of egg caught in his moustache. It waggled as he spoke, "I mean, a blind man coming out on a search."

Joe wondered if he should tell Fredrich about the egg. It fell off.

Schwartz felt the egg on his lap. His hands were very quick to recover it and place the morsel in his napkin. "My brother, William . . ." Mister Schwartz paused. He held out his hand. "My name is Fredrich, not Fredrick as Eric says; Eric prefers the anglicized version."

Joe took the hand. "Well, Fredrich, my name is Joseph and I like to be called Joe."

"Thank you, Joe. Is there something to drink?"

"Yes. Lemonade in little glass jars." Joe took the elastic from the top of the jar and removed the waxed paper. "The Wag does it up real fancy." Joe undid a glass jar for himself. "You were saying?"

"My brother, William, was meant to be on the search party. I was to come along for the outing."

Joe wondered about the rueful little smile playing across the other man's face.

"He brought me to the dock and then begged off, saying that there was an important meeting he had remembered— just in the nick of time."

Joe made no comment, waiting for Fredrich to reveal only as much as he wanted to.

"My wife, Emma, thinks William wants to be the big cheese in the company and cut me out of the loop . . . do things while I am away." He sighed. "After William's perform-ance this morning, I'm inclined to believe her."

"I've learned that you quickly find out who your friends are and you should cherish them and hold them close. It takes longer to know your enemies."

Fredrich smiled. "Yes, and you hold them even closer." He leaned forward as he heard footfalls. "I will look forward to your company on other occasions, Joe," he said quickly before they were interrupted.

"We are finished our picnic, Mister Small-wood." Eric Oland was holding a wine glass in one hand and a marine chart in the other. "Oh dear, Fredrick, you were eating out of the worker's basket. No matter, it was probably plain but nourishing fare, I would wager."

"It was just fine, Eric."

"Well, then, let's get on with it. I would like to do some grappling near Ives Knoll and then off Point Pleasant Shoal. I believe if she foundered, she could be at either location."

Joe motioned to Mark. "Let's do it, then."

Lady Betty was not found that day.

June 29, 1914
Halifax

The door to the store was open to the salt air of a beautiful, sunny morning. Vladik was hunched over his newspaper and, on the counter, off to one side, were some coins from customers who had bought things with exact change.

I must teach him how to do the cash, Joe thought. "G'mornin' Vladik." *There must be something really interesting in the paper if he isn't even going to lift his head. Or grunt. Perhaps they have found Lady Betty.* "Did they find *Lady Betty?*"

"Mister Smallwood. Good morning, sir."

Joe noticed that the little man was just bursting with happiness or, perhaps, pride.

Pointing at the newspaper, Vladik said, "My people kill the . . . monster."

He must be joking. "What are you going to do with the body?"

The Russian pointed at the headline. "He dead."

Switching the paper around, Joe read the headline out loud.

HEIR TO THRONE
IS ASSASSINATED
IN CAPITAL OF
ANNEXED BOSNIA

Excitedly, Vladik began waving the newspaper and asking questions with a mixture of Russian and English words. Joe pulled out his packet of Black Cats and gave him one. "Take it easy! I'll read the whole thing and then let you know what went on."

Vladik sat down and lit his cigarette. He inhaled deeply, which gave him a fit of coughing, but as soon as he could take a breath, he began again with the questions.

"No questions! Stop!" Joe gave the little fellow a reassuring smile. "I will tell you what's going on." It was a long article: the entire column down the right side of the paper and over to the second page. From time to time, Joe looked at his helper and thought the little fellow was going to burst. When Joe put the paper down, Vladik looked up at his employer and cocked his head much as a dog would watch his master break a dog biscuit in two before tossing a piece to the animal.

"Archduke Ferdinand and his wife were shot by an eighth grade student called Prinzip. They were visiting Sarajevo. Prinzip was from another province called Herzegovina . . ."

"Da! Bosnia, Herzegovina . . . elopement. *Lady Betty* elopement. Same."

Joe realized where the use of "elopement" came from and, having read the article, understood the intent. "Well, yes. They say the Austrians annexed the two places." When Joe saw the look on the other man's face, he tried again. "Stolen or taken." He tried again. "Steal."

"Ferdinand tell father, Emperor Franz Joseph . . . steal Bosnia and Herzegovina. Emperor Franz Joseph steal. Now Ferdinand dead. Good. Mother Russia steal Bosnia back . . . and keep Servia. Is good."

His English is getting better. "That's wonderful English, Vladik. Wonderful." He picked up the paper again. "Anything else you want to know?"

"Yes, please." Picking up the change from the counter and dropping it into Joe's hand he asked, "Three *Herald* . . . sale. Is good?"

Joe counted the pennies while wondering at the sudden change of subject. It dawned on him: *with the death of this Ferdinand fellow—as far as Vladik is concerned—everything is in the hands of Mother Russia and Vladik is now content. Vladik is just getting on with the business of daily living.*

"Good, Vladik." He opened the cash and set up the till. Then he explained everything to Vladik so that he could run the counter. When they were both satisfied, Joe announced that he was leaving for a while. He walked up the hill to the university, where one of the lady librarians he had been dating vouched for him with the chief librarian so that he could have a student's card for the day. Joe wanted to know more about Austria, Bosnia/Herzegovina and why Mother Russia would be looking after things. It was much more complex than he had supposed.

It took the rest of the morning but Joe learned that the Germanic peoples of Austria and Germany, led by their royal families, had been expanding their empires.

As far back as 1870, when there had been fighting over the French province of Alsace Lorraine, the world newspapers had accepted the German acquisition of Alsace Lorraine as a buffer province on its western border at the expense of the Republic of France. Journalists noted that France, by killing off the French nobility earlier in the century, had lost all hope of any sympathy or support from the royal houses of Europe. Consequently, when the royal German army beat the republican French army, Alsace Lorraine was recognized as a German province.

But! The German royal house had scarcely digested Alsace Lorraine when they made moves to increase German influence in Africa—again at the expense of the French. This time, however, royal family loyalties did not enter into the resolution of the African squabble because German expansionism threatened the colonial interests of Britain and Italy as well as France. The German royal family lost prestige when Germany was forced to give up African territory to the French Republic.

Then the Austrian annexation of Bosnia and Herzegovina in 1909 was a move by the Germanic royal houses to gain access to the Adriatic Sea. As anticipated, the other European royal houses failed to act. Russia, which might have come to the rescue of the Slav peoples of the threatened provinces, had been weakened enough by a recent war with Japan that it also failed to intervene. Now, a cocksure Austria, emboldened by its Bosnia/Herzegovina success, was intent on the subjugation of Serbia, a little country recently created on the southern border of the expanded Austria.

Joe closed the journals, one by one. *Now that the instigator of Austrian ambitions, Archduke Ferdinand, is dead, that should be the end of it.* He pushed his chair back and stood. He smiled to himself as his librarian friend, Charlotte Norman, quickly appeared by his side.

"I'll put them away, Joe," she whispered.

Since he was dying for a cigarette, Joe was pleased he didn't have to fuss with anything. He mouthed a thank-you and patted her hand. As he passed out the door into the lobby, he pulled out his packet of Black Cats and selected a cigarette. He reviewed the Balkan situation as he lit his cigarette. *So this wasn't the first time that these European royal families had squabbled over territory. If there were going to be a war between some little place called Serbia and the huge Austrian Empire of Emperor Franz Joseph, it would be no contest; the Emperor would win.*

He blew out his match and flicked the blackened matchstick in the general direction of the big ashtray at the entrance to the reading room. *So the Austrians get their access to the Adriatic Sea. Then what?* The cigarette paper was stuck to his lip. He gently pulled it away. Removing some stray strands of tobacco from his mouth, he then took a deep, deep drag. *Nothing like a good cigarette,* he thought as he started back to see how Vladik was getting along at the store. He had one more thought about the Balkan squabble before he stepped out into the fresh sea air; *Russia probably won't react this time, either.*

July 1, 1914
Carolyn
On the North West Arm

"What will we do now, Joey?"

Giving it some thought, Joe finished tidying up the *Carolyn's* stern-fast³ before he answered. *This is promising to be a washout. The Wag festivities were cancelled because of the weather so here I am, on a dark and chilly Dominion Day in a fancy boat, with a delightful companion . . . and nowhere to go.*

"Did you hear me, Joe?" The murmur of *Carolyn's* engine

and the spluttering of the exhaust into the water made Charlotte raise her voice just slightly to be sure she was being heard. She studied this handsome man she believed she was falling in love with. *He's nodding his head so I know he's thinking about a reply,* and she waited. *He has such nice hands,* she thought, as he used them to put the rope that he called a "stern-fast" into a tight little circle flat on the rear deck. *There is no one at Dalhousie or Kings who possesses more natural intelligence than Joe Smallwood.* It was apparent to Charlotte that he lacked formal schooling but he made up for that by investigating anything that he hadn't heard of before or wanted to understand better. She had met him at the library one morning when he had been searching for a copy of the founding charter of the Waegwoltic. He had read the whole thing and every newspaper account about the country club that she could find for him; *Joe Smallwood leaves nothing to chance.* She smiled as she recalled him saying, "*I always do my homework.*"

He looked up and gave her his devastating smile. Her heart fluttered. Charlotte put her hands to her bosom to hide her turmoil.

"There's nothing going to happen here, on the North West Arm, my dear."

Did he call all the girls "my dear," she wondered, *or just me?* "That's all right, Joe. It was a nice thought and I was so pleased when you invited me . . ."

"Later this afternoon there's a ball game between the Capitals and the Wanderers but, in the meantime, why don't we just cruise around to the harbour and see what's going on."

"I'd enjoy that, Joe." *I would like anything as long as I can be with you . . . but a nice girl from a good family doesn't make that kind of remark. As it is, father would be upset to know that I am alone with a man on a powerboat . . . and not with friends at the Wag.*

Joe increased the throttle and turned *Carolyn's* prow toward the western passage to the Atlantic.

"Take the wheel, Charlotte," Joe said as he disappeared into the cabin.

That's just like him. He treats me like an equal . . . not like the boys father approves of . . . who think I'm some sort of doll to be cherished. She took the wheel and watched as the shoreline sped by. Quickly they were abreast of Martello Tower and still Joe hadn't come back. *He said he meant to take the boat to the harbour . . . but . . .* Charlotte kept *Carolyn's* prow pointed to where she believed the Atlantic Ocean should be. "Out there, somewhere," she said to herself. She licked her lips as the salt spray came across the foredeck, laughing into the breeze. *I could get to like this . . . if Joe were always here.*

Joe staggered a bit from *Carolyn's* pitch into the waves as he came out of the cabin balancing two steaming mugs and a tray of sandwiches. "The boat salesman told me the marine stove was easy to handle," he said in a grumbling tone.

Charlotte relieved him of a mug while steadying the wheel with her left arm. Her big hat threatened to come loose but Charlotte didn't have a hand free to catch it.

Joe reached over and caught the tail of the ribbon, rescuing the hat for the moment, but there was just too much to handle: the wheel, the mugs, the tray, and the hat. Joe was drawn close to Charlotte, almost nose to nose. He looked into her eyes and tossed his mug of coffee over the side, freeing his hand to caress her face. Slowly, gently he raised her chin and kissed her, lightly, on the lips. He kissed her again, enjoying the salty softness of her lips. Joe leaned back to measure her reaction to his advances. He noticed her nose—a trifle small— was shiny wet from the spray, while her blue eyes were closed as if she were still savouring his kiss. He smiled to himself; *when those eyes are open, they are almost too big for her face, giving her a wide-eyed, innocent look that belies the complex woman she is.*

Her eyes sprang open. "Dammit!" Charlotte made a clutching movement over her head with both hands as her hat flew off, the mug bouncing off the wooden deck, splashing coffee over the bottom of her dark brown dress.

Joe stepped in closer, taking the opportunity to slide his arms around her waist. He was surprised at how slight she was under the tunic-like jacket. He felt the pressure of her breasts against him as he pushed her back against the wheel.

"Someone has to keep a hand on the wheel," Joe said by way of explanation. He still had a grasp on the tray but the sandwiches had long since joined the coffee underfoot.

Charlotte returned the kiss while pushing against Joe's shoulders so she could lower her arms. "Joey, there are people watching us."

Joe chortled. "Not out here, my dear."

"There's all those men in boats, just over there." Charlotte pointed over Joe's shoulder.

When Joe looked, he could see rowboats and barges, filled with armed men, heading to the shore just off York Redoubt—one of the forts that protected Halifax Harbour. Leaving Charlotte at the wheel for the moment, he reached into a small locker and took out his binoculars. He focused on the boats, guessing that they were intent on landing just below the gun emplacements on the shoreline. When he scanned the hillside, he could see smoke which he believed was coming from the cannons and small arms of the defending Nova Scotia militiamen. Joe rubbed his eyes as if he couldn't believe what he was seeing. *York Redoubt was being attacked! But by whom? The Yanks?* He knew from his time at the library that they had invaded Canada several times before. He raised the telescope, hoping to find an explanation.

Carolyn almost swamped as Charlotte turned the wheel, heeling the boat into the swells. "We must get back to the city and warn the army!"

Joe, looking back over the stern at the boats, shook his head. "It'll all be decided long before we get to the Dockyard. If we are going to be of any help we must do something now."

"It would take cannon to stop those boats."

"I don't even have a flare gun, Charlotte." Joe took a couple of steps toward the stern. "I've been meanin' to get one but I haven't had the time."

Putting her hand on the throttle just like she had seen Joe do, Charlotte grasped it. "This makes the boat go faster?"

"Yes, but wait a minute!" Joe put his hand over Charlotte's and pulled back on the throttle, slowing *Carolyn*. "The nearest boat is low in the water. I could swing in there and . . ." Joe turned the wheel. "Get every life jacket, my dear," Joe said, all business now that he had decided to do something about the invaders.

Charlotte had opened her mouth to say something but now that *Carolyn* was heading back to intercept the strange boats and Joe had pushed the throttle all the way, she was probably discouraged from saying anything further by the roar of the engine and the determined look on her companion's face. *Carolyn* was flying through the swells, her motor giving off a deep-throated growl. Charlotte thought, *it might be a good idea to get some life jackets.* She turned away and, bending her head, entered the cabin. When she returned to the cockpit, she could see Joe was holding the wheel with the one hand and manipulating the binoculars with the other. Charlotte dropped the half-dozen grey life jackets on the deck and grasped the wheel.

His hands now free, Joe made some adjustments on the knurled rings of the binoculars taking a long, long look at the occupants of the nearest boat. "They are all in uniform. By God, they are a fierce-looking bunch." He lowered the glass and handed it to Charlotte. "I want you to wedge yourself in there," he pointed to the bulkhead by the entranceway to the cabin, "and keep your head down."

"What are you going to do?"

"If I can get in close enough, our wash should swamp that low one." He pointed to the nearest boat. "They've seen us!"

Sure enough, one of the soldiers was pointing in their direction.

Joe checked the throttle and found a little bit more thrust available at the top of the mark. The motor responded and *Carolyn* dug a little deeper in the swells each time she crested.

"Wash? What do you mean, wash?"

"See that big wave behind us? It might be big enough to sink their boat if I can get in close enough. If we can do that, our boys on the beach will have a better chance to beat the other two boats off."

"What'll happen to us?"

"Wedge yourself in and don't look up, my dear."

Joe put both hands on the wheel and aimed *Carolyn* at a point about twenty-five yards in front of the other boat. He hunched his shoulders and crouched behind the windshield.

"Joe!"

He cast a quick glance over his shoulder. Charlotte was sitting up looking at something through the eyeglass.

"You had better get down, my dear."

There were a dozen soldiers in the first boat now watching *Carolyn's* approach. One of them had raised a weapon. No, it was an officer's swagger stick.

"Joe!"

There was enough urgency in Charlotte's voice for Joe to take his eyes off his target. Somewhat exasperated that she would want to have a discussion at such a moment, Joe asked, "What the hell is so important, Charlotte?"

"I know one of the men in the second boat. It's Colonel King."

Joe didn't stop *Carolyn's* forward rush but he did take the proffered binoculars. Making a quick adjustment, he identified the man standing in the stern of the second boat, brandishing his fist at the onrushing *Carolyn*, as one of his regular customers at the store; Colonel Billie King of the 66th Regiment, the regiment known as the Princess Louise Fusiliers—the PLF. Joe cut power and, once the surge of the wash had caught up to her, turned the *Carolyn* away from what now appeared to be an army exercise and not an invasion.

Charlotte was the first to speak. "The King's Harbour Master should have put out a *Notice to Mariners*."

"Probably did," a dispirited Joe said, "but I didn't think to read the notices this last week."

"It's my fault we came out this far."

"I look like a fool."

"No, Joe. I think you are a brave man. To think that you would come to the aid of the defenders of York Redoubt . . ." She squeezed his hand. Leaning forward, she kissed him on the cheek. "I think you are wonderful."

Behind them, on the side of the hill at York Redoubt, the crackle of gunfire could be heard. Joe took one last look through the telescope. "The men from the boats are running straight up that hill against the fort."

Charlotte squeezed his hand again and then began picking up the life jackets. "I met a number of the PLF at the library when they were doing some war studies. I got the books for them and put them away after. I remember Major Simmonds said that offence is the stronger form of warfare because the attacking force has higher morale than the defending force."

"Yes, but to charge up a hill like that . . . right into the guns of the enemy . . ."

"Colonel James Wolfe said that pushing on smartly is the road to success. He said a leader can't know how serious an obstacle is until he has a try at it."

"I thought Colonel King was in charge of the PLF."

Charlotte cast a quick look at Joe's face to see if he was being funny. After the slightest hesitation, she gave him a straight answer. "No, Wolfe was here in 1757."

Joe pressed his lips together and looked ahead over the prow at the Martello Tower.

Charlotte thought it wise to proceed. "Later, when Wolfe was a general, he led his men up a hill at Quebec and won Canada for England. He was fond of saying that a good leader would allow something in his plans for chance and fortune . . . and the valour of his men." Charlotte tossed the last of the life vests into the cabin. She put her hand on Joe's shoulder, turning him slightly. "You have that valour, Joe. You were willing to charge into the middle of a large body of armed men . . ."

Joe gave her his best smile. "Yeah, but I thought they were attacking the PLF."

"You see, you have the valour."

"Not really. Most of the PLF are good customers of mine . . ." As Charlotte grabbed and pulled on his ear he finished, " . . . and I didn't want to lose any of 'em."

When Charlotte had finally let go of his ear, Joe asked; "Did you learn anything more from this Simmonds fellow?"

"I did find it most interesting. He said that the essential objective of the force taking the offensive is the existing hostile force . . . not the fort, not the hill, but to destroy the enemy army."

"Yes, but to run uphill against . . ."

"I remember Major Simmonds saying that today's leader must benefit from the lessons of the last war. He said that our biggest mistake in the Boer War was to concentrate on capturing the Boer cities. The reason the war went on so long was we didn't destroy the Boer army first."

"So you charge right at them?"

"That's what Major Simmonds was teaching his junior officers."

"That's hard to believe."

"Major Simmonds is a graduate of the Royal Military College at Kingston. He's a professional. He must know what he is doing."

"Well, it's all quiet back there now. I wonder who won?" And it remained quiet behind them on the slopes of York Redoubt as Joe steered *Carolyn* to her mooring just north of the Waegwoltic.

Once at the club (Charlotte's father was a member), they learned that the ball game between the Capitals and the Wanderers had been postponed because of weather. They discussed the possibility of taking the excursion ship, *Davis Macnab,* to the dancing pavilion on MacNab's Island, but by this time they were chilled to the bone. Joe offered her a taste of his flask but Charlotte, concerned that her father might sense the dark rum on her breath, declined. A miserable ride in an open cab, the only vehicle available, put a very wet end to a dismal Dominion Day.

At the door to her home, her lips blue with the cold,

Charlotte told Joe that she had enjoyed his company and was pleased that they had been able to get to know each other better. Her voice sounded sincere and Joe was elated that she was pleased.

He suggested that they might go out again.

"We will have to wait to see the nature of the occasion, Mister Smallwood," Charlotte replied, primly.

The door opened behind them. "You're wet, Miss Charlotte." An older man in a severe black suit stepped back to allow his master's daughter to come in out of the rain.

Charlotte stepped in. She held the door open with a slight pressure from her hand. Smiling at the drenched young man she said, "Thank you for seeing me home, Mister Smallwood. Thank you so very much." She turned away from the door allowing the manservant to close it.

As his shivers overtook him, Joe heard the lovely contralto voice behind the door: "I'm home, Mama."

July 4, 1914
Carleton House

H.H. Marshall and Joe entered the foyer of Carleton House. The hotel manager, Mister Pass, spoke to them as they handed their hats to the bellman.

"I hope you gentlemen are agreeable." If Mister Pass had been wearing a wider smile, the ends would have met at the back of his head. "I have been asked to place you at the Schwartz table directly in front of the fireplace."

For once, H.H. was at a loss for words.

Joe wasn't having a problem. "Mister Fredrich is here?"

"Yes, and he is waiting for you." As he led the two gentlemen into the dining room, Mister Pass assured them that the rest of their party would be well served at their usual table. He glanced back, quickly, to see if there was a reaction. Reassured that all was well, he pulled one of the chairs back and, with a grand flourish, indicated the seat was for the senior of the two gentlemen, facing the front of the room as it did.

"It's Joe Smallwood and H.H. Marshall," Joe said to Fredrich, who was sitting at the table.

As they shook hands Fredrich playfully brought up the subject of *Lady Betty*. "I was told you were given credit in the *Herald* for conducting a thorough search for the missing boat."

H.H. guffawed but said nothing, waiting for the Smallwood rejoinder.

Joe reached into his side pocket and brought out a leather billfold. "Actually, I clipped it out because I'm going to show my Dad that I hit it big in the big city!" Joe pretended to puff up his chest as he unfolded the four-inch newspaper column. "Yessiree! Here's the part about me . . . right on the front page of the *Halifax Herald*." He held it to the light and read.

"On finding no trace of the yacht in the immediate vicinity . . ." Joe raised a hand and pointed at his own chest and emphasized the next few words, ". . . *a motor boat was secured*," he grinned and lowered his hand, "and a careful search was made of all the coves and inlets of the Arm and finally the outside harbour was gone over without the slightest trace of the *Betty* being found. Fully three hours was spent in the fruitless search."[4]

With humour in his voice, Fredrich said, "They never seem to get the right spelling of anyone's last name."

"Look right here," he jabbed his finger at the page, "they got Oland's name right." Joe gave a big sigh as he continued reading.

"After exhausting every possible means of obtaining any information or clue as to the sudden departure of the yacht, Mister Eric Oland referred the matter to the police."

Fredrich leaned forward. "My father-in-law, Warren Gray, told me something interesting."

"Excuse me; your father-in-law is Warren Gray, the oarsman?"

"Yes. It's nice you remember him, Joe."

"When I was a boy I read some pulp stories about him. I would sure like to meet him."

"Right now he's on his way to England to watch the race for the Grand Challenge Cup at Hemley-on-Thames, but I will be pleased to arrange it when he comes back. He retired as sergeant major of the 66th Regiment but continues doing some victualling for the navy ships."

"In the pulp story, there was a girl."

"Yes, there was Hannah who became his wife. She died a few years back."

"I'm sorry. And I'm sorry I got you off track. I think you were going to tell me something about *Lady Betty.*"

"Yes. Before he left, Warren told me that Captain Latter of Pilot Boat number 1 saw a white yacht resembling *Lady Betty* off Meagher's Beach on Sunday. We believe now that she was stolen."

"Did the disappearance of the yacht have anything to do with the escaped prisoner?"

"Hard to say, but you can depend on the *Herald* to make as much of a story out of it as they can."

The men paused in their conversation while the beef consommé was being served.

Fredrich had tucked the end of his napkin into the top of his vest, feeling with his hands to ensure that he was well covered. "One of the advantages of being almost blind," he said, indicating the napkin, "I am permitted table manners to suit my disability."

H.H. laughed. "I only get to do that at home."

Joe tucked his napkin under his collar. "I didn't know there was any other way," he said with his biggest grin.

H.H. hesitated, quickly checking the room. He left his napkin in his lap. "Joe tells me he saw you at the Academy of Music on Wednesday afternoon."

"Ah, yes. I went to hear my daughter Edith sing. My Edith is very shy and needs the support of her father and mother from the audience when she sings." Fredrich waited the moment or two for the consommé bowls to be removed.

The waiter paused behind Joe's chair. "There was something wrong with the consommé, Mister Smallwood?"

"No. Not at all, thank you."

The waiter took Joe's untouched consommé away.

"Ira Hubley brings out the best in her; in fact, she will only sing for Ira."

They paused for a moment as the fish entrée was served.

"The descriptive number was enchanting," Joe enthused.

"Edith has the lead in that number." Fredrich paused. "If you saw us, you should have come over. We had excellent seats and several vacant."

"I wasn't alone, Fredrich."

H.H. jumped in. "You didn't tell me you were with someone, my dear friend. What are you keeping from me?" He leaned forward, doing a good imitation of a villain's leer. "It's not all business under that businessman's suit?"

Joe tried to change the subject. "The haddock is beautifully fresh, isn't it?"

H.H. indicated the boiled dressing. "Help yourself to the sauce, Joe."

"No thanks, H.H.. I like it plain."

"Let's have some plain talk, then. Was your companion . . ."

"Enjoying the play?" Fredrich interrupted. He didn't want the younger man to feel that there was to be an inquisition.

Joe gave Fredrich a glance of appreciation. "It was *The Lottery of Love*. Sidney Toler Players. It was very fine."

"Yes. The *Herald's* commentary said it was funny, hearty, and clean. Just the sort of play for you to take a . . ." Fredrich, obviously as curious as H.H. about who might be keeping company with this young bachelor, allowed his curiosity to overcome his discretion, " . . .an acquaintance?"

"I had two tickets and I invited someone from the university to come with me. Sort of a repayment for some favours," Joe finished lamely and then, quickly changing the subject, "you know what I learned at the library the other day?"

As the entrée dishes were removed and during the serving of the roast beef, boiled potatoes, new peas, and leaf lettuce, Joe explained his interest in the Balkan situation. In particular, that Serbia had kept its army of 250,000 men on a war footing for the last five years. Austria/Hungary, on the other hand, had recently placed its army of 895,000 on a war-footing and was beginning the call-up of another million soldiers. "Imagine! An army just sitting there for five years, waiting for something to happen." Joe sat back a little, allowing the server to place a fruit dish in front of him. "Now there'll be a couple of million Austrians sitting around."

"Did you see the photograph of the Archduke in the *Chronicle?*" H.H. almost instantly regretted having mentioned his preference for the *Chronicle*, it being the newspaper that had campaigned against Sir Robert Borden's plan to build Canadian Dreadnaughts for the Imperial Navy.

"No, I didn't." Joe grimaced. "I don't like the *Halifax Chronicle*. In times like these, Canada should have a battleship . . . just like New Zealand has a battleship . . . to be assigned to the Royal Navy for the defence of the Empire."

Fredrich could sense a political argument shaping up. He realized that there would not be many people in the port city of Halifax who weren't in favour of Canadian fleet units in the Royal Navy, but he knew that H.H. Marshall shared no man's opinions; he had enough of his very own. Moreover, H.H. was a true Grit, a Laurier man . . . and if Wilfrid Laurier felt that Canada should have its own navy, then H.H. Marshall wanted a Canadian Navy . . . and to hell with the Tory Haligonians who would spend Canadian dollars on a tin can for the use of the Royal Navy. So Fredrich hastened on, "The *Herald* carried pictures of Austria's royal orphans. My wife Emma said Princess Sophie was adorable in her lace dress while Prince Ernest and Prince Maximilian looked very grown-up in their little sailor suits."

Joe made *tsk, tsk* sounds between his lips. "I saw that. The caption was a real tearjerker. It said something like"—Joe raised his hands as if writing the words across the wall of the dining room—"orphaned by an assassin's bullet . . . which killed both parents . . .dead." Joe rearranged his knife and fork on his plate and the server came, almost immediately, to retrieve the dishes. No one commented on the fact that Joe had barely touched his meal. "There was a picture of the German Crown Prince, his wife, and their four children on an inside page." Joe chose the strawberry pie from the dessert selection and then added, "I think all the royal families are related, you know. Miss Norman was telling me . . ." His face went red.

For the rest of the meal, H.H. and Fredrich prodded and questioned Joe to discover the extent of his involvement with a daughter of one of Halifax's prominent commercial families. Joe kept his head down, eating every morsel of his strawberry pie and drinking another full glass of milk. As his friends poked and prodded, trying to get him to commit himself— one way or another—about his female companion, Joe came to realize that Charlotte Norman was beginning to assume a significant role in his daily life. Perhaps he loved her.

July 8, 1914
Barrington Street
Halifax

That's what Joe was wondering as he listened to Charlotte describe the afternoon performance of the Academy of Music to the senior librarian: *do I love this woman?*

"There were talking pictures! Not only could I see the military band playing their instruments but I could also hear them! The soldier on the tuba was exerting himself so much his face was dark from the effort."

Joe thought, *Charlotte is so, so . . . alive and vivacious and I am always happy to be with her. Is that love?*

"They showed us some musical blacksmiths, a dancing bear and, at the end, the flag was waving big and bright while we sang "God Save the King." It was thrilling!" She turned and put her hand on Joe's arm, squeezing it slightly, feeling the texture of Joe's muscles, making it almost a caress, sending messages, Joe imagined, along to his heart.

Joe looked down at those oversized eyes and felt they had impaled him. He barely heard the librarian's next question about the performance.

"Talking Pictures . . . are they Mister Edison's?"

Joe was at a loss. "I . . . don't . . . know who made the pictures, Mister Mahen," he said as he continued to feel Charlotte's lightest touch, see her face looking up to his and smell her breath so sweet. "I . . .

Charlotte, without taking her eyes off Joe, answered for him. "It is Edison's Kinetophone. And, at the end, there was continuous applause." She released Joe from his bondage by slipping her arm through his and turning him toward the library door.

"Mister Smallwood has an important meeting at his place of business, Mister Mahen. I hope you will excuse me for the moment while I see him to the door."

Outside the door, Charlotte patted Joe's hand while she said, "You should hurry back to the shop, Joe. Father tells me that H.H. doesn't like it when any of his managers leave the premises for long periods of time."

"True enough, but Frank is there, as well as Vladik. There shouldn't be any trouble." Obviously, Joe didn't want to leave.

Charlotte pushed him down the first step, "Well, then, my dear boy, *I* have work to do and I won't get it done by lollygagging out here with you." She put on a stern schoolmarm's face and pushed him down another step. "Now, go!" She turned her back and strode to the door.

Joe watched her leave, hoping that she might relent, but she disappeared into the shadows of the entrance. He marvelled at her retreating figure—upswept brown hair with one of those big hats perched on top, well-defined shoulders and waist, ample hips—and he imagined the long, long legs under a skirt short enough to reveal a flash of calf. *Oh my, yes! Charlotte Norman is more woman than . . . than anyone I have ever met! Yesirree, my Dad wouldn't want me to throw this one back!*

Joe smiled to himself as he went down the hill to the shop. *Imagine Charlotte having a serious discussion with my father about the shortcomings of the Intercolonial Railroad!* He grinned at the thought of the Duke's reactions. *Or telling him that there should be a Canadian battleship in the Royal Navy like Prime Minister Borden wanted because it would have given Canada a proper say in the Imperial War Councils. Besides, it really would-n't have been a Canadian ship at all; it would have belonged to Nova Scotia, she would argue. Let Canada pay for it and let the British think that they could control it; but the sailors would be Nova Scotians and the ship would be out of Halifax.* "Ha!" he said aloud. *That would be a conversation to savour. Duke would have a fit!* As Joe went up the walk to the shop he concluded, *Newcastle isn't ready for a Charlotte Norman, not yet anyway.*

Joe pulled on the shop door, the bell tinkled, and Vladik was the first to say, "Welcome back, Mister Smallwood."

"Yes, welcome back, Mister Smallwood," Frank chimed in. "Vladik was reading for me. Did you know they found the boat you was searching for?"

"*Lady Betty*? No, I didn't have time to read the paper this morning."

"A young fellow stole it but didn't know how to sail. Damn near ruined the boat; canvas in tatters and gear all missing. Found him off Liverpool."

"She was taken to sea?"

"Yep, by an escaped prisoner from Rockhead Prison. The stupid bugger thought he might be able to reach Calais and disappear in the States . . . but he'll be back where he started at the end of the week."

Joe cast his eyes down. *Roy Curry believes the Herald created an incident to embarrass certain members of the Waegwoltic. It should now appear—even to the likes of Mister Curry—that the whole world does not really revolve around the city's so-called elite.* He went deeper into his own thoughts. *An escaped convict steals a boat and tries to get away. The newspaper reports the story and the Olands and the Currys believe it to be another example of the . . . the peasants . . . poking at their betters.* He raised his eyes.

". . . police are going to pick up the . . ."

Joe lowered his chin as he allowed himself to sink deeper into his thoughts. *Not that they don't deserve some poking for the way they assume for their own use all the good things in Halifax. What the established families didn't reserve for themselves, they let the common working class have . . . if they could afford it. Obviously, hardworking people like . . . like me, Joe Smallwood . . . with little education and a questionable background, would never fit in, never be a member of the Wag, never be accepted. The city's upper crust would always be on the defensive about their social position.* Joe looked out the display window as an expensive car honked its horn in passing. *They probably believe that everything is an action or reaction to them in their insular world and not to anything else.* He sighed. *Wouldn't it be nice if I were Joe Somebody instead of Joe Small-wood from backwoods New Brunswick?*

He sensed he had missed something in the conversation. "Eh? What did you say, Frank?"

"Did you find a better place for Vladik to live?"

Everyone had taken a liking to Vladik so Joe was not surprised at Frank's concern for the little Russian.

Joe smiled at them both. "I think I might have found just the thing! There's a small house, on Shore Road in Dartmouth—with a view of the harbour—three bedrooms. Junior Forsyth told me he has been advertising it for $25 a month but has had no takers. He would rent to Vladik for $19.50 if Vladik could move in right away."

Vladik was shaking his head, sorrowfully, as if there were something wrong.

Joe thought he knew what was bothering him. "Mrs. Carmichael will let you move out right away." He put his arm around the smaller man and gave him a squeeze. Joe looked up to bring Frank in on the joke. "All the women are putty in this man's hands." He let go and gave Vladik a good-natured shove. "I do believe it's the accent."

"You're right! It just slays 'em," Frank joshed, but he could see that there was trouble in the Russian's eyes. "What's the matter, Vladik? Don't want to leave your room at the Carmichaels'?"

Both men paused, giving Vladik plenty of opportunity to speak. Joe realized that there must be some sort of serious problem. *What could it be?* They waited as Vladik unfolded a piece of paper and held it out for them to see.

"From . . . Ottawa," he said.

Joe took the letter. He scanned one side and then the other. It was written in Russian but there was a coupon attached that Joe recognized; it entitled the bearer to a ticket on any Cunard ship departing Halifax for Europe. "This bearer coupon expires August fifteenth." He gave Vladik a questioning look.

Vladik had a hangdog look about him as he pointed to the letterhead. "Mother Russia." He spread his hands in a helpless gesture.

Reading the letterhead, Joe and Frank could see that it was an official document from the Russian Embassy in Ottawa.

"I must go home . . . army."

"He's going to Russia?" Frank questioned.

Joe swallowed hard, thinking of all the things he had read at the library. *Mobilization! If they are recalling Russians from Canada . . .* he pulled out his cigarettes. *So! Russia isn't going to take it lying down, this time.*

Vladik was obviously sorry to leave this generous man who had helped him . . . but Russians must answer the call of the homeland. Vladik butted his cigarette, suddenly not liking the taste in his mouth.

Frank, aware only that someone thought enough of this little fellow to pay his boat fare to Europe, took a deep draught of his cigarette, thinking what a wonderful trip it would be!

Joe, realizing that he would probably never see his little friend again, wondered if there was some argument he could make to keep Vladik in Halifax. When Vladik butted his cigarette and moved to the front window of the shop to gaze at the harbour, Joe joined him.

"Vladik, you don't have to . . ."

The Russian put his hand up to stop Joe. "Mother Russia needs Vladik."

Joe was annoyed at that kind of talk and let it show. "Son of a bitch, Vladik! Russia can leave one soldier in Nova Scotia."

For the first and last time, Vladik used his friend's Christian name, "No, Joe. Family in Russia and Vladik in Nova Scotia is no good. No good." He turned and looked up into Joe's face. "Real bad for family." Vladik looked away. "You are my . . . friend." He turned to face Joe and offered his hand. "Thank you, too much."

Joe grasped the extended hand in both of his. He felt a huge lump in his throat. All he could think of to say was, "Not thank you, too much, Vladik. You should say, thank you, very much."

Three days later, Vladik was gone.

Endnotes

1. The article—"WAS *LADY BETTY* FORCED VICTIM OF AN ELOPEMENT"—is taken directly from the *Halifax Herald* of that date.

2. Joe Smallwood was disappointed that he was not permitted to be a WAG member. He had bought the boat, the equipment, and the clothing but said the closest he came to the WAG was "to pick them up and drop them off at the WAG." He was generous with his boat and that's why I considered using the *Lady Betty* story and allowed him to be master of the motor boat that was secured to conduct a careful search of all the coves and inlets. I have no way of knowing who actually took part in the search . . . it was most unlikely that Mister Schwartz was involved other than in this story but I needed his attendance for storyline reasons.

3. Stern-fast is a rope used to confine the stern of a vessel to a wharf, pier, or buoy.

4. The quotation about the search for *Lady Betty* is also taken from the *Halifax Herald* of that date.

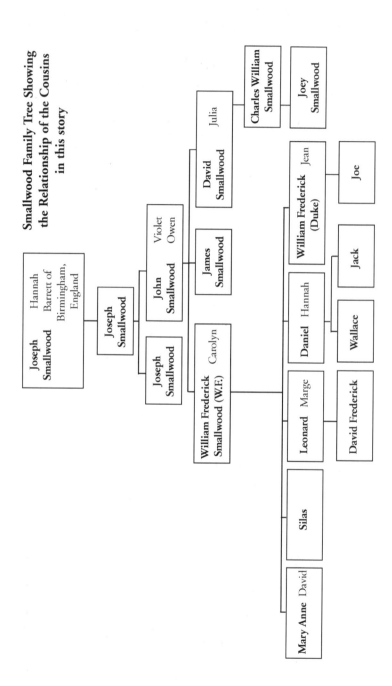

Smallwood Family Tree Showing the Relationship of the Cousins in this story

Chapter Three
The Cousins

July 30, 1914
The Sugary
New Brunswick

As usual, Silas Smallwood hadn't come to the family party.

Mary Anne was standing in the kitchen listening to the laughter of the men who were sitting under the old maple tree at the back of the house. It sounded like one of the boys was telling a story. She took two or three steps to the open doorway to identify the storyteller—her brother Danny, of course. The tale seemed to be about a salesman, a farmer, and a hungry calf. She couldn't hear the punch line because Danny had seen her and lowered his voice. She turned back to the kitchen where the Smallwood wives, Jean, Hannah, and Marge, were rolling the last of the pigs-in-a-blanket. Mary Anne had the wood stove ready and, as soon as the sausage rolls were popped into the oven, the other women would be able to leave the hot kitchen to join the men. Mary Anne planned to tend the baking since it was her kitchen . . . her stove.

In a peevish voice, Mary Anne complained, "It's not far from Harcourt. Silas should be here with the rest of the family." Her tone of voice hardened. "The next time I see that Silas, I am going to give him the old what-for, I will."

Hannah, Daniel Smallwood's wife, was quick to comment. "Danny says that Silas doesn't like it when the party is here, at your farm. Silas would rather we met at the home of one of the men."

Surprisingly, Duke's wife took a deep, deep breath as a prelude to saying something. The other women stopped what they were doing to listen to what the reclusive Jean Smallwood had to say.

45

Jean opened her mouth and then closed it again without a sound. She lowered her head and stared at her hands which showed traces of flour and dough.

Despite the fact that Mary Anne put her finger to her lips to keep the other women from interrupting Jean in case she should choose to speak, Marge asked, "What is it you want to say, my dear?"

Another sigh. "Silas knows that Mary Anne will get mad at him. She always does. That's why he doesn't come."

The women waited to see if there was going to be any more.

Mary Anne's face was turning crimson as she restrained herself from commenting.

Jean looked up at her sister-in-law. "Mary Anne, you are mad at him already, aren't you?" Jean wiped her hands on a towel and stepped away from the table. "It is hot. I am going upstairs to lie down." Jean folded the towel and, without another word, walked out into the hallway.

Mary Anne followed the tiny woman to the foot of the stairs. "You may use either bedroom at the front of the house, Jean. They will be the coolest." She watched the silent figure until it disappeared at the top of the stairs and then she returned to the kitchen just in time to hear Marge say, "That's more out of her than we have had for a long time."

Marge closed the oven door. "The sausage rolls are in and we should join the gentlemen."

"I will tend them."

"No, Mary Anne. You should join us where it is cooler. They will be fine." When it looked as if Mary Anne would object, Marge picked up the egg timer. "We'll take this with us. No sense missing the conversation."

The ladies filed out into the soft summer air.

". . . finished the installation of the telephone cable between Caribou in Pictou County and Wood Island on P.E.I." Joe Smallwood took a sip of his lemonade. He had the attention of his cousins who were seated on the grass around him; they were interested in the big-city things Joe might tell them. The Smallwood brothers, Leonard, Daniel, and Duke, were off to one side in the wooden garden chairs but they were also intent on what Joe had to say. They all rose as the women approached, the brothers offering their seats to the ladies.

"Thank you, gentlemen," Mary Anne said with a smile. Directing her comments to her nephew, Joe, she asked, "Does that mean we can now speak on the telephone to people all over Prince Edward Island . . . or just at Wood Island?"

"I don't know how it works from here in the Miramichi, but in Halifax I just pick up the receiver and ask the operator to be connected to, say, Charlottetown, and in a moment I'm talking to my party in Charlottetown."

"Wow!" Wallace Smallwood, Daniel's eldest son, was known for his general enthusiasm. "Wow!" he repeated. "That's progress!"

Jack, Wallace's younger brother, always vying for attention, tried to think of an appropriate question. It took him a moment. "Yes, but . . . when you place the call . . . the operator . . . what's . . . the cost?" he finally said.

Joe smiled at his old friend. "Y' know, Jack, I thought it would be expensive but it's only ninety-five cents for a three-minute call."

"I don't get ninety-five cents for a whole day's work." David Frederick looked over at his Dad, Leonard, and seeing no sign of any disapproval stood up and brushed imaginary dirt from his coveralls. "And there sure as hell isn't anyone in P.E.I. that I would waste the better part of a dollar on . . . .."

Leonard's face was dark with shame for his son's intemperate language in front of the ladies. He was quick to apologize to his older sister. "Mary Anne, my son means no disrespect."

"Then he should mind his tongue, Lenny."

"I am sorry, Aunt Mary Anne," said a hangdog David Frederick.

David Frederick was Marge's favourite and she let it show as she came to his rescue. "Did you know that our David enlisted in the 73rd Militia Regiment?"[1]

Mary Anne's attitude instantly changed. "Oh, my boy! I am so proud of you!" She looked around the family group and said, "We are all proud of you." She stood up and put out her arms for David Frederick to come for an embrace.

David hesitated until his father indicated that he should approach his daunting aunt, who took him into her arms, saying, "I am sure that you will not be the only Smallwood to keep faith with the Empire." Aunt Mary Anne stood on tiptoe to kiss the tall young man on the cheek. "My father . . ." She pushed David back slightly so she could speak to the entire family. She started again. "W.F. believed that our destiny is with the British Empire. When the call comes, I hope you will all see your duty as sons of empire the way David Frederick has. I read it in *The Gleaner* just this morning . . . on the other rim of the Atlantic the Motherland is in peril and the call of the blood will reach her sons."

Duke was very obviously uncomfortable with his sister's unbridled display of patriotism. "I don't think it will come to a war."

Daniel could see the fire in his sister's eyes so he was quick to try to shield his brother against Mary Anne's rising indignation. "Duke, I don't think any of us know whether or not there will be war."

"I think I know."

All eyes turned to stare at Joe who, by the shocked look on his face, obviously wished that he had kept his mouth shut. Joe hadn't meant to get involved, but he didn't want to be witness to his father taking a shellacking from Aunt Mary Anne. "A month ago, Russia sent recall orders to Russians living in Canada."

"How would you know that, Joe?" Mary Anne patted David Frederick's arm as she stepped around him to face her favourite nephew who seemed to be putting on big-city airs. Hands on her hips and leaning forward, she dared the young whippersnapper to take up her challenge. "How could you possibly know that?"

Joe did feel intimidated but he continued. "My helper,

Vladik Sopotov, was recalled. It cost Russia a lot of money to send that man home to Russia to be there by the middle of August. He sailed from Halifax on the *S.S. Olympic*—all found. They wouldn't spend that kind of money if they didn't mean to actually go to war this time."[2]

Duke smiled at his son. "What do you mean, 'this time,' Joe?"

Joe raised his chin and began. "In 1909, Austria annexed Bosnia and Herzegovina, both of them Slav countries. Russia, as the protector of the Slavs, should have come to their defence but didn't."

Duke was fascinated, seeing an aspect of his son he hadn't seen before. "And Russia didn't save the Slavs in . . . those two places . . . because?"

"Because she had suffered a defeat at the hands of the Japanese." Joe pulled out his Black Cats and offered them to his father. "So, when Russia didn't mobilize its army in 1909, Austria gained two new provinces without a fight."

Daniel indicated that he would appreciate a cigarette so Joe handed the package around. Soon all the men except Wallace were smoking—the ladies not participating.

Joe glanced at his Aunt Mary Anne and could read something other than anger in her face; perhaps interest . . . or even admiration. He kept on. "Now, in 1914, Austria has invaded the last little country between her and the Adriatic Sea—historically the Germanic peoples have wanted a port on the Adriatic Sea and the Slavs have been getting in the way."

With a new sense of appreciation for his son, Duke pressed for more information. "What has all this to do with England?"

"Russia has called her sons home to the army. I know that because Vladik had to go back." Joe took a deep drag on his cigarette. He spoke as he exhaled the smoke through his nose and lips. "So, this time, Russia has mobilized. If Russia goes to war against Austria to rescue Serbia, Germany and Italy will go to war against Russia. France will support Russia and so will England . . . and . . . the Empire will support Britain."[3]

Marge held out the egg timer. "The Smallwood summer super special will be ready in about thirty minutes as soon as we can serve up the pigs-in-a-blanket. Boys, get some lettuce and cukes from the garden."

Duke got up to join the good-natured trek to the garden but Joe put a restraining hand on his father's arm. "Dad, I need to talk to you."

"Of course, Joe." He sat down in one of the wooden chairs. "What is it?"

Joe examined the end of his cigarette until he was sure they were alone; still he lowered his voice almost to a whisper. "When Vladik Sopotov was recalled to Russia, I had such a firm belief that there would be war that I sold all of my stocks and bonds that very day."

Duke waited for his son to continue.

"I took the money and made a deposit on a huge order of imported products like sugar, tea, coffee . . . in fact, as many imported items as I could think of."

Duke was flabbergasted. "Based on the fact that a Russian went home?"

"Based on the fact that the Russians started full mobilization a month ago."

Duke stubbed his cigarette on the trunk of the tree and dropped the butt on the grass. "When are the goods being delivered?"

"A lot of them have been delivered. My shop is filled to the rafters already." Joe looked shamefaced. "I'll be in trouble soon because I won't have the money for the next delivery." Joe dropped his cigarette butt to the grass and, while he ground it in with his foot, he added, "I thought the war would come quicker than it has."

"You are being squeezed and need money from me."

"Yes." Joe didn't meet his father's gaze. "If you can."

Duke rubbed his chin. "I can manage two hundred dollars." He could see his son's face sag. "Maybe, in a couple of days, I could make it five hundred, but no more than that."

"I can't tell you how much that helps, Dad," Joe said,

allowing a look of relief to flood his face but he wasn't letting his real feelings show; even five hundred dollars wouldn't be enough.

Aunt Mary Anne stuck her head out of the kitchen door. "Little William!" She still called Duke by his boyhood name. "Little William, would you get a couple of quarts of maple syrup out of the well house?" Without a pause she went on, "And you, Joe, tell your cousins to quit horsing around. I want those fresh vegetables, now."

Both men were quick to respond, "Yes, Ma'am."

* * *

After a meal of sausage rolls and ham drenched in maple syrup with fresh vegetables and homemade bread and butter on the side, the brothers and their wives retired to the front room to look at family photographs. The younger set, the cousins, went back out under the tree to sip some spruce beer and share jokes they had heard since the last reunion. At one point, when there was a lull, David Frederick brought up the subject of "the war."

"Can you believe the way the old gal went on about the British Empire?" he asked in a subdued voice.

Joe showed some displeasure at the use of the term "old gal." "I wish you would refer to her as Aunt Mary Anne."

Wallace didn't want the spirit of the occasion spoiled so he was quick to respond to David's question. "If you didn't join to fight for the motherland, why are you in the militia, David?"

"If I attend the parades and the training, I get almost two dollars a week. That's good money and easier than farmin'."

Joe cleared his throat. "I watched a training exercise at York Redoubt a short while ago. Didn't look like easy money to me."

"What was it like?" Wallace and Jack asked the same question at the same moment.

Even David was eager to hear about training at Halifax where they had real, honest-to-god forts. "What kind of tactics did they use?"

Joe recalled what Charlotte had told him. "The important thing is to destroy the enemy force so, wherever the enemy is, the attackers charge right at them and kill or capture them."

"If that's the case then, Joe, they couldn't pay me enough." Jack let out a beer belch and the rest of the boys smiled at him. "If the defenders are in a fort, it doesn't sound like a good thing to do." He burped again.

"That's why you need lots of big guns." Wallace held his bottle up to the light to see how much was in it. He put the empty down and signalled his younger brother, who was sitting next to the beer hamper, for another. "When I go in the army, I want to be a gunner."

Jack got up and handed his brother an opened quart. Then he sat down next to him and put an arm over his shoulder. "A gunner?"

"Yep. I will be dishing it out with the big guns." He burped. "No running up hills for me." He burped again. "Maybe I've had enough beer."

Joe pulled his flask out of his pocket. He said, "General Wolfe won Canada for the British Empire by charging up a hill at Quebec." He handed the flask to Wallace. "It's rum. Navy stuff."

The kitchen screen door creaked. "You boys should come in now."

Joe grabbed the flask back and stuffed it in his pocket. "Christ! How does she know!"

"I heard that, Joe. Don't you ever think you will be too big for me to teach you not to swear." The screen door squeaked closed. "You and Jack get the carriages ready. Everyone will want to be home before it gets too late."

The boys waited to see if there was going to be something else. After a moment, Jack grinned at his old friend and they set about their chores. "What are you going to do, Joe?"

"My lady friend would expect me to join up."

"You didn't say anything about a girlfriend."

"You didn't ask."

"Christ! That's the first time you never told me . . ."

"Jack!" The well-recognized voice reached them through an open window. "Your mother would be mortified if she knew you used language like that!"

They grinned.

It was just like when they were kids.

* * *

Joe liked spending the night at the Sugary. It wasn't just that Aunt Mary Anne was such a good cook, or that the Sugary was quieter than his digs in downtown Halifax. No, it was something else. He sniffed the fine aroma of bacon and eggs, hot rolls, and cinnamon as he stopped at the top of the stairs waiting for Jack to catch up. He didn't take his eyes off the country scene framed by the window when the floors creaked at his cousin's approach.

"You snore, Jack," Joe said over his shoulder.

"Only when I have a few beers," Jack replied, agreeably. "How come you were awake to hear me?" The two of them had shared the double bed in the guest bedroom just the way they had often done while they were growing up.

"'Cause you were hoggin' the bed." Joe carried his vest and suit coat over his arm, his overnight case in his other hand. He started down the stairs. "I don't remember you takin' up so much of that bed during our afternoon naps."

Jack made a little boy's voice. "You gonna tell Auntie on little Jackie?"

They were joking in that vein as they entered the kitchen. Seated at the big farm table, with loads of bacon and eggs in front of them, were David Frederick and Wallace.

"Sleepyheads! I've already been down to the crossing and picked up the paper." Wallace stuffed a forkful of egg into his mouth. He chewed as he read from the front page. "Austria Hungary considers itself . . . blah, blah . . .in a state of war with Servia."[4]

"That's simply disgusting, Wallace." Aunt Mary Anne had been cutting more bread and she stood at the side counter with the knife poised over the loaf. "Simply disgusting!"

"I didn't say it!" He peered at the page. "This statement

was issued by Count Berchtold, Minister of Foreign Affairs for Aus . . .'"

"Don't be funny, Wallace. You know what I mean. You shouldn't be talking with your mouth full." Mary Anne began to vigorously cut the bread. "You were brought up better than that." She heard the snickers from Joe and Jack. "Probably the company you keep," she said, turning to face the two cousins in the doorway. "Now, you two sit in your usual places and let's not hear any more foolishness until you are fed up."

"Yes, Aunt Mary Anne," were the dutiful replies.

"And Joe, remember that you have a train to catch."

* * *

At the Newcastle train station there was more news about the war. The boys studied the pamphlet that had been tacked on the face of the old, yellowed advertisement for Intercolonial Railway excursions to Pictoo (the "u" had been removed or fallen off over the years). Again, it was Wallace who read from the paper.[5]

"Austria has formally declared war on Servia and has seized Servian barges on the Danube. Austrian troops are pre-pared to cross the Danube opposite Belgrade."

"I wonder if my regiment will be called to the colours." The other boys couldn't help but hear the pride in David Frederick's voice.

Wallace traced the next sentence with his finger. "King Peter of Servia says he will crush Austria."

Joe gave a half-laugh. "Only with the support of Russia. Is there anything about Russia?"

They were quiet while Wallace scanned the rest of the poster. "Montenegro has mobilized her army to support Servia," he finally said.

"Where's Montenegro, Joe?" Jack wore a self-conscious smile as he added, "I thought it was in South America."

Joe wasn't too sure but he put on his poker face and replied, "Everyone knows it's . . . near Serbia."

Jack studied his friend's face. Suddenly he pushed him against the kiosk. "You don't know! You smart ass!"

There was a tussle until Jack noticed that the platform attendant was walking in their direction. "Mind the railcop!"

The cousins stopped, Joe giving one last push at Jack. "Nothing about Russia?" he asked Wallace as he ignored Jack's glares.

"Not that I could see, but it looks pretty serious."

They stood there—sort of waiting for one of them to begin the goodbyes.

David Frederick repeated, "My regiment will be called up, I'm sure."

Wallace shook his head. "I don't think they will do it that way. They will want volunteers from all over Canada for one, big regiment. I'm going to find out where they are accepting volunteers for the big guns . . ."

"The artillery," interrupted David.

"Yes, the rrr . . ."

"Artillery," said David, helpfully.

The "all aboard" came sooner than expected. With quick handshakes all around, Joe grabbed the handrail and swung himself up the steps, tripping at the top.

As the porter closed the apron and half-door, Joe reappeared to the cheers and catcalls about what a terrible soldier he would make. He endured the jokes at his expense with a big smile and small waves. He was still standing there, watching the New Brunswick countryside sweep past, when the porter came to close the half-door.

"Headin' home, sir?" the porter asked, politely.

Joe looked at the man. He shook his head. "No. Headin' away."

Endnotes

1. David Frederick did (in real life) join the 73rd Militia Regiment. The information was taken from the personal records held at the Canadian National Archives.

2. In real life, Joe Smallwood became aware of the Russian recall and did invest in imported goods.

3. In reality, Italy actually came into the war on the side of the Allies.

4. Newspapers used the word "Servia". If the speaker were reading from the newspaper, I believe he would have said "Servia" instead of the more usual "Serbia".

5. In the advertising text for excursions on the Intercolonial Railway, Pictou had been spelled just the way the Upper Canadians pronounced it: Pictoo. The error went unnoticed by Upper Canadians for years, to the amusement of Maritimers. Eventually, a "u" was pasted on all the posters. The poster was introduced to the readers of Book VI of the Abuse of Power series, *Rebels, Royalists, and Railroaders.*

Chapter Four
Cousin Joe
And So It Begins

August 1, 1914
W.H. Schwartz and Sons
Halifax

"Come in, Joe." Fredrich Schwartz rose from his seat behind the big desk. He indicated with his hand that Joe could take one of the two plush chairs on either side of a small table. "How was your trip?"

"Had a lovely time visiting with old friends and family. We didn't talk about much other than the Serbian situation." Joe sat in the nearest chair. "The Sugary had a good maple syrup season and the crops are really coming along."

When he was seated, Fredrich came around the desk and walked directly to the empty chair. He positioned himself carefully in front of the chair before he sat. "The Sugary? That's the name of the town?"

"My Aunt Mary Anne named her farm the Sugary. The whole area used to be called the Sugary but they changed it to Maple Glen. The Sugary is just my aunt's farm now. Anyhow, the boys talked about nothing but the possibility of a war."

"It's not good news. The Serbians blew up a bridge on the Danube yesterday."

"Then the fighting has started."

"The naval batteries on MacNab's Island were manned last night."

"And I heard the engines supplying the power for the big searchlights at Ives Point—running all night long. This morning, I saw guards at King's Wharf and at the Naval College as I dropped off some orders in the Yard."

Fredrich cleared his throat. "That's what I wanted to talk

to you about, Joe." Fredrich cleared his throat again and then hesitated before he said, "Your supplies . . .."

"There's a problem?"

"Not exactly. There might be some objections from my brother if you don't accept delivery of your order in a day or two." The older man could sense the protest rising in Joe Smallwood's throat. He raised his hand. "I know I agreed that you could delay acceptance of your supplies for thirty days but . . ."

"Fredrich, I have no place to put the stuff. My storage area is full to overflowing."

Fredrich sighed. "I wanted to check with you. My brother has mentioned it twice now; in fact it was the last thing William complained about before he left for Montreal."

There was a timid knock on the door.

"But I'll look after William," Fredrich said quietly before raising his voice. "Come in, please."

The door handle turned and the door swung wide as a girl in a middy blouse—with sailor's collar and tie—struggled to keep hold of a soup bucket, a purse, and a package of sand-wiches while attempting to stop the door's swing.

Joe jumped up and caught the door with one hand and rescued the package of sandwiches with the other. "Let me help you, Miss," he said as he was drawn closer to the young lady by the weight of the heavy door.

"That must be Gladys." Fredrich waited for confirmation but the girl was involved with the door, the bucket, the purse, the wrapped sandwiches, and the unusual closeness of the very masculine gentleman with deep brown eyes.

For his part, Joe was aware of her beautiful skin and the sheen of the thick, reddish hair pulled back into a neat coil of pigtails at the nape of her neck. He had stopped the door and he was quick to step back from the now flustered girl. When she didn't respond to Fredrich's question, Joe's wicked sense of humour took over.

"Well, Mister Schwartz, it's an angel disguised in a blue skirt and top with a sailor's collar. Her hair is the most beau-tiful red I have ever . . ."

"Auburn," the now thoroughly embarrassed fifteen-year-old interrupted. "It's me, Papa."

Fredrich took a moment to preen his moustache before he said, "Yes. Mister Smallwood, I would like you to meet my second daughter, Gladys. Gladys, Mister Smallwood is a business associate and friend."

Joe glanced at Fredrich but could discern nothing more than a proud father introducing his daughter to a friend. *Friend, indeed!* Joe was surprised that he qualified as a friend of one of the Schwartz brothers. He returned his gaze to the fresh, young face. "I'm very pleased to meet you, Miss Schwartz."

Gladys curtsied. "Mama says to be sure to eat all of your soup; it's chicken." She put her hand on the doorknob. "She says . . ."

" . . . it's good for what ails you," father and daughter said in unison.

"And take your medicine," the girl added as they both laughed.

Joe gathered up his hat and gloves, preparing to leave. He extended his hand to the older man.

"Mister Smallwood wants to shake hands, Papa," Gladys Schwartz said from the doorway.

Joe felt stupid because he had done it again; of course, Fredrich wouldn't be able to see what Joe was doing. He grasped the other man's hand in both of his. "I appreciate what you do for me, Fredrich." He released his grip and turned to go.

"My daughter will see you out. As for me, I have my orders from my Emma, the commander-in-chief."

Joe laughed as he closed the door and followed the young girl through the outer office where several employees were reading from an official-looking notice. They glanced up as Joe approached. Joe asked them, "What's the news?"

"There's a run on the Bank of England. People are panicking; converting their money to gold!"

"The Montreal Stock Market has closed," another said.

Gladys watched for Mister Smallwood's reaction. He seemed only mildly interested. When they were outside she was curious enough to ask him.

"What did they mean by a run on the Bank of England?"

"During a war it is better to have gold and tangible things like sugar and wheat rather than money. So, some people are buying gold because they think there might be a war. When there are a lot of people converting their money to gold at the same time, it's called a run on the bank."

She seemed to digest this, her eyes cast down while fingering the little purse she was carrying. "Papa doesn't think there is going to be a war."

"Yes. That's what he told me, too."

"But he did say that, if there is to be a war, they who would reckon with England must reckon with England's sons." She turned her hazel eyes on him, forcing him to the realization that she was a strikingly beautiful child. "Do you know what that means?"

"I suppose it means that if England goes to war her colonies will support her in battle."

"Colonies like Canada?"

"Yes, and Australia and New Zealand."

Gladys studied his face for the longest time. She finally turned away, saying, "I am truly pleased to have met you, Mister Smallwood." She curtsied. "Papa says you are an up-and-coming businessman." Apparently a trifle embarrassed by her own forwardness, she curtsied again. "Good day, Mister Smallwood." Without waiting for a reply, she hurried up the hill toward the Citadel.

Joe shook his head. He turned downhill toward Water Street. "What a looker she's going to be," he said to himself. "With those eyes and beautiful hair she'll break some fellow's heart." On impulse he glanced over his shoulder and, when his eyes located the figure of the girl in blue, she was looking back at him.

August 4, 1914

Joe pointed at a picture at the top of page three of *The Herald* where men with rifles and long bayonets were peering over a wall at some unseen enemy in the foreground.

"Charlotte, it says that some plucky Servian soldiers are . . ." Joe hesitated because the cab bounced in and out of a pothole in the road, " . . . fighting tooth and nail for their beloved country." He folded the paper and handed it to her so she could take a closer look. "Funny looking uniforms." Joe took a deep breath. "But they don't look the least bit scared."

"It's a posed picture, Joe."

Joe retrieved the paper. Unfolding it and appearing to scan the rest of the page, he compressed his lips as if he had nothing further to say.

Charlotte recognized his deliberate motions as a delaying tactic he often used when he was presented with a fact or a situation he wasn't prepared for. When it seemed that he really wasn't going to comment any further, Charlotte changed the subject.

"I didn't hear where you told the cabby to take us."

"I thought you might like dinner at Carleton House." He gave her his brilliant smile. "And yes, these Serb guys are aiming right at where the camera would be. I guess it was posed." He grinned. "But, on the other hand, the photographer could have been an Austrian and then you could say it's remarkable the picture isn't blurred."

Charlotte snickered.

Joe raised her gloved hand and kissed it. "You are a sweetheart, Charlotte."

"Thank you, kind sir." She said nothing more nor made a move (so as not to discourage any further caresses) until he had released her hand with a tiny pat. Then she suggested he turn to the next page. "Union Carriage is advertising a sale . . . fifteen to twenty per cent off carriages and delivery wagons. Wasn't that what you were waiting for?"

Joe leaned forward in a conspiratorial motion so the cabby wouldn't be able to hear. He pointed at the cabby. "Even the cabbies know that the best thing to have is a motor car. I bet if you ask him, the driver would replace his horse and cab with a motor car at the first opportunity." He leaned even closer. "And, with some wise investments I have made in additional goods for the shop, I think my opportunity has arrived." When Charlotte didn't seem to be overly impressed he added, "I am considering a Lozier Light Six." He was right; she wasn't impressed. "Or perhaps a 1915 Maxwell, which will hold the road at fifty miles an hour.

"You already have wagons. Take them to Crowell Brothers and have them refurbished."

Joe made a face.

Charlotte wasn't being deterred. "Crowell Brothers have Sherwin Williams paint and they would do a fine job . . . and there's not a road in Nova Scotia where you can do fifty miles an hour safely."

"Whoa!" The cabby leaned back and said, "The Carleton Hotel, Mister Smallwood."

"Thank you, driver." Joe descended first and helped his lady out of the cab. He closed the door and handed a dollar to the cabby. "If you are passing by in about an hour . . ."

"I'll be here, Mister Smallwood."

Meanwhile, Charlotte had already passed through the hotel door into the lobby, where the assistant manager welcomed her with "How's your father, Miss Norman? Business is good?"

"Yes, Georges. Everything is fine."

"I didn't realize you were acquainted with our Mister Smallwood."

"He comes to the library all the time."

"This way, if you please. Do you have a preference for seating?"

"I'm sure Mister Smallwood will leave that to you, Georges."

As they entered the dining room, Joe noticed that the Schwartz brothers were seated at the table by the fireplace at the far end. "Anywhere here would be nice. Near the window," Joe said.

"There is so much noisy traffic and pedestrians staring into this end of the room, Mister Smallwood. Might I suggest . . ."

Fredrich must have overheard. He half rose. "Joe! Please join us here."

Joe took Charlotte by the arm and steered her to the blind man's side. "Good day," he said to William Schwartz. "I am not alone," he said to Fredrich.

Fredrich dabbed his moustache with his napkin. "Delightful! Is it the mysterious lady whom you have kept from us?"

Charlotte nodded to both gentlemen and allowed the assistant manager to position her chair.

"Yes. Miss Charlotte Norman, may I present . . ."

William Schwartz was quick to say, "I have already had the pleasure. He extended his hand. "It is nice to see you again, Miss Norman."

"I am delighted to finally meet you, Miss Norman." Fredrich leaned forward as if to see better. "Are they seating you next to me?"

Charlotte's deep-throated chuckle was delightful. "Would I be safe, Mister Schwartz?" Not waiting for the reply, she allowed the chair to be pushed in and she gracefully sat down, arranging the folds of her dress and taking off her gloves. "I am here, right beside you." She touched the blind man's wrist lightly, allowing enough time for her warmth to register before she placed her hand in her lap.

Joe was struck by the simplicity of the gesture. *Charlotte has put Fredrich completely at ease.* He cast a glance at the elder Schwartz, wondering what she would do to take the sour look off his face. Joe didn't have long to wait.

"Mama tells me that you let her win at whist, Mister William!"

"Not at all. She is perhaps the Wag's finest whist player."

"Mama says the very same thing about you!"

Aha! Joe busied himself with the napkin in his lap and hoped his amusement wasn't showing. *Charlotte strikes again!*

She's got him worshipping at the Norman altar. This is going to be a fun luncheon. Maybe the talk will centre on Wag activities and not on the war.

"Your father has rejoined his regiment? The Fusiliers, if I remember correctly."

"My, you have a wonderful memory, Mister Schwartz. Yes, he was a lieutenant in the Princess Louise Fusiliers and he has spoken to the Commanding Officer about his return but . . ." Charlotte again touched Fredrich, who was instantly alert to the young woman's comments. "My father's eyesight isn't what it used to be." She picked up Fredrich's hand, squeezing it before putting it down. "There are a lot of good men who won't be permitted to join up." She leaned forward as if to speak confidentially to Fredrich but raised her voice so it could be heard across the table, "But we expect the rest of our boys to come to the aid of the Empire . . . don't we, Mister Fredrich."

"Harrumph!" William Schwartz squirmed in his chair, apparently searching for a waiter. "The Empire is not always best served by putting on a uniform." His eyes continued to search the room. "Some of us must feed the sinews of war by keeping the supplies moving. Schwartz and Sons must . . ."

Charlotte interrupted, "Do its part, I know . . ."

William continued, " . . . do its part and I am the only one to lead the company . . ."

Both Joe and Charlotte saw the hurt in Fredrich's face but it was Charlotte who was the first to speak.

"Schwartz *and Sons* is what I have always heard you say, Mister Schwartz."

"Of course, but our company is an important wheel in the machinery of the British Empire. During a war one can't expect that wheel to be kept turning by a blind . . ."

Charlotte rose, followed almost immediately by the three gentlemen. "Silly me! I never admire those women who interrupt proceedings by going off to the powder room but here I am . . . excusing myself while I go off to the powder room." She nodded at the three of them and, as soon as Joe had moved her chair, she walked away.

The three men resumed their seats. The waiter and the assistant manager appeared but were waved off. No one spoke for several moments.

Fredrich cleared his throat. "William, I understand . . ."

"No, I don't think you do. If you understood anything at all about the Schwartz business you wouldn't make hare-brained deals."

There was a long, long silence. Fredrich waited while William Schwartz seemed to be choosing his words carefully, or perhaps reconsidering his position.

As far as Joe was concerned, he just wished he were somewhere else, and sat with his head down. *I can understand about brothers, even if I don't have one. Jack is almost like a brother and we do have our differences. . . .. sometimes even arguments, but . . .* He jerked his head up. William Schwartz was speaking to him!

"You take advantage of us, sir," he hissed.

"I take advantage of you?"

"Of our company. I check our warehouse and am gratified to see we have great stocks of imported goods. Perhaps, for once, my brother had foreseen the huge profit a wartime market would bring. . . . But no! I find that they are not the property of Schwartz and Sons as I had believed but are invoiced to some Johnny-come-lately . . ."—the veins on William's forehead became very prominent—" . . .who hasn't even paid for them yet." The elder Schwartz choked on the last few words and put his napkin to his lips, stifling a series of coughs.

Neither of the other two men spoke as William's shoulders shook from his struggle to control the coughing spell. Joe had been shocked into silence by the viciousness of the verbal attack, while Fredrich was astonished that a Schwartz would display such a total lack of social grace in a very public place.

William took several deep breaths but gave the impression that he had nothing more to say.

Fredrich spoke quietly but forcefully. "I want you to know, William, Mister Smallwood discussed his opinions about the near-term market and, while I thought his opinions had merit, I did not share them. I didn't believe we would have a war that would interfere with our markets because there have been a number of petty conflicts in the last several decades that caused us no concern. I believed this Serbia affair to be another one."

"More fool you! Obviously our Mister Small-wood has intelligence sources that are to be envied."

"He trusted me with the information that served as the basis for his business decisions and, while I could not gainsay them, I did not share the conclusions he drew from them." Fredrich smiled at Joe. "Completely correct conclusions, as it now seems."

At this point William's voice became petulant. "Since those stores have not been paid for, I want them freed up for resale, immediately."

"If you had checked, brother, you would have seen that Mister Smallwood's invoice has a payment due date of . . ."

"That doesn't matter! We hold the stock in our storeroom and it hasn't been paid for!" William lowered his voice. "The Royal Navy needs those stores and will pay a premium for them."

Joe could see Charlotte coming out of the Ladies' Room. He leaned forward and said, softly, "I meant there to be no loss or inconvenience to Schwartz and Sons." He touched Fredrich's sleeve to get his attention. "I will co-operate any way you want me to, Fredrich." Joe rose as his lady approached.

Charlotte was all a-bustle adjusting her costume and her gloves. "Dear me! I am so forgetful, and I do hope that you gentlemen will excuse me if I ask my escort to return me home. It is my oversight . . ."

"Of course, Charlotte." Joe looked William right in the eye. "And I will help Schwartz and Sons in that other matter in whatever way Fredrich suggests." Joe touched Fredrich's sleeve. "I leave it all up to you, Fredrich. Perhaps I could drop by your office tomorrow?"

"That would be just fine, Joe. See you tomorrow," Fredrich said as the young couple turned to leave.

Charlotte was the first to say anything as she approached the foyer. "Well! He doesn't mind dishing it out!"

Joe smiled. "You didn't hear the half of it."

"You mean he kept picking on his brother after I departed?"

"Amongst others."

Charlotte stepped out onto the sidewalk. She whirled around to face her companion. "You mean . . ." she had started to say when she was bumped by a passer-by, who stopped to excuse himself before hurrying on; it was the chief librarian, Mister Mahen. He tipped his hat.

"Oh! I'm terribly sorry, Charlotte. Pardon me, but I must . . ." Mister Mahen was going to move right along but stopped and stepped closer to the two young people. "Have you heard?" he asked as he looked up and down the street, carefully studying any person who seemed to be looking his way. "They came to the university this morning and arrested Mister Otto."

Charlotte opened her mouth in surprise. "What did he do?" Raising her voice she demanded, "What would the police want with Carl Otto?"

"Sh-h-h! Not so loud, please, Charlotte. I'm going to have to find a lawyer for him. Austen, Dunbrack and Brown wouldn't take his case when I asked them to help." He paused in his examination of the faces of the other pedestrians and looked right into Charlotte's eyes. "Maybe your father would know someone who could help? I'm sure that Mister Otto isn't a spy." He looked away again. "Well, pretty sure, that is. I really don't know the man well enough to . . ." His voice trailed off as he resumed his scrutiny of each passer-by.

"What did the police say when they arrested him?"

"It was the military police. They said he was German and must be taken into protective custody."

"Carl is no more German than you or I."

"That's what Mister Otto said but the soldier asked him to spell his first name."

Joe couldn't stop himself. He asked, "What could that prove?"

"He spelt it with a 'K.'"

"Oh, for pity's sakes!" Charlotte stamped her foot and then growled, "This is so stupid!"

"They had already taken his wife Shirley into custody because I could see her in the back of the van when they loaded Carl."

"But Shirley is a Jamieson!" Charlotte gave Joe an apologetic look. "Joe, I'm going to have to run along to see Papa. The Jamiesons are relatives on my mother's side." Charlotte waited for Joe's nod and then she took Mister Mahen by the arm. "You come right along with me, Mister Mahen, and tell my father everything you heard."

Joe waited in the sunshine for the return of his cabby. On the drive back to the shop he was musing on what the world was possibly coming to when it dawned on him: there couldn't be a name more German than Fredrich Schwartz!

August 5, 1914

Entering the Aberdeen Building on Buckingham Street, Joe was shown directly into his friend's private office. Bearing in mind the Karl Otto incident of the previous afternoon, he was relieved to find the older man seated at the desk. Fredrich was holding a newspaper.

"What did you tell the military police, Fredrich?" When Fredrich didn't respond immediately, Joe explained himself. "The military police were picking up Germans and people with German-sounding names yesterday. Did they come after you?"

"I wasn't troubled by them, Joe; but at an early morning meeting of the family, it was decided that we should henceforth use the anglicized version of my name. Father was advised by the chief of police that it would be the politic thing to do."

"So, hello, Frederick Schwartz?"

"No, actually, it would be Fredrick." He grinned. "Just the one letter has all the significance in the world . . . at least in the port city of Halifax." Fredrick appeared anxious to change the subject. "I have been reading this newspaper . . ."

Joe blurted out, "But I thought you were blind!"

"Well, that's what a lot of people believe, particularly when my brother encourages the fiction that he is the only Schwartz of the present generation with any foresight." Fredrick chuckled at his humour. "Actually, it suits his vanity to have people believe that I am totally blind," he gave a small wave of his hand, "and mostly, in buildings and at night, I *am* totally blind. However, in bright sunlight I can see light and dark, figures . . . in fact, with the proper help, I can even read a little."

Fredrick pulled a huge magnifying glass mounted on a retractable arm to a position over the copy of the newspaper that he had been holding. "Let me read this to you. It might be of some interest." He glanced up at Joe. "You know that England declared war on Germany this morning?"

Joe nodded in the affirmative.

"This is particularly appropriate." Adjusting the magnifying glass and the newspaper to the light from the sunlit window, Fredrick read from the paper. "According to the *Iokalanzeiger*, an important Berlin journal," Fredrick leaned over the paper, painstakingly identifying each individual word, "the Germanic peoples will begin the final fight which will settle forever Germany's great position in the world. When Germany's sword glides into the scabbard, she shall stand before the world the mightiest nation, and shall at last be in a position to give the world peace, enlightenment and prosperity."[1]

"That's arrogant," Joe commented. "I liked what the King said in his speech following the declaration of war. He spoke of the security the Royal Navy would give the Empire."

"Was it in the papers this morning?" Fredrick's voice was apologetic as he added, "I read the English newspapers on alternate days and today is a German day."

It was then that Joe noticed other newspapers on the desk, the top one in German, another in French . . .

"Sons of mercantile houses like Schwartz are obliged to learn a number of languages . . . even if blind." He smiled and paused a moment before he asked, "Do you have the King's words there?"

Joe unfolded the paper he had been carrying under his arm. He pointed to the blurb at the head of the columns. "It says, August 5. Britain declares war. I have every confidence that the British Fleet will revive the old glories of the navy. I am sure the navy will again shield Britain in this hour of trial. It will prove the bulwark of the Empire. King George."

"Oh, I say! How terribly British!" Fredrick was going to make another comment but was interrupted by a discreet knock on the door. Fredrick responded, "Yes, come in."

A young male clerk opened the door and stood just inside the threshold. "Your guest would like some refreshment?"

Fredrick sought Joe's preferences for tea and biscuits and instructed the young man. Until the clerk's return, the two men discussed the possible effects of the war on the port city. Eastern Passage had already been closed to all ship traffic and the Senior Naval Officer for the port of Halifax had issued the first of what were probably going to be long lists of restrictions.

"Until the port settles down a bit," Joe said, "I don't intend to do any cruising in my motor launch."

Fredrick nodded his head in agreement as the clerk returned with a tray of biscuits and tea. They busied themselves with the ritual of teacups, sugar tongs, and stirring until the young man had closed the door on his way out.

"What do you plan to do, Joe?"

"I have to be honest with you, Fredrick. I don't have enough money to pay for the supplies."

"Actually, I was wondering about your . . ."

"Pardon me, but I expect more cash in the next few days."

"Then let us settle this matter right now. Pay for the stock you want by the date on the invoice and accept delivery. Our company will broker the remainder of the stock and you will be charged a fee based on the proceeds of the sale." He put his teacup down with an air of finality. "If that is acceptable to you, then the matter is settled."

Joe breathed a sigh. "That is more than fair." Joe put his cup down and indicated that he was finished. "Will a broker-age fee satisfy your brother's concerns?"

"It certainly will. If you hadn't had the foresight to order the extra stock, Schwartz and Sons wouldn't have a broker's fee." Fredrick smiled ruefully. "Yesterday, after lunch, my brother suggested that you should be charged a carrying fee. A broker's fee will make him even happier."

"As I said, you are being more than fair."

"Good. The matter is settled."

Joe noticed that the other man preened his moustache with one hand while he fiddled with his watch fob with the other. *Perhaps he has something else to say on the matter.* Joe waited. It wasn't long in coming.

"But earlier, when I had asked you about your plans, I didn't mean to discuss what you were going to do with your merchandise. What I meant to ask you, Joe, was what are your plans now that England is at war?"

When Joe didn't respond, Fredrick explained. "The young man who served our tea is a Schwartz. This is his last day with the firm."

"He enlisted?"

"Last night. One hundred men of the Princess Louise Fusiliers marched out of the Armoury to join the Royal Canadian Regiment at Wellington Barracks. I am proud to say Private Charles Schwartz was one of them." Fredrick touched his eye as if there were a tear. "My sister-in-law is so proud of her son." He sighed. "The boy is handsome in his uniform."

"I heard the band playing but didn't go along to see what it was all about." Joe paused and then said, "So, one hundred of the PLF went regular army. Well, there's never been any doubt that the Empire would come to the aid of the mother country but . . ." Joe hesitated.

"But you don't intend to enlist."

Joe brushed at a biscuit crumb. "Well, it's not that I don't want to enlist." He bent over and picked up the crumb between his thumb and forefinger, depositing it on the saucer.

"It's because . . . well, the King is right, you know."

"Meaning?"

"His navy will isolate Germany from her colonies and keep the British Empire safe. Meanwhile, the professionals will fight the war on the continent and it will be over before any volunteers can get to the fight."

"I see."

"You don't agree that the war will be over in a month or two?"

"Not as quickly as that . . . but certainly by Christmas."

"Then you can understand why I don't plan to get involved. Besides, I have so many things I want to get done in the next little while and I don't want this European fracas to get in the way."

Fredrick might have said something else but Joe had stood up to take his leave.

"I really appreciate what you have done, Fredrick. I want you to know how much your friendship means to me."

"It was just good business, Joe. Your foresight made us both a lot of money."

"Well, I know it was more than that and I thank you."

Joe stood at the door and looked back at Fredrick Schwartz. The sun was streaming in the window making Fredrick's hair and moustache look almost white. Joe could see the daughter, Gladys, in the handsome face. *I wonder what the older daughter . . . what was her name . . . Edna? I wonder what she looks like. No, not Edna. Edith. Edith Schwartz. That was her name.*

With a casual "see you at the luncheon on Thursday," Joe was off about his business.

Endnotes

1. *The Herald* quoted the German newspaper *Iokalanzeiger* later in the year. I used it here.

Chapter Five
Girding for War

August 10, 1914
Halifax

Joe stood in the middle of his near-empty storeroom. He scratched his head in wonderment as he recalled how quickly his customers had cleaned him out. *Big, big turnover and lots of profits but . . .* "What'll I do for an encore?" echoed back to him before he heard Frank's voice from the front of the shop.

"What'dja say, Joe?"

Taking one last look at the storeroom as if hoping to find a bale or two he had perhaps overlooked, Joe gathered up some blank price cards and walked out into the shop. He put on a false jovial air as he shouted back, "Woe betide the businessman who doesn't keep up with the flood of price changes!"

Joe and Frank had come into the shop an hour before the usual opening to do mark-ups on the stock remaining on the shelves. By the end of the day, if his customers continued with their frenzied buying, his shelves would be cleared. He picked up the Schwartz and Sons catalogue and studied it as he moved toward the front of the store near the display windows, where the light was better.

"No sense looking in there, Joe." Frank held a copy of the morning newspaper. "That catalogue's been cancelled."

"Since when?" Joe asked in a disbelieving voice, but he reached for the newspaper anyway.[1]

"Since right away, it seems. Shoulda put your order in on Friday, big fella."

Joe read down the ad. He took in a deep, deep breath and then let it all out. "I hate to do it but we'll put an order in to Wentzells." Then he noticed the little box near the Schwartz and Sons ad. It didn't take him long to read it.

Price List Cancelled

Our friends will please take notice that on account of our beloved Empire being in a state of war; and all raw material used by ourselves in the manufacture of "PEERLESS' SPICES and COFFEES, having to come across the seas from France, the East and West Indies, it will be impossible to get supplies, only at risk of capture and greatly advanced cost, freight, insurance, etc.

WE HEREBY CANCEL ALL PRICE LISTS; and we will be compelled to advance our prices to a war basis. We EXCEEDINGLY REGRET HAVING TO DO THIS, but at the same time
Schwartz's Peerless Spices
Coffee and Cream Tartar
(if we can continue to get supplies) will be up to the same high standard of quality attained by us during the last SEVENTY-FOUR YEARS.

God Save the King and Our Great Empire
and Give Him Victory in A Just Cause.

Yours faithfully,
W.H. SCHWARTZ & SONS

WENTZELLS LIMITED

On account of war conditions we have cancelled and withdrawn all catalogues for the present.

Frank must have seen the dismay on Joe's face. "What's the problem?"

"They have cancelled their price lists, too." Joe put the paper down. "And they're closed for the day." He picked up the paper again. "By the looks of this ad, the Schwartz brothers must be having troubles with the authorities."

"What'dya mean, troubles?"

"Well, their ad is full of patriotism and good wishes for the future of the Empire—almost as if they are trying to buy the good will of the public." Joe tossed the paper to Frank. "Take a look at the Schwartz ad and then compare it to the Wentzells ad. They're both saying the same thing: cancelling their price lists."

"I don't see what the trouble is."

"The Schwartzes have a German name and probably think they have to be more patriotic than anybody else." Joe handed Frank some of the price cards. "You know, the military police have been taking people into custody because they have German names."

"Yeah. Heard that." Frank held the price cards up. "Shouldn't we wait until we find out about the War Tax?"

"No. Can't wait. We'll have to do it again later."

Frank opened the drawer under the counter and pulled out the stencil set. He closed the drawer. "But Joe, isn't Wentzell a German name? Shouldn't they have every bit as much a problem as Schwartz?"

"Maybe so." Joe shook his head. "I don't know what's going on around here any more. You know George Martin? Sure, he was born in Austria but he's been living here for thirty years and he's a naturalized Canadian. But when he reported to the Armoury volunteering to fight for the Empire, he got thrown in jail for his trouble." Joe continued to shake his head. "Some of the things the authorities are doing don't make much sense." Joe grabbed the paper. "Just look at this notice from Rudland."

"The Rudland who's Chief of Police?"

"The very one. Well, he's now the Assistant Provost Marshal and he has announced that . . . wait a minute. I'll read it to you." Joe flipped the paper open to page three. "It says here . . . should sentries, pickets, or patrols be obliged to use their weapons and to open fire, their aim will be directed at, and not over the heads of, offending parties."

"Imagine gettin' your balls shot off by one of Rudland's boys!"

Through the display window, Joe saw Charlotte coming up the front walk. "Take off to the back, will you, Frank?"

"Sure thing, Joe."

"Here, take the paper." Joe gave Frank a push and said, with a smile, "Practise your reading. If you practise real hard, you might graduate from kindergarten . . . in a few years."

The ring of the telephone drowned out Frank's retort. Joe picked up the receiver. "Hello?" The doorbell tinkled and Joe nodded his head and smiled at Charlotte, waving at her to take a chair at the back of the shop. Again, to the telephone he said, "Hello? Yes, this is Joe Smallwood." A pause and then, "What a surprise! Never thought you would go to the expense of a long distance call but I was expecting to hear from you . . . maybe a letter."

Charlotte wandered around the shop looking at the various things for sale, pretending not to eavesdrop. She was just about to try one of the jelly candies when she overheard something that was interesting.

"I don't want to go way up there, Wallace."

Charlotte moved closer to the telephone. *Someone named Alice is trying to talk Joey into a trip! I don't know any Alice . . . and Joey had better not plan to go away with one!*

"Yes, I heard what he said, too . . . no, I heard he said it wouldn't last long."

Intent on listening to what Joey had to say, Charlotte blundered into the bread rack, knocking it over. As the loaves of bread tumbled every which way, Joe looked up to see what was going on. He gave her a huge grin and signed that the spilled bread wasn't important.

On her part, Charlotte was so embarrassed at her clumsiness that she missed whatever else was said in the telephone conversation. When, finally, she had returned most of the bread to its proper place she heard, "I wish you all the best, Wallace. You'll keep in touch with me?" Joe took the receiver away from his ear and looked at it. Then he carefully put it back on the hook. He gazed out the window. "I think we got cut off."

"Who's Wallace, Joey?"

Still looking out the window, Joe said, slowly, "He's my cousin. I wasn't around him too much while we were growing up but in the last few years I got to know him better. He works in a pharmacy and he's going to volunteer for the Expeditionary Force."

"He's going to be a volunteer. Isn't that wonderful!"

"The militia told him he has to go to Quebec City to enlist." Joe turned and walked away from the window. "I told him I wasn't going." He reached under the counter and took out a fresh package of Black Cats. He slit it open. "Want one?" When the young woman seemed to hesitate, Joe leaned closer to her and whispered, "I know you smoke, my dear. I can smell it in your hair."

Charlotte gave him a glare, stepping back as she retorted, "Then you'll have to go to Quebec City, Joey, if you mean to fight for the Empire."

"Well, I'm not going."

After a moment's hesitation she held out her hand. "I'll have that cigarette, please."

Joe lit the cigarette for her and then lit his own. "Wallace and I had agreed to go together but . . ."

"But what, Joe?"

He sensed that he was getting into something he didn't understand, but plodded on anyway. "Sam Hughes, the Minister of Militia, says that the war will be over quickly. Even the Canadian Regulars might not get to the battlefield before it's won. I don't see why I should disrupt my life and traipse over to Germany and back . . ."

He continued with his argument but Charlotte wasn't hearing him. Instead, she was almost overwhelmed with the thought that Joey, the man she admired so very much, the man who was willing to take on, single-handedly, armed invaders when they seemed to have threatened Nova Scotia shores last Dominion Day, wasn't going to answer the Imperial call for help! She butted her cigarette.

When Joe saw his lady butt her unfinished cigarette, he knew he was "for it."

"Now, you just listen to me, Joey Smallwood." She dug in her bag and pulled out a folded piece of paper. "This is what that new student minister said from the pulpit yesterday. They handed out copies as we were leaving the church . . . and a good thing too, because I have it here to show you." She thrust the paper into his hands. When it seemed that Joe wasn't eager to read it, she snatched it back. "It was a wonderful sermon. In fact, I believe the speaker is a friend of yours . . . Mister Roy Curry . . . which should make it even more meaningful to you . . . and he said things the way we felt . . . that we are all of the English race and the Mad Dog of Militarism, Kaiser Bill, must be put down before he destroys everything British in this world we love and cherish."[2]

Squinting a little now as she focused on the paper, Charlotte's hands shook with the emotion she felt. "With the enemy at the gates, with the safety of our homes and loved ones menaced . . ." She stopped. "No, that's not the part I want you to hear." She scanned the page and turned it over. "We have put our hand to the plough—and there is to be no swerving from our purpose, no turning back. Comrades all! Brothers All! The regulars of the garrison, the trained militia-man, the raw recruit, and the civilian have clasped hands in this the Motherland's worthy cause."

She looked up to make sure he was listening. Satisfied that he was paying proper attention, she resumed her reading.

"Hovering as guardian angels over all are the tender, strong women of the race, eager to assist, to care for, and if possible to protect the fathers, brothers, sons and husbands, not alone as individuals but as a Great Sisterhood, the One Great Brotherhood." She put the paper down. "Oh, Joey! We can be a part of the great up-welling of loyalty and devotion to our Empire!"

When Joe didn't answer, Charlotte stepped closer to him. She raised both hands and cupped his face, drawing him to her. "If you don't feel it in your heart, dear Joey, then reason it out with your mind." An imploring note crept into her voice. "Laurier and Borden had a silly political fight and, because of that, Canada is not contributing anything to the Empire's naval defence. There will be no Canadian ships, no Canadian sailors." She released Joe's face and stepped back a pace. "If we send no navy, then Canada should send more soldiers than any other part of the Empire." She kissed him, lightly, on one cheek and then the other . . . almost like a benediction. "My brave Joey will be a soldier of the King"—she hugged him and whispered, "and come back to march down Barrington Street with the other heroes wearing the laurels of victory."

The storeroom door creaked as it was opened. Frank stuck his head into the room. "Can I come out now? My wife expects me home for lunch and if you want me to help you with the pricing . . .."

Joe and Charlotte separated.

"Come in, Frank." Joe patted his companion's hand. "Miss Norman and I can finish this discussion later," he gave Charlotte a smile, "can't we, my dear?" Joe made a great show of spreading the price cards on the counter and opening the stencil box. "I'll give you a call tonight, Charlotte, if that's all right with you."

Charlotte took a moment as she fussed with her gloves. "You men have a lot to do and I don't want to hold you up." Once at the door, she gave them a gay little wave and left.

Joe worked with the stencil for a few minutes. "Frank."

"Yes, Joe?"

"You going to volunteer?"

"If they'll take me, I'll go."

They worked along in silence for another moment or two.

"Y'know Joe, maybe I'll get to see Vladik. Can't be that big a place."

Endnotes

1. The Schwartz and Wentzells newspaper ads are taken from *The Herald* of that date.

2. The sermon Charlotte attributes to Roy Curry is actually based on newspaper editorials of the day.

Chapter Six
Cousin Joe and Cousin Wallace
We're Off to Beat the Kaiser

September 5, 1914
Newcastle Train Station

Joe stepped down from the train, glancing first one way and then the other, looking for Wallace. There was a crowd of people at the far end of the platform near the first class. He grasped the fact that most of them were Smallwoods only when Jack took several steps in his direction and, raising his arm to point, hollered, "There he is! There's Joe!"

Jack ran ahead to be the first to embrace Joe, which caused Joe a moment of reservation; but then he returned the hug.

"Wallace said you weren't going."

"I know, Jack."

"What changed your mind?"

Joe pushed away from his cousin and, giving him a rueful smile, complained, "They talk at you in the church, in the theatre, in the shop . . . my customers, my friends, my girl-friend, shit!" He spoke with a nasal herringchoker twang. "Every son of empire must rally to the grand old flag!"

Joe Smallwood always spoke of himself as being a herring-choker from New Brunswick. The rest of the family thought of themselves as bluenosers, having been born in Nova Scotia within forty miles of the sea.

"But isn't it exciting?" asked Duke.

"Yeah, but . . . .." He grinned as he turned to greet the rest of the family. "I told them I wasn't a son of empire but here I am . . . on my way to Quebec." He put out his arms. "Auntie Mary Anne! I've missed you!"

There were hugs and kisses all around. Joe looked for his mother and then caught his father's eye.

Duke shook his head.

Joe threaded his way to his father's side and shook hands with him.

Duke was the first to speak. "Your mother doesn't understand about the war. She remembers that Kaiser Wilhelm is the King's cousin. I can't seem to make her understand that there would be war between them."

Joe bowed his head in understanding but Duke felt he had to go on with the explanation.

"She said that members of the same family might have bad feelings but families resolve things without fighting . . . but then she drifted off to talk about your Uncle Silas and Aunt Mary Anne as if, somehow, King George and Kaiser Bill were in the same room with them having the usual stupid arguments." Duke squeezed his son's shoulder. "I hope you don't mind that I didn't try to get her to come with me this afternoon."

"That's just fine, Duke . . . er, Dad."

"Are you going to be all right?"

"Sure thing. Wallace and I will look after each other." Searching the crowd Joe asked, "Where is Wallace?"

"I loaned him the car. He wanted to go out to Vera's to say goodbye rather than try to do it here at the train station."

"That's a good idea. Charlotte came to the station and she got plenty teary-eyed."

"She's the lady-friend you wrote about?"

"Yeah. I'm sorry, now, that I didn't get a chance to bring her to the Miramichi." Joe stood on tiptoe and tried to look over the heads of the people. "I hope Wallace doesn't miss the train." Then he added, "I'm pretty serious about her but I don't know if she's 'the one' for me."

"You're serious about the young lady from Halifax? This . . . Charlotte?"

"Yes, and now that I'm going away, I might not ever know if she is the one."

"Something will tell you." He hesitated, but doggedly continued, "I thought I knew about your mother."

Joe was shocked at Duke's admission. He looked around to see if they could be overheard. Leaning forward and in a lowered voice Joe said, "I always believed . . ."

Duke Smallwood hushed his son with a movement of his hand. "I loved her but I never really knew the woman I loved. Maybe she changed over the years and I didn't know it . . ." Duke tried to put some jocularity into his voice but failed in the attempt. "She changed and changed again over the years but, every now and then, the old gal comes back." He put his hand on his son's sleeve. "I love her and"—here he paused and his eyes drifted off into the past—"there never was anyone else—just my Jean." Duke glanced down at his feet. When he directed his gaze back at his son, Joe knew that his father was firmly back in the present. "You heard David Frederick's eyes aren't good enough for him to transfer to the regulars?"[1]

Joe didn't want the moment to pass; there might not ever be another chance for father and son to come to an understanding. "I want to tell you . . ."

When Joe hesitated, Duke pressed.

"What do you want to say, Joe?"

"You're the best father a son could ever have." It was Joe's turn to look at his feet. "If I shouldn't come back, I wanted you to know that."

Probably for the first time in his life, Duke Smallwood was embarrassed. "Train stations bring out the very best in people." When Duke saw the hurt in Joe's eyes, he hastily remarked, "Thank you, son."

Father and son, standing apart from the family throng, were silent.

Finally, Joe asked, "But they're going to keep him in the militia? David Frederick, I mean."

"Yeah. His eyes are good enough for guarding bridges but not good enough for shooting Germans. He's on duty today at the dam or he would be here to see you off."

"And Jack is going to continue working on the road?"

"Yes. Railroad employees won't be accepted in the Expeditionary Force. Did you know that he's a union shop steward?"

"All aboard!"

Joe was startled by the trainman's call. "Shit! Where is that fart of a Wallace?"

"Joe Smallwood!"

Joe nearly jumped out of his skin. "Yes, Auntie?"

"You might be a grown man going off to war, but if your mother ever heard you using such language, she would be mighty upset."

Before Joe could give an answer, the second call came.

"All aboard for Campbellton and points west. All aboard."

The station agent passed close to Duke, touching his hat, "Get what's yours that's goin', goin', Mister Smallwood." He nodded at Joe. "Good luck to you in the war, Joe. Give the Kaiser hell." He paused, examining the faces around Joe. "Where's your Cousin Wallace? Thought he was goin', too."

With a certain lack of conviction in his voice, Joe said to the retreating agent's back, "He'll be here."

Duke motioned to the porter. "Sleeping car passenger," he said.

Joe reacted immediately. "No, I only have coach class. I couldn't get a sleeping car reservation."

"I upgraded you and Wallace." Duke grinned. "Remember, your Uncle Dan is an inspector now."

"But I already have a ticket."

"Turn in the unused portion for a refund, Joe," Duke said as he handed Joe's coach class ticket back to him. The other ticket he put in the porter's hands. "Car 41, please, lowers one and three," and he gave the man a dollar. "You'll look after it, won't you?"

The porter folded the bill, "Yessir, I sure will."

Duke scanned the crowd. "Hope I haven't wasted my money on that young pup Wallace. He said he'd be here." Duke pushed his son up the steps into the car's vestibule as they heard the engineer's bell. The trainman boarded last, lowering the vestibule trap door over the steps and closing the half-door. As soon as the trainman was out of the way, Joe leaned forward, searching for any signs of his missing cousin.

Hands reached out in farewell. Good wishes and final words filled the air. The train shuddered, then again. Joe was going off to war, alone. His stomach turned over and he thought he might be sick. He swallowed hard. He was retasting the pickle from lunch when he caught a glimpse of Wallace at the entrance of the stationhouse, running hard, with a bag in each hand held high in front of him.

Joe grinned as he watched Wallace pass quickly through the crowd. "He's coming! Help me get the door open!"

The trainman released the latches, opened the half-door and raised the step's cover.

"He'll make it, no trouble," Joe said to the trainman.

"Lots of time," the other man agreed.

Wallace stopped in front of Duke. He dropped both bags and reached into his trousers pocket.

"Oh my God!" Joe clapped his head with his hand. "What in hell is he doing?"

The train was moving.

Wallace cast a despairing glance in Joe's direction. He dug in the other pocket and then in his coat pockets then back to the trousers.

Duke pushed him in the train's direction, urging him to leave, but Wallace was obviously still searching his pockets.

The trainman cleared his throat. "I'll have to put the put the trap door down, Mister. We're leaving the station. ICR regulations. I have to put it down."

Joe was standing in the trainman's way watching Wallace pick up his bags and start running again. "Just give him a chance. He can run like the wind."

"He'll have to. The train is picking up speed." The trainman took out his watch and flipped it open. "Right on time." He looked out at the struggling Wallace. "Seen it before. They never make it." He closed his watch and returned it to his vest. "Naw! They never make it." He shouldered Joe out of the way and put the trap door down and then closed the half-door. "I seen it all before," he said as he pushed open the other door to the coach and proceeded to the rear of the train.

Joe pressed his face against the glass but the station was beyond his view. He pushed the coach door and went in search of his berth. "Car 41, the Duke said." He moved along conscious that he was feeling a very real sense of loss. Whatever was going to happen from here on in, Joe Smallwood was on his own. "What a hell of a way to start an adventure!"

The conductor, trainman, and porter came swarming up the aisle. Joe got out of their way by taking a seat.

The trainman, catching Joe's eye said, *sotto voce,* "I never seen this before! We been red-flagged!"

Joe followed on. "What does that mean?" he whispered.

The conductor, in a peevish tone, complained, "We've been told to hold." He watched as the trainman opened the half-door and raised the trap door. "There must be something on the track."

The porter jumped down and placed the step-and-a-half on the ground for the conductor, who then regally descended to the gravel. He looked toward the front of the train to where he could see that the engine crew was letting off great clouds of steam and then to the rear where he was chagrined to see Wallace huffing and puffing as he staggered down the track. "Well!"

Joe whooped and ran down the track to give his cousin a hand.

The three ICR men stood with their hands on their hips, the trainman and porter grinning from ear to ear, watching as the Smallwood boys boarded the train.

Wallace turned and waved at the tall man who was standing on the tracks near the emergency signal box.

Duke waved back and then tinkered with the box.

The train engineer sounded his bell.

"We are clear," snarled the conductor who, with a grand flourish, examined his watch. "We are two minutes forty-five seconds late." He signalled for the train to proceed and mounted the steps. "I will have to write an incident report." He regarded the two young men with some hostility. "Do either of you know that man at the box?"

"Who? Us?"

"I wouldn't see more innocent faces at Sunday School." He seemed to be considering something. "You boys going to war?"

Wallace was too short of breath to answer.

"We're going to be in the artillery," Joe said with a great deal of pride.

The conductor seemed to be studying his watch. Traces of a smile lurked at the corners of his mouth and his eyes twinkled—sort of. He turned on his official face. "Trainman!"

"Yes, sir."

"We left the station on time, did we not?"

"We certainly did, sir."

"Then, by now, your trap door should be down and the vestibule secured." He snapped his watch shut. "See to it, if you please," and he departed.

As far as Joe was concerned, everything was in its proper place: the conductor was gone, the train was moving and the cousins were together. Joe took Wallace's bags. "I think our car is this way." He stopped to say something else and Wallace bumped into him.

"Sorry, Joe. I seem to be all thumbs today."

"Why did you stop running?"

"I had to give Duke his car keys."

"Where were they?"

"I forgot I left them in the car."

Joe sighed. He struggled with the two bags and the door.

Wallace seemed not to notice, waiting patiently until Joe got the heavy coach door open and the baggage through.

Joe, his face red with exertion, pronounced, "I have a real feeling that you're going to need me close by if you're going to survive this war, Wallace."

Endnotes

1. Militia records in the National Archives record that David Frederick Smallwood was not accepted by the regular army. His eyes were not good enough.

Chapter Seven
Michelle

September 7, 1914
Camp Valcartier, P.Q.

Line up to eat. Line up to pee. Line up to wait and then line up to wait some more . . . what's next? Joe was lined up again but didn't know what kind of line-up it was. Someone said it was for the dentist . . . gotta have good teeth if you were going to fight the Germans. "Might have to bite them," said the man behind him in line. Joe tapped the shoulder of the big man in front. "Can you see what we are lined up for?" Joe asked.

"I don't know jack."

"The name's Joe."

"That's all right, jack," the man said as he turned away to step forward a couple of paces.

Joe recognized the tent-like structure they were approaching as the mess tent and the next structure, part tent and part wooden construction, was a temporary field kitchen where great quantities of food were prepared that Joe couldn't make himself eat much of. Milk and cookies would have been nice but there hadn't been any. Joe had eaten a little bit of the stew but had tried to fill up on bread and what passed for apple juice. Wallace, on the other hand, had dug right into the stew, saying it was delicious. After the meal, they had been assigned to a tent with seven other men sleeping on cots that had mattresses as thin as a coalminer's pay envelope.

At first, the uncomfortable cot kept Joe awake and, just when it seemed like he might be drifting off to sleep, Wallace got up complaining about having the jimjams and raced to the latrine, giving up what seemed like half his body weight to the latrine and the other half to the clouds of mosquitoes. Joe, worried about his cousin, stumbled through the darkness to the latrine several times. His tent mates became quite verbal about Joe's activity so he eventually climbed onto the cot and waited for sleep to come. No matter how much he wanted to help his cousin, he was forced to allow nature to determine Wallace's fate. In the morning they were both haggard and worn-looking.

None of the other men had any troubles. They ate, slept, and lined up with no physical complaints of any sort. The seven men from their tent all had "old country" accents—mostly Scots. This one in front of Joe in the line had said he was from the Midlands, wherever that was, where everyone was "jack."

An arm with sergeant's stripes was thrust between Joe and the Midlands fellow. "From here back, abo-o-o-ot turn."

Joe and the men behind him turned around.

"Quick march! Left, right, left, right . . ." and off they went to a tent that was called clothing stores. They lined up in front of clothing stores until it was time to line up for lunch. When they finally got to sit at the mess tent, Joe was so hungry he ate two helpings of the shepherd's pie.

The afternoon was spent getting a haircut. In the haircut line, the men could see what was happening since the barber's customers sat on a wooden chair in the middle of an open area. Mounds of different coloured hair surrounded the legs of the chair.

Wallace returned from his most recent trip to the latrine, joining Joe in the line. "God! Look what they're doing!"

"I know. I've been watching."

The barber's clippers were placed against the side of the customer's face just in front of the ear and then were passed up the one side to the middle of the head. The barber stepped around to the other side of the chair and did the same thing again.

"They look like dog shears!"

Joe swallowed but didn't make any comment. His eyes were as big as saucers as he watched the clippers go from the back of the neck to the forehead. A couple of more passes and the man stood up to be quickly replaced by the next in line.

The chair's new occupant had several friends in the yet-to-be-done line who made jokes about coming all the way from Winnipeg to get clipped in Quebec.

"You men!"

The good-natured joshing stopped and all eyes were on a small man with corporal's stripes.

"Yes, you men with the peach fuzz! I want a right marker!"

One of the newly sheared men moved quickly to stand in front of the corporal.

The corporal turned smartly to the right and moved off a few paces where he again faced the men. "Fall in!"

Most of the men were militia-trained but there were a few who drew the attention of the NCO.

"That means lining up in threes, ladies."

Some shuffling and pushing by the militiamen quickly produced a military-looking formation.

"My name is Hastings. Corporal Hastings." He pointed his finger at the group, "You will be going to the mess tent to do your papers." He put his hands on his hips. "If there are any of you who don't know how to read and write, fall out and go to the guard house. We have over thirty thousand men here . . . more comin' every day . . . and we only have room for twenty-six thousand in the Force." He seemed to study the face of each recruit as he added, "Do yourself a favour and drop out before you're found out." Surveying the formation, Hastings saw there was room for one more body in the blank file. He pointed at the barber. "Hand the clippers to the next man and fall in."

The recruit who had been an acting barber fell in with the formation.

The man who received the clippers held the instrument in his hands, just staring at it.

Hastings raised his voice: "You men are now a squad. Squad! Attention! Right turn! No ladies, the other right! Quick march!" Hastings called the step, "Left, right . . ." but didn't march off with the group. He looked at the man with the clippers. "I know, son, you never cut hair before. Do ten heads and then hand it to the next man, who will do yours. I will want thirty more fuzzy heads when I come back." Without waiting for an answer or an acknowledgement, Hastings marched briskly away, calling out, "Left, right, left, right . . . swing those arms . . . you're in the army now . . . left, right . . ."

* * *

"Toss me some paper, Wallace."

Wallace had been sitting on the toilet with his head in his hands. He raised his head slightly, just enough to allow his eyes to go the rest of the way. "I only have the one roll, Joe." Wallace picked it up and tossed it across the aisle into Joe's waiting hands.

At this time of night they had the latrine all to themselves. This particular latrine could accommodate twelve men at a time: five toilets down each wall and two across the bottom. A single light bulb in the ceiling cast a harsh light on their stubble-covered heads and pasty-grey faces in need of a shave.

"You're a fine-looking corpse, buddy."

Wallace groaned as he passed more fluid, "Tell me about it, Joe." He waited for the spasm to pass. "How's your stomach cramps?"

"Still there. I shouldn't have eaten the shepherd's pie . . . I know better but I was mighty hungry." Joe was wistful as he added, "If mother were here, she would heat up some cocoa, add a lot of milk, give me three or four of her honey rolls," Joe sighed, "and I would be fine."

Wanting to talk about anything but Valcartier and the war, Wallace prompted, "And she always had fudge on the go."

"Yeah. Fudge, cookies, but her chocolate cake was the best. She would take pieces of sweet chocolate and melt them down and then pour it over the two-egg-cake while the cake was still hot."

"I had it once."

"I had it all the time. Mother wasn't much of a cook. If I wanted a meal, I had to go to Aunt Mary Anne's. "

"Um, yes, pigs in a blanket; spicy sausage in pastry with a honey-mustard sauce."

"I could never eat that. My plate was always chicken in a blanket with honey." Joe tossed the paper back. "She made it special for me. Always looked like pigs in a blanket, but it was chicken." He stood up, pulling his trouser suspenders over his nightshirt. "You still goin'?"

"Yes."

"You have it much worse than I do. I just have my same old cramps and nausea."

"You're lucky . . . but I don't have any nausea."

"I'll wait with you a while, if you like." Joe sat back down on the toilet seat. "Well, at least we got something done today; we got a haircut."

"Did you see that fellow from Dartmouth? The money he had?"

"He was pretty proud of himself. He said he fell in with as many pay parades as he could find. Got a small fortune. He's playing pontoon with some others right now."

"What's pontoon?"

"You would probably know it as twenty-one. I used to play twenty-one at Logieville in the good old days, when I was young." Joe laughed. "My Dad said I was never young . . ."

Wallace grunted. "You had better go along, Joe. I'm going to pass more shit. By the feel of it, I'll be a while and you should get some sleep."

When Joe hesitated Wallace insisted he leave.

Joe went off to bed.

In the morning Joe looked quite refreshed.

Wallace, on the other hand, resembled death-warmed-over.

* * *

"We're in the dentist line again."

"I don't think so. I think it's the doctor line this time."

The line moved forward about ten paces.

"On the way over here, did you see the men with swords?"

"Officers. That's the way they do their PT. They do sword drill."

"I heard one of the permanent guys explain what PT was."

Joe waited for the punch line but he finally had to ask,

"Okay. So it's not physical training. So what else is it?"

"Physical torture."

"Uh, huh."

"Corporal Hastings told us we would have Physical Training right after we see the doctor. That's why I think we're in the doctor line."

"Dentist."

The line moved forward about ten paces, where they could see a sign in front of the building: HOSPITAL 2.

"See! It's doctor."

The next time the line moved the cousins were inside. Where the line split, Joe and Wallace went toward the screened area on the right.

Wallace became edgy and nervous. "How do I look, Joe?"

"You still look pasty. Hold your breath to get more colour in your face."

"Right." He squeezed his cheeks with his thumb and forefinger. "I read about that in a romance. The heroine pinched her cheeks to give colour to her face while her man went to the firing squad."

"How's that?"

"She wanted to be pretty for his last look at her."

"Well, you're pretty," Joe said by way of humour.

Wallace went in first.

When it was Joe's turn, he entered the screened area just as Wallace was going out the other side. Wallace gave him the thumbs up sign. *Great,* Joe thought, *we got it made!* Joe was happily smiling when the doctor took his card.

"Another Smallwood? Drop your trousers."

During the physical, Joe coughed, bent over to touch his toes, ran on the spot, had his pulse taken and then was told to climb up on the table and lie flat on his back.

Joe was lying there, thinking about how lucky it was that Wallace got through the physical, when the doctor pushed hard against Joe's abdomen—hard enough to make him wince. When the doctor did it again, Joe asked, "Is it necessary to push that hard?"

"Have you had cramps?"

"Well, yes, but we all have had some trouble with the food."

"Diarrhea as well as cramps and nausea?"

"How did you know about the nausea?"

"Sit up."

"I've always been a picky eater but I get along just fine, doc."

"I'm going to have to reject you."

Joe couldn't believe what he had heard. He swallowed twice and then said, "Don't do that, please. I will adjust to the food."

"It's not the food for you, my son. It's your stomach. You've got ulcers. If I checked your stools . . ."

"Doc, I know other guys who came in here with stomach troubles." Joe almost said "my cousin has more troubles than me," but thought better of it and finished, lamely, "why me?"

"The others will get better. You won't." The doctor saw the utter desolation in Joe's eyes and went on, "Believe me, son, the food here is the best you're going to get. You're rejected."

"But my cousin and I . . . we are supposed to go in the artillery together. I promised . . ."

"Orderly! Next!" The doctor put his hand on Joe's shoulder. "Sorry, son. Next."

Joe pulled on his trousers. He was buttoning his fly as he went through the screen.

Wallace clapped him on the back. "I don't know how I made it, but I did. Watch out Kaiser Bill! The Smallwoods are coming!" He pointed at the squad being formed at the side of the boardwalk. "Guess we should fall in. Time for our Physical Torture."

"I was rejected, Wallace."

Wallace knew from the tone of voice that Joe wasn't joking. "Shit!" was all he could manage to say. "Shit! Shit! Shit!"

"You! You two!" It was Hastings. "You horrible little men have nothing better to do but gossip?"

Wallace whirled around to say something but Joe grabbed his arm. "No, Wallace. That won't do any good."

"I don't repeat myself; are you having a pleasant chat?"

Despite his sense of despair, Joe was tempted to tell the corporal that he had just done that very thing but he held his tongue. "Better go, Wallace."

"Double time, recruits!"

Wallace ran along the boardwalk and took his place in the squad.

Joe stood there.

"I gave you an order!" Hastings marched over and stood nose to chin—Hastings looking up at Joe with a terrible fury in his eyes. "I don't get disobeyed, recruit!"

"I was rejected, Corporal Hastings."

Hastings' face ceased to show any emotion. "Now that's a good man. You go along to your tent, lad. Say your goodbyes to your mates this evening."

Joe felt a tear.

Hastings could probably see it forming. "Believe me, there are other things to do than be a soldier. It's just that some of us—like me—don't know no better. Go along, now."

* * *

Joe waited at the tent, quietly smoking one cigarette after another. When Wallace and his tent mates finally came sauntering down the boardwalk, he could see they were carrying their uniforms.

"Try it on, Wallace. I'll bet you'll look marvellous."

Wallace held the trousers up against his waist.

Joe laughed; he couldn't stop himself because the pants were built for a chubby five foot three while Wallace was a slim five foot ten.

"They don't have enough uniforms. I'm supposed to keep them and when I get the chance, turn them back into stores for a proper fit."

"What are you going to wear in the meantime?"

"Corporal Hastings said to wear whatever parts of the uniform that fit."

A permanent soldier stopped in front of the tent. "How are you gettin' on, son?"

"Just fine, thanks. We got our clothing issue."

"Looks a tad small, don't it?"

Wallace nodded his head. "I might have to wear my civilian trousers . . . and I don't think the tunic and boots are much better."

Corporal Hastings came around the corner of the tents. "Anyone here know horses?"

When no one answered, Hastings was obviously annoyed. "I asked a question, ladies! You would do well to come to attention and give me an answer right smartly."

The recruits were quick to admit they didn't know horses. Joe hadn't responded so an apprehensive Wallace spoke for him. "Joe, here, is a fine horseman."

"Yeah, but I leave in the morning."

Hastings drew himself up to his full five foot three. "You might be leaving tomorrow, son, but tonight you don't say 'yeah' and you do say 'yes, Corporal Hastings'!" The corporal's voice was calm but there was a threat to the tone.

Joe caught the tone. "Yes, Corporal Hastings, I can handle horses."

"Stand up, son, and say your piece again."

Joe got up quickly. "I can handle horses, Corporal Hastings, and I meant no disrespect, Corporal."

"That's fine, son. Come along, I need you."

Joe knew better that to ask what for? but he didn't have to. As they walked briskly to the cavalry tents, the corporal explained the problem.

"The horse soldiers have misplaced their mounts and are searching for them on foot."

"Wha . . .?"

"All of the cavalry horses are gone from the corral. We need to augment the search party." They were moving along so rapidly that they were almost running so Joe missed the next thing the corporal said as he lost his footing off the side of the boardwalk.

"Beg pardon, Corporal, but I didn't . . ."

"Son, I have found fourteen men from the infantry and two from the artillery to help the cavalry find their horses. You will join a search party, which will proceed on foot to recapture the beasts."

"But it will be dark in a couple of hours."

"Then we had better get a move on, son," Corporal Hastings said as he resumed his quick march to the south end of the camp where the horses had been stabled. When they approached the corral, Joe could see some fifty or sixty men with pieces of harness and ropes in their hands receiving instructions from a major of cavalry.

As far as Joe could understand from the briefing, Camp Valcartier was eight miles long and nearly four miles wide—lots of room for a bunch of horses to get lost in. The cavalrymen were assigned to search that area. The rest of the men, addressed by the cavalry major as "you others," were divided into three groups: the first to cross the Jacques Cartier River by way of one of the oil-drum pontoon bridges to look for the wayward animals in an unspecified area north of the camp; and the second to cross another oil-barrel pontoon bridge and search a similar area to the south.

Joe was assigned to the third gang. In less than fifteen minutes he was on his way across the river by way of a windlass-operated cable ferry to search to the east of the camp. Later, in the twilight of the day, he became separated from his fellows. Darkness overtook Joe on the road to St. Gabriel.

Three days later

Joe and Wallace walked arm and arm into the mess hall. Wallace had been delighted to see Joe, worried as he had been about what might have happened to his cousin. They were early for breakfast but they still had to line up at the steam counter where the food was dished out. Wallace was dying to ask a million questions but he had to wait; there were too many people around.

"My, you look good, Wallace." Joe stepped back to get a better look. "Your uniform fits! Boots look good too!"

With a wry smile, Wallace lowered his voice and stepped closer to Joe, turning his head to one side so that only Joe could hear what he had to say. "You remember that friendly, regular force soldier who came by and asked how things were doin'? Well, his friendliness had a price."

"What do you mean?"

"He said he could take me back to clothing stores and get me everything I needed; the right size and good stuff, too."

"That was nice of him."

"Yeah. I said that was nice of him but I also warned him that I had been told by the clothing stores sergeant there weren't enough supplies; we would have to wait for as long as a month before we got better fitting uniforms."

Wallace picked up his tray. Putting a plate in the middle of the tray, he stood in front of the food handler, holding his tray out for some eggs, bacon, and fried potato. He shuffled along getting some bread, coffee and a couple of apples. At the end of the line, he turned around to see how Joe was doing.

"I'm not really hungry, Wallace." Joe had only taken a mug of apple juice.

"Tummy out of sorts again?"

"No, I'm just fine but I don't want to start anything."

"Good idea." As they walked over to a table at the end of the hall, Wallace explained how he had obtained a good uniform. "The regular soldier asked me how much it was worth to have a good uniform." Wallace put on that wry little smile of his and added, "I didn't know he wanted money until he said, was it worth two bucks to look good in the pictures I was going to send home?"

"The bugger!"

"I said I didn't have a camera."

"Good! That should have taken him down a peg!"

"He said that for three bucks he would get me the uniform *and* have my picture taken. When it looked like I wasn't going to take the deal, he offered to throw in the picture for free."

They put their trays down on the table. Joe pulled a small paper sack out of his pocket and placed it, very carefully, on the table next to his tray. "How did the picture turn out?"

This time Wallace wore a disgusted look on his face. "There wasn't any picture because there wasn't any camera." He sighed. "And it still cost me the three dollars because the clothing stores corporal wanted a dollar for his troubles." Wallace picked up a piece of bacon with his fingers and put it on a slice of bread. He folded the bread and took a big bite. "Did you find any horses?"

"Oh, I found some horses." Joe opened the paper sack. He stuffed his mouth full with one of the beautifully fluffy biscuits that he had brought back with him. He spoke around the delicious contents of his mouth. "I left one of the horses in a barn so the farmer could use it to get his crops in." Pretty sure that his cousin would be satisfied with his bacon and bread sandwich, Joe offered a biscuit to his cousin, regretting his act of generosity the instant Wallace accepted. Joe looked away as Wallace broke the biscuit in half and nibbled on it, wasting huge crumbs on the mess hall tabletop.

"Why would you leave an army horse at a farm?"

"For two full days I had all the roast chicken, milk, butter, biscuits, and fresh vegetables I could eat and I slept on a comfortable, thick mattress . . ." he bobbed his head up and down, "believe me, it was just like being at Auntie Mary Anne's on a Sunday morning."

Wallace's eyes popped. "You mean you paid for your food and lodging with a government horse?"

"I don't know what to think of you, Wallace, that you would believe I'm a horse thief."

With a big, big grin Wallace answered, "I'm the only person in the whole of Quebec who could vouch for your true character at your court-martial . . . confidence man, gambler, crooked jockey and now, unless I hear to the contrary, horse thief." He ducked as Joe took a swing at him.

When Joe couldn't land a blow, he snatched up the remains of Wallace's biscuit and stuffed it in his own mouth.

Wallace complained, "I hope you catch everything I have going."

"Well, I won't catch any brains!"

"Can't improve something that isn't there!"

They were enjoying the moment but they knew it had to end because time was short and, if Joe were going to tell his cousin about St. Gabriel, he would have to do it right away.

"I was walking up the road. The sun hadn't gone down yet but I was wondering what I should do. You know, I didn't have much in the way of instructions because I don't think the cavalry major expected people who weren't cavalrymen to find any horses." Joe searched his pockets for his cigarettes but then realized he had left them at the farm. Wallace, of course, didn't smoke. Joe said aloud what he was thinking, "Of course, you don't smoke." He glanced over at one of his tent mates who always said "jack" and made the "v" motion of two fingers to his lips. The man tossed his pack to Joe.

"Anyhow, I met Michelle." Joe took out a cigarette and, with a nod of thanks, tossed the package back.

"Michel?" Wallace could see some movement at the end of the mess hall. They would be called out soon. "Tell me quick, Joe, did he have the horses?"

"*She* was astride one and leading two others."

"I might have known there would be a woman involved!"

"What a woman! Golden hair, blue eyes, and a beautiful smile . . ." Joe paused, "and riding bareback." He shook his head from side to side. "And she knew how to ride."

"How does a lady ride bareback?"

"She had some sort of rig with her dress . . . or maybe she had trousers on . . . I didn't notice . . ."

"You didn't notice?"

"When she smiled at me, it was like seeing the whole rainbow." Joe's eyes misted. "Each person sees different things looking at a rainbow, you know." When Wallace didn't say anything Joe went on, "You know, sometimes you see a little bit of rainbow while the person next to you, only a few feet away, sees the whole thing."

"So you saw a woman who looked like a rainbow."

Defiantly, Joe took another biscuit out of the sack and bit into it without offering any to his cousin. He chewed and chewed.

Wallace was just as stubborn and said nothing as he played with a biscuit crumb on the table.

"Five minutes!" It was Hastings at the end of the mess hall. "Five minutes, Company C!"

Wallace seized the opportunity to break the stalemate. "Hastings thought you had gone home."

Joe kept on chewing.

"When I told him that your things were still in the tent, he reported you to headquarters as missing. I suppose you had better tell him you are back, safe and . . ."

Joe interrupted. "Michelle asked me in French what a mackerel was doing on the road to St. Gabriel. I couldn't think of an answer in French fast enough so I said I was looking for army horses . . . and what was an angel doing on the road to St. Gabriel with three army horses." Joe butted his cigarette. She switched to English and asked me, 'Are you in the . . .'"

" . . . in the army? You don't have a uniform on." Michelle gave the stranger a disarming smile. "You look like you belong behind the counter of a boulangerie and not out rounding up horses."

"And you, mademoiselle, look like you are leading army horses away from the army camp."

Rather flustered, the young girl stuttered and hesitated. "I . . . I . . . My Aunt Hortense asked me to lead the horses up the road . . ."

"Because?" Joe was enthralled and wanted to keep her talking. Michelle (she soon told him that she was Michelle Bourgeois from just north of Winnipeg visiting her Aunt Hortense) had double dimples in her smooth, golden-coloured cheeks and strong, well-formed hands that the horses seemed to appreciate since they responded to her every signal.

"You're leading the horses away . . . because?"

"We would take them back to the army, later." And then, like a proper English schoolgirl, she added, "I promise." She steadied the horses as Joe approached them. "My aunt saw them on the road, unattended, and there was no man on the place and she sent me out to round them up." When she saw that Joe was going to raise more questions she hastened on, "And I am taking them to my Cousin Joseph's farm . . . his horse died and one of these mares might be able to do some farm work . . . there's no real harm . . . just a couple of days . . ."

"Or until your Cousin Joseph gets all his work done?"

Again, there was that gorgeous smile. "You want a great meal?"

"You bet I do!" Joe had gotten quite close to the horses and now he extended his hand and made some soft, crooning noises. The second one on the lead took a step toward Joe.

Michelle let the horse move.

Joe cupped his hand under the horse's nostrils and, with his other hand, caressed her forehead.

"She likes you."

Joe swung his leg back and then forward, grasping the horse's mane as he vaulted onto her back. "Throw me the reins," he said as the horse took several little steps, startled as she was by the man's quick movements and his weight on her back. As soon as Joe had the reins, the horse was calmer and responded to Joe's caress on her neck and the little crooning noises he made with half-closed lips. "Yeah, I think she does." Pulling the mare's head around, Joe inquired, ""Now, which way to this meal you were talking about?"

The girl beckoned Joe to follow her down the trail to where a man was fixing a gate. She said something to the man. Joe came up alongside in time to hear the man say; "C'est un maudit Anglais, Michelle?"

"This is Joe and he understands French, cousin."

"Then, I say English so he make no mistake." Cousin Joseph put both hands on his hips. "Is that a maudit Anglais, Michelle?"

Michelle gave her cousin a look of exasperation. "If you want a horse to help you with your harvest, I think you had better be nice to the Lieutenant. We have brought three horses for you to try; the Lieutenant thinks the one he is riding might accept farm work . . . at least for a while."

Joe felt uncomfortable as he was subjected to a long, close examination from very dark and hostile eyes, but he didn't flinch or turn away.

Allowing a smile to creep up his face, Cousin Joseph slapped his thigh. "Har! You are . . . bland-bec! No officer, Michelle! He say officer? He got . . . conscript . . . hair!"

Joe passed a leg over and slid to the ground. He extended his hand to the farmer. "Je m'appelle Joseph Petitbois de Nouveau Brunswick."

Cousin Joseph ignored the hand. "You got horse for me?"

"I have a horse I can lend you for a while."

Cousin Joseph took Joe's hand. "I am Joseph Bourgeois and I need horse."

"He's hungry, Cousin."

"Come eat, Anglais."

Joe nodded his head and smiled at his companion. "I could certainly use some good..."

"... use some good food."

"You did barter the horse for room and board!"

Wallace looked around the mess hall to see who might have overheard. Somewhat relieved that there was no one close enough to hear his exclamation, he asked in a whisper, "Do they still hang horse thieves? But more importantly, they wouldn't put your soldier cousin in jail, would they?" He grinned. "What did you do for three days? I mean, what did you do just to keep yourself busy?"

"We did manage to get one of the horses to do some farm work."

"And?"

"That left two whole days for . . ."

"For what! For what, Joe?" Wallace cast another look at the door to the mess hall; "I will be called away any minute and might not ever see you again."

Joe gave a good imitation of a villain's leer as he said, "You should try that line on the young girls. Might get you somewhere."

Wallace leaned forward and grasped Joe's arm as if to twist it. "Now get on with it! Tell me what you did for two whole days."

Joe could see that Wallace was losing his patience so he settled into his story as quickly as he could. "Michelle and I borrowed a couple of saddles and we visited every nook and cranny of this valley. She's got more relatives around here than a hunting dog has fleas."

"She was showing you off to her family? And she's French and Catholic? Now, there's a storm coming to the Miramichi; Auntie Mary Anne will never . . .."

"It isn't like that, Wallace." Joe shook his head. "The Bourgeois, they all hate the English."

"Good thing you're not English."

"You're not listening to me because it doesn't work that way. According to them, I am 'an English' from Halifax . . .one of the Maudits Anglais . . . Goddamn Englishmen . . . and that's not a very good thing to be."

Corporal Hastings entered the hall. He was about to give an order when a sergeant called him to the door, where they began talking.

"Hurry, Joe. Tell me! Why would they hate the English?"

"They came to Nova Scotia in 1640 something."

"Who came, Joe?"

Patiently Joe explained, "Jacques Bourgeois founded a little settlement at the east end of the Bay of Fundy and called it Colonie Bourgeois. By the mid-seventeen-hundreds, the French had lost a war and their village, by then named Beaubassin, was burned to the ground and the Bourgeois were forced to move to what is now New Brunswick."

"And they still hate the British for that?"

"It wasn't the British who made them burn Beaubassin and move the first time. It was the French."

"So there was another time?"

"Yes. The expulsion of the Acadians . . . you know, Evangeline and all that stuff. We took it in school."

"Yeah. The French wouldn't swear allegiance to the British Crown so we moved them out."

"No, it was the Acadians who wouldn't take the oath . . . actually, the Acadians said they would take an oath, but the New Englanders didn't care. The New Englanders were going to ship the Acadians out and take all the land along the Fundy for themselves."

"New Englanders? I thought the Acadians hated the English." Wallace waved his hands in front of his face as if to make it all go away. "It really doesn't matter! That was a long, long time ago . . . water under the bridge."

"I want to tell you, it matters to these people. They don't forget."

Joe could see Corporal Hastings make an about-turn and move briskly to the middle of the hall. Time was short.

"Like I said, Wallace, the Bourgeois were burned out again and shipped out to Massachusetts in 1755. They have a family story and the bad guys in that story are the English."[1]

"Do you really care?"

Joe thought for a moment before answering. "Michelle is a marvellous girl. She works with children. She is good with animals . . . and great with me . . . if I had half a chance . . ."

"Company C! Fall in outside."

Wallace scraped back his chair and stood up. He squeezed Joe's shoulder. "Follow your instincts. You seldom make mistakes, Joe. Whatever you decide, write and tell me."

Joe stood up and gave his cousin a hug. "I'm sorry I'm not with you, Wallace."

"I know."

They shook hands.

"Good luck."

"Write me about Michelle."
"I will."

Saint Gabriel

Michelle released the footbrake on the flatbed wagon. She had to encourage the army horse to take up the strain but soon they were travelling down the rutted dirt road toward Quebec City. The light, light breeze and the movement of the wagon kept the horseflies away but wasn't enough to offset the warmth of the sun. Before they reached the turnoff for the windlass ferry to the island, Joe was in shirtsleeves. With his sleeves rolled, his collar removed, and the straw hat he had borrowed from Joseph Bourgeois perched on the back of his head, he was cheerfully greeted by the locals as another visiting Bourgeois and was studiously ignored by passing army personnel who might otherwise have noticed the horse wearing a Canadian government brand.

"Those boys think we're a local farm couple, Michelle," Joe said after an army service wagon moved over to let them pass on the road.

Michelle's lips moved as she gave the horse a little verbal encouragement but she didn't respond to Joe's comment.

After a while Joe asked, "You didn't tell me if you were married, or anything; are you? What I mean is . . ."

"My father calls me his spinster daughter because I am over twenty-one with no husband in sight."

"Oh!"

There was relief in Joe's voice that Michelle could hear. She grasped Joe's arm and squeezed it, letting go almost immediately. "You're a sweet man, Joseph Smallwood from New Brunswick, but don't you go getting any ideas."

"Why not, Michelle?" Joe took the reins and stopped the horse. "You could do worse than me, Michelle." He took her hand in both of his and held it firmly, as if he wasn't going to let go, ever. "I don't know what love is. I do know that when I saw you on the St. Gabriel road my heart almost stopped . . . I had to speak to you . . . had to . . ."

"I'm not the first woman you've been attracted to," she said, a mischievous smile playing at the corners of her mouth. "Tell me that I am the first woman to give you a flutter and I'll drop you right here and you can walk the eighteen miles to the city."

Joe considered his answer before he made it. "I am a very successful Halifax businessman with no ties. What I mean is, I could leave Halifax tomorrow and go wherever you are, be whatever you might want me to be . . ."

"And you would be the father of my children?"

"Well, yes."

"And I would be your wife?" Joe was going to answer but Michelle hurried on, "With a litter of children?" She smiled but this time it was a grim little smile. "All the Bourgeois women have litters; they must do their part for the *revanche de la crèche.*"

Joe looked puzzled as he translated, "The revenge of the cradle?"

"The Acadians will win back their lands by eventually outnumbering the Maudits Anglais."

Joe tried to make a joke of it. "If it's a sort of war you want, I surrender!" He put both hands up, "Take me prisoner, Michelle."

Michelle picked up the reins from where they had fallen. She pursed her lips to signal the horse but, thinking better of it, she turned and planted a soft, quick kiss on Joe's lips. "You will know what love is when you find it, Joe." She encouraged the horse to move. "As for me, I am a modern woman and, with my teacher's profession, I will be . . ."

"But . . ."

" . . . and maybe I might want to be somebody else—maybe a lawyer—because I can be anything I want to be and I refuse to be trapped into a life where the high point will be the annual rise and fall of my belly."

Joe opened his mouth to say something but changed his mind. They drove along in silence and, at the turn of the road, came upon three dusty, rejected army recruits who were walking the long distance to Quebec City, where they would, like Joe, catch the train back to their home towns.

Michelle stopped the wagon and offered the men a lift. During the rest of the journey, the talk was of the early end to the war and the victory of the forces of the British Empire over the brutish Huns. Even at the end, when the others had collected their baggage and gone off to the inn, Michelle Bourgeois would not permit any further discussion of love or attachment.

"I will say our goodbyes now, Joe." She gave him another peck on the lips before climbing back onto the wagon.

"Where will you go, Michelle? It's too late to start back now and the horse needs some feed and a good rubdown."

"I will spend the night at my cousin's." When she saw Joe's little smile at the mention of another cousin, she smiled back. "Yes, I have forty-two first cousins . . . at last count."

Joe's stomach was in turmoil but he didn't allow his distress to show on his face. "I can't lose you, Michelle. I will write to you at St. Gabriel . . ."

"I won't be there, Joe. Don't try to write."

She gave him one last little smile. "I will return the horse to Valcartier," and then there was that English schoolgirl voice, "I promise." She released the brake and snapped the reins. The horse moved off, smartly.

* * *

It was a forlorn Joe Smallwood who boarded the eastbound train the next day. He started the trip believing he had lost his true love to some phantom ambition that had possessed "his" Michelle but, by the time the train passed through Rivière du Loup, he had come to recognize the same traits in Michelle that he admired in his Auntie Mary Anne: the main one being that she always dealt with a man's world on her own terms. He grinned. "They surely have minds of their own!" *Yes, Michelle was Aunt Mary Anne all over again—same chassis and springs but with a modern, 1915 finish.* He sighed, deeply. "Ah, Michelle! It would have been an exciting time!"

Eventually, he pushed thoughts of Michelle down and

away, allowing other subjects to well up. *Should I stretch my legs at Newcastle and perhaps leave a note at the barbershop for my Dad? No, Angus would ask too many questions; a carefully crafted letter from Halifax would be better. And Halifax? Maybe I should send a telegram to Charlotte letting her know that I am coming back. Ye gods, no!* He winced when he recalled the gold brooch with his picture in it. Charlotte had taken to wearing the brooch for the whole of Halifax to see the romantic image of her citizen soldier—her sacrifice to Empire. No, he didn't relish his return to Halifax.

Suddenly, Joe felt the need for a drink of rum. He rose. Balancing himself in the aisle between the chairs, he was gauging the bounce of the floor before he began his quest, when he heard Duke's voice from out of the past: a *good engineer will make up time on the straight-a-ways.*

"Yeah, well, Duke, this engineer is sure as hell makin' up time."

The door to the Pullman opened and closed.

Joe turned to face a trainman on his way forward.

The trainman smiled. "Anything I can do for you, sir?"

Joe stepped back out of the aisle. He knew better than to ask the trainman where he might find some rum as he recalled another of the Duke's sayings: *the railroad's death on rum.*

"No, thank you. I mean to stretch my legs for a bit."

"Dining car's three cars down," the trainman said as he passed. "They're serving dinner right now. The porter would have your bed made up by the time you got back."

Joe, clinging to the little metal handgrips on the corners of the chairs for support, watched the trainman walk down the aisle as the car cavorted to some devilish jig. *My! That man is nimble,* Joe thought. *Must come with years of practice.* Maintaining a precarious balance, Joe followed in search of some rum. Two cars down, Joe was getting the hang of better balance and movement in the bouncing cars when the train went into a curve and he lost his balance—falling into one of the chairs.

"Steady up, recruit!" Seated in the chair opposite was a man who would have had steel-grey hair if someone hadn't sheared most of it off. "You horrible little man! What do you think you are doing?"

Joe pulled himself around so that he was sitting facing the man. "Next thing you'll say is . . . you're in the army now, ladies."

The smile came off the other man's face. "No, I guess neither of us made it. For me, it's my feet. What's your problem?'

"My gut."

The stranger extended his hand. "Robert Bowie from Austenville."

"Where's that?" Joe took the hand and shook it, warmly. "Joe Smallwood."

"Across the harbour from Halifax . . . up on the hill behind the town."

"Dartmouth?"

"Some calls it Dartmouth."

Joe made as if to stand up. "I was on my way looking for a drink."

Robert Bowie pulled a black business satchel from under the seat. He opened it and, with a grand flourish, produced two small glasses. "The boys gave it to me as a going-away gift." He spread the top of the satchel wider so Joe could see. "Gin, rum, and whisky and four little crystal glasses. A real special going-away gift . . . 'cept I'm goin' back." He handed the glasses to Joe. "Rather embarrassing, don't you think?"

"Yeah. I know what you mean. My lady friend has been going around wearing a gold brooch with my picture in it."

"Ah! She's proud of her soldier boy and wants the world to know it."

"Except I'm going back, too."

"We should drink to that. What's your poison?"

"The rum would be nice."

"Rum it is." He broke the seal on the bottle of dark rum and, taking into account the gyrations of the train, carefully poured both glasses half full, not spilling a drop. "We shouldn't feel bad about goin' back, you know."

"Why is that?"

"The army has approval for only twenty-six thousand and there's already over thirty-two thousand recruits at Valcartier." He sipped his rum and then knocked it back, swallowing hard. "A lot of the boys are going to be rejected."

"Yes. I heard that, but I wasn't going with the infantry. I volunteered for the artillery."

Robert topped up the glasses. "That's even worse!" He clinked his glass against Joe's and cheerfully sang out, "Bottoms up!" When he saw Joe's hesitation, he asked, "Got troubles with your gut?"

Joe growled, "Nothin' that the rum won't cure," and he downed his drink, holding his glass out for a refill. He swallowed a couple of times to keep the harsh drink down. "What's wrong with the artillery?" he eventually managed to ask.

Robert showed some concern for his new-found friend. "You got stomach problems? Maybe you shouldn't drink."

"It's never stopped me before," Joe waved his hand as if to dismiss the trouble, "and I don't have a problem with it right now . . ." but he did put his glass down. "What do you mean it's even worse for the artillery?"

"The artillery militia units were mobilized in their home cities."

"But I saw artillery personnel at Valcartier. I could tell by their red shoulder straps."

"I thought red was for infantry."

"No, the infantry have dark blue tabs. Besides, I saw the big sign with the artillery guns on it."

"Well, you're right about that! It had the artillery motto: Where Duty and Glory Lead."

"There was no English on that sign."

"Quo Fas et Gloria Ducunt . . . Where Duty and Glory Lead." Robert poured another drink for Joe and then one for himself. "It was Latin."

"How come you know that? Only doctors and priests know Latin."

"I studied to be a priest."

"Oh!"

"Yeah. That usually stops all conversation." Robert waggled his finger, "You goin' to drink that drink?"

Joe grabbed the glass. "You just watch me." He downed the contents of the glass. After a couple of breathless moments, Joe stated, "So you agree the artillery is at Valcartier. So what's the problem?"

"The problem is, my fine-feathered friend, the artillery units at Valcartier were already on a war footing when they arrived. They don't need no mo' men! Anybody who signs up at Valcartier will be an infantry grunt . . . not a gunner . . . not a cavalryman . . . not a doctor or Indian chief . . . just a grunt." Robert peered into the satchel. "That's the end of the rum. We'll have to switch to gin or whisky."

"It doesn't matter to me. I don't drink for the taste."

As Robert broke the seal on the second bottle, Joe gave some thought to what he had just learned. "So me and Wallace go to Valcartier to be artillerymen and the army knows all along we have to be infantry."

Sagely nodding his head, Robert poured two more drinks. He gave Joe a glass. "I might have got the glasses mixed up." He pointed at the glass in Joe's hand. "That one might be mine."

"Doesn't matter." Joe slurped a bit as he as he sucked up the gin. "And Wallace doesn't know."

"That's right. Wallace doesn't know." Robert cocked his head much like a puppy seeing his first cat, "Who's Wallace?"

"My cousin. He passed the army medical but he doesn't know he will be infantry and not artillery."

"Well, he'll find out soon . . ." Robert belched—". . . enough."

Joe was doing some rapid swallowing, as if he were trying to keep a raw egg and oyster down. "I must get some milk." He stood. "What about you?" The train was still gyrating but Joe didn't have any difficulty marching down the aisle to the end of the car. He looked behind to see if Robert were following.

Robert put the two glasses in the satchel and pushed it under the seat. He leaned over, shaking his finger at the bag, instructing it to remain under cover and not to do any entertaining in his absence.

Joe laughed at the sight. It reminded him of Aunt Mary Anne telling him to behave and, of course, he would behave—and so would the bag.

"It will behave, Robert,' Joe light-heartedly shouted the length of the car. "Come on! We need something to eat." As he turned to continue on to the dining car, the car's motion seemed to become more jerky and erratic. *Oh, God! I had better get some milk inside me,* he thought. To his drinking buddy he hollered, "And then I think I just might go right to bed."

Joe didn't get his milk. He didn't get past the next toilet where he lost the contents of his stomach. He cleaned himself and returned to his lower berth. All night long, as he floundered between sleep and the painful awareness of just how much he had imbibed, he knew there would be no relief in the morning. Come morning he would have to deal with his ulcerated stomach as well as a dreadful hangover. Joe Smallwood would have no time to worry any further about his cousin in the infantry.

Endnotes

1. The story of the expulsion of the Acadians from mainland Nova Scotia is told in book #1 of this series: *The Acadians.*

Chapter Eight
Cousin Wallace
Soldier of the King

September 22. 1914
Camp Valcartier

It was happening so quickly.

The short, red-faced officer asked the questions and the Warrant Officer, seated at the desk, wrote Wallace's replies on the government document labelled Attestation Paper.

"What is your name?"

"Clarke Wallace Smallwood."

"In what town, township, or parish and in what country were you born?"

"Newcastle, New Brunswick."

Wallace gave the answers to the next questions in what he hoped would pass as a clipped, military manner. However, what was of immediate concern to him was that he had heard rumours the artillery didn't need any more men. Perhaps he should ask the officer . . . *Oh-oh! From the look on the officer's face, I guess I missed something!.*

"Beg pardon, sir. Would you please repeat the question?"

"I said do you now belong to the active militia?"

"No, sir, I don't."

"Let's not make a speech, recruit. A simple 'yes' or 'no' will suffice."

The officer looked down and continued reading from the Attestation Paper. "Do you understand the nature and terms of your engagement?"

His mind racing, Wallace thought it might be the time to ask about the artillery. "Sir, I would . . ."

The officer looked up, "Keep it simple, recruit."

"Yes, sir."

"An acceptable answer to the question would be 'yes' or 'no.'"

"Yes."

Eyes down again, the officer read the next question. "Are you willing to be attested to serve in the Canadian Over-Seas Expeditionary Force?"

"Yes."

The Warrant Officer wrote the answer and slid the paper across the desk. The officer put his finger on the form. "Step forward and sign your name using your normal signature."

As soon as Wallace had finished and had stepped back, the officer signed as witness. He then handed Wallace the second form he had been reading from. "Read the declaration using your full name in the blank."

"I, Clarke Wallace Smallwood, do solemnly declare that the above answers made by me are true and that I am willing to fulfill the engagements by me now made, and I hereby engage and agree to serve in the Canadian Over-Seas Expeditionary Force, and to be attached to any arm of the service therein, for the term of one year, or during the war now existing between Great Britain and Germany should that war last longer than one year, and for six months after termination of that war provided His Majesty should so long require my services, or until legally discharged."

The officer pointed to the paper in front of the Warrant Officer. "Sign the declaration, recruit, using your normal signature."

When the form was returned to him, Wallace noticed that the officer's name was Barton. He was thinking that Barton might be a New Brunswick name as he read the oath. "I, Clarke Wallace Smallwood, do make oath, that I will be faithful and bear true allegiance to His Majesty King George the Fifth, His Heirs and Successors, and that I will as in duty bound honestly and faithfully defend His Majesty, His Heirs and Successors, in Person, Crown and Dignity, against all enemies, and will observe and obey all orders of His Majesty, His Heirs and Successors, and all the Generals and Officers over me. So help me God."

"Sign the form, soldier." The officer picked up another sheet as if he were going to consult a list but changed his mind, putting the paper back on the desk. "You will be given a regimental number as soon as you are assigned." He extended his hand, impressing Wallace with the firmness of his grip. The officer released his grasp and stepped back. "Now, let's see a proper salute, soldier."

Wallace was impressed with the dignity of the moment and did his best to remember his corporal's instructions on military deportment. He saluted and waited for the captain's return salute before he dropped his arm.

"Carry on, soldier, and good luck."

After completing a shaky about-turn, Wallace marched out of the office. Outside the administration building, he paused and sucked in a huge breath from the beautiful day. He felt wonderful; the birds were singing, the sun was shining, and Clarke Wallace Smallwood was a soldier of the King!

Chapter Nine
Cousin Joe
Pleased to Meet You

September 22, 1914
Halifax

Joe Smallwood slammed the window shut on the racket being made by a demanding bluejay. "Damn jays! Neighbours shouldn't feed them so close to the houses," he grumbled. He pulled the blind down to darken the room and to further shut out the bird's piercing calls.

Joe had been home for several days but he had told no one of his return nor had he been anywhere but to the corner drugstore for some milk of magnesia. He ran his hand over the stubble of his beard. "Must look a sight," he muttered. The empty milk bottle on the table reminded him that he must soon shave if he were to go out to get some groceries before the stores closed. He threw himself down in the chair and turned on the table lamp. "I'll go later," he said as he fumbled for something to read from the magazine rack at the side of his chair. What he found made him laugh. He read the first paragraph aloud, as if to a Sunday school class.

"Canada's Artillery Division will compare very favourably, both in equipment and effectiveness, with the British and French artillery. The Canadian 18 pounders, all modern and of recent purchase, are capable of firing an 18.5 pound shrapnel shell 6,200 yards." Joe sighed as he carefully folded the paper and jammed it back into the magazine rack. He closed his eyes as he recalled the look of disappointment on his cousin's face when Joe had said, "I was rejected, Wallace." Joe lunged up out of his chair and repeated Wallace's reaction: "Shit, shit, shit!" He strode purposefully to the bathroom where it was a miracle he didn't lose a lip or an ear as he shaved. He was almost finished when he spied the razor blade package on the shelf. He read from the cover, "Durham double edge blades. So safe, you can shave in the dark." With a devilish gleam in his eyes, Joe reached up and turned out the light.

Having proved a point, Joe dressed carefully so that he didn't get any blood on his shirt. By the time he was ready to go out, he had the first pains of the stomach distress that was a sign that he needed more milk of magnesia. He took the last of the medicine directly from the bottle. Not bothering with his hat or cane, Joe hurried down the walk but, instead of turning uphill to the pharmacy, he went downhill in the direction of his shop. "Might just as well face the music," Joe murmured. He did hesitate once he reached the door to the shop but when he recognized Fredrick Schwartz at the counter, he went right in.

"Fredrick! I'm so glad to see you." He grabbed the older man's hand and shook it warmly. "I'm glad to see you, my friend," he repeated.

"Joe Smallwood! By the sounds of it, you are in one piece." He held onto Joe's hand, grasping it with his two hands.

"Yeah, but he looks like hell!" Frank patted Joe on the shoulder. "It's good to see you, Joe."

"You still here, Frank? I thought . . ."

"I was rejected, Joe. They aren't taking married men, 'specially those with no military training."

"Have you been ill, Joe?" Fredrick's non-visual sensory skills were at work and his hands told him that Joe was running a temperature. "Do you have a fever?"

"Well, yes, I guess I haven't been well these last few days but I'll be up to my usual self in a day or two. *Which isn't good enough for the army.* I was rejected for medical reasons."

Frank was quick to say, "They're rejecting one in ten, the paper said. Lots of the boys are coming home."

Fredrick let go of his friend's hand. He nodded in agreement with Frank's comment and added, "Yes, and the good people of Halifax gave the first of the rejections the cold shoulder thinking they had let the Empire down and all that."

"But there are too many of us now for the garrison wives to snub." Frank looked around as if a spy might overhear him before adding, "They are such a bunch of old biddies."

A broad-shouldered, powerful-looking man came through the storeroom door. "Who's an old biddy?" Running his fingers through his grey hair, the man joked, "There are no towels in your washroom, Frank."

Frank was quick to respond, "Take it up with the manager, Mister Gray," indicating Joe.

"The manager? Ah!" Warren Gray made a great pretence of checking Joe over before saying, "So, you're the Mister Smallwood that I hear so much about from my granddaughter, Gladys. Pleased to meet you, finally."

It was Joe's turn to give the other man a very critical examination. "And I have read so many stories about the great Warren Gray that I can hardly believe I am finally in his presence."

"There!" Fredrick was wearing a broad smile. "We just came in for some smokes and to ask Frank whether or not he had heard anything about you, Joe, when you appear on the scene and I am able to fulfill my promises." With a flourish, Fredrick indicated first one man and then the other, "Warren Gray, of Pryor Crew fame and hero of many, many pulp magazine escapades, please allow me to introduce Joseph Smallwood of the Miramichi, an energetic, sterling businessman who is making his mark in this grand old city."

There was a lot of laughter and good-natured joking before Joe had the opportunity to ask, "You were in England, Mister Gray. How are things in the old country and how much danger was there during your Atlantic passage?"

"I came home on board the Allan liner *Mongolian*. Captain Hatherly knew me as a Gray from Sambro and he did me the courtesy of allowing me the freedom of his navigation deck. Consequently, where the rest of the passengers were aware that the ship showed no lights at night and travelled at top speed the whole trip, I had the privilege of knowing the nature of our route; the captain sailed well north of the regular ship lanes to avoid any encounters with German warships."[1]

Fredrick explained with some pride, "My father-in-law was invited to witness the rowing competition between England and the United States."

"The race was held in England?" Joe could see that this was Warren's favourite subject because he warmed to it immediately.

"Yes. Harvard rowed against the Union Boat Club at Hemley-on-Thames." Warren stroked his chin. "I was sure the Americans were going to win because they had accepted and adapted the Eton stroke and it was this English style of rowing that carried the day for them. By rowing in the English manner, the Americans won the cup for the first time in decades."

Warren's enthusiasm for rowing showed in his voice as he added, "It was so thrilling and a fine race." He then assumed a mock serious tone. "And, if the Germans had just left the world alone for another week or two, I would have been able to stay in England and enjoy the sights. As it was, even with my letters of credit, I wasn't able to draw any more funds and had to procure a passage on the *Mongolian* before my money ran out."

"What's the temper of the English, now that war has started?"

"Excitement. Every man I met of military service age was looking forward to the great adventure on the continent. The Boche are going to have to fight really hard to keep the war going until Christmas."

Joe seemed to be very thoughtful as he agreed with Warren's observations on the probability of a short war.

"You say you agree with me, young man, but you seem very pensive. What's bothering you?"

"I don't really have anything that's bothering me . . . except that I won't be there with the rest of the Empire . . . but . . ." Joe finally blurted it out. "The Germans are so damned thorough and the last time they beat the French in jig time."

Warren spoke in a reassuring tone. "Just consider my experience. The Royal Navy rules the waves and I had no trouble at all travelling back home, even with a war on. German ships are being captured everywhere they try to sail."

"I suppose you're right."

Frank thought he would contribute his two cents' worth. "The imperial navy has cut the Germans off from their colonies and they will run out of war . . . war . . . you know . . . war stuff."

"War material," Fredrick said, "and I agree with you. Germany will be cut off."

Feeling good about Fredrick's support for his opinions, Frank became even bolder. "Yes, our Canadian militia is well organized." Frank looked around to see if he had everyone's attention, and he had. "Colonel Sam Hughes said our men are well equipped and ready to trounce the Hun." He stuck his thumbs in his suspenders. "He said we could probably take the Huns without the help of the British or the French."

Joe thought of Wallace, holding up his fat, five-foot-three trousers to his slim, five-foot-ten frame. "There are supply problems at Valcartier."

"Maybe so, but Sam Hughes will fix all that!" Frank snapped his suspenders and buttoned his suit jacket, running his hands down the front in a smoothing motion. "Our boys know how to fight. Just point them in the right direction and it will all be over in a snap." For emphasis, he snapped his fingers.

Joe didn't want to sound like a defeatist so he had very little to add to the ensuing enthusiastic comments about Sam Hughes and how "good old Sam" might just be the best officer to lead the Canadian boys into battle. But Joe wasn't so sure about Minister of Defence Hughes and his cronies. Not only were there supply problems, but there were other, serious practical difficulties; *like misplacing all of the cavalry horses.* As Joe stood at the front door and said his goodbyes to Fredrick and Warren, he had another thought: *like that Dartmouth soldier getting away with attending a whole lot of pay line-ups.* He closed the door, watching as the two men walked away. *Like Wallace taking artillery training when he would probably have to be an infantry grunt.*

Joe smiled as he thought of the word "grunt." He wondered who had thought that one up. *Wallace won't like running up hills and over cliffs.* Joe was still smiling at the thought when Frank came back from the storeroom.

"What's so funny?"

"I guess there's nothing funny about it."

When Frank put on his hurt puppy dog look, Joe relented and explained.

"My cousin might have to go into the infantry."

"So?"

"He won't be very happy about that." *No, he'll probably tell them to take the infantry and shove it, if I know my Wallace.* And Joe was smiling again.

Endnotes

1. In previous books of the *Abuse of Power* series, the men of the Gray family were introduced to readers as harbour pilots of the Port of Halifax.

Chapter Ten
Cousin Wallace
But I Don't Want to Be Infantry

September 25, 1914
Camp Valcartier

Wallace was standing at the back of the mess hall and couldn't believe his ears. With no thought whatsoever for military etiquette he raised his voice. "But I don't want to be infantry!"

The major, standing at the podium, didn't hesitate. "Take that man's name, Sergeant Major, and remove him from my presence!"

The sergeant major, six foot three of shiny brass and quivering moustache, strode toward the offensive life form. Hastings and another corporal formed up on the sergeant major, echelon right. In this formation, Wallace was whisked out of the mess hall into the bright sunlight before the officer at the podium could take a breath to continue his announcement that the artillery would not be accepting any more personnel. As the door closed behind them, Wallace could hear the major repeat his opening statement: "Gentlemen, those of you who have not yet been assigned will go overseas as infantry."

Wallace attempted to go back but the two corporals had him by the elbows and he continued in a straight line down the walk. Only when they were beyond shouting distance of the hall did the sergeant major indicate that the troublemaker be turned to face him.

"I don't want to be . . ." was all Wallace was able to say before something sharp and hard was jammed into his ribs behind his arm and out of sight of the sergeant major. Every time Wallace tried to say something, Hastings (because it was Hastings on that side) reapplied the object with greater and greater pressure until Wallace gasped with the pain and was quiet.

125

The sergeant major spoke to Hastings as if Wallace didn't exist. "Mister Hastings, to have one of these unruly sods interrupt the major is not on."

"Yes, Sar'major."

"In my old regiment, we had 'em run the gauntlet behind the barracks . . . out of sight of the officers."

"Yes, Sar'major."

"Never had one speak up against a field officer." He rocked back and forth on his heels. "Never."

There was a moment or two of silence between the two British Army regulars.

"The Canadians don't hold much for spit and polish and proper discipline, Sar'major."

"Are you saying, Hastings, that we should forgive them their trespasses?"

"No, Sar'major, but this here's a good man, better than some of 'em . . ."

"But not as good as most of them, I hope, Corporal."

"He'll measure up." When the more senior NCO didn't comment, Hastings went on. "He'll measure up and I give my word on that . . ." but the ongoing silence told him there had to be more. "I have his name, Sar'major, and he'll be on report." The sergeant major still didn't speak so Hastings continued, "And I'll take him behind the latrines myself and make him see the error of his ways."

"You must do what you think is necessary, Corporal. Carry on."

"Yes, Sar'major." Hastings took the object out of Wallace's side. The order, "Defaulter, right turn!" was followed almost immediately by "left, right, left, right . . ." in almost double time cadence.

When they reached the tents, Wallace thought they might stop, but Hastings took him further down toward the latrine. Wallace was halted and given the "right turn" to face the corporal who then struck him, hard, in the mouth. Startled and off balance from the turn, Wallace fell down.

"Let me help you up, son." Hastings extended his hand.

Wallace ignored it and stood up, not knowing what to expect.

"Come into the latrine and put some water on that lip. Lean forward so you don't get blood on your uniform. I don't want to hit you again, but you gotta look sufficiently chastised for the sergeant major." When Wallace gave the corporal a questioning look, Hastings said, "Yes, he'll come looking for you tomorrow to make sure I kept my promise to take you aside."

As Wallace put some cold water on his lip, Hastings talked. "Of course, you tripped and hit your chin on a tent peg. That's your story and you will stick to it." Hastings caught Wallace's eye in the mirror. "You understand?"

"Yes, Corporal."

"Don't go around making an ass of yourself again because I won't be able to help you a second time."

Wallace's lip was swelling. "Thish is help?"

"In this man's army a troublemaker has things happen to him that would break his mother's heart."

"Permission to speak, Corporal?"

Hastings smiled. *The boy is learning.* "Carry on, soldier."

"I am not going in the infantry."

Well, maybe he isn't learning fast enough. "You signed the paper what says you promise to serve in the army and in any part therein . . . at His Majesty's pleasure."

Wallace could remember when he had read that. He had been about to ask the officer—*what was his name?*—*the one that talked like a New Brunswicker? I was about to ask him about the rumours of no more artillery vacancies . . . Barton! That was his name!*

"Did you hear me, soldier? You're in the army now and you'll do as you are ordered."

"I don't much care, Corporal; I won't go overseas in the infantry. I want to be a gunner."

"You're not hearin' me, son; you'll go overseas in the infantry or you won't go at all."

"That's fine! The war will be short and I can be home by Christmas."

"You're forgetting the sergeant major, soldier. He has you in his sights. Your goose is as good as cooked."

Wallace felt despair because it was true; *there had been a dirty gleam in the sergeant major's eye when he had spoken of running a gauntlet. Surely, that sort of thing wasn't still going on in this day and age!* "The officer, Barton, who took my . . ."

"Captain Barton, soldier."

"Excuse me, I meant no disrespect, Corporal Hastings. Could I please speak to the captain?"

"That's not on, soldier." Hastings put his swagger stick under his arm. He straightened his cap and brought himself to attention. "You will report to the field kitchen, immediately, and place yourself on duty. Tell the chief cook that you are a slacker and will do kitchen duty for the weekend. After breakfast on Monday, you will attend defaulter's parade in front of the orderly tent. Understand that the charge hearing is not a trial. You are guilty. When the punishment is given, you will answer 'very good, sir.'"

"Very good, Corporal." Wallace was learning.

* * *

"Very good, Captain Barton."

Captain Barton glanced at the sergeant seated at the end of the table who was recording the judgement: two days forfeiture of pay plus two days extra duty had been the awarded punishment. Embarrassing a field officer in front of assembled troops had given rise to a litany of offences and the young private had been found guilty of each of them in turn. *At least the lad had displayed good form during the charge hearing, probably because of earnest coaching by one of the British NCOs responsible for shaping up the Canadian boys.* Barton studied the little corporal who was one of the British Army regulars who had been quickly posted to Canada when the balloon went up. *I believe his name is Hastings. We could do with another dozen just like him,* the militia officer mused as he waited for the recording sergeant to finish the paperwork.

Barton accepted the forms from the recording sergeant,

signing the bottoms of the fanned papers. As he bunched up the forms and handed them back, he addressed the corporal. "Our boys need all the professional help you can give them, Hastings."

"Sir!"

He had forgotten how difficult it was to converse—militia officer to regular NCO—in any meaningful way. Considering what to say next to finish what he had started with the NCO, Barton idly opened the defaulter's personnel file, noting that he had, himself, witnessed the Attestation Form. There were so many in such a short time that it was hard to remember any of them. *Yes, Smallwood from Newcastle.* He remembered now. "Excuse us for a minute, gentlemen." When he noted the surprise on the militia sergeant's face (Hastings' face remained impassive), Barton explained, "I wish to speak to the defaulter alone, gentlemen."

"Sir!" was the British regular's response as he immediately departed.

The militia sergeant gave the officer a quizzical look but then followed the regular's example.

"Stand easy, Smallwood." Barton steepled his hands in front of his lips, elbows on the table. "Are you related to Duke?"

Wallace couldn't keep the surprise off his face. "Yes, sir. He's one of my uncles."

"Well, his wife was Jean Lawson, who is my aunt."

"I never saw much of her." Wallace thought he should explain but the officer interrupted.

"Neither did I," and then Barton thought he should explain further. "Duke Smallwood was very protective of his Jean."

They both smiled.

Barton got up and assumed a more friendly approach by sitting on the edge of the table next to Wallace. "Do you have any idea how the army handles troublemakers?"

Wallace snapped to attention. "I request to be assigned to the artillery, sir! It's what I joined up for."

"At ease, Smallwood." Barton waved his hand in a dismissing manner. "You joined up to go overseas. Infantry or artillery, does it make any difference as long as you go over to fight the Hun?"

Still in the position of attention but allowing his head to turn so his eyes could find the captain's, Wallace said, "Duke's son Joe told me about a military assault at a Halifax fort."

"An attack?"

"It was a military exercise on Dominion Day."

"Oh, yes, I heard about it. The assaulting force was wiped out." Again the dismissive hand gesture. "That doesn't matter. There aren't any more vacancies in the artillery."

"Joe and I talked about it one night at the Sugary. We decided that we would go with the big guns and the bigger the better, but Joe was rejected for medical reasons. I am the only one going." Wallace resumed the proper stance for being at attention. "I won't go overseas unless I am artillery, sir!"

Obviously annoyed, Barton stated with deliberate finality, "Soldier, you will go where you are ordered. Dismissed."

Proving that a good corporal overhears everything, Hastings pulled the tent flap back and took control of the defaulter: "Left, right, left right . . . swing your arms, man!" and marched him away.

Closing the personnel file, Captain Barton handed it to the recording sergeant. Before he let go of the file, Barton said, "On second thought, let me take another look," and he retrieved the file from the sergeant's still outstretched hand.

"Of course, sir," the sergeant said as he awaited his officer's pleasure.

"Where would his regimental number be, sergeant?"

"At the top of the file, sir, left-hand corner . . . but since this man hasn't been assigned . . . there would be none."

"Leave the file with me, sergeant. I will return it to the orderly room."

"Of course, sir."

September 28, 1914
Quebec City

A great deal of planning had gone into the movement of the Canadian Expeditionary Force from Valcartier to the English port of Plymouth. To begin with, it was scheduled that every day, starting September 25, trainloads of men, equipment, and munitions would depart for Quebec City, where the thirty or more transport ships lay waiting. Rigorous loading schedules had been devised and in a matter of a very few days, the transports would depart for the Gaspé, where they would rendezvous with warships of the Royal Navy. The weather forecast for the crossing was good and trains were scheduled to meet the disembarking troops at Plymouth and whisk them off to Salisbury Plain, where serious military training would begin immediately.

As the operation got under way that very first day, the men detrained at the station, gathered up their guns and stores, and marched through the city streets to the piers. The streets were lined with civilians throwing flowers and wishing their warriors well while the soldiers sang "O Canada" and "It's a Long Way to Tipperary" as they marched along.

On the piers, the soldiers lined up and waited for the little ferries to take them out to the ships, everyone singing and waving as if it were all one gigantic carnival. Certainly it was a great day to be Canadian—that very first day.

On the second day, the planners claimed the first serious glitch was the fault of the estimators. The estimators pointed to the misleading data supplied by the ships' pursers which indicated to the army, for example, that the Canada Steamships Line's *Bermudian* could handle 1161 troops and their matériel. The reasons for the foul-up were not complicated: for the seamen, capacity meant measurements in cubic feet and pounds; for the army planners and estimators, the numbers meant square feet because men and guns weren't stacked one upon the other; but for the men of the Strathcona Horse, it meant a miserable night sitting cheek by jowl anywhere they could find space on the badly overcrowded ship.

On that second day, 599 weary Strathconas had to be moved from the *Bermudian* to some other ship, yet to be named. Dumped back on the pier, with no hot food and not the least bit appreciative of the enthusiasm of the new arrivals singing "O Canada" and "Tipperary," the Strathconas quarrelled with anyone who came within ten feet of them. Then it began to rain and what had been a dark and dreary day became a cold and wet night.

The Cleanup Squad, men who for one reason or another were not leaving Canada with the Expeditionary Force, had to create some sort of meaning to the muddle on the pier. First, they had to stop all movement of the second day's contingent toward the end of the pier where the disgruntled Strathconas were. That took a bit of doing and men like Wallace Smallwood acted, at times, like a human fence between the two groups. Then, when the name of the new ship assigned to the Strathconas was promulgated, the lines had to be re-formed to board the ferries. By the time the Strathconas were finally on their way to *Lapland* and the men of the second contingent were being shunted to the front of the pier to await the return of the ferries, out of the darkness marched the artillery.

It had been a long day and night for the artillery, who had marched the eighteen miles from Valcartier, their bands playing and the men singing as they slogged through the mud of the narrow country roads. Now, even with their horses and guns spattered with mud and the men thoroughly drenched, the artillery nevertheless proudly marched onto the pier, only to be met by the stony faces of the men of the second contingent who had spent the day on the pier. The music faltered and then bravely continued as the artillery formed up in sequence of batteries, the last battery of the Second Battalion remaining in column between the houses of the lower town because there was no more room on the pier.

After the *Bermudian* fiasco, the planners had been reviewing the capacities of the other ships, making changes to departure and loading schedules, causing delays all the way down the line, but it had been too late to do anything about the artillery. Now that they were on the pier, they would just have to wait their turn. Consequently, it was several more hours before the planners found the next serious glitch: some of the hatchways were too narrow for the guns while other holds were not suitable for the horses.

Finally, on the twenty-ninth of September, when their loading was completed, some of the transport ships slipped their moorings and drifted downstream, bands playing and the men cheering as they disappeared into the dusk on their way to the rendezvous at Gaspé. More and more of the great ships moved away. Wallace raised his arm and waved at the nearest ship as it gave a blast from its horn, momentarily drowning the plaintive wail of a piper playing from the prow of the ship. Wallace thought he saw the piper wave but he couldn't be sure. *Oh, it was a wonderful moment . . . all the work . . . all the troubles with the men on the pier . . . and the stupid guns not fitting through the hatchways . . . It was all worth it,* he thought.

"Cleanup Squad!"

Wallace knew who it was without turning around. "Yes, Corporal Hastings!" He double-timed to where Hastings had gathered a number of the Cleanup Squad around him.

" . . . that's according to the Department of Militia," he was saying, "and we have to get it done."

Wallace sidled up to his new friend, the man from his tent who called everyone "jack." "What's going on, Ned?"

"The 18 pounders have to be accompanied by their own stock of shells . . . fifteen hundred shells for each gun."

"But the ships carrying the artillery batteries are gone!"

"Not all of 'em, jack. We're to load shells on the tugboats and ferry 'em to the ships. Start right now puttin' the stuff on the tugs, Hastings says, while he finds the ships what has the guns." Ned hawked and spit off to one side. "Shit! Another screw-up!" Beckoning Smallwood to follow him, Ned cheerfully barked, "We get this done, we might have us some shut-eye."

October 3, 1914
Quebec City

All the ships were gone except for the large transport *Manhattan,* which had been pressed into service to take on miscellaneous cargo, such as items that were left on the pier (didn't fit on the assigned transport and had been returned); last-minute items (pallets of flour given as a war gift to the mother country); CEF members who had worked on the pier (supervisors, planners, administration clerks, etc); or vital war matériel that had been orphaned by the end user (tons of artillery shells).

Captain Barton reviewed the faces of his little command, the Cleanup Squad. "You all did good. I want to tell you that we accomplished miracles in the short time we were here." Barton consulted a piece of paper in the palm of his hand, "Seven thousand, six hundred and seventy-nine horses and thirty thousand, six hundred and seventeen men moved through here and I like to think that we were of some help in getting them to the right place at the right time."

Someone in the rear rank called out, "Not the Strathconas we didn't!"

Barton nodded his head, "Right! Most of them to the right place at almost the right time . . . and in good order."

There was general laughter.

"There's just the one ship left and there are plenty of harbour personnel hanging around to service it, so we won't be needed." Barton gave a theatrical sigh, which brought another laugh from the men. "Now that it's done, we'll spend the night at the Citadel and tomorrow we should find out whether or not we will return to Valcartier. Since there isn't much for us to do back there right now, maybe we can stay in Quebec City for a few days."

(Cheers from the men.)

Barton was distracted by the approach of an infantry major accompanied by an officer of the merchant service.

Barton brought his squad to attention and then made a right turn to face the more senior officer. He saluted.

The major returned the salute and, with no preliminaries, described the problem. "The captain of *Manhattan* will not accept artillery shells and fuses unless the movement and storage of such stores is supervised by artillerymen."

Captain Barton hesitated, wondering if he should try to enlighten the major on such a simple military matter. *The shells were inert until . . . oh, very well!*

"Sir, the shells are harmless until the gunner uncaps the fuse."

"I know that, Captain."

The merchant service officer smiled. "And I know that . . . but my captain says he will have two or three artillerymen accompany this cargo or he will leave it on the pier."

Barton was going to make the reply that all artillerymen were on ships out near Gaspé when he had a thought. "I will attend to the matter, sir. May I be excused?"

"Carry on, Captain." The major turned and said casually to the merchant services officer, "We should move along to *Manhattan* and let your captain know that his request has been satisfied."

Barton handed the parade over to an NCO and went in search of the sergeant clerk. When he found the clerk he asked, "Do you have copies of the personnel records . . . the travel copies?"

"No, sir."

Barton felt he was being strangled by stupid circumstances. *The damn sergeant doesn't have the damn records he is supposed to have so I can't assign two or three men to the Manhattan. For want of the men, the damn ship's captain will not deliver the shells to the guns. For want of the shells, a lot of goddam Huns are going to live longer than they should.* In a small voice he asked himself, "Where in hell would the records be?"

The sergeant thought it was a question and he answered, "The records are with the admin unit on the ships, sir."

Captain Barton saw a glimmer of hope. "What about the records of the men who didn't go overseas?"

"Oh! Since we didn't know if we were going back to Valcartier, I brought them with me."

Barton seized the sergeant's arm. "You have the personnel records for the men of the Cleanup Squad?"

"Yes, of course, sir." He thought the officer was showing the stress of the last week so he humoured him. "I have the records of the Cleanup Squad with us, yes, of course."

"Pull the file for Smallwood."

The sergeant clerk flipped open the cover of a file case. He ran his finger down to "S." "Smallwood," he said as he pulled the file. He opened it. "That's funny!"

"What's wrong now, Sergeant?"

"There's a regimental number written across the top of this file. It shows recruit Smallwood has a number that belongs to the Second Battalion, Canadian Field Artillery."

"Good. Make the entries for him to be assigned to . . . to the 8th Battery."

"Yes, sir, Captain Barton." If sergeants were ever guilty of giving an officer a sly look, this sergeant was guilty. "You will authorize the entry?"

"Yes. Pick a second recruit and put him in the same battery."

"Very good, sir." After a pause, the sergeant said, "I won't know what number to assign the second man. The lists are gone with the convoy."

"Just take Smallwood's number and add one to it."

"Yes, sir."

When *Manhattan* sailed for England independently of the convoy on the 5th October 1914, she carried a large quantity of artillery shells. Custodians of this cargo were no. 41593 Private Edward Smithers and no. 41592 Private Wallace Smallwood, 8th Battery, 2nd Brigade, Canadian Field Artillery.[1]

As the *Manhattan* cut her ties with Canada and moved downstream, the two privates leaned against the rail, watching the moving shoreline. Without taking his eyes off the scene, one of them remarked, "It just goes to show you, jack; stay close to me and you'll always come up smelling roses."

Endnotes

1. Smithers and his service number are fiction.

Chapter Eleven
The Three Cannoneers

January 1, 1915
Salisbury Plain
England

Ned Smithers tossed aside the flap of the tent, bursting in on the hunched-over figure seated at the field table.

"Good Christ, Ned! Must you do that?" Wallace tried to shelter his papers from the water being spattered everywhere by Ned's trench coat but most of the exposed pages were smeared. "Dear Cousin Joe" was obliterated and the rest of the page suffered almost as sadly from the deluge.

Ned wasn't much concerned. "You know that puddle at the end of the walk . . . well, it's not a puddle." Ned raised his voice. "It's a bloody lake!" He indicated his groin. "An' it's as deep as this!"

In spite of himself, Wallace couldn't keep from laughing.

Ned laughed too. "I almost had to goddam swim to get out!" He noticed the letter paper. "Who you writin', jack, your Ma?"

"No, I'm writing my Cousin Joe, telling him what has happened so far."

"There's nothin' to tell; we came and we saw nuttin' but the mud of Salisbury Plain."

"I told him about the rain and mud." Wallace picked up the second page. "And I wrote about how our main fleet entered Plymouth Harbour on 11 October but, by the time we arrived a few days later on the *Manhattan*, enough Canadians had been jailed for bein' drunk and disorderly, we were marched right from the boat to the train station and shunted off to Salisbury." Wallace glanced up as Ned let out a huge sigh.

"Disappointing it was, yes indeed! Instead of having some jollies in Plymouth, we had a miserable seven-hour train ride and were plunked down here." Ned shucked off his wet out-erwear. "Did you tell him what the Brits had planned for us colonials?"

Wallace nodded his head "yes" as he read from another page:

> "The Brits thought it very important to inform
> us that the officer who was named as the
> Commander of the Canadian Division, the Earl
> of Dundonald, was from a family with a long,
> illustrious history of imperial service in the
> colonies. But, when they later named Lieutenant
> General Edwin Alderson as the commander
> instead, they made no such claim to fame on his
> behalf. We didn't know which was the insult:
> putting a Dundonald in charge because he knew
> how to handle us colonials, or putting Alderson
> in charge despite the fact he didn't know
> anything about handling us colonials."[1]

Ned blew his nose into the corner of the tent, clearing one nostril at a time. He wiped his nose and chin with the back of his hand.

Wallace tried to ignore what he was doing.

Having completed his personal hygiene, Ned asked, "Are you goin' to tell him about . . ."

Wallace interrupted. "Remember when they found out that we didn't have much artillery training?"

"They was some upset!" Ned pointed at his friend. "You wanted to be a rider."

"Yep, sure enough did." The letter to Cousin Joe fell to the floor as Wallace clasped his knee with his hands and rocked back and forth on the little campstool. "I did believe it would be exciting to be a rider."

"You and me, both." Ned drew his sword bayonet from its scabbard and wielded it as if he were attacking a swarm of mosquitoes. "Take that! And that!"

"You know we aren't expected to defend ourselves with that pig-sticker."

"Uh, huh!" Ned's imaginary enemies were now more substantial as he made jabbing thrusts as if he were a Roman legionnaire. "Pig-sticking is probably the only use it will get." He stopped and gave Wallace a serious look. "Those carbines we were issued with today . . ."

"Forget it! They aren't personal weapons. They're to be tightly strapped on to the gun carriages. We aren't meant to defend ourselves with them, either."

"Oh? Well, mister smarty-pants, what the hell good are they?"

"If we have guard duty or have to perform escort duty, that's what they're for." Wallace closed his eyes as he quoted a line from the artillery drill manual they were supposed to memorize: "Carbines are not meant to be used for defending the guns and are to be securely strapped to the carriages because if gunners have recourse to small arms, they would neglect their proper duty of serving the gun."[2]

"The goddam riders are armed with revolvers!"

"Yes. I asked one of the Brits about that. He said if the riders are doing their duty, they could still have one hand free. With one hand free and a revolver, they could defend the guns and horses. Seems logical to me. It's one of the reasons I wanted to be a rider." Wallace picked up Cousin Joe's letter and blew some water off the pages. He smiled as he said, "If I were a rider, I would get to have a pistol—just like an officer."

"Ya know, jack, it's your mother's fault the brass wouldn't let you be a rider."

Wallace's initial reaction was one of anger at some sort of suspected slight to his mother, Hannah. "What do you mean?" When he had given it a moment's thought, he softened and, assuming a false British accent, he quoted again from the drill manual. "Drivers should be short, squarely built men as the horses should not be over-weighted."

It was Ned's turn. "Gunners should be tall and of good physique."

Getting right into the spirit of the moment, Wallace imitated the order that had been given to the inexperienced artillerymen during their very first muster parade on Salisbury Plain. "Tallest on the right, shortest on the left, in single rank, size!"

Ned laughed. "Ring-around-the-rosie and there you were—the tallest on the right."

"Yeah. Next tallest was the French Canadian." Wallace scratched his head. "What's his name."

"Albert. Al-bear."

"That's him! Al-bear."

"And then there was me, Edward Smithers, the Third!"

"Too bad for you that you weren't Edward the Fourth."

"Yes. If I had been fourth, I'd have been a rider."

They considered for a moment how disappointed they had been that only the last five men in the line had been short enough to be assigned as riders to the batteries of the 2nd Brigade of the Canadian Field Artillery.

Wallace broke the silence. "Albert was really funny, wasn't he?"

"Yeah."

"Remember when the Brit ordered us to number from the right? So, I said, 'one,' but Albert didn't say anything. I thought the Brit NCO was going to have a fit!"

Ned sniggered. "Yeah. Then the Brit came over and stood nose to nose with Albert and shouted, you stupid fart! What comes after 'one'?"

Wallace laughed. "An' Albert said, 'Who cares!'"

"Who cares what comes after one?" Ned shook his head as he pictured the look on the Brit's face. "Yeah, Albert had balls!"

"These Brits have no sense of humour." Wallace could hear someone sloshing through the mud at the bottom of the walkway. He turned his head toward the tent flap as he waited to see who it was. "I suppose that's why we had the lecture that Canadians should exhibit more self-discipline."

"Yeah, jack. Us colonials don't show proper respect for our betters." Ned cocked his head to one side. "Hear that?

Somebody just went for a swim." He grinned. "Somebody comin' up the walk just fell into my lake. Believe me, It'll take 'em a while to get out."

"Should we go help him?"

"Naw. It's probably a Brit an' that's a Brit lake."

It was Wallace's turn to grin as the cursing at the bottom of the walk assumed a very Brit accent.

"Sounds like an officer."

Wallace nodded his head. He tried to arrange the pages of his letter in a neat stack. "When does Albert get off detention?"

"Tomorrow."

Without any announcement the tent flap flipped up and a very wet Brit lieutenant entered, spraying more water onto Wallace's letter home. The Brit stood there, waiting for something to happen and, when it didn't, he complained, "Don't you Canadians know to stand when an officer enters a room?"

"This isn't a room," Wallace said sotto voce as he and Ned stood up.

The officer bristled. "What did you say?"

"Hope we move soon. Any news as to when we'll be moving into the barracks, sir?"

Mollified by the open-faced earnestness of the two Canadians, the officer pointed in a general way toward the area of the camp where the barracks were being built. "Yes. Your hut is finished. My sergeant has four slackers working on cleanup but he needs you to carry the stove in."

"Right away, sir."

The two Canadians began to hustle, getting into their boots and trench coats.

Satisfied that they would be right along, the Brit backed out of the tent, letting the flap drop behind him.

Both men immediately sat down.

"How long do you think?"

"About ten minutes. When we don't show up, that gung-ho Brit will consider it more efficient if the slackers move the stove. You know, muddle through with what's at hand . . . get the job done."

Wallace sighed. "Imagine! Real walls!"

"Dry floors!"

"Heaven."

They laughed.

When they considered it the proper time, they gathered up their kit and headed off to their new barracks where Wallace used his unfinished letter to fire up the pot-bellied stove.

January 13, 1915
Salisbury Plains[3]

Wallace removed the stiff-necked Canadian tunic. He slipped on the looser, more comfortable Brit jacket, flexing his shoulders and then stretching his neck, first one way and then the other. He gave a grunt of satisfaction; he was glad they had complained about the Canadian tunics. *The Brits sure know how to make military uniforms,* he thought. He threw the old tunic into the garbage can. *The Brits make good boots, too.* He glanced down at his Brit boots, wiggling his toes in comfort. There had been no need to complain about the Canadian boots; they had disintegrated in the Salisbury mud. Feeling particularly satisfied with himself, he scoffed one of Ned's pieces of maple sugar. As the sugary mess trickled down his throat he murmured, "God Bless the Duchess of Connaught" (The duchess, as the wife of the Governor General of Canada, had shipped 12,000 pounds of Canadian maple sugar to her boys. Wallace's share had been consumed days ago but Ned had conserved his issue as if it were gold.) Wallace considered snaffling another of Ned's pieces but thought better of it. He hummed the tune *Hundred Pipers* as he used his pig-sticker to open his first parcel from home. For a moment, he thought there might be a letter from Joe but, when he recognized his mother's handwriting on the inside package, he forgot all about Joe.[4]

"There must be some candy!" *Yes! Right on top—something wrapped in heavy brown paper.* Neat script identified it as coming from the Sugary so Wallace knew what it was, straight away. With a guilty glance in the direction of Ned's cache of sweets, he opened the package from The Sugary first so he could replace the piece of maple sugar he had purloined.

"There, Ned. Don't say I never did nothin' for yuh 'cause Auntie's maple sugar is the finest in the world." He contemplated the returned piece, sitting there, different from the rest of Ned's supply, larger, lighter and lacking a vice-regal crest on its tempting surface. He had just popped it into his mouth when Ned entered the barracks.

"Almost time, jack!" Ned had his new Brit jacket over his arm. As he tore the Canadian-made tunic off, he paused long enough to pick up a piece of maple sugar and break it into two, offering the larger piece to Wallace. "We've got ten minutes before muster! The colonel's going to speak to us."

Shaking his head and feeling terribly guilty, Wallace pointed at his mouth, making chewing motions as he answered, "I'm almost ready! The Brit jacket is a dream! Don't you think?"

"Wait'll I get it on!" Once he had it on, Ned ran his hands down the length of the jacket. "Boy! They sure know how to make things right for the military . . . and we're going to use the Brit cars and wagons this afternoon on manoeuvres."

"The ones the Brits issued to the CFA?"

The trumpeter gave the warning call. Ned didn't have time to answer the question. Instead, he shouted, "Move it, jack! We don't want to be late for the colonel!"

Smallwood and Smithers dashed out of the barracks, Ned still doing up the last of his buttons. They fell in to the left of the right marker, brigade strength, to hear what the colonel was going to say about the war exercise.

As soon as Colonel Creelman had taken command of the parade, he ordered the men to break ranks and gather 'round. The colonel raised his voice. "Can you men at the back hear me?"

"No-o-o," was the quick reply, followed by laughter.

"Good! I have some important information that I only want . . ." the colonel looked around and picked the nearest officer to be the foil for his humour, " . . .Captain Healey to know." More laughter, and then the colonel began his briefing.

"On the plains, this afternoon, we are going to have a war. The opposing forces are imaginary so the VIPs will only have us to watch from that small hill over there." He pointed off to the west where chairs and two canopied enclosures were visible. "From that vantage point, the VIPs will have an unobstructed view of everything we do . . . or don't do."

Colonel Creelman shifted his weight as he pointed in the other direction. "Over there, between the blue flags, is the start point for the infantry. They will form up, shoulder to shoulder, behind that line. At zero hour, we will commence our bombardment of the enemy's defences. We will maintain a rate of fire of five rounds per minute until we see the signal flare that the infantry are advancing in successive waves seeking to subdue the enemy, which are those bales of hay. Cavalry units will respond to a perceived threat on the right flank of the infantry's advance while we will limber up and advance at the trot to a new position on the left flank to provide close support to our infantry in the event the enemy should mount a counterattack." Colonel Creelman put his hands on his hips and surveyed his men. He thought *what a fine looking group. I am proud to be their commander.* "Any questions?"

A lance corporal, known to be a wiseacre, asked, "Will live rounds be used, sir?"

"Live rounds will only be used on those of my command who screw up during this exercise, corporal." Creelman turned to his second in command and gave the order, "Dismiss the men to their duties, Major."

* * *

The sound and smoke of the artillery batteries of the 2nd Brigade, Canadian Field Artillery, had been almost overwhelming. Battery after battery, gun after gun had fired round after round at the imaginary enemy while the columns of infantry had marched to the start line. The signal flare had risen into the cold, clear afternoon sky and the guns had fallen silent. The gunners watched as the infantry formed line. Bayonets were drawn and affixed, adding to the glitter of the cavalry that had drawn up on the far right. The crisp air carried the huzzahs as successive lines of infantry, shoulder to shoulder, marched determinedly forward. As the first lines reached a series of small pennants, the men broke into a run, attacking the bundles of hay with vigorous thrusts of their bayonets. Wallace noted that the infantry weren't doing any shooting in this little war, probably because when the Canadian rifle, the Ross rifle, was fired, the bayonet had a tendency to fall off. He grimaced; like the tunics and the boots, someone had better decide to get rid of the Canadian rifle and issue the boys with the Brit gun before they got into the real war.[5]

Bugles sounded through the cold air and the darlings of the battlefield, the glittering, galloping cavalry, swooped across the plain throwing great clods of the partially frozen soil high in the air. Beautiful!

A shrill, English-accented voice gave the command: "Forge wagon stand fast! Second Division limber up!"

Ah! By that order Wallace knew that the wagon carrying a field forge for the purpose of shoeing horses and making good any damages to the metalwork of the battery equipment was going to remain at the start line. The artificers, farriers, and shoeing smiths would not have the thrill of crossing the battlefield at the trot.

Wallace swallowed, hard. Some thrill! He would be hanging onto the seat handles of the ammunition wagon as the driver maintained his wagon's position in the formation of six artillery guns, six ammunition wagons, and the outriders; maintaining his position with no thought to the boulders, bushes, and branches reaching out to dislodge Wallace from his perch. Of all the duties that Wallace performed as a gunner, the ride to action was the hairiest!

The senior NCO, the No. 1 of the sixth gun, was antici-
pating the next order as he motioned to one of the outriders
to bring him his horse. No. 1 would ride into action on the
left of his gun while No. 2, also an NCO, would ride to the
left of the ammunition wagon. At this time, No. 2, with no
orders from his No. 1, stood by his gun with the rest of the
gunners, although by the amount of fidgeting he was doing,
obviously wishing that he could also be in motion. He didn't
have long to fidget.

"8th Battery! Rear limber up!"

Rear limber up! Ned and Wallace knew the manoeuvre
was simple in principle, but their mouths always went dry as
the two-wheeled carriage that was fitted to carry the gun's
supply of ammunition approached where they were standing
at eight to ten miles per hour. The driver was supposed to
turn the horses in a half-circle and halt the limber as close as
possible to the rear of the gun. Ned and Wallace's job was to
lift the trail of the gun to hip level while the driver backed the
limber so they could place the steel-reinforced trail eye over
the limber hook. Once the hook was engaged, gunners No. 3
and No. 4 would jump up on the limber to be ready for their
ride into battle while Ned and Wallace moved smartly out of
the way.

With thoughts of the VIPs watching their every movement, Wallace tried not to flinch as the head of the left lead
horse passed within inches of his face in her wheel to the rear.

"Back! Back," the driver bellowed as he strove to be
the first gun of the battery to be limbered up. The horses
responded but, when the boys dropped the eye onto the limber hook, the limber was still travelling in reverse and the
weight of the gun failed to stop it. Ned managed to jump out
of the way but Wallace tripped over an expended shell casing
and fell. The limber wheels missed him but he was still under
the limber and would be in the way of the gun carriage when
the next order was given.

"The Second Brigade will advance by the right, advance
in column of sections . . ."

Wallace knew he was in serious trouble. *Oh Christ! Which way?* He began to scramble on his elbows and knees. He could hear Ned's voice and then felt his friend's hands on the collar of his tunic as he was roughly dragged backwards.

Ned jerked Wallace to his feet. "You're lucky the Brits made that jacket!"

"Yeah! Good material," Wallace tried to say as they raced for their seats on the ammunition wagon but his breathlessness wouldn't let him.

" . . . 8th Battery! Advance by the right in column of sections, advance!"

He managed a grunted "Thanks!" as he threw himself onto the seat.

The sixth gun, wheeling to the left, followed the single line of guns toward the enemy positions. A few minutes later, when the order was given to form column of sections, the sixth battery, along with the other even-numbered guns, moved up abreast of the gun in front of them. *Like Roman charioteers,* Wallace thought. *All I need is a javelin or a slingshot to properly play the part!* He patted his sword bayonet; *it will do in a pinch.* It was then that Wallace realized he was actually enjoying the ride because the ground was remarkably even; there wasn't a stone or a rut to menace his continued existence. The driver called out, "Flat as a pancake, by Jesus!" as if to confirm Wallace's thinking. They were able to raise their eyes and take an interest in what was going on up ahead. They watched as the cavalry charged a knoll where the gunners could see the flutter of little flags; according to one of the briefings, this represented the location of the enemy's artillery.

The driver shouted, "Christ! Imagine being on the receiving end of that!" It was awesome as the cavalry thundered over the flags, trampling them into the stiff ground. Having delivered death and destruction to the imaginary enemy gunners, the cavalry formed up for their return to their own lines.

Ned pointed. "Those blue flags! That's where we move into line before we take up our positions."

Sure enough, by the time 8th Battery had reached the blue flags, the order to "form line" had been implemented. Then they halted. The guns were unlimbered and swung around in a half-circle by the trail until they were pointed at the enemy. The limbers were wheeled to the right and placed in positions behind their guns. The ammunition wagons nos. 1, 3, and 5 had been moved forward to support the six guns of the battery and were four or five yards further back. All the horses were unhitched and led away to the rear, where the location for the picket line had been marked with white flags.

Ned and Wallace ran to the steel box that was the limber and opened the back section doors. Crouching behind the steel doors that hung down enough to form a shield for the men working behind it, Ned extracted a blank shell from one of the basket tubes. He paused in front of Wallace.

"Gotta make it look good for the spectators."

Wallace pretended to set the range dial and then consulted the inner scale to get the proper fuse setting.

Ned cradled the round. "Don't want this baby going off too soon and hurting the wrong people."

A Brit observer shouted at them, "We're not playing games, gentlemen. Those are demonstration rounds. There is no need to set the timing device. Please do proceed."

Ned wasn't having any of that. "Sorry, sir! We might be usin' demo shrapnel on dem approachin' ima-gin-ary infantry sojers . . . but we needs the prac-tice for da real ting . . . dontcha tink?"

Wallace frowned at his friend's attempts to sound more of a colonial than he was, but it worked! The Brit officer spurred his horse to move away.

"Dear me! They don't speak the King's English!"

"Dear me," Ned mimicked the officer, "set the fuse for six hundred yards my dear fellow."

"Yes, of course, my little sweet petunia!"

"What are you turkeys doing?" was shouted at them like a clap of thunder. It was their No. 1!

"Putting some realism into the action, sergeant."

"Don't give me none of that horseshit, Smithers! Pass the goddam round to No. 4. Let's get on with it or I'll have your backside for bacon!"

Ned scrambled to do as he was told, passing the round to No. 4, Albert Fournier.

"You guys! Always farting around!" Albert then grunted as Ned passed him the round more vigorously than usual.

"Who cares!" Wallace shouted from where he was extracting the next round from the basket tube, meaning to tease Fournier about his most recent run-in with authority.

That's when they heard the order to range the guns and they knew that the sixth gun might not be ready because it did not have a round in the breech!

Number One gun fired.

"Oh shit, shit, shit," Ned groaned.

Number Two gun fired.

"We're going to be in big, big trouble."

No. 3 grabbed the round from Albert and helped No. 2 ram it home.

Number Three gun fired.

Ned grabbed the next round from Wallace's hands and turned to face Albert.

Number Four gun fired.

He was dismayed when he saw that No. 2 had only now closed the breech. Ned could see where the tripper had entered the recess in the face of the carrier and now stuck out from the left-hand side of the breech, ready for No. 2 to fire . . . but . . .

Number Five gun fired.

. . . would there be time for No. 2 to work the laying screw until the telescope pointed at the target? No fuses to set, but was there time to match the elevation to the amount shown on the yards indicator on the range drum?

Albert, Ned, and Wallace stood still, waiting for the fiasco to unfold.

The battery commander looked up from his watch and nodded at the sixth gun. Number Six fired, in sequence and on time.

No. 1 faced his crew. Grimly he passed sentence on his gunners. "If there is any more horseplay, I will have you shot!"

Ned's eyes widened as he asked Albert in a subdued voice, "Can he do that?"

Albert Fournier didn't know what could happen in a wartime army but, just in case, he thought he had better put up some sort of defence.

"Sarge, we were the last gun to arrive at the firing position and we didn't delay anything by practising the complete procedure."

"Shut up, Fournier! I was forced to call the shoot without proper aim or elevation."

"Yeah, I know Sarge, but we are shootin' blanks . . . there's no enemy . . . no target . . ."

No. 1 compressed his lips. "Stop trying to feed me horseshit as if it were fresh hay." He indicated that the gun crew should prepare the gun for the next round. "Get on with it, Fournier, or I will have you on report."

No. 2 pulled the breech lever from left to right. The cylindrical breech screw moved through a quarter of a circle. While No. 3 swung the screw around to the right so the cam on the hinge-pin engaged the outer end of the extractor, which prized the cartridge case out of its seat, No. 2 sponged the barrel and inspected it for debris. As soon as the extracted casing was ejected to the rear, Albert presented the next round to the No. 3 gunner.

"The Sarge is a bit of a horse's ass himself," he probably meant to say only to No. 3 but the sergeant heard him.

"You're on report, Fournier."

"Yes, Sergeant."

Ned and Wallace smiled. *Old Al-bear was at it again.*

Wallace felt a sense of well-being; with Ned's continuous good luck and Al-bear's sense of humour, nothing would ever wear down the three musketeers . . . make that the three cannoneers . . . not even that old meanie of a sergeant.

Endnotes

1. Readers of the second novel of this series might remember how Major Dundonald died during the British attack and capture of Louisbourg in 1758.

2. The instructions concerning the proper use of carbines are quoted from the artillery manual held at Canadian Forces HQ.

3. This part of the story is based upon the documents and reports held at Canadian Forces HQ, Ottawa, concerning conditions and incidents during the training of Canadians on Salisbury Plain.

4. Joe Smallwood always regretted that he and Wallace lost touch.

5. The information that the bayonet tended to fall off every time the Ross rifle was discharged was taken from documents held in the Canadian Forces HQ library.

Chapter Twelve
Rear Limber Up!

February 12, 1915
St. Nazaire, France

"This goddam boat is going in first!" Wallace picked some hay off his jacket. On the S.S. *Archimedes,* the accommodation for the horses had been quieter and drier than the smelly hold that had been assigned to the soldiers. Not being stupid, the three gunners had spent their nights with the horses.

Albert picked some more hay off Wallace's back. "We are last on pay parade, first for inoculations." He stuck a piece of straw between his teeth as he continued his litany, "First on parade, last to be dismissed; first on the duty roster and last to be granted leave."

Ned nodded his head in agreement. "First to be crammed into a tiny little boat and now we are the first to land on the continent? What do you think is waiting for us on the docks? Three squadrons of Kaiser Bill's cavalry?"

Thinking back, it had seemed like forever since they had been loaded on the trains (6th February) and then dumped on the pier at Avonmouth, near Bristol. When half of the 2nd Brigade had been stuffed into the transport ship *Archimedes,* while the remainder embarked on the larger ship *City of Dunkirk,* the Canadians had expected an immediate departure for the continent, but it wasn't until the 11th that a destroyer had been made available to act as their escort. Their little convoy crossed the channel and anchored in the roads of St. Nazaire around 2030 hours on the 12th. Now, at midnight, it looked like *Archimedes* would be the first to dock.

As the ship warped into the dock, the boys could see the area looked as if it had been swept clean of human existence: a few lights, a big trash barrel, several stevedores, but no shelter, no canteens, no brass bands welcoming the Canadian volunteers to Europe. On top of that, the rain showers were mixed with snow and the wind was mercilessly cold.

At 2 a.m., when they were assembled on the dock, it seemed more like snowballs mixed in with the rain. It was hellishly cold.

Gun six, 8th Battery's No. 1 walked briskly to where his gun crew was standing. "Break out the tents. We've been ordered to bivouac here 'til the boys come in from the *City of Dunkirk*."

"That could be hours and hours from now."

"Get used to it. You're in the army now."

By noon, 8th Battery had been informed that their tents on the wharves of St. Nazaire constituted a "rest area" and they would be permitted to spend the next night there. Guards were posted but there was no real need for them; the citizens of St. Nazaire left the area completely to the Canadians.

It wasn't going to be until the 15th of February that the rest of the Second Brigade would disembark from the *City of Dunkirk*. By that time, 8th Battery would have been detailed to board a French train, destination unknown.

February 11, 1915
Halifax, Nova Scotia

"Five, jack, ace of hearts, ace of trump, king . . ." Joe Smallwood had been explaining the top power cards of the game when Roy Curry interrupted.

"I know all that!" There was a noticeable whine in his voice when he complained, "But why does a three beat a ten?" He pointed at the last trick. "I played a ten and you say you win the trick with your three. That can't be right."

Edith Schwartz, giving the man dressed in unrelieved black a look of compassion, tried to soften the moment. "Mister Curry, I know it's difficult but . . ."

"Difficult! The game is impossible!" Roy was obviously annoyed and not the least bit soothed by the older Schwartz daughter's efforts to explain the game of 45s.

"High in red, low in black," Gladys Schwartz explained.

Joe noticed that Roy immediately responded to Gladys, seeming to devour her every word.

Gladys, unaware of Curry's preference for her explanations over any other, continued, "For clubs and spades, a two is the best card after the queen. If diamonds and hearts are called, the ten follows the queen of trump."

It dawned on Joe that Roy Curry hadn't set his cap on Edith Schwartz, no, not at all. He was gunning for the young one! Joe glanced quickly at Edith. She seemed to know it too, because her next comment had a touch of venom for her sister.

"You are suddenly an expert on the game of 45s, Gladys. Father only taught you the game at Easter and suddenly you are interpreting the rules for the gentlemen."

Fredrick, sitting by the fireplace, put his newspaper down and, clearing his throat, intervened in what might turn into a family squabble.

"I'm sorry my dear Emma isn't here this evening; particularly since this is your very first visit, Joe. She is at Sambro. But there are some refreshments in the pantry that the house girl made for us. Ladies! Would you please see to it? We could take some tea with it here by the fire, don't you think?"

"Yes, Papa."

"Yes, Father."

The girls rose.

Roy bolted out of his chair. "Please let me help." Despite the female protestations, he followed the young ladies into the kitchen, closing the pocket doors behind them.

Fredrick waggled a finger in the general direction of the stuffed horsehair sofa across from him. "Might as well make yourself comfortable over here, Joe, nearer the fire. They'll be a while." He opened the lid of a silver-plated cigarette box. "Care to join me? I'm going to have a pipe." He smiled, broadly. "I made sure I had your brand of cigarette." Soon, they were making small clouds of smoke that drifted toward the fireplace and then streamed up the flue.

The older man cleared his throat, several times. "I

thought . . . perhaps . . . since you are. . . ." Fredrick worked at his pipe. He started again. "When I suggested that you might want to visit this evening, it was under the assumption that . . ." He tapped his pipe. "I was speaking with Miss Norman on Monday and . . ."

It was Joe's turn to clear his throat.

Fredrick fell silent, waiting. *He must know about the army lieutenant.*

"I didn't get to see Charlotte right away . . . after I got back . . . wasn't feeling well enough to. . . ." Joe spread is hands and shrugged his shoulders. "This is a small town . . . and she must have felt slighted that I didn't tell her . . . right away . . . that I had been rejected. Anyhow, after a while, she returned my picture."

"The one she was wearing in her victory brooch."

"Yes, and she . . ."

"I know about the army officer."

"Well, yes." Joe sighed. "She said they would probably announce their engagement before he ships out."

"I was told that . . ."

Joe turned his head as they heard some fumbling at the pocket doors.

Fredrick chatted along as if they were continuing the same conversation. "My brother tells me your powerboat is gone from the Arm. What happened to it?"

Joe didn't hesitate to follow the lead. "I offered her to the King's Harbour Master for patrol duties until they're able to get enough small craft to do the job properly. Haven't seen her lately myself."

The sisters had re-entered the room and Gladys picked up on the subject.

"Oh, if you do get your boat back, would you please take me for a ride?"

Fredrick made a face. "Daughter! You must not be so forward!"

Roy Curry was still at the doors, pulling them closed. He turned quickly as he saw his chance. "I do declare, Miss

Schwartz, but I had suggested the very thing to my good friend Joe, just the other day." As he moved across the room he gave Joe an oily smile. "I had said it would be a grand idea if we took some of our friends out on the Arm. I bet if I ask him again, nicely, he would oblige us."

"I am somewhat delicate when it comes to the ocean," a suddenly very shy Edith Schwartz announced. "I am not sure it would be a good thing for me to go out in a small boat."

Roy disposed of the problem of the delicate sister. "That's a shame," he said, and, without a pause suggested, "With your permission, Mister Schwartz, I will drop you a note inviting . . . the Schwartz ladies . . . for an outing."

"Whenever I get my boat back," Joe added.

"Of course, Joe, we would need your boat," Roy agreed over the brim of his teacup.

February 15, 1915
Abbeville, France

Wallace jumped down from the train and joined Albert, who was surveying the rolling countryside as he scratched his fleas.

"Beautiful," Albert sighed. "A beautiful place."

"Holy shit, it stinks around here!" Wallace held his nose by way of emphasis.

"Oui! Tu as raison, mon vieux! C'est merde. It is the shit that smells."

"What d'ya mean, Bert?"

Albert pointed at the large mound of hay in front of the farmhouse. "That might look like hay but actually it's a pile of manure. As it ripens, it drips down into the underground tank. When it is good and ready the farmer pumps it up"—and here Albert pointed at the pump handle in the middle of the pile— "into a honey wagon."

"And they spread it on the fields."

"That's it, Wallace. That smell is the smell of money to a French farmer. He can't help but like it."

A French farmer was standing near the siding with his

hands on his hips watching the soldiers. Albert pushed his field cap to the back of his head, sauntered over to the Frenchman, and began speaking to him.

Wallace watched them for a while but, when he saw Ned coming down the tracks, he walked along to meet him.

"What's the word?"

"We're not staying here. We have to march along to a place called Borre where we will do some training." Ned stared down the tracks and watched their French Canadian friend as he walked back toward them. "What's the matter with Albert? He looks pissed off."

They waited for Albert to say something but he didn't volunteer any information.

"What did you learn from the old geezer?"

Albert scowled. He turned away so he was looking in the direction of the old farmer. "He said I couldn't speak proper French. He said he wouldn't speak to a dog like I was speaking to him." When Albert returned his gaze to his friends, they could see the hurt in his eyes.

"You don't have any accent when you speak English and I bet your French is twice as good," Wallace said.

"I think your French is perfect," Ned volunteered.

"La Belle France!" Albert growled. "They can stuff it!"

February 22, 1915
Le Bizet, France

"Quit your griping, jack. We're here to learn from the Brit gunners. They stopped the Huns cold so they must know what they're doin'."[1]

Wallace cupped his hands around the teapot to garner as much heat as he could. "I wasn't really complaining, Ned, but did you see the crap the Brit gunners have to take from their officers?"

Some of the Canadian batteries had been seconded to Royal Field Artillery to learn from the more experienced units. The 7th and 8th Batteries had come to Le Bizet and were attached to the 14th Brigade, RFA. The Canadian boys were impressed with the professionalism of the Brit gunners; in particular, their ability to take advantage of available cover that was excellent from views on all planes. On this day, there had been little chance to watch the gunners serve their guns since visibility was restricted by extensive fog. On the negative side of the experience, a young British officer had gone to great lengths to demean his gun crews in the presence of the Canadians. It had left a very bad taste in the mouths of the more independent-minded Canadian gunners.[2]

"Who the hell did he think he was?"

"Oh, he knew who he was. He's Lieutenant Sir Timothy Ellsworthy and he expected the common soldiers to say sir, yes sir, when they addressed him." Albert had been standing next to the Brit gunners who had been subjected to a royal dressing down for no good reason that Albert could see. "I think he was pissed because his crews couldn't shoot."

"It wasn't their fault. There was too much fog."

"I would refuse to put up with that kind of shit, I would," an incensed Wallace Smallwood declared. He quickly backed down from that position when Albert assured him that the Brits lined their insubordinate men up against walls and shot them.

Ned summed up their feelings. "The sooner we get away from these people and get back to our own kind at Borre, the better."

It wasn't until the 25th that the men of 8th Battery finally got to see the Brit gunners in action albeit it was the howitzer and heavy batteries that silenced the enemy guns at Frelingham. The day was snowy and very cold but the visibility had been excellent.

"Just like having ringside seats," Albert had said.

On the 27th, the Brit guns were in the process of demolishing some enemy earthworks when 8th Battery received orders to return to Borre. The battery limbered up right away and departed with a sense of relief that no confrontation had occurred between Canadian soldiers and Brit officers.

* * *

Ned and Wallace were swaying with the movement of the wagon as it moved away from the British positions. A cold rain had just started and Wallace pulled his trench coat closer to his neck. With nothing in particular to look at, he was watching one of the outriders when he saw the rider slump in his saddle and fall off—the horse running along with the gun carriage as if nothing had happened.[3]

Waving the wagons on, No. 2 dropped back to check on the fallen man.

Outrider Gordon Graham was the first 8th Battery casualty, a victim of a German sniper. The Grim Reaper had found the Canadians.

March 1, 1915
Borre, France

"Someone must know where we're going." Albert was always the one who wanted to know why things were happening. If the brigade was moving on, he wanted to know where. "I'm going to ask No. 1."

"Sit down, Albert," Ned and Wallace said in unison. They had finished knocking down their tent and were folding it. It was a two-man job so the fact that Albert had nothing to do was probably the cause of his restlessness.

"No. 1 has no time for us right now, Albert. Besides, if he knew where we were going he'd tell us, right, Ned?" They tied the last of the straps and, after giving each of them a little tug, began to do their personal kit.

"Albert, you stow the tent while we get our leggings on."

Five minutes later, a trumpet sounded "stand to."

Second Brigade hitched up and then moved off at precisely 1100 hours toward Strazeeler. It was a comfortable ride; although the road was narrow and the rows of trees were very close together, the road surface was in good condition, making for smooth going.

"This is the way to see France."

"You got that right, jack."

"Wonder how cold it is?"

"Not cold." Ned went "huh, huh," to try to see his breath. "Not cold enough to see my breath."

The ammunition wagon stopped; the officers up ahead had given the signal to halt.

After a few minutes of inactivity the driver said, "Oh shit! We're going to turn around!"

"Not on this narrow road! Brigade HQ must be bats!"

No. 1 came riding back. "8th Battery will lead." He pointed at the driver of the ammunition wagon, "You will be at the head of the column. We're going back to Borre."

The driver, a redneck from Alberta named Mathew, didn't question his No. 1. He chose the largest space between two of the trees and drove his horses over. It took some doing but, with the help of the gunners, the 6th gun's vehicles were soon pointed in the direction of Borre. Not all gun carriages and wagons had as easy a time of it as did the 6th gun, but soon the column was on its way back.

Ned was enjoying the situation. As No. 1 rode past on his way back to his position, Ned flagged him down.

"Would you please tell Bombardier Fournier our destination, No. 1?"

"What for, Smithers? We're going back to Borre."

"Please tell that to Fournier."

No. 1 knew Albert Fournier as something of an old woman so he grinned. "I'll do that, Smithers," and rode along.

At Borre, Albert slipped off the gun carriage, running over to the ammunition wagon. "I suppose you arranged that."

"What do you mean? " Ned replied all innocence and good fellowship.

"He came over and told me we were coming back to Borre . . . and then ordered me to take Graham's place on guard duty tonight." Albert studied his friends' faces. "You didn't have anything to do with that?"

Both men replied, "We can honestly say we had nothing to do with putting you on guard duty tonight." Ned raised his right hand and swore, "So help me God."

Albert switched his attention to Wallace. "Do you swear, too?"

"Yes." Wallace put what he hoped was a pious look on his face and raised his right hand. "So help me God."

The trumpet sounded "stand to."

The column turned around again and, by 1300 hours, was headed back down the road to Strazeeler. No. 1 came by, telling the men that the column would pass through Strazeeler to the village of Merris where the Second Brigade would receive further orders.

At Merris they were instructed to march to Doulieu.

At Doulieu there were further instructions to follow a road that would take them north of Sailly-sur-la-Lys and the river Lys to where they had been assigned billets in various farmhouses and buildings. That was good news for the gunners, who were now cold and tired.

"No more tents! I just love it when we get to sleep inside."

"Yeah, jack. I need a nice warm fire. It seems to be gettin' colder."

Wallace looked back at the village sign; it read "Doulieu." "Nice-looking little place but nobody even waved at us. It's as if we don't exist!"

"We're the phantom army, jack."

Wallace glanced back one more time. The village and the sign were gone! Where they should have been was now a wall of swirling white stuff devouring everything in its path as it sped down the road toward the ammunition wagon. Wallace didn't have time to warn Ned or Mathew before the violent snowstorm engulfed them. The horses were startled too; the wagon lurched this way and that, almost throwing Wallace off the seat. He held on and the driver quickly recovered control of the animals, but Ned had gone over the side.

After the initial onslaught of foul weather, the visibility improved. Wallace could see Ned was a few paces back rubbing his bum as he walked toward them. The column had stopped, or rather, the three wagons that Wallace could see in the heavy snow had stopped—gunners had jumped down to steady the horses, and No. 1 was riding back to check on the end of the column. No. 2 was gone. His horse had bolted and it was ten or fifteen minutes before he would return to the unit.

"Christ! That was something else, eh, jack?"

"You okay?"

"Yup!"

"Get the wagons moving again!" shouted an irritated No. 1. "There's no sense staying out here in the snow when we have nice, warm billets waiting." He continued to the fore to consult with the battery commander.

The storm had hit the column at 1530 hours but had cleared up completely at 1630 hours. The Second Brigade moved rather easily through the new snow until 1815 hours, when the head of the column reached the billets. For the last thousand yards, the going was tough; snow mixed with mud made a slurpy mess of the surface of the steep, narrow road. Equipment and animals required extra care that evening before the men were able to take advantage of the comfort of their new billets.

Within the hour, however, tea had been brewed, pipes were lit, and the cares of the day were washed away. It had been a long, tiring march but it was over.

Albert found it hard to drag himself away from the fire and don his wet gear to report for guard duty, but he did so without too much griping. Wallace and Ned felt guilty but, as Ned said after Albert had gone out the door, "Shit happens. Someone had to pull guard duty and Albert won the fur-lined piss pot."

At 2130 hours, 41038 Bombardier Albert Fournier, 8th Battery, was accidentally shot and killed by a sentry removing cartridges from his rifle.[4]

Endnotes

1. The War Diary for the 2nd Battalion reads, in part, for the 21st of February: "Brigade HQ and 7th and 8th Batteries to Le Bizet and attached to 14th Brigade RFA. WX clear and fine."

2. War Diary for this date reads: "Other ranks were attached to the men doing the same duties and learning all possible from the experienced soldiers. Inspected batteries and found their cover was excellent from views

on all planes. Learned many helpful hints. Around noon, howitzer opened fire on enemy's trenches firing 20 rounds. WX foggy and cold."

3. "Outrider (G Graham) killed en route from St Nazaire to Hazebroule" is the War Diary record of the first loss to 8th Battery.

4. The War Diary stated: "At 9:30 41037 Bar Paddon 5th Battery was accidentally shot and killed by a sentry removing cartridges from his rifle." I moved the incident to the 8th Battery.

Chapter Thirteen
The Salient

March 14, 1915
Northwest of Sailly, France

The weather was clear and warm—which was a blessing—and the good news was that, after a short briefing by an officer from the staff of the General Officer Commanding, the battery would limber up and proceed to the front.

Since the beginning of March, 8th Battery had been held in reserve at the crossroads northwest of Sailly while, as Ned regularly complained, "The rest of the guys were having all the fun." Now Ned was fairly dancing with excitement because, for the first time, 8th Battery was going to move up to where the action was. "Well, what are we waiting for?" Ned fumed. "We should be . . ."

"Oh, stow it, Ned!" Wallace had been subjected to his friend's gung-ho attitude for almost two weeks and it was getting a trifle wearing. They had been walking along to the canteen area where the Intelligence Officer was to give them a briefing when Wallace had experienced a flood of anger and frustration that Ned should always be such a goddam adolescent. Wallace instantly regretted his outburst and looked over at his friend to see if there was any resentment, but there didn't appear to be any. So he continued, "First we hear from the IO and then . . ."

"He'll probably be late and won't have much to say. They never do, you know."

"Maybe so. Look! He's here and he has maps and stuff."

Not allowing himself to be impressed, Ned said, "About time we got the low-down."

They joined the gathering as the lieutenant introduced himself. "My name is Patterson and I am the 8th Battery Forward Observation Officer."

Ned wore a self-satisfied look on his face as he whispered to Wallace, "See! We only get to talk to a FOO."

"Put a cork in it, Ned!"

Lieutenant Patterson pointed to a position on the map and then made a wide circular motion. "This is Belgium and this area"—here he made a smaller circle—"is known as the Ypres Salient. Last year, when the Allied offensive pushed the Germans back along this whole front, the Germans were pushed further back in this little area. While the rest of the line is roughly straight, we bulge into German-occupied territory between these two German strong points enough that, throughout most of the bulge, or the salient as we like to call it, the Allies take fire from the Germans on three sides."

The lieutenant nodded to the two soldiers who had been holding up the map and they folded it and moved off to one side.

"Last year, fighting in the salient was pretty desperate but I guess the Germans have given up on pushing us out because there has been little Hun activity since just before Christmas." He rubbed his hands together, "So, now it's going to be our turn. English and French regiments will be coordinating something to irritate the opposition. I don't have any of the details but you can count on some exciting days ahead.

"Today, you will move up and take a position next to 6th Battery while 7th Battery will fall back into reserve. As your Forward Observation Officer, I will be with the infantry sending back information by field telephone about enemy movements and targets and giving you your overs and unders."

He swept the group with his eyes, seeming to make contact with each soldier. "You get out there and do your job . . . I'll do mine . . . we'll hammer their fortified positions. . . ." Suddenly, Lieutenant Donald Patterson, Forward Observation Officer, 8th Battery, Canadian Artillery picked up the hem of an imaginary dress and pranced to the edge of the platform. He stopped and raised his voice. "We'll pulverize their positions! We'll demolish their defences so our infantry can cake-walk to Berlin if they want to!"

Wallace was the first to jump up. "Huzzah!" he shouted, waving his arms.

"Huzzah!" sprang from a dozen Canadian throats. "Hooray! Hurrah!"

It wasn't until March 25th that Wallace found out why the attack failed.

March 25, 1915
Bank of the River Lys

"I got somethin' wrong with my mouth." Wallace gingerly felt along the gums at the side of his mouth with his fingers. "Ish rawr an' sorf."

Ned was leaning back, enjoying the warm, spring-like day. He didn't open his eyes when he asked, "What did you say?"

"I said my fuckin' mouth is raw and sore."

Unlocking his fingers from behind his head, Ned picked up a ceramic mug stamped with the letters SRD and handed it to his friend. "Rinse your mouth with this." He grinned as he added, "but don't spit it out!"

Wallace accepted the cup and lifted it to his nose to smell the contents. "God! It's not diluted!" He took a sip, rolling it around and around in his mouth before swallowing. "How did you get rum that wasn't diluted?"

"I did somebody a favour."

There was a lull in the conversation as Wallace took a large sip and held it on the lesions in his mouth. When he finally swallowed he asked, "Like, what did you do to get some Service Rum Diluted that isn't diluted?"

"You remember when we were in action last week, and the General Officer Commanding did his inspection?" Ned didn't wait for Wallace to confirm; he just pressed on, "Remember when one of the GOC staff officers stepped off the wooden walk and got his boots muddied?"

"Washn't there." Wallace was feeling his gums with his fingers again. He nodded his head. "That sure helped, buddy. Thanks."

"The major was some upset. He waited until the GOC had gone along and then he turned on that young lieutenant, MacDonald, just as if he were an old hound dog finally catching his first squirrel. Talk about the fur flyin'! He gave him shit!"

"What for?"

"For not cleaning up the area for the inspection."

"Cleaning up a trench?"

"Yeah. He promised to put MacDonald on report for not filling in the shell hole." Ned smiled as he remembered the look on the young officer's face when Ned had come to his rescue. "I said . . . bold as brass, mind you . . . I said, Major, sir, the Kraut batteries were searching for 6th Battery this morning, throwing shells in every crazy direction . . . and an unexploded shell had even gone so far as to burrow into the ground right where you were standing." Ned guffawed. "That major jumped back so quick," Ned made flapping motions with his hands, "he damn near flew . . . but I assured him that the lieutenant had looked after the bomb before the inspection. Our only regret . . . I said, the only regret was that we just didn't have enough time to fill in the hole before the good major came along." Ned laughed. "I even suggested the lieutenant should get a medal for his effort . . ."

"You didn't!"

Ned considered his reply before admitting, "Actually, no, I didn't, but it would have been the right thing to do, the lieutenant being so brave and all."

"I never know when you're pulling my leg or when you're not."

"I'd never pull your pisser about pusser rum, jacko! That Lieutenant MacDonald was so appreciative he diverted some SR our way before it became SRD." Ned pretended a studied, thoughtful air as he said, "Y'know, SRD doesn't mean Service Rum Diluted; it means Seldom Reaches Destination. Har! Har!"

Wallace took another sip. It was his turn to appear thoughtful. "Don't you want any?"

"Nope! Had three of those SRD mugs to begin with."

In measured tones Wallace said, "You had three cups of service rum and you're just now telling me . . ."

Ned knew he had just stepped into it further than the major had. In an apologetic voice he said, "You know I always share with you, Wallace. Like I always share my good luck with you . . . 'n anything else I have . . . like you always took as much maple sugar as you ever wanted." Ned paused.

Wallace turned his head away as he scowled. *In artillery terms, I've been bracketed. Time to limber up and get out of here.* He quickly changed the subject. "Did the good lieutenant give you any information about the Franco-Brit attack and why it failed?"

"He didn't . . . but his sergeant told me some stuff that was mighty interesting. In particular he told me why the lieutenant was so appreciative of my saving his butt."

"Appreciative enough to give you *three* cups of rum, eh?" Wallace instantly regretted his loose mouth; it probably was the rum doing the talking for him. He was relieved when Ned let it go.

"True, but you asked me about the attack. You want to hear?"

Properly chastened, Wallace nodded his head. "I do. I remember we were ordered to bombard the Krauts in front of us so they would think it was the Canadians attacking over here . . ."

" . . . while it would actually be the Brits and French attacking at Neuve Chapelle. And it was Lieutenant MacDonald who had us maintain the high rate of fire; at least he carried the can for it."

"How could he get in trouble for permitting a high rate of fire? We were supposed to support the Franco-Brit attack with a diversionary bombardment."

Ned was enjoying himself. "Not really, jack. The sergeant explained that the official orders were to create the belief that we were about to assault but the unofficial orders were to husband our ammunition. Headquarters only allowed fifteen rounds per gun for the diversionary fire." Ned sighed. "Our young lieutenant believed it was immoral to tell the Brits one thing and do another, so he approved the use of our reserve ammunition and ordered up more."[1]

"And, of course, when the other batteries saw us shootin' it up, they used up their ammunition, too."

"Yes, and as soon as the brigade found out about the orders for more ammunition, they cancelled the shoot. Our young lieutenant was put on report, or whatever it is they do with officers."

Wallace thought for a moment as he sipped the last of the SRD. "I get it. If the major had also put'm on report maybe he'da found himself lined up against a Brit wall bein' introduced to the Enfield rifle the hard way."

"You got it! Enter the hero of the day," Ned patted his own chest, "who saved the career and maybe even the life of a MacDonald boy from Sunbury, Ontario."

"Too bad us Canadians couldn't'a saved the Brits and the Frenchies from defeat. If 'n we'd not held back our guns . . ." Wallace put his SRD cup down and straightened up, "If 'n we hadn't let'm down, maybe the attack woulda gone through and we woulda broke the Hun line."

"Nothin' of the sort, jacko." Ned picked up the cup and examined the inside to see if there was anything left. He put it down. "The Brit gunners opened a hole in the German line a mile wide. Could've been the beginning of the end of this whole war but like the sergeant tells it, there was a lack of offensive spirit in the officers."

"Dear, dear Sir Timothy would rather play at bowls 'til he could see the whites of their eyes."

The two men heard the trumpet sounding mess call. Ned started to get up but Wallace remained seated on the grass.

"Not goin' to the field kitchen, jack?"

"It was mutton stew and biscuits at dinner. Whatda you think it'll be for supper?"

They both said, "Leftover mutton stew and biscuits," while Ned added, "and it waited all afternoon in the pot." Ned leaned back too. "Good idea not to eat it. Don't think I'll bother to go over."

They continued to sit there. The sun had finally gone down; dusk was upon them.

Wallace raised his head. "What about the daily rum issue?"

"Walk all the way over to the field kitchen for some SRD?"

"A quarter ounce of rum."

"Diluted with water."

They reached their decision at the same time.

"Naw."

Endnotes

1. The following was reported in the War Diary about the planned lack of artillery support for the Franco-British attack. "Artillery hampered by a shortage of shells. It is more important that while we create the belief that we are about to assault, we should at the same time husband our ammunition and from ten to fifteen rounds per gun should suffice for this task. Fired twice as many. After, rationed to three."

Chapter Fourteen
The Attack

April 22, 1915
Ypres Salient

"Ah, there you are, Smallwood." Colonel Creelman smiled at the tired-looking gunner. "You had a spot of trouble with the 6th gun, 8th Battery."

"Yes, sir. The gun crew were killed, sir, by a coal box. It took out the gun, too."

"When the German batteries search us out and deliver . . . call it what you like; HE, Black Marias, coal box or Jack Johnsons . . . when the Germans search for our batteries, and when they find one of us and we get hit by their high explosives, we lose friends."

"Me and my buddy were at the limber."

Creelman put on a wan smile. "That's why you and your buddy survived."

"He got concussion, sir. Won't be right for a while. Light duty."

"Yes, well, I have to transfer you to another gun. Your old 8th Battery gun will be replaced in a few days but, until then, I need you in the 6th Battery." When the colonel saw the distress in Wallace's face he hurried on, "It won't be permanent, son. You'll go back to your friends at 8th Battery as soon as more replacements arrive. Until then, I'm gathering up a half-dozen bombardiers and posting them to . . ."

"Excuse me, sir. I'm not a bombardier."

"You have performed well, and your officer has recommended you to act as a replacement at 6th Battery."

Some of the tiredness left Wallace's face. "Thank you, sir."

The colonel raised his chin and called out, "Sergeant!" He pushed back his chair and strode toward the door-like opening at the front end of the metal hut. "That's the trouble with having my headquarters in this boiler; it's sunk into the ground and covered with several feet of dirt, so no one hears me when I call out." He pushed the door. "There he is, near the barn." He looked at the new bombardier and again noted how weary he looked. "Sit down at the other table. I won't be long," he said as he went out the door.

Wallace did as he was told, thinking how very different the Canadian officers were from the Brit officers, when the colonel stuck his head back in.

"That's the War Diary on the table. I don't usually have it here, but I needed to make a notation. You might read the diary if you want to make sense of what we have been doing this last while." Then he was gone again.

The War Diary was shaped like a cashier's book with lines and columns. Each entry was dated. A brown stain was on the open page. Wallace noted that the writing changed on one of the dates near the stain. He started to read some of the recent entries.[1]

18 April 1915
Relieving the French. 8th Battery registered the trenches at map reference d10a86 to d4c54 also two houses in the rear. At 5 pm, we took over the telephone system. The French group finally moved away at 9pm. The billets we took over from the French were in a very unsanitary condition and filthy dirty.
  8 horses and 13 mules arrived as remounts for the brigade.
  Quiet. Several aeroplanes both hostile and friendly. Fine and warm.

Wallace smiled as he read a note pencilled in at the side of the page. *Those are the colonel's initials.* The note read:

We relieved a French Brigade on 18 April and already everyone is itching and scratching. The place was absolutely filthy when we took over. The straw used for bedding had not been changed in months and was lousy to the limit.

Wallace chuckled. *Boy! He's some pissed at the French!*

19/4/15
9:15am enemy shelling on the right. 8th
replied.

20/4/15
Heavy German shelling at about 4:30pm
until 9pm. One gun 8th Battery destroyed.
Clear and warm.

What a way to describe the deaths of my friends on gun six.
Wallace read it out loud: "One gun 8th Battery destroyed." *Shit!*
Didn't even write down their names! He heard some noises and
looked up but there was no one coming. He read some more.

21/4/15
Canadians are replacing the French batteries
in the line. 8th relieves the 11th Battery
position at 8pm.

22/4/15
Change-over continues with various batteries
registering their guns.

Of course, the War Diary entry for the 22nd is unfinished, it
being only slightly after 1100 hours.
Wallace felt the fresh, warm air flowing through the open
door of the makeshift headquarters, which brought with it the
sounds of excited voices. He thought he might read some of
the earlier War Diary entries, but instead he got up and
walked to the door to see what was going on. Over near the
barn a messenger was giving information to members of the
HQ staff and, at the same time, pointing off to the left of the
Canadian lines where there were increasing sounds of artillery.
In the sky, several German warplanes soared unopposed over
the Allied lines, most probably selecting targets for the report-
edly two hundred Kraut guns firing into the salient.
A sergeant left the group and marched—as only a sergeant
can march—in his direction.

"Hi, Sarge."

"Bombardier, this is a diagram of how to get to the 6th Battery." He handed the slip of paper to Wallace. "And here's your orders assigning you to the 6th." He handed Wallace the sheet of foolscap. "Give it to your officer at your new section."

"But Sarge! I wasn't meant to be assigned to the 6th. I belong to the 8th Battery."

The expression on the sergeant's face didn't change. "There are four boxes on the movement form and I ticked off 'assign' and, according to the colonel's orders, the lieutenant approved it. The 6th owns your body, Bombardier. Deliver it. You are dismissed."

Wallace shouldered his gear and went off to find the 6th. He stopped at the edge of the farmer's field and looked back at the sunken boiler. The colonel was mounting his horse and several messengers were beginning their run. One of them was headed his way. Wallace waited until the runner came abreast and then joined him in his trot.

"Where are you headed?

"5th and 6th Batteries."

"Mind if I tag along?"

"If you can keep up."

Wallace hitched his pack up tighter as he trotted down the path with the runner. When they came to the end of the path, the runner explained, "The batteries are down the end of that little track but it gets swampy in there." He slowed to let Wallace catch up. "Just over that rise is a nice little country road that takes us north and then I cut back behind the French lines. I keep my feet dry that way."

"Sounds good to me," Wallace said.

The runner didn't reply but took off at the trot. As they came over the rise, they saw that the road was crammed with civilians fleeing south.

The runner stopped and placed his hands on his hips. "Should have gone by the swamp. Gettin' up that road is going to be pretty tough, now."

"Christ! What are they escaping?" The sudden passage of

artillery shells overhead seemed to give full answer to Wallace's question, but the motley crowd of refugees streaming by paid little notice—either to the flight of the shells or to the line of destruction as those shells struck.

Passing the two Canadian soldiers at that moment was an old lady sitting high on a handcart, her sweating son between the shafts, both dressed in their Sunday best. When a woven basket fell off their cart, they took no notice. Following the cart were three children: they shuffled past the basket, their eyes cast down but unseeing. One of the two deep-chested dogs pulling a two-wheeled cart, meant to hold children in happier times, sniffed at the basket before passing on, crushing it with the cart. The contents of the basket, some fine linen and table-ware, presented an obstacle to the next vehicle, a wheelbarrow being pushed by a young woman with bewildered children clutching her dress, but she just pushed harder on the handles to get by. After two wagons, hauled by a brace of fine horses, had run over the spot, the basket, linen, and tableware were unseen amongst the other debris on the road.

The messenger lifted his forage cap and scratched his head. "These people are gettin' out of the way of somethin'."

Wallace put his hand out to stop the runner as he stepped into the road. "But our officers told us the Krauts had given up trying to push us out of the salient . . . they gave up months ago."

"In this part of the world, armies come and go and the people have learned to get out of the way to survive. You can bet the Germans are coming through here."

The runner tried to move but Wallace held his arm more firmly. "What makes you such a goddam expert?"

"I was a gentleman cadet of the Royal Military College and my forte was studying the development of arms and war-fare." He nodded toward the fleeing civilians. "They know the Krauts are coming through here.

"How come you're not an officer?"

"I volunteered before I graduated." The messenger shook his arm loose and stepped into the road. He put on his cap and, with both arms, raised his rifle above his head. "Make way!" he shouted and, as if by magic, a little island of space formed around the two Canadian soldiers, allowing them to make slow progress north against the flow of people on the congested road. After a while, Wallace gave the messenger a rest by stepping to the fore and raising his carbine in the air. At some indiscernible point, the messenger led Wallace off the road across another field—no different than the four or five fields they had already passed.

"We're in behind the French lines now. All we have to do is move along behind this little ridge for a couple of hundred yards and we'll find the Canadian batteries."

Now that they were away from the human noises of the road, Wallace could hear the Canadian guns above the German barrage. "We're given' it back to 'em!" he said with glee.

"What the fuck!" The messenger stared, open-mouthed, as an NCO of the French Territorial Division came running away from the front. He was carrying no weapons because he was using both hands to tear at his collar and the front of his uniform which was saturated with some yellowish-green gunk. Another, and then another French African soldier came stumbling, running, and falling toward them.[2]

"What's wrong with them?" And then Wallace smelled the chlorine; the Frenchmen were saturated with chlorine. "They've been gassed."

"My God, look over there!"

Two clouds of yellowish-green smoke were drifting slowly southwards, close to the ground. Shadows in the terrible fog struggled and fell, jumping up only to fall again, each attempt to escape less energetic. Several of the shadows broke out of the fog, revealing the purple face of a white officer or the ashen faces of the black soldiers. If they fell, they would lie on the ground squirming until overtaken by the fog, where their torture was masked by the thick folds of the poison gas. More groups of soldiers staggered clear of the horrible fog, eyes bulging, the sounds of their choking, retching, and coughing masked by the fury of the German bombardment which was now enfolding the French line.

"This is a rout!" The messenger gestured toward the right where the Canadian lines were. "Move it! If we stay here we will be gassed!" As they ran, they were not aware the German bombardment had stopped but they did see more figures come out of the greenish haze: upright, featureless figures with weapons extended in their direction. The first one, and then the second and third, raised their rifles to aim at the Canadians.

Wallace waved his arms, "Je suis Canada!" *Oh shit,* he thought. *They're not French! They're Germans! And they're going to kill me!* Wallace threw himself to the ground as he tried to bring his carbine around to where he might be able to use it. He went cold all over as he recalled that he wasn't armed. After the way Albert had died, Wallace had decided to never carry a loaded weapon and now he was going to regret that decision. Getting up on his knees, he looked ahead, but the threatening figures were gone. The greenish fog was dissipating and there was no one in sight but his messenger friend. And what the hell was his friend doing? Feet pumping like he was running a marathon while doing dog paddle motions with his hands, he wasn't going anywhere because his face was jammed hard into the ground.

Warily, Wallace stood up, making sure there wasn't any further German threat before he went over to help his friend. With his carbine again slung over his shoulder, he heaved his friend to his feet. "Christ! That was some scare, wasn't it?" he said as he turned the other Canadian around. There was no face! Where a nose, mouth, and chin would have properly been, there was a mangled mess. Maybe there were eyes, or an eye, but Wallace's mind didn't register the fact. All he saw was the lack of face and the blood coming from nowhere and everywhere. He reached up to brush the dirt and twigs from the . . .

That's when the messenger grabbed Wallace's hand with both of his and, with impressive strength, placed Wallace's hand on his carbine.

"It's not loaded."

The hands failed, dropping uselessly away; the knees bent as the messenger sank to the ground. He would have fallen forward but, by this time, Wallace had his wits about him and he knelt to support his friend. "Sweet Jesus, I couldn't . . . anyway."

A long, long stream of air came out of the gasping, wheezing area above the chest.

Wallace had made up his mind to carry the messenger to an aid station but, with a flutter like a wounded crow in a farmer's field, the messenger died.

Oh God! I don't even know his name! With a start, Wallace realized that he wasn't alone. Half a dozen soldiers marched resolutely toward him, the goggles of their gas masks slightly fogged, their rifles at the ready. He thought to run but, when he didn't move, the Germans pressed on as if they had an appointment in the town. He could see more Germans in the distance. Taking a quick look at the backs of the nearest Germans, Wallace flew like the wind toward the Canadian guns. He thanked God when he found a Canadian officer.

"The Krauts are . . ."

"Soldier, do you have the messages?"

"No, sir. The messenger was shot. The Germans are . . ."

"Were you with the messenger when he was shot?"

"Yes, sir. The French . . ."

"But you aren't a messenger and you don't have his messages."

"No, sir. I am a bombardier assigned to the 6th Battery."

"This is the 5th. Just over there," he waved a hand in the general direction, "another seven hundred yards." The officer turned on his heel. "I hope you have your papers," he said as he marched off. "If the Brits find you, they will charge you with desertion in the face of the enemy."

Wallace felt desperately tired and annoyed with the officer. *Why would there be Brits walking around here looking for deserters?* He trudged along. *Of course, the Canadian Brigade was infested with Brit advisers and observers. But would they check for papers? Officers are such pissants.* He saw another officer. This time he drew himself up and marched over. The officer took the salute.

"Yes, soldier?"

"Bombardier Smallwood reporting on loan from the 8th Battery."

"Good man! I'm Lieutenant Geary and you'll be with the third gun. They're short."

"Sir, there are Germans behind the French line."

"The French line? Don't worry about it. The French will counterattack." Now, move smartly! There's a body snatcher working our gun positions."

Wallace couldn't help himself. The very thought of a sniper's cross-hairs zeroing in on his back caused him to scrunch his shoulders.

The officer noticed and gave a reassuring smile. "The infantry are smoking him out now. Hopefully, they'll get him before he gets another one of us."

"But, sir. What about the Germans on the left?"

"Not our problem. The French will counterattack."

"Sir, the Germans used chlorine gas on the French."

"It's against the rules of war to use poison gas. You must be mistaken. I suggest you get to your gun, Bombardier, where you'll be less of a target for the body snatcher."

Bloody officers have answers for everything. "Yes, sir."

* * *

By midnight, Wallace was more aware of the rattle of rifle fire, seemingly all around them. Gunners would spin around and fall or stagger or clutch at some part of themselves but, despite the losses, discipline was maintained and the guns continued to be well served. Fires burned in the distance—a tree, a barn, a house—while flares spouted into the sky making long eerie shadows in the semi-darkness. During a lull while they waited for a resupply of ammunition, his No. 1 complained, "We're one thousand five hundred yards from the enemy and I can't understand why we're getting so much rifle fire."

Wallace shouted from his position on the other side of the gun, "The Krauts are behind our left flank."

"Nonsense! They would have to overrun our infantry and the 5th Battery . . . and the 5th is still there!"

"They used poison gas and overran the French."

A trumpet sounded "stand to."

Wallace lips moved, "Glory be to the Father and to the Son and to the Holy Ghost," as a form of thanks that the 6th Battery was moving out.

"Rear limber up!"

Wallace was doing his checks: *tampions and breech covers on, breech fittings and sights secure, elevating gear, brake shoes and brakes cleared of mud . . .*

When he heard the driver's orders to the horses, "Back, back," he knew he'd better hop onto the axle tree seat and be prepared to hang on for dear life because the nearest country road was several hundred yards south of the current firing position across very rough terrain. He was barely into his seat when the limber lurched forward, the lead horse getting into the spirit of escaping from German rifle fire, which was now supplemented with shelling. Bushes were tearing Wallace's arms and legs and then it was down into a ditch—the gun carriage seemingly flying over his head right behind him—up the other side, crashing onto the flat of the road, one of the horses bleeding from the neck and shoulder, obviously flagging in her efforts to drag them to safety. Gunner No. 3, the one who should have been sitting by the driver was gone. There was no sign of No. 1, who should have been riding off to the left but, as Lieutenant Geary led the other guns of the battery across a farmer's field to avoid the extensive shelling of the country road, No. 1 appeared on the right of the injured horse. He signalled the driver to stop.

Two outriders helped No. 1 cut the injured horse out of the traces.

The other gunner, the one sitting near the driver, jumped down. "Don't hurt Speckles!" He raised his arms, as if to prevent No. 1 from getting any closer to the horse, but he was too late; one of the outriders drew his pistol and shot the horse in the temple.

"Get back up on the limber, Ritchie!" No. 1 shouted at the driver. "Get out of here before they get our range! No. 1 grunted and grabbed his wrist; his hand hanging down the wrong way. Guiding the horse with his knees, he spurred her along the wheel tracks in the dirt. An outrider caught up to him and took the reins, leading No. 1 at a much faster pace; the limber and gun carriage following right behind. Once back out on the road, they were met by another outrider.

"We've been ordered to select and occupy gun positions near Wieltje." In the darkness, the second outrider couldn't see that No. 1 was wounded.

"You'll have to lead; I'm taking Sarge to an aid station," the first outrider said as he turned the sergeant's horse out of the way of the limber.

"Shit! Bad luck, Sarge." The second outrider gave the "follow me" to the limber driver.

* * *

It was remarkably quiet at the next gun position and Wallace said so to his new No. 1.

"It's quiet here because we are so far away from the fighting. We are positioned in support of the *second* line of defence."

"Our first line of defence is gone? Overrun?" Wallace couldn't stop his concern from showing in his voice.

The new No. 1, a corporal who hadn't had the chance to put up his sergeant's stripes, failed to hear the anxiety in the voice of his No. 3. "Naw! Our boys are holding the line. It's the goddam generals. Our last two fire orders were for targets out of range. I don't think they know where we are."

A voice called out, "It's a good thing we have a navy!"

Wallace thought it sounded a lot like old Al-bear and almost said so . . . but none of these men would have known Albert Fournier. He tapped his tin cup against the side of the gun carriage.

"Right!" Their No. 1 had heard the sound. "Brew up, gentlemen. Don't wander away, now."

* * *

At 0250 hours, the order was given to "stand to" followed almost immediately by "rear limber up."

The sky was too light from flares and fires for Wallace to check the stars for direction but still dark enough that Wallace couldn't be sure what country road they were on. When he saw Speckles' body, he knew they were headed back to the same gun positions they had driven out of a few hours ago. This time he was ready for the plunge into the ditch and the dash across the rough terrain. Once at the gun positions, they were subjected to heavy rifle fire and shelling but by 0330 hours, 6th Battery was ready for business, and that business wasn't long in coming.

No. 1 crouched behind the gun shield, cupping his squall lantern with his hands so he wouldn't draw fire from the enemy as he read his fire orders. "What time is it?"

"0440 hours, corporal."

Wallace saw the look of aggravation on No. 1's face and thought being addressed as corporal instead of as sergeant had ticked him off—but that was not so.

"This fuckin' order says we should support an attack at 0430 hours."

Lieutenant Geary shouted, "Anybody see Allied movement out there?"

Not many gunners stuck their heads above the guns' shields but someone must have because a voice replied, "Not a thing, sir."

As it got lighter, the men of 6th Battery could confirm there was no movement of Allied troops in front of the Canadian batteries. The gunners hunkered down behind their guns, seeking as much shelter as they could from the probing German bullets and shells.

It was 0600 when the next fire orders were delivered.

"Get this, No. 1! You know the attack that was supposed to take place at 0430? Well, according to this, it has been postponed to 0500 hours."

This time, there must have been at least two gunners who peeked over the shields because one of them was shot in the head for his trouble. The other gunner confirmed that it was all quiet along the Canadian lines.

Each gun of 6th Battery was then ordered to shoot thirty rounds at map reference V19c after which German harassment of the field guns waned and there were no further gunner casualties. When the German assault failed, the men of 6th Battery felt a sense of joy and exuberance they hadn't felt since that night in Quebec City when they had marched onto the pier with the bands playing and the civilians cheering. Oh, it was a glorious war!

"The bastards have given up!" Wallace did a jig and then a clumsy pirouette, much to the amusement of his crew. He rubbed his belly. "Could we get some food up here, No. 1?"

"Off you go, Smallwood. See if you can find something hot."

Wallace was returning from the commissary wagon with two pots of beef stew when the Germans commenced heavy shelling of the Canadian trenches. Within minutes, the 5th, 6th, and 7th Batteries of the Canadian field artillery retaliated. Wallace sat in the ditch until the action faded away.

The boys reheated the stew over a small burner and, later, slept by their guns.

April 24, 1915

Wallace wasn't sure he was awake or if he was dreaming. He rubbed his eyes with his sleeve but it didn't help him decide if he was in trouble or if it was a nightmare.

"The Krauts are coming! They're using gas bombs!"

Okay, so it has to be a nightmare, he thought. He was going to ignore it all but the brilliance of a flare in the night sky made his eyes wince. *Oh God! My eyes are open and the Krauts are coming . . . and they are using poison gas!* "What time is it?"

"After 0400," someone answered. "You can just see down there the green stuff in our trenches."

The 6th Battery waited. Soon figures could be seen scurrying out of the Canadian first-line trenches.

"Our boys are retreating!"

"Only to the second line!" Wallace recognized the voice of the lieutenant. "We have a request for support. No. 1's report to me!"

The artillerymen watched as the Canadian infantry took up a line about five hundred yards from the guns.

"Look! Our boys are lying down!"

Wallace couldn't see anything. He realized there was no supporting German artillery. "Why aren't the German guns firing?"

"The Kraut observers can't call the fall of shot because of the clouds of gas." No. 1 took up his position. "Load shrapnel! Set fuses for 600 yards. We will fire into our old first-line positions as soon as we see Germans in them."

"Can't see anything; just that green stuff."

"We wait until we can see the Kraut infantry."

When Wallace heard a bird sing from somewhere behind him, he realized just how quiet it had become. *Some horny male bird wasn't going to let a war interfere with his love life. That bird had a chance to be heard right now because the Canadian batteries were holding their fire; the Germans couldn't shoot because their forward observers couldn't report where their infantry was. Smart bird! Wasn't missing the opportunity.* Wallace smiled to himself as he waited.

In almost full daylight, the only soldiers the men of the 6th Battery could see were the Canadians lying on the ground wherever they could find shelter, but the green haze had almost reached them. The first soldier did a lot of squirming before he jumped up and ran, zigzagging to the rear. He threw himself behind a small bush, wiggling around until he faced the proper direction. The next Canadian to run from the gas cloud was cut down by gunfire from an unseen enemy. He fell on a small knoll and was chewed by bullets until he stopped moving of his own accord. After that, the Canadians who were enveloped by the thinning gas clouds could be seen pissing on various bits of clothing and holding the wet material over their mouths and noses.

There! Wallace was sure he saw a glint of light from within

the green haze, perhaps a reflection from the eyepiece of a gas mask. He watched as men in greenish-grey climbed over the parados and out the back of the first-line trenches, marching toward the Canadian infantry.

"Double-check your fuses!"

Wallace had been preoccupied watching the German advance so he was a bit startled to be caught daydreaming . . . but also slightly irritated that No. 1 would consider it necessary to remind the gunners to check the shrapnel fuses. He was more than slightly irritated when the lieutenant added, "Wouldn't want any short fuses because then our infantry would be hit with their own shrapnel!" But Wallace did check the fuses.

The prone Canadian infantrymen fired into the advancing line of Germans. Many Germans fell. More fell when the Canadian eighteen pounders unleashed their shrapnel. Round after round was fired into the advancing lines of Germans, but still some came forward, to be cut down by the rifles and machine guns of the waiting Canadians. When there were no more Germans to be seen, the cease-fire order was given. By 0510 hours, the gas had dissipated enough for the Canadians to advance and reoccupy their first-line trenches.

The men of the 6th Battery stood and cheered the victory they had helped win. Their joy was short-lived.

Lieutenant Geary rode over to Wallace's gun. "Guns 2 and 3, limber up! The Krauts are breaking through on our left! No. 1's report to me!" Above the din of battle, Geary gave his briefing to the No. 1's standing near gun 3, 5th Battery. "The Krauts are pushing on our left. There's a hole in the 8th Battalion's front and the goddam Krauts have found it. 5th and 7th will move their fields of fire as far to the left as possible. 6th Battery will send two guns to a position between map references D19b68 and D20a28." He pointed at the No. 1's from guns 2 and 3 . . . "Move! Now!"

Wallace heard the order and felt a thrill of fear. *We are to give direct support to the infantry! We're already limbered up; I guess we're waiting for our No. 1 to lead us to the party. I wonder if I have time for a pee. Too late,* he thought as the limber moved off at a fast trot but broke into a gallop when they came under heavy small arms fire. Lieutenant Geary rode by at the gallop. He waved the guns on to the firing position without any of the usual procedure of the commanders reconnoitring or layers carrying their sights with them as they assumed the position on the ground from which the gun would eventually shoot. No, the two guns were driven right to the lieutenant who pointed to where he wanted the guns positioned.

"Action front," he shouted. "Commence firing as soon as you have a target! Number 2 gun, percussion. Number 3 gun, shrapnel!" The two guns had brought the one ammunition wagon, which was their fair share of the battery's resources, so Lieutenant Geary ordered, "Supply from the wagon." At the same time, he beckoned one of the outriders to come for orders. When that rider was shot by German rifle fire, he tried again, ordering another rider to return to 6th Battery for more ammunition wagons. Wallace was close enough to hear him shout, "The one wagon won't give us enough ammunition. Hurry! Bring us what you can!" That was all Wallace could hear because his gun went into action. Out of the corner of his eye, he saw that the limbers and horses were led off to the rear. The first rounds were taken from the limber, Wallace's crew using HE so they weren't concerned about ranges and fusing. *God! There's no trouble finding targets . . . there are Germans everywhere!* His crew switched to shrapnel after a few minutes of rapid fire.

Wallace's No. 1 was hit and down! Wallace vaulted the trail and took over the pointing of the gun. The No. 2 continued the searching, ramming home, and elevating of the gun. In a few minutes, when No. 2 was wounded, No. 3 took his place while continuing to uncap the fuses when in the bore.

Wallace looked behind; there were no men at the limber to order forward to help—they too were down. *Where was the accurate German fire coming from?*

It was as if the German riflemen and Wallace became aware of each other at the same instant. Wallace could see that the Germans were reloading while keeping their eyes on the Canadian gunner.

Wallace thought of trying to use the carbine strapped to the cannon but discarded the thought immediately. He would have to stop the Germans with his gun. The riflemen had rounds in the chamber; they raised their weapons and fired, almost in unison.

Wallace threw himself to the rear of the gun, reaching for the handspike as he fell. His acting No. 2 fell, wounded by the rifle fire. Gripping the handspike, Wallace levered the trail of the gun so the cannon was pointed in the direction of the riflemen. The German rifles were loaded again but, by this time, Wallace had the shield of the gun between him and the bullets. He was unharmed by this next volley. Satisfied that the cannon was pointed properly, he now had to cross over the gun and see to the ramming home and elevation . . . and the fusing . . . *ah shit! I'll never make it!* But he saw that the wounded No. 2 was elevating the gun. Wallace saw him fall away to the right and thought his No. 2 had been wounded again. When he heard the gunner shout, "Ready," he knew the gunner had moved away to avoid the recoil of the gun. Wallace stepped back and pulled the lanyard.

"Goodbye, German warriors! Hello, merry widows!"

Gunners from the fresh ammunition wagon lifted the acting No. 2 off the trail where he had fallen after being wounded again. His inert form was pushed off to one side. Wallace looked to be relieved as the No. 1 but there were no NCOs.

One of the newcomers hollered in Wallace's ear during one rather quiet moment while he was searching for a target. "The 7th and 8th Batteries have withdrawn. We have their ammunition. The other guns of the 5th and 6th are still being served but they are short of ammo. They won't be able to keep up this high rate of fire for much longer."

When Wallace counted three rounds left, he ordered, "Stand to! Rear limber up!"

Lieutenant Geary rode over. "What are you doing, No. 1?"

"Sir, I have fired off my ammo."

"Do you know where to go?"

"No, sir, I don't." He thought, *I hope they give me time for a pee before they line me up and shoot me.* "But I thought it was a good idea to leave here if I didn't have any ammo."

"You have no shells?"

Wallace thought he had better admit the truth. "I have three HE, sir."

"That's close enough, No. 1." He turned his horse away to go to the other gun. "I will lead as soon as gun 2 is ready."

Wallace could hear the lieutenant give the "stand to" and the "rear limber up" to the other gun.

They rode off in the direction they had come earlier in the day. When the lieutenant saw what was left of the 5th and 6th Batteries, he positioned his guns with them. They seemed to be facing some unseen threat in a wooded area. The two arriving guns were supplied with shrapnel shells and told that there was an enemy force in Kitcheners Wood. If the enemy attacked—and they might—the 5th and 6th Batteries would receive them over open sights. "Make every shell count," they were told. "We don't expect any reinforcements and we are short of ammunition" was the ominous warning.

"Wrong place, wrong time," Wallace said to himself. He stepped over to one side and had a long, long pee. *At least I got that out of the way.*

"Here, they come!"

Wallace's first reaction was that there were so many of them. They came out of the woods in waves of silver bayonets. The sun was behind the German attackers, allowing them to cast long shadows on the ground as they came down the slight incline toward the Canadian guns. The setting sun took on a red glow and each infantryman was silhouetted against the blood-red sky.

Lieutenant Geary said it for the gunners. "That's the most perfect target I have ever seen."

At the first order to fire, the front line of Germans ceased to exist.

The Canadian guns, firing twenty rounds a minute, soon ran out of ammunition and still the Germans were coming. In the Canadian silence that was broken only by German rifle fire, Wallace could hear the questions from the gunners, things like "Should we break out the carbines, No. 1?" and "Limber up, sir?"

From behind, out of the dust of arriving wagons, a young reedy voice sang out, "Three wagons of ammunition, sir!" A subaltern had driven all day from an ammunition depot at Vlamertinghe, dodging enemy fire, to bring ammunition to the Canadian guns—arriving just in time. With the fresh rounds of shrapnel, the rest of the German attacking force was wiped out. No third line emerged from the woods.[3]

Within the half-hour, German long-range guns had found the Canadian position. Under heavy shellfire, the batteries withdrew.

April 28, 1915
Aid station near Potijze

"Ned! Is that you?" Wallace had just had his forearm bandaged and was looking for the mess tent. It was a beautifully warm day and he was in no hurry to return to his work party. It seemed like such dull work: identifying and relaying telephone lines between the HQs and the units. "Ned!" He shouted louder.

Edward Smithers turned to face his old friend. "My God, it is you! I had thought you would have been dead by now." He extended his hand but changed his mind and gave Wallace a big hug. "I asked around for you, Wallace, but no one at the 8th knew where you were."

Wallace was touched that Ned had actually used his name for the first time. "I have survived one gun crew and two guns," he said. "Right now, I have been given light duties until my arm gets better."

"What happened to your arm?"

"Gunshot. Not bad though." Wallace assumed a pose, as if he were having his picture taken for a magazine. "Can you imagine what 'light duty' means?"

"You're going to tell me."

"We are laying new field telephone wires." Wallace slapped his friend's back, "And guess what we are doing at the same time? We are putting labels on each wire so the German spies will know which ones to cut."

"HQ idea?"

"Yep. It's a good thing we have a navy." Wallace slipped his good arm through Ned's. "Come on. Let's go along and get some chow."

When they were sipping on a mug of tea, Ned admitted to his friend that he was frightened about serving near the front. "Yesterday, Div Arty reported that we were shelling our own lines. I saw the wounded coming in to the aid station. Shit! Imagine being shelled by your own guns!" He took a gulp of his tea, scalding his mouth. "It's bad enough having to watch for German incoming but to think that . . ."

"You'll be all right, Ned. Get back to the 8th and you'll be all right."

"As long as I don't have to go into the trenches."

"You think you're ready to go back on full duty?"

"I try to tell that doctor I'm not ready but he don't listen."

Wallace didn't like the way Ned's eyes wandered when he talked about the front lines. "When are you coming off light duty?"

"They took me off today."

"Have you been reassigned?"

"Yes. We've lost enough guns that they are using gunners for other duties. I've been assigned as a runner for the 6th Battery."

"That's great!"

Ned turned a pea-green colour. "I've been assigned as a runner for the FOO of the 6th Battery. I'll be at a forward observation post." His eyes wandered around and around as he kept on talking. "I'll be closer to the Germans than anyone else in our army. The guns will get me. They'll get me good! If our guns don't, the German guns will. I was concussed real good, you know. My head won't take another bang like the last one."

"Don't worry, Ned. Mistakes don't happen very often."

"Div Arty ordered all sights and range dials to be tested. They said our guns are killing Allied troops."

"So they were tested; that's good, isn't it?"

"It doesn't matter. The guns will get me. If they get me one more time, my head won't take it."

Wallace thought he might change the subject. "Remember when we said that if we stick together, we would be fine." When Wallace saw Ned smile, just a little, he built on it. "I would share in your good luck if I stayed with you, you told me. I need that good luck now. I'll volunteer for runner duty and we will be together." Wallace squeezed Ned's arm. "And we will be lucky."

May 3, 1915
6th Battery forward observation officer's station
near Ypres-Pilkem Road

"Smithers! 7th Battery FOO station reports that the enemy is shelling their position. I want you to . . ."

"Sir, I can't go over there. Another bang and my head won't take it."

"Soldier, if I wanted you to go over there, you would go over there."

"But sir, you don't understand, I can't take another bang."

"I'll go, sir."

"You mind your own business, Smallwood. Smithers will do his duty just like any other soldier and I order him to go to Div Arty and tell them that 7th Battery has been shelled and their lines are out too. They will be repaired as soon as possible."

"Go to Div Arty . . . in the rear? Of course, sir! I'll go, quick as a flash."

The FOO finished writing out the message and handed it to the runner.

Ned started to scramble out of the dugout when the FOO put a restraining hand on his arm. "Wait!" He picked up his glasses and scanned the area in front of their position. "I had better see if there is anything to report from here before you go."

Ned slumped down in the bottom of the dugout. "Yes, sir."

"Ah. There is movement straight ahead about two hundred yards." He handed the glasses to Wallace. "What do you think?"

Wallace's lips moved as he counted. "Forty or fifty, maybe more, sir. They think they are behind the berm, but we can see them from here."

The FOO checked the grid map while Wallace continued to study the area with the glasses.

"There's more, sir." Wallace put his finger on the map and traced the position for the officer. "Five hundred yards southeast from C9d0."

The FOO wrote the reference down. "500 yards SE from C9d0 and," he consulted the map, "the first one is C9c22." He folded the message and put it in the map case. "Off you go, Smithers. We want concentrated fire as soon as possible."

With the runner gone, the FOO usually treated himself to a hot cup of tea, but this afternoon he was edgy. The Krauts had gone to a lot of trouble to saturate the area behind the places where it would be logical to have forward observation posts. It was almost as if they wanted to ensure the wires were cut so the FOO would be out of touch.

Wallace must have felt the same way because he said, "It's almost as if they don't care if they are seen while they mass their troops."

"Yes, Smallwood. They believe they have cut our telephone wires."

Wallace gave the officer a rueful smile. "And they have."

* * *

Smithers moved as quickly as he could until he was out of range of any enemy rifle. Then he stopped to take a breath, feeling safer than he had felt all day long. "They wouldn't waste a shell on one man now, would they? It's better to be alone because when I am alone, I'm a smaller target." He considered taking a cigarette but thought better of it. *If I'm caught having a cigarette, they'll think I'm skulking and that could earn me a place in the frontline trench. No, I'll keep moving, but . . .* he smiled a sly little smile . . . *I'll stretch out my little . . . vacation . . . as long as I can.*

* * *

Wallace studied the only building in sight, a small farmhouse on the edge of the road from Pilkem to Ypres. He shook his head. "Can you believe it, sir? The Krauts are using that farmhouse as the rally point for the main body of their troops."

"Let me see." It was the lieutenant's turn to be astonished. "What a target!" He saw his runner was checking the grid map. "Is it close to the two references we have sent back?"

"Not really. We would have to say C9c21 for the farmhouse."

"We'll watch the fall of the first shots and then I will send you off with the correction." Lieutenant McGrath checked his watch. "Smithers should be there by now."

* * *

"Goddam it! The Krauts are moving." McGrath studied the area with the glasses. "I can't see the ones behind the berm any more and I don't know which way they're going . . . but they are on the move." He checked his watch again. "I must assume that something happened to Smithers. You'll have to go." Lieutenant McGrath began to write out the message.

* * *

Smithers reported to Lieutenant Geary. He handed the message without comment to the young officer and then stepped back to reduce the size of the target area.

Geary saw the time on the bottom of the message. "What took you so long to get here, soldier?"

"I came as fast as conditions would allow, sir."

Geary grunted with disgust. He would have to see that this runner was replaced but he didn't have time to think about that right now. Here was a juicy target that might just get away if he didn't handle it quickly. He ran to the nearest gun.

"No. 1! We have an immediate fire order! Here are the coordinates. Massed enemy troops! Fire when ready!" Geary ran along to the next gun.

The No. 1 at the second gun read his coordinates and selected his target visually. *Piece of cake!* He called for shrapnel, 1000 yards, no ranging shot, three rounds in quick succession. He could see that the crew of the other gun was getting ready, but No. 1 was smug in the knowledge that his gun would be ready first. He ordered his gun crew to move more quickly; he wanted his rounds to reach the target ahead of the others.

* * *

Lieutenant McGrath placed the message in Smallwood's message bag. He patted him on the shoulder. "Move quickly. I can't understand why we don't have rounds passing over our heads right now."

"I'll get there in time, Lieutenant."

* * *

No. 3 gunner removed the fuse cover and the breech was closed. The crew stepped back and, when the lanyard was pulled, the first of the shrapnel was on its way to the enemy target 1000 yards away.

* * *

Wallace crawled out of the dugout and slung his rifle over his shoulder. He looked in the direction of the guns; there was no activity, but then he didn't expect to see any since the guns were very well concealed to avoid being detected by enemy aeroplanes. He started to run, bent over at the waist, so as not to attract the attention of enemy riflemen. Several paces along the communications trench, he heard the first of the shells pass almost over his head. Instinctively he ducked and then smiled at his reflex action. He heard it explode near the Ypres road. He smiled. When he arrived at the guns, they would adjust their targets to include the farmhouse.

* * *

No. 3 gunner opened the breech and the spent shell casing was ejected to the rear. No. 2 swabbed the empty breech, checking it for debris and then the second shell was presented, No. 3 removing the fuse cover before the breech was closed. In a second, another shell was on its way to create new holes in Kaiser Bill's army. It was at that moment that the gunner at the limber realized that he had made a mistake with the second and third shells. By this time, the third round was in the breech and No. 3 was removing the fuse cover. The breech was closed and the crew stepped back. Just as the lanyard was pulled, the gunner at the limber shouted, "Short fuse! Short fuse!"

* * *

The second shell passed over Wallace just as he left the communications trench and was beginning his run across the open ground leading to the trees where the guns were hidden. The incorrect setting on the fuse caused the shell to explode almost overhead. The shrapnel caught Smallwood on the back of his head and across his shoulders. He fell, badly wounded. He didn't hear the third shell as it came his way nor did he have time to feel the pain caused by the second shell. He was dazed by the impact and the concussion but he rolled over on his back and stared at the sky. At that moment, the third shell exploded.

Wallace Smallwood raised his arms over his face, perhaps in response to some warning of the flood of metal that was going to cut and tear into his totally exposed body, perhaps as a futile remedy for the pain that was coming from the dreadful wounds to the back of his head and shoulders. There was no opportunity for thought or reason as the shrapnel struck him. All the cares of that day and of that war were wiped away in an instant.[4]

Endnotes

1. I copied the entries from the microfiche of the War Diary held at the Archives. There was an irregular splotch on one of the pages but, of course, I couldn't tell what colour it once was. The writing style changed on the next page.

2. The storyline of the gas attack is based on the incident report and various accounts held in the Canadian Forces HQ Library.

3. The actual record of the fight: "The ammunition of the 7th and 8th was to be handed to the 5th and 6th Batteries who were ordered to remain. The section of the 6th which had gone forward having run out of ammunition was also ordered to retire. The remaining section of the 6th switched its position to cover the woods and one section of the 5th Battery. At 7:30 reinforcements arrived and at 5:05 pm 3 wagons of ammunition."

4. War Diary entry. "1/5/15 FOO 6th Battery reports premature bursts from a battery on our left wounding a man standing near him near observation post." Records showed that Wallace was the only man wounded near that post that day.

Chapter Fifteen
Cousin Joe
More Than One Way . . .

May 1916
Carleton House Hotel

"Oh, if only you guys were here."

Joe Smallwood was sitting alone at a table in the dining room of the Carleton Hotel thinking that, despite the great feeling of independence he had gained during his years in Halifax, he would still like to be able to bare all his troubles to his cousins, Wallace and Jack. *Well, maybe not Wallace any more. I probably won't ever be able to confide in Wallace because . . . because Wallace has spent months in an English hospital recovering from his wounds and . . . and we haven't kept in touch very much. I know I've changed and so has Wallace. Besides, Wallace always needed looking after while Jack had a sensible way of doing things.* Joe was taking a sip of his tea as he recalled one of the times he had followed Jack's sensible advice and some of the tea went down the wrong way as he started to laugh. The people at the next table looked at him, sideways, wondering if he was all right, but with his napkin to his mouth, he waved his free hand trying to assure them that he wasn't choking to death—just choking.

When the coughing fit had subsided and the other patrons had resumed paying attention to matters of greater interest, Joe went back to thoughts of Jack. Yes, Cousin Jack had a ready answer for everything; *like the time Aunt Mary Anne was being bothered by a skunk.*

Jack had had the bright idea that if the skunk were shot, right in the head, it wouldn't have time to squirt, which was what their aunt was concerned about in the first place—the skunk stink being that close to the house. Of course, the skunk squirted the side of the house, a dog and two surprised boys. There was no sympathy at The Sugary, only remorse.[1]

Joe sighed into his teacup. *Jack would know how to handle my current problem—an older woman.* He cast a glance at the door to see if his guest had arrived but there was no sign of her. He caught his reflection in the mirror near the door and adjusted his wing collar and cravat. He took a moment to study the rest of his appearance: dark blue suit, blue cravat, wing collar, brown wavy hair, dark brown eyes set in a tanned complexion acquired on his motor launch. *That's where my troubles started: on my boat. Roy Curry—that self-righteous novice clergyman who was escorting Mrs. Emma Schwartz and her daughter Gladys—was a guest on my launch one Sunday afternoon.*

The older Schwartz woman had been all steel and polite courtesy. She had commented on the unusual family name. "Small-wood isn't a Halifax name," she had said.

Joe remembered it as if it had been moments before. He had replied, "No, Mrs. Schwartz, it's more common . . .

. . . more common in New Brunswick."

Joe was getting his guests settled, making certain that the ladies had pillows to cushion themselves against the mahogany seats.

"Common." Emma Schwartz cast a meaningful glance at her daughter who was accepting a pillow from the boat owner. "What do you do . . . professionally . . . Mister Small-wood?" The mother was very aware of her daughter's interest in the young man so she patted the seat next to herself and motioned the young lady to move over. "You would be more comfortable over here in the shade, Gladys," she said.

"Oh, no need to bunch up. I will raise the awning, Mrs. Schwartz." Joe touched the girl's gloved hand as he passed the pillow. "Your daughter makes a pretty picture, sitting all alone in the stern, doesn't she?"

Gladys blushed. *He is so handsome,* she thought, as she noticed how his white yachting trousers fit his slim body perfectly. The blue jacket sported an aquatic crest while his white shirt was open at the throat with a red and white kerchief jauntily peeking out. He was not wearing the sailing hat but it had been thrown casually over the steering wheel where she could see it had the identical crest.

"You just stay right there, Miss Schwartz, and I will have us in the shade in a jiffy." Joe unsnapped the canvas cover and lifted the frame. "In answer to your question, Mrs. Schwartz, I have a smoke shop on Water Street."

Roy Curry sat next to the matron, offering her a mint from a small package, his voice a soft purr as he informed the daunting Mrs. Schwartz, "Our Mister Smallwood is from out of town and sells smokes to the Water Street locals."

"Penny candies and sundries, Mister Curry." Joe gave the other man a broad smile, "It's much like a neighbourhood store."

"And Water Street is the neighbourhood?" Curry quickly changed the subject as he saw the hostility behind the Smallwood smile. "You have a nice boat; how very kind of you to invite us."

"Always like to have pleasant company," Joe said, bowing in the direction of both ladies. "As for the boat, I would have invited you sooner but the King's Harbour Master has had the use of her for the better part of a year. Used her on harbour patrols and the like. Insisted on paying me a dollar although I had offered it as a contribution to the war effort."

"To have a boat like this, you must do well in penny candies." Roy spread his hands in an all-encompassing gesture. "I would never be able to afford something as grand as this on a minister's stipend."

Joe had finished raising the awning. The space next to the auburn-haired beauty now being taken by the man in black, Joe perched on the captain's stool near the wheel. From there he was able to gaze at Gladys Schwartz without raising the mother's ire.

Gladys had rich auburn hair, drawn back and tied in a neat bun at the nape of her neck. A saucy blue and white sailor's hat perched on the side of her head was apparently chosen to complement the occasion of an afternoon on the water, but actually it was her attempt to remind him of an earlier meeting before she had grown up. She was wearing a light blue dress, closed at the wrists and throat, which was drawn in tightly at the waist by a white belt. The shell of a jacket or tunic hung loosely from her shoulders, open at the front, accenting her generous form.

Joe had meant to spend the afternoon harassing the clergyman but the tables were now turned. Curry had seen the mutual attraction between Joe and Gladys and it was now Curry who was doing the needlework and Joe's skin wasn't very thick. At times during the afternoon, Joe thought he might have to throttle Curry.

"Money isn't everything, Roy," the sympathetic mother said. She turned her whole body so she could confront the out-of-towner. "Small-wood? I have never heard of a Small-wood." She straightened her body and leaned back in the seat, fluffing the cushion as she asked, "Are there any in Nova Scotia?"

Joe recognized that his opponent (because that was what Emma Schwartz became from that moment on) was going to play a mean game and provide close support to whatever tactics her partner, the Reverend-to-be Roy Curry, implemented. Any reference to out-of-town, penny candies, or social background would score points with the mother who was the daughter of Warren Gray, a man of solid reputation in the province, and she had married into the Schwartz family . . . all pretty upper crust and well removed from penny candies.

"I am the first Smallwood in the city," was Joe's half-jocular reply.

As far as Emma Louisa Schwartz was concerned, that should be the end of it. She prepared for the final thrust. She cleared her throat.

"Are you ready, Mister Smallwood, to . . ."

" . . . Mister Smallwood, to order now?"

Joe shook himself out of his remembrances. He looked up to find Mister Pass standing next to his table. "Thank you Mister Pass, but I am waiting for . . ."

With the appearance in the dining room doorway of a tall, elegant Gladys Schwartz, impeccably dressed for an afternoon in the city and obviously intent on meeting someone in the dining room, Joe stammered his thanks to Mister Pass and joined Gladys at the entrance archway. Taking one of her gloved hands in his, he turned to lead her to his table.

Firmly and politely, Miss Schwartz withdrew her hand and indicated that she would follow him to the table.

The maitre d' quickly appeared on the scene, apologizing to the lady that he hadn't been aware Mister Smallwood would be joining her. He bowed to Joe and asked if he could be permitted to correct the situation and lead them to a more suitable table.

When they were seated near the magnificent stone mantel fireplace, Gladys was the first to speak.

"We sit here, next to the mantel, because it is part of the lore of the city that a Gray helped bring this mantel home from Louisbourg in the 1750s."[2]

Joe wasn't much interested in anything or anybody but the beautiful woman seated in front of him. "Tell me, Gladys. Did Mrs. Schwartz say that you could attend the theatre with me?"

Gladys smiled as she said, "You, Mister Smallwood, aren't much interested in history."

"I studied it in school and paid attention when I had to." He instantly regretted that he had mentioned school so he tried to change the subject. "The Sidney Toler Players will be at the . . ."

"Where did you go to school?"

"In Newcastle, New Brunswick." To forestall any discussion of his schooling or lack of schooling he said, "My parents still live there. My Dad is the locomotive foreman and now in charge of the roundhouse since a lot of the boys volunteered to go to war."

Nodding her head, Gladys said; "Mother wanted to know why such a fine-looking young man hadn't volunteered. Roy Curry had volunteered, Mother said, but his church asked that he be made exempt until he had finished his training." She began taking off her gloves as the waiter brought the menus. "Mother thought you could have been spared from the important business of selling cookies and expressed surprise that you weren't already in uniform." She accepted her menu and opened it. "Mother also said that I cannot go with you to the theatre unless I have a chaperone."

"Did your Mother suggest who should accompany you?"

"Roy Curry."

"Um, yes."

They were still holding the menus in their hands and the waiter made a great show of moving away from the table so they would have more time to choose their meals.

Joe put his menu down and reached across to touch her hand. Gladys placed both of her hands in her lap. "I am well known in this city and do not touch a man in public unless I am in need of assistance or guidance."

"I have a lot to learn, I guess."

"No, Joe, you are going to do just fine. It's Mother who will have to learn." She picked up the menu and opened it. "Let us order and then, afterwards, over something sweet, we shall have to plan how we can overcome Mother's opposition to you."

The meal flew by and soon they were eating chocolate mousse, Gladys coming as close to smacking her lips as her upbringing would allow.

"Understand this, dear Joe. Roy Curry is Mother's choice for my life partner. Any other interest will be strenuously opposed."

"You mean you want to continue seeing me."

"I think we go well together. I enjoy your company . . . ."

Joe grinned. ". . . And you enjoy aggravating your mother." By the look on Gladys' face, Joe thought that perhaps he had gone too far with his sense of humour.

It was Gladys' turn to grin. "And I enjoy aggravating my mother." She reached across and squeezed Joe's hand, briefly.

His heart sang and it showed.

She studied his face, intently. "You think you love me, don't you."

"Yes, I love you, Gladys."

"Then let's go over the problems." Gladys counted on her fingers. "Your family is not established here like the Curry family is. Could your parents visit the city? Stay at the Lord Nelson? Entertain a select list of my parents' friends?"

Joe thought of his mother's depressions and dependence on the private nurse, Lottie Borland. "No, that isn't possible."

She selected the second finger. "You must have a reason for not joining up. I don't want to see you in the army but there has to be a reason."

"I tried to enlist but they wouldn't take me. Me and my cousin . . ."

"My cousin and I . . ."

Joe started again. "My cousin Wallace enlisted and went to France. He was badly wounded at Ypres. He's been promoted several times. I think he's a sergeant now, still in England getting over his wounds. You can tell your mother that a Smallwood is fighting . . ." His voice trailed off as he realized that he was not making much sense. *What would Mrs. Schwartz care about a cousin who is in the army?* Lamely, he finished, "Anyhow, I tried to go but they wouldn't take me because I have a bad stomach."

Gladys held the third finger up and thoughtfully looked at it, during which period Joe didn't move or speak. She closed her hand and began to pull on her gloves. Wistfully, she said, "Mother will never accept you. As much as I think you are an interesting man, Joseph Smallwood, I'm afraid all we will be able to share in this lifetime is appreciating the extent of the aggravation our time together will give my Mother . . . and the enjoyment of each other's company." She indicated that Joe should pull her chair back, waiting for him to do so before she spoke again. "I will have the additional benefit of seeing the dull Roy Curry discouraged sufficiently that perhaps he will discontinue his pursuit of my hand in marriage." She grimaced. "I do so hate the idea of being a pastor's wife."

When they were outside, Gladys took his arm. "You may walk me home, Joe. While we walk along, we shall discuss your schooling and the sources of your money that allowed you to have a partnership with a man like H.H. Marshall at such an early stage of your life. By the way, just how old are you?"

* * *

The problem of the chaperone was overcome when Joe invited both daughters to the theatre. Edith was delighted at the opportunity to get out of the house and readily accepted—subject to Mother's approval, of course. Emma Schwartz approved.

It was at the third outing that Edith met Cecil Havill, a local businessman, who just happened to be seated in the usually empty box seat next to Edith. Edith was thrilled, rapidly falling in love with the shy young man who had believed that a member of the Schwartz family wouldn't have taken him seriously. He had attended the theatre that night under protest . . . and as a consequence of Joe paying for his ticket and drinks at the intermission.

In the following weeks, Edith blossomed. Where Before Cecil she had been a quiet girl, a gifted pianist with a superb voice who only performed occasionally for Ira Hubeley, she rapidly graduated to singing at the church and the church gatherings, to a paid substitute singer in choirs, to a professional singer in wide demand across the city. And all it took to maintain her confidence was a glance into the wings or into the audience and find the upturned faces of Gladys, Joe and her dear, dear Cecil.

Edith's success and popularity surprised her mother who, however, recognized the whole thing as a boon. Emma Louisa Schwartz had believed that the quiet, reserved Edith would never find a man and, as far as Emma was concerned, Cecil Havill, a product of a fine Huguenot family, was a man of prospects (being a part owner of a printing supply company aptly named The Printing Supply Company). Being part owner of a company was solid and respectable. People would always read and printers would forever need supplies. "Not like selling penny candies, Gladys," Emma Louisa often told her second daughter. "Do you want to be nursemaid to an invalid? A bad stomach! Not even the army would take him!"

As the months went by, Gladys became a professional singer every bit as much in demand as her sister, performing in the hotels, in theatres, and at the best weddings. Joe Smallwood revelled in the girls' successes but it had the opposite effect on Cecil who, in his shyness, backed away from it all. Since Cecil wasn't there, Edith didn't accept many engagements and Gladys and Joe were alone more often. By now, Mother Schwartz had been forced to the conclusion that the penny candy salesman was going to be the only man in her second daughter's life . . . and perhaps there wasn't going to be a man in Edith's life after all. She handled the situation; she pronounced Emma's Law: "Edith is the eldest daughter and she shall be married first" (which made Cecil even more skittish) "and there will be no discussion on this matter." Then Emma Louisa Schwartz declared war on the penny candy salesman. "You, Gladys Evelyn Schwartz, may inform the penny candy salesman that I will not be subjected to any more of his smarm."

* * *

Meanwhile, the other war had become very real for the people of Halifax.

The tread of the thousands of feet as the soldier boys left the barracks, the trucks, and the trains, and marched to embarkation, brought citizens out of their homes. They joined the parade to Pier 24 where the soldiers lined up and were counted—lined up and counted again—while they waited their turn to board the transports that would take them to war. The Red Cross had erected a stage and Gladys sang popular songs to the throng. Often the men and the well-wishers would join her, applauding themselves and the singer when they were finished. She was the declared sweetheart of the soldiers as they prepared to leave their homeland. The boys all promised to come back to her, calling that message out across the widening gap as the ship separated from the pier. With the ship fading away down harbour, the crowd fell silent before dispersing, perhaps giving a prayer for their boys who would soon be a target for German naval units lurking off Sambro Light. Yes, the citizens of Halifax had gotten used to the military regulations that ran the city . . . and the blackouts so the Germans couldn't bombard the city from the ocean . . . and the shortages of food . . . and the line-ups for virtually everything . . . . But it was at the moment of departure . . .when the singing had stopped and the Red Cross workers were turning out the lights . . . that the most familiar poster in the city became very real. "Don't talk! Loose lips sink ships!" the sinister shadow of a spy seemed to be saying. And it was true! Canadian boys were being killed on their doorstep and the citizens of Halifax believed there might be a German spy behind every door.

The threat of the German spies was probably on Gladys' mind the day of her dental appointment.

* * *

"Open your mouth, Gladys." Emma Schwartz leaned forward to peer into the girl's mouth. "Let me smell your breath." Emma carefully inhaled and considered the result before proceeding. "We were very fortunate to find another dentist now that Doctor MacKenzie has gone into the army. We don't want bad breath or an unkempt mouth to discourage this new dentist from taking appointments from the rest of the family." Emma leaned back. "That's fine, dear." She waved a hand at her daughter in the general direction of the front door. "He will probably just do a check-up this first visit because he said he wasn't taking appointments just yet; he is a refugee from Holland and his office isn't ready." Emma clutched at her daughter's sleeve as she passed by in the hall so that she could speak to her, face to face. "I insisted that he take you today, so be on time." She released the sleeve, permitting her daughter to continue toward the front door. "Don't come home without a date and time for a second appointment, Gladys," she admonished.

"I won't, Mother." Gladys closed the door and descended the steps, two at a time, to the street.

There was some vigorous tapping on the front window but Gladys pretended not to hear, although she did proceed down the walk in a much more sedate manner. Once out of sight of the house, she held her skirt up a few inches so she could take longer strides. She smiled to herself as she realized that Joe Smallwood was changing the way she approached life. *That man is a devil, always into some sort of mischief!* Lately she had been helping him in his store on weekends right after her voice lessons at the Halifax Conservatory. She was amazed how people would walk blocks past competitors' stores just to pass the time of day with Joe at his new store at the corner of Morris and Barrington. He was amazing. He was successful. He was in love with her!

At the risk of getting dusty shoes, she cut across the Upper Common and began the long climb up the western slope of the Citadel. At the top, she wasn't surprised to see several sentries checking to make sure no one was taking pictures or making sketches of the location of the ships in the harbour. From her vantage point as she went down the hill near the Town Clock, she could see all the new construction that had been going on because of the war. Doctor Lowen was in one of the new buildings. Checking the numbers, she had no difficulty locating the building and then the proper floor. As she approached the door to Doctor Lowen's office, she noticed the gilt letters were bright and new. She knocked, but when no one answered, she pushed the door open and went in. There was no receptionist or assistant in the first room which looked like it would eventually be the reception room. In a moment, a large, gruff individual came from the other office and introduced himself as Doctor Lowen. In a heavily accented voice, he explained that most of his equipment was still in boxes and asked that she excuse the disarray. He led her into another, smaller room where Gladys could see that the chair was brand new—feeling very comfortable and reassuring as she sat down. The doctor was thorough and efficient, quickly checking her teeth and making some notes on a scribbler he said he would transfer to a file folder when the rest of his supplies arrived.

Fifteen minutes later, Gladys was at the bottom floor of the building, relieved that the doctor had done his check-up without causing any sort of discomfort. *"There is nottink that can't be vait until later in der month,"* she recalled him saying. She opened the door but let it close by itself as she turned around and bounded back up the stairs. *Mother told me not to come home without a date and time for my next appointment! I can't face her without one.* When she pushed the door open and stepped into the reception area, she could hear two men talking. *They're speaking German,* she thought. *It's hoch deutsch just like Father speaks!* She leaned forward, peeking around the corner. She saw Doctor Lowen looking through a telescope— perhaps at the ships in the Narrows and Dartmouth Cove. A second man was making notes in the scribbler.

In a flash, she turned around and ran out of the office, not stopping until she was under the stairwell one floor down. She heard the men coming down the hall above her. They stopped at the top of the stairwell—probably listening for some movement on the stairs.

Gladys hugged the wall and held her breath. There was the sound of a footstep on the tile; *one of them is coming down! A few steps more and he will see me!* She shivered with fright.

The gruff voice of the doctor reverberated off the walls of the stairwell. "You ver mistaken. Kome back. We haf verk to finish."

Gladys remained under the steps. She heard the office door close. She waited. She heard them lock the door. She waited some more. Then, very quietly, she went down the stairs and slipped out the door.

Once at home, Gladys might not have mentioned the experience to her Mother since nearly *everyone* had some sort of spy story to tell . . . but she had to give a reason for not obtaining a date and time for the next appointment.

Freddie informed Major Cooke, a friend of his at the Provost Marshal's Office, who arranged for the Dutch dentist to be monitored for a period of time. Doctor Lowen and his associates were arrested as German spies.

With the spies in custody and Emma searching for another dentist, the excitement seemed to be over. It was a bit of a surprise when Major Cooke dropped by to brief Mister and Mrs. Schwartz that their daughter might be in some danger.

"What do you mean, Gladys might be in some danger?" Emma could see that her Freddie was upset; she could tell by the way his blue eyes wandered around the living room as if they were searching for something to focus on. She put her hand on her husband's knee and patted it, reassuringly. Emma repeated the question, "What do you mean?"

Major Cooke cleared his throat, obviously uncomfortable with what he was going to say. "We can't be sure that we got all the spies. If there are more, they might want to retaliate against the source."

"By 'the source,' you mean our daughter."

"Yes, and the best way to protect the . . . your daughter is to send her to someplace like Montreal for six months at government expense."

Fredrick Schwartz sat upright and fixed his eyes upon the shadowy figure. "Montreal!" he exclaimed.

By the tone of Mister Schwartz's voice, Major Cooke surmised that going to Montreal was not the least bit acceptable to the father. He hurried on. "Or I could assign a plain-clothes guard who would guarantee her safety and report on her every contact."

There was silence in the room as the parents assimilated the information.

Emma was the first to speak. "The second choice interests me."

"The guard?"

"Yes. He would go everywhere with my daughter?"

Major Cooke assured her that the escort would be a professional and nothing would get by him.

"We will take the six months of guarding."

Rising to leave, Major Cooke shook hands with the parents. "I will have a man on the job before morning."

Emma, thinking of her daughter's regular routine, said, "No, it won't be necessary. The guard can find her in a little shop on Barrington Street at noon." Emma Schwartz smiled a contented smile as she went to get a piece of paper to write down the address of Mister Small-wood's new store.[3]

* * *

Gladys and Joe put up with the presence of the guard, the restriction that Edith would have to get married first, and the continuous barrage of Emma Missives directed at Joe's supposed "lack of substance" until, on the last day before the departure of the guard, Joe thought that he would seize the high ground and make a frontal assault. He asked permission of Fredrick Schwartz to propose to Gladys.

Permission was granted.

As everyone anticipated, Gladys accepted, professing undying love for her Joe. When the excitement of the moment had passed, she also expressed great admiration for his pluck because she knew Emma Louisa would not likely accept defeat.

Behind closed Schwartz doors, Mother Schwartz resumed the offensive; since there was an engagement ring (impressive, she had to admit), there would have to be an engagement announcement.

Gladys and her father waited for the shoe to fall.

"I do not give permission for you to set a date."

"Why can't we set a date?" a distraught Gladys asked.

It was like a death sentence, pronounced in measured, tomblike tones, a syllable for each beat of time, "I am not con-vin-ced that Mis-ter Small-wood is a man of sub-stance." Emma then folded her arms and looked out the window.

Endnotes

1. In real life, I didn't know which cousin (Wallace or Jack) would have been involved with Joe in his shenanigans. Wallace was the eldest being Hannah and Daniel's first born. However, the story was going to reflect Joe's actual life in great detail and it was also going to follow Wallace into the

army and I still needed a character to help tell the story of the Depression. So I borrowed Jack from his real life where he had a wife (Effie May McKinley) and ten real kids. From this point on, Jack is a fictional character.

2. As a boy, I thrived on the stories about Halifax. One of them told how the fireplace was removed from Louisbourg during its second capture in 1758 before the fortress was levelled to the ground. Readers will remember in book 2 of the Abuse of Power series, *The Colonials and The Acadians*, I allowed Joshua Maugher and his henchman Amos Skinner, to perform the "liberation" of the fireplace for their own ends. Now, in book no. 7, I give credit for the liberation of the fireplace to the Grays just to demonstrate that, with constant retelling, folk stories change over time.

3. The spy in the dentist's office story is repeated here much in the manner it was told to me by Emma Louisa and verified in later years by Gladys when I had decided to start writing things down.

Chapter Sixteen
Cousin David James
Happy to Have Been of Service

July 1916
Halifax Police Station

"I was hoping it was the right thing to do, Mister Smallwood. The prisoner claims he doesn't know you but his name is Smallwood, the same as you, so I thought I'd better let you know. It's a small town . . ." Sergeant Paul McMurray pulled out a chair so Joe could sit. The sergeant then walked around the desk and sat down himself. "Of course, I don't mean that any member of your clan would necessarily tell a lie, but I thought . . ." McMurray scratched the back of his head as he tried to work his way past any sort of insult to Joe's family but he was having a rough time of it. He shrugged his shoulders. "And then again, Mister Smallwood, he was caught breakin' and enterin' and he might've thought it necessary to tell somethin' less than the truth to the police if you know what I mean . . . under the circumstances, you might say."

"That's fine, Sergeant. I do appreciate being taken into the confidence of the police force. I'm glad you thought to telephone me."

"You do grand things for the police charity; even go to more trouble for us than some of the regular . . ." The sergeant was really flustered, now. "What I mean is . . . you help even though you're . . . non-Catholic . . .." He realized he was getting in deeper and so he stopped.

Joe thought he would try to help the sergeant out of his predicament. "The police charity generates a lot of money for the orphans. I'm proud to help."

Sergeant McMurray took the opportunity to get right down to business, "The perpetrator is a soldier on his way overseas." McMurray scratched his chin. "And I suppose that

217

says a lot of good about the man." He picked up an official-looking piece of paper. "And his name is David James Smallwood." The sergeant cast a quick glance at Joe. "He wouldn't be a brother, now, would he?"

Joe nodded his head as he said, "No, but he's a very dear cousin of mine."

"Captain Hanrahan says he will not record the incident if you vouch for the man."

"Certainly."

"And go good for the damages he caused."

Joe wasn't so quick this time. "And that would be how much?"

"That's what the boys like about you, Mister Smallwood. You're straight up and down when it comes to matters of money. The captain said fifteen dollars."

"That's a lot of money."

"Maybe twelve, if the other Mister Smallwood returns the books he stole, er, had in his possession when he was apprehended." Sergeant McMurray could see the questioning look on Joe's face so he hurried on. "He broke into Anita Brown's book store . . . had in his possession several textbooks on accounting and bookkeeping."

Joe had a quick thought. "You say he's shipping out?"

"His papers put him with the 89th Overseas Battalion."

"Probably wanted something to study on the trip across the Atlantic—you know, keep himself busy so he wouldn't have to dwell on what these brave lads have to face once the ship clears the mouth of the harbour."

McMurray bobbed his head in agreement. "If you vouch for him while he's in the city, we will release him. There'd be no paperwork; just the money for Miss Anita to repair her door window."

"I'd be pleased to pay the fifteen dollars and I will vouch for him."

"That's good, Mister Smallwood. I'll have him brought out right some quick." Sergeant McMurray waved to a uniformed policeman through the iron grille of a heavy oak door.

In less than two minutes, the Smallwoods were meeting for the first time, although Joe went to great lengths to create the impression that they were well known to each other.

"Cousin David! What's the news from home? The last time I spoke with your father, he said to me, he said . . . 'Joe, I want you to visit us any time you can. A Smallwood from New Brunswick is always welcome at our house.'" Joe could see that this David Smallwood was no fool; he picked up on the deception very quickly. The two spoke of fictitious meetings and letters until they were outside. Then Joe took the other man by the arm and turned him until they were facing each other.

"Let's hear your story pretty quick! I work hard at making the Smallwood name mean something around here and I don't need . . ."

"You've heard of Smallwood's Boots? From Newfoundland? I'm one of those Smallwoods."

"And you're a thief, if the charges are accurate." Joe studied the other man's face, carefully, trying to take the measure of the man. *Nice-looking fellow, but I bet his face hasn't felt a razor in days. Ugh! Look at his uniform. He must have slept in . . .*

"Do we have to talk on the street? Couldn't we discuss this somewhere else?" Then the stranger flashed a Smallwood smile. "A little further from the police station, if you don't mind."

Joe's cabby was still waiting for him so Joe waved him over and they both climbed into the car.

"Carleton House, if you please, Billy."

"Yes sir, Mister Smallwood."

"What happened was . . . "

Joe shook his head and pointed at the back of the driver's head. "Tell me about your family."

"When I was a lad, my father, David, owned a lumber mill in Gambo, Newfoundland. It was a good business and he made a lot of money when he sold it. He had six sons and a daughter but I was the only one he couldn't tolerate. The old man told me to get out and learn about life and stop trying to tell him how to run his business. So I got out twenty-nine years ago and went to Calgary, but there wasn't much work in the trade my father had picked out for me."

"Which was?"

"Lumber inspector."

"So how did you earn your living?"

"I did some clerking." David grinned. "But mostly I would diddle the wives of rich men . . . .."

Abruptly, and with a sharp glance at the back of the driver's head, Joe changed the subject. "I volunteered, you know, but . . ."

The cab's brakes squealed as they drew up in front of the hotel. "Carleton House, Mister Smallwood."

"I'll need you in about an hour to take me home, Billy."

"Of course, sir."

The men got out of the car, Joe leading his cousin to the door of the hotel, where the doorman's face froze into an imitation of a smile.

Joe believed that he was going to have some difficulties because of David's unkempt appearance but the manager hurried over to greet them.

"You are early for dinner, Mister Smallwood."

"We would appreciate a quiet table and some food, Mister Pass." Joe flashed his smile. "Whatever you can arrange for us would be appreciated."

"Of course, I will see what I can do."

"Thank you, Mister Pass."

Once alone at a table off to one side of the dining room, Joe pushed for some sort of explanation as to why a Smallwood had broken the law, but David preferred to tell his story his way.

"At the time of my difference of opinion with my father, we owned a lumber mill at Gambo, Newfoundland. Rather than listen to my ideas, Father exiled me to the mainland. I wasn't expected to come back until I had learned something about life."

The two Smallwoods were silent until the waiter had finished with the table.

David continued, "Now he's a big shot in St John's runnin' Smallwood's Boots Company with my brothers. I'm not ever going back. That man can rot in hell before . . ."

"Much the same thing happened to me. I was sent out west while I was still a boy. My father told me I had to learn what was important in life before coming home."

"Are you going back?"

"I did go back . . ."

"More fool you."

Joe Smallwood was angered by the other man's attitude. Somewhat testily, Joe snapped, "You come to my town dragging the Smallwood name into the police stationhouse and then have the gall to be lippy?"

David pushed away from the table, the chair scraping across the pine boards of the floor as he rose. "I can do as I please, Mister Fancy Pants Smallwood."

Joe looked into the steel-grey eyes. He thought, *the man's quite short, only five foot nothing at all.* He remembered that William Frederick, his grandfather, had often said that the Newfoundland brother had been the shortest of the three brothers. *He has a wide, wide set of shoulders on him, though.* Joe made a placating motion with his hands. "You do owe me, David; you owe me at least fifteen dollars' worth of story." David wore a quizzical look so Joe went on, "You did twelve dollars' worth of damage when you broke into the bookshop."

"The door was unlocked." When Joe didn't seem to believe him, David protested, "I tell you it wasn't locked." He sat down again. "There was a light on and I thought someone might be there. I tried the lock and the door opened. Since I was in, I turned on some lights and found the books I was looking for. I was going to leave a note, promising to pay, when the police came onto me." He rubbed his wrists. "They were pretty rough until they found my name. Then they put me in a cell, and you know the rest."

"I paid for your books, too." Joe handed him the three books.

David took the books without a second's delay. "I'll pay you back."

"What do you need the books for?"

David paused, but just for the moment. He took a deep breath and began by declaring that he was forty-four years old. "I'm not a kid looking for adventure."

"Excuse me, but that prompts me to ask, why did you volunteer?"

Again, David James appeared to hesitate, probably considering his options, before continuing.

"In my most recent amorous adventure, there wasn't a rich Mister Tyhurst who would pay to protect his wife's unsullied honour. No, there was only Mrs. Tyhurst . . . and I turned out to be just another notch in her corset. I thought if I told her that I had joined the army, she would postpone her wedding plans." David shuddered as he recalled. "I couldn't imagine a worse fate than being married to that woman." He shrugged. "So, I had to join up and, before I could get shipped out, she took me before the army padre, demanding that I honour my promises to her . . . to marry her." Now smiling at the recollection, he said, "Soon's I got her to agree there wasn't time for a wedding, I signed over five dollars a month on pay assignment." He shrugged again. "With the Holy Joe sitting right there, I couldn't do much else."[1]

"Ah ha! I now see why you want the accounting and bookkeeping texts. You want to learn how to undo the pay assignment."

With a show of disgust, David said, "Naw!" He seemed to ignore his surroundings as he sucked on a morsel of food caught between his teeth, occasionally probing with his fingernail to dislodge more of it. When he realized that Joe was watching and waiting for an explanation, he wiped his finger on the napkin. He leaned forward as if he were revealing a national secret. "Ya see, Joe, I realized I needed something . . . some sort of skill the army could use. My lumber inspector qualifications would put me behind a rifle in the trenches." He leaned back and raised both hands in defence of the thought. "No sir! Not for me! I had to do something. Well, it cost me a bottle of rum, but an admin clerk wrote on my enlistment form that I was also an accountant." He grinned. "I'm not goin' into the trenches if I can help it. I figure they won't have enough accountants and, when they find out how good an accountant I am, they'll put me in headquarters miles away from the fighting."

"But you're not . . ."

" . . . not an accountant. That's right. But I'll be able to pass for one before I get to England by studyin' those books."[2]

"Was it necessary to steal them?"

"I told you! I didn't steal them!"

"Then why didn't you just walk into the bookstore and buy them?"

"I meant to, but I spent all my money on a Dartmouth doxy; meant to be only one night with her but . . ." David shrugged his shoulders. "I'm supposed to be in barracks ready to board the *Olympic* when that ship comes in." Again the shrug. "Not much time left and I had to have those books. It's a matter of life and death. I hafta be behind a desk in this war . . . not behind a rifle."

"I would agree with you there. I was going into the artillery."

"What happened?"

Joe signalled to the waiter. "Put this meal on my account, please." He allowed the waiter to pull his chair back and then rose. "That's another story. What shall I do with you now, cousin?"

David didn't wait for assistance from a member of the hotel staff but pushed his own chair back. "If you deliver me to the first military policeman we see, I will be taken care of."

As they proceeded to the front of the hotel, arriving customers made no secret of their disapproval of a soldier who did not have a cap and appeared unshaven with at least a day's growth showing where the face should have been clean. It didn't help that David had undone the top buttons of his tunic so he could stuff the books down the front.

Joe noticed the attention his companion was receiving. "This is a military town. I'm afraid you're getting the once-over and not passing inspection. Shouldn't we go to my digs and get you cleaned up?"

"We don't have to bother. The military police won't be concerned with my appearance when they find out that I'm AWOL." With a modest looking smile, David explained, "I should have reported to the barracks several days ago. They will be delighted when you hand me over."

"I won't drop you into a pack of trouble."

"Oh, I have to get back tonight. My outfit will be going any time now and if I am not there to go with them, I could be charged with desertion. No, no, I have to get back."

Joe waved for his cab. "Well, I still think . . ."

"There's a couple of military police." David Smallwood squeezed Joe's elbow and, with a hop and skip, trotted down the street to accost the two policemen.

After a moment of conversation, one of the policemen took his club from his belt and, with his other hand, seized David's arm. The second policeman didn't immediately draw his club but he was quick to position himself on the opposite side of the renegade. When David attempted to give Joe a small wave, the second policeman grabbed that arm and twisted it behind David's back. David rose up on his toes to relieve some of the pressure on his wrist but the MP lifted until the hand was as high as the shoulder blades.

"Let's go along quietly, chum," the MP growled.

"I am being quiet!"

Joe didn't see the short, sharp blow to the back of David's head. He watched as David was half-dragged up the hill toward Windsor Barracks. When the three figures turned the corner, Joe whispered, "Goodbye, cousin." He walked to his waiting cab. He looked once more at the corner. "And goodbye fifteen dollars."

Endnotes

1. Mrs. Tyhurst was included in David Smallwood's military records as being the recipient of a $5 pay deduction.

2. On the enlistment papers for David James Smallwood (obtained from the National Archives), it was neatly filled in with "lumber inspector." Some time later, it would seem, someone had added the word "accountant" just a little off to one side in a less neat script.

Chapter Seventeen
Cousin Joe
76 Walnut Street

July 1916
Halifax

Joe gave her plenty of warning. "Would you and Gladys like to go for a Sunday afternoon drive, Mrs. Schwartz? I hoped you would be free this Sunday but we can go the next Sunday if you would rather."

Never a person to turn down a drive, Emma replied, graciously, "Thank you, Mister Small-wood. This Sunday would be lovely."

On Sunday, they saw all the sights. Returning from the North West Arm, where Joe had pointed out his newest powerboat moored at the Royal Yacht Squadron, he drove down Coburg Road and then turned onto Walnut Street. He stopped at no. 76 and suggested that they should go in for a visit; the house had just been built and was vacant.

Emma knew she was being manipulated but she was curious. She grumbled and pouted but she went.

"The house is beautifully finished," Joe said. "There's a weather entrance with double doors . . . leaded glass. You can see the front parlour fireplace from the foyer. The staircase is four inches wider than standard; made to look rich. The family kitchen is big; you could seat an army around that kitchen table. The second fireplace in the dining room is a nice touch." Joe ran his fingers through his greying hair. "I spared no expense on the house; it cost over $5,000 not including the furniture." Joe hastened to add, "The only room that isn't furnished is the nursery."

After showing Emma and Gladys the entire property, they stood on the front veranda, where Joe made his pitch.

"Mrs. Schwartz, I love your daughter and will make her a good husband. As pledge of my good faith, this house and its contents, free and clear of any liens and mortgages, will be registered in the name of Gladys Smallwood."

Gladys was as surprised as her mother. She was so excited; she kept twisting and untwisting her afternoon gloves waiting for her mother's answer.

Emma didn't take long. "You have my blessing, Joe Smallwood. I think you have the capacity to make her happy." She walked toward the car. Emma turned back and gave Joe a lovely smile. "It's a grand house. I wouldn't mind living here myself."

On the way back to the car, neither Joe nor Gladys could imagine any circumstance where Emma Louisa Schwartz would be a resident of 76 Walnut Street.

Endnotes

1. Over the years, the story about Emma Louisa's introduction to the house on Walnut Street was a family favourite and was even narrated in the presence of the grand old lady—once.

Chapter Eighteen
Cousin Jack

October 1916
Moncton
New Brunswick

"It is a management prerogative to organize the work force and make changes . . ."

"Make changes any way you see fit?" Union steward Jack Smallwood smiled to himself as he saw the dark-suited man on the other side of the table wince. "You think you can just go ahead and do anything you like?" The man winced again. *Not much of a poker face,* Jack thought. *I wonder how far I can push him.*

"We intend to implement the changes at the beginning of the month."

"You weren't going to tell us about them; just put up a notice saying 'here's the way it is, boys.' Like it or lump it, the Canadian Government Railway management knows what's best for you."

"We are talking about it now."

"Only because we found out and asked for the meeting. Mister, you do not deal with the union in good faith. Even back in the days of E.G. Russell, the union and its members . . ."

"Our employees."

"The union got advance copies of changes . . ."

"You have your copies . . ."

"Advance copies of any change so that we could give you the benefit of the collective experience of our members."

"Our employees."

"You're right. They are ICR employees, who are aware of ICR problems. Why don't you listen to them? They are your employees with years of experience. Take them into your confidence . . ."

"I don't think we can go that far...." The company man studied his fingernails as he asked, "It's Smallwood, isn't it?" He sighed. "You must understand that we have managers and supervisors who are paid to give us the input that allows us to run the Canadian Government Railway efficiently. You can understand that, can't you, Mister Smallwood? Your work as a . . ." He waved his hand making little half-circles to encourage the union leader to speak up.

"Section hand."

The management man smiled for the first time since the meeting began. "Your work as a section hand hardly qualifies you to make suggestions about the organization of the Canadian Government Railway . . . or much of anything else, for that matter."

"You little pip-squeak! I'll match my knowledge of the Intercolonial Railway against yours any day of the week!" Jack half-rose in his chair and leaned forward, wagging his finger at the man opposite. The two men on Jack's side of the table pulled him back down into his seat. Jack thought, *I'll have to give credit to the little bugger. He didn't flinch that time!*

The little bugger was a very slight man with a thin face made to look even more pinched by the narrow glasses he wore. He was one of the new breed of railway men whose railroad experience was acquired on a first class pass from Ottawa to Moncton to handle a "union thing." Hired right out of school, this was his first field trip, but the novice management man felt no anxiety as he faced off against this unschooled union official who was merely a section hand. *I will soon put him in his place,* he thought.

Assuming what he hoped was a confident expression, the pip-squeak, (actually he had a name—Guy Sullivan—but Jack didn't bother to learn it or use it) said, "With your aggressive tendencies you should join the army to fight the Boche. We'll soon be sending men through Halifax to help the English. You should not hesitate to join them."

God, he looks smug! I would dearly love to challenge him on his use of "the English" instead of "the Mother Country" but I'd better stick to our agenda. "You must delay implementation of the changes until the union has an opportunity to review your proposals."

"They are not proposals."

"According to the agreement the union made with E.G. Russell back in oh two . . ."

"That was during the days of the Intercolonial Railway." Sullivan seemed to sit taller, straighter as he pronounced, "We are now the Canadian Government Railway. I wish you would use the correct terminology."

"We prefer the Intercolonial."

"It is more correct to say Canadian Government Railway."

Jack took several moments to examine the papers in front of him. *There's nothing to be gained from that line of argument.* Jack picked up a smudged and dog-eared paper and read from it: " . . . any major change in working conditions will be submitted to the representatives of the union before implementation." Jack paused for effect. "Seems simple to me; we get to see the proposal, then you get to implement it."

"It's not a proposal. It's our plan to adjust the size of the sections so they are even. At the present time, some sections are as long as eight miles while others are only four. We are arranging them so that the average is six miles."

Jack gave the man his best smile. "That sounds perfectly reasonable to me. Does that sound reasonable to you, boys?" Jack looked from left to right, seeking the agreement of his companions. "Sure sounds good to us."

Jack leaned back in his chair. He breathed a huge sigh of relief. "And I thought we were going to have a big problem over this." He held out his hand for the copy of the plan that was on the table in front of Sullivan. "We'll just put our initials on the plan and you can go right on ahead and make your changes. The union will help in any way it can."

Sullivan picked up a copy and held it in his hand. He was hesitating. "But . . . this does not constitute union approval of a management decision."

"What do you think the Manager was thinking when he wrote the order, er . . . the instruction to provide a copy to the union before any major change can be made? Certainly he did not anticipate proceeding if there were valid objections to a particular change. The old manager had planned to stop and listen and in this case . . . we agree with you, completely. It's a grand idea!" With his hand still extended, Jack leaned forward until he was almost touching the paper.

How pleased my superiors will be when I return to Ontario—almost a return trip—with the "union thing" all settled. Mister Sullivan handed the sheet to Jack without further comment.

Jack put his full signature and title of Senior Steward, Local 27, Brotherhood of Railway Trackmen of America. He handed the sheet to his companions to sign. Looking up at the slightly uncomfortable Sullivan, Jack asked, "Do you have a second copy?"

"Of course. I have several signed copies."

"May I have another, please?"

The management man handed the section hand a second copy. Jack promptly began to sign it as he had the first one. "We will each need a copy for our records." When he was finished, Jack handed Sullivan one of the copies.

Sullivan rose, indicating that the meeting was over.

The three union men remained seated.

"Actually," Jack said, "the main reason we asked for a meeting today was on another matter. You see, one of your section hands, Archibald Peters, was laid off because he owed a grocery bill."

Mister Sullivan slowly backed toward the door. "I am not ready to speak on local matters which are the concern of the Division Chiefs." Still facing the union men seated at the table, he twisted the doorknob and opened the door behind him. Turning slightly to one side he said, "Have Mister Hunter join me." He closed the door and walked to his chair. He resumed his seat. "If you will wait a moment, I should be joined shortly by one of the Division Chiefs. I would expect in future, if there is to be more than one subject at a meeting such as this, you submit an agenda, well in advance."

Before Jack could reply, there was a knock on the door and a burly man whom Jack recognized as the Division Chief entered. *The pip-squeak must have had Mister Hunter cooling his heels in the outer office all this time!* He smiled.

Guy Sullivan experienced an irrational urge to punch the smile off the bastard section hand's face. He shook his head and smiled back. *Maybe I am the one who should volunteer to fight the Boche,* he thought. *Good thing railroad employees are considered essential and are to remain on their jobs for the year the war is expected to last. The government couldn't permit a wholesale migration of patriotic men from the railroad to the army. Wouldn't do.* "Mister Hunter, these men say we are experiencing a problem with an employee—" Here Sullivan raised a quizzical look at the section hand.

"Archie Peters."

The Division Chief leaned forward and, in ponderous tones, explained the situation as if he were speaking to young boys in a Bible class. "Section Hand Peters owed a grocery bill. Upon complaint to the railway by the retail establishment, the situation was reviewed under the provisions of a General Manager's Circular which states that debts for fuel, rent, necessary furniture, food, doctor bills, druggist bills, wearing apparel, and necessary repairs to property, are bills that the ICR . . . er . . . the Railway, should force the men to pay, but regarding the purchase of liquor, borrowed money, and articles such as pianos, organs and other unnecessary things, the retailer selling them should know the circumstances of the party to whom they sell and, of necessity, should make their own arrangements to collect these."

One of the men with Jack began to speak but Jack held up his hand to silence him. Hunter continued.

"I interviewed Section Hand Peters. There being no indication he was a drinking man, I accepted his promise to pay five dollars a month on the bill." Hunter shrugged his shoulders. "But he failed to carry out his promise."

"So he was laid off."

"Yes, I ordered his supervisor to lay him off until he did carry out his promise."

Jack smiled. "If he is laid off, he won't be able to earn the money to keep his promise."

Irritated again by the smile, Sullivan commented, somewhat harshly, "He was given his chance. The matter was handled in accordance with regulations." He placed his hands on his thighs as if preparing to stand and leave. "I don't know why we are continuing with this conversation. I have a train I'd like to catch."

Jack raised his voice, getting Sullivan's attention. "Brother Peters' problems weren't handled in accordance with regulations. The General Manager's Circulars are interpretations of the regulations. They are guidelines or explanations. They are not ICR Regulations. They do not have the force of law. They are meant to help managers come to rational decisions." Without a pause, Jack spoke directly to the Division Chief. "Mister Hunter. I'm sure if you had been told that his only daughter, Elsie, has consumption and needed to go to Montreal to see a doctor, you would have made more allowance for Archie."

"No, I don't think so. The General Manager's Circular is definite . . ."

"You mean, after seventeen years, eleven months and six days of dependable work by this employee, you didn't wonder why he was suddenly in some sort of trouble?"

"No. He promised to pay the grocer five dollars a month and failed to do so."

Jack gave a sigh of exasperation followed by, "The union will pay the monthly five dollars on behalf of Brother Peters."

Guy Sullivan sat forward on his chair and leaned both elbows on the table. "Is this the last item you wish to discuss with management, Mister Smallwood?"

"Yes, it is."

Sullivan picked up his case. He stood. "Mister Hunter, it is my recommendation to you that you reinstate Peters and continue his employment for as long as the retailer is paid the monthly five dollars. However, at the first sign of default . . ."

Jack stood up. He walked around the table, extending his hand.

Sullivan didn't hesitate. He took the proffered hand and shook it once and then twice.

Jack didn't release the hand. He held it and said, with a great deal of sincerity, "I hope you can come to Moncton again and help us with our problems. Local 27 appreciated your presence here today. Thank you."

Sullivan made some polite noises as the union men left the office. Once outside, one of Jack's companions chortled, "I thought he was going to choke when you told him how much you liked having him here."

The other steward laughed. "That's the last thing a management man wants to hear: the union likes him and wants him around."

Jack protested, "No, no. He was good enough to listen. I meant what I said."

A runner came breathlessly up to the three men. "Mister Smallwood! You're needed right away!"

"What is it, son?"

"I was told to say that Duke and Danny are out of town. Mary Anne needs you right away."

5 Hours Later
The Sugary
New Brunswick

Jack had arrived at the Petrie farm to find his Aunt Mary Anne lying on the kitchen table. She was covered with a blanket. Arthur Petrie took Jack to one side and explained what had happened.

"I found her on the barn floor. She was conscious and told me that she had fallen from the loft ladder an hour or two earlier. Her legs wouldn't work and she had terrible pain anytime she tried to move."

"Oh!"

"I got help from the neighbours and we brought her in here where it was warm. We put her on the table where we could keep everything straight. She's not always conscious, now. She comes and goes. Her colour isn't good."

Arthur ran his hands through his hair, a note of despair in his voice. "I sent word for Uncle Dan and the doctor. Where's Uncle Dan? She wants to see him."

"He's in Saint John. I will send him a telegram as soon as we find out what's wrong. Where's the damn doctor?"

"He sent word back that he would be here as soon as he could. He's at the Landry farm across the valley. Missus Landry had twins but won't stop bleeding."

"Get the flat wagon out, Art. Bring some blankets down from the bedrooms and spread them out. Make it all flat and even. Get some ropes and pillows so we can fix it so she doesn't move as we ride along."

"Shouldn't we wait for the doctor?"

"If you have noticed a change in her colour and she has periods when she is gone . . ."

"Yes."

"Then we'd better get her to the hospital."

"All right. I'll get going on it. You had better go explain about Uncle Dan."

When Jack stood over his aunt, he was shocked to the core. The only colour on her face was her eyebrows. Her eyes were closed as if in sleep but her breathing was so shallow. He took her hand and rubbed it, gently. There was no response.

A neighbour woman standing there, helplessly looking on, said, "She hasn't spoken for an hour."

Jack said to her, "Make some coffee. If my Aunt Mary Anne is still with us, she will wake when she smells her favourite brew. Make it strong." Jack continued to stroke her hand.

Soon the delicious coffee aroma filled the kitchen. Jack bent down and whispered in his Aunt's ear, "Mary Anne, the coffee's ready. It's that special Schwartz blend that you like."

She stirred. Without opening her eyes she replied, "That's nice, Danny. You always make nice coffee."

"Yes, my dear. It's that special blend that was too good to use in the ICR dining cars."

"Oh, lovely. Thank you." She slept for a few moments.

"Danny!" There was urgency in her voice. "I am Mary Anne."

Jack's heart leapt with the pain of it. His indomitable aunt was losing her awareness. "Yes, I know."

Obviously aggravated, Mary Anne insisted once again, "I am Mary Anne," and then continued. "I am Mary Anne because my mother named me after my grandmother, Mary Anne Charlotte d'Auvergne."

"Yes, dear. Maybe you should stop talking for a bit and we can have some of that coffee."

Angry again, Mary Anne responded, but this time with a weaker voice. "You men! Always so proud of the male line, always talking about the Smallwoods." She took a deep breath. "Mary Anne Charlotte d'Auvergne married Captain Sir Henry Prescott." A smile flitted across her face. "He became an admiral, you know. Men don't become admirals without a strong woman behind them." Here her voice faded and she seemed to be asleep again.

Arthur came back from the barnyard. "Everything is ready, Jack."

"I think we should wait for the doctor, Arthur." With head downcast, Jack added, "I don't think it will do any harm to wait."

A tear came down Arthur's cheek. "I understand." He went to the other side of the table where his mother lay and took her hand.

Mary Anne awakened. "Danny?" She looked at her son and then looked frantically around the room. "Danny?"

Jack went to her side and took her other hand. "We're here, Mary Anne."

She closed her eyes and seemed to relax. "You remember." It was an order, not a statement. "My mother was Carolyn

Prescott, daughter of Captain Sir Henry Prescott, the Governor of Newfoundland. My grandmother was a d'Auvergne." She paused as if to take a breath. "I was Mary Anne . . ."

Jack waited but there was no more.

Both men stood there holding the hands of Mary Anne Smallwood.

Finally, Jack put the hand down, carefully. He said, "I promise to remember."[1]

Endnotes

1. Mary Anne was eighty when a cow kicked her. She was loaded onto a flat wagon and taken over winter roads to the hospital in Newcastle. In real life she survived her broken hip. She died in her bed in 1922.

Chapter Nineteen
Ronald Cameron

31 July 1917
North Sydney Harbour
Cape Breton

The young lad ran his fingers through his unruly red hair as he stared at the blank sheet of paper. His grimy hands had made a black smudge on the corner of the page and he considered going back to the main cabin to beg another piece of paper from the captain, but he knew he didn't have the time. If he were going to write the letter, he would have to make do with what he had. He wet his thumb and tried to get rid of the smudge but that only made it worse. He sighed. He began to write.

S.S. Hilford,
North Sydney,
Nova Scotia.

Dear Mother;
 I promised I would write as soon as I could and here it is already the end of the month and it is my first opportunity.
 Arriving at Sydney I had no trouble finding the offices of the North Sydney Tow Boat Company. I expected to be assigned to a boat after some shore training but so many of the seamen have enlisted, I was assigned to the S.S. Hilford right away. She's a fine boat (I am supposed to speak of the tug as if she were a woman!). She is stronger than she looks because she was built to tow barges around the harbour or push bigger ships when they need help getting to their mooring. Sometimes we act as a water taxi taking crews from ship to shore when there are not enough bumboats. (I'm truly sorry, Mother, but that is the proper name for the little harbour craft that carry crews between ship and shore.)
 My captain is the owner of the Hilford. Since I do not know enough to be a seaman, he has signed me on as Cook's

Boy. I will help the cook in the galley (kitchen) and the rest of the time serve as an extra deck-hand while I learn about seaman's duties. Captain Gordon knows I am underage but said that I am just the right age to serve as a "galley slave" on the *Hilford*. (He thought that was funny but I have found there is plenty of work. Do not worry, Mother, I get lots and lots of good, hot food because I am in the galley right before and after each meal.)

My ship has been ordered to sail to Halifax on the tide this day. We will work with the large convoys that are forming at Halifax. Oops! I am probably not allowed to say that. Loose lips sink ships, they say. Anyhow, we will sail to you know where, today.

I will let you know if I will be able to come home to Lot 38 for Christmas.

I must close now, to get this mailed before we sail.

All my love, Mother. Say hello to the family. Please tell Bina Gallant that I will write as soon as I can.

Your loving son,

Ronald Cameron
(soon to be) Deck-hand
S.S. *Hilford*

Chapter Twenty
Taking Horses to the War

November 30, 1917
Newcastle
New Brunswick

Hannah Smallwood stood behind Daniel as he ate his breakfast. She touched his shoulder, lovingly, as she surveyed the empty places around her kitchen table.

The children—those little people who had grown up around this table—are so quickly gone, she thought. *It seems like yesterday that my eldest, Lucy, would be the first down the hall rubbing the sleep from her eyes wanting to know what was for breakfast even though she knew that the fare never varied. It was always a trainman's hearty meal: bacon and eggs, pancakes and maple syrup, brown bread and farm butter, tea, milk or coffee and apples.*

Hannah smiled as she remembered that Lucy wanted apples, every morning.

Now Lucy's husband is in France and Lucy is serving as a nurse's aide in Camp Hill Hospital at Halifax.

Next would come Sadie . . . always complaining that her sister had left a mess in their room. Her complaint usually concerned some piece of underwear that she would not handle because—well—because Sadie didn't handle other people's dirty underwear. She would sit opposite her sister and annoy her as much as she could until Danny intervened. She always wanted prunes before anything else. (I believe she learned from the ladies' page of the newspaper that prunes would keep her regular—Sadie always wants to be regular.) By the time she had her prunes, she would put a nice smile on her face and be quite a sociable little thing.

Sadie hasn't married, yet. She's gone to visit her Aunt Aylane in Maryland (who also hasn't married). My little Sadie acquired

241

*her teaching licence in Maryland. She's teaching school while liv-
ing with her old maid aunt. (That's what Aylane calls herself and,
by now, it is probably appropriate to recognize her as such.)*
Hannah sighed. *Aylane has too much schooling for her own good.
Hard to find a man these days who can tolerate an intelligent **and**
educated woman.*

"What's the big sigh for, darlin'?" Daniel put his fork
down, grasped his wife's hand, and gave it a squeeze. "Anythin'
wrong?"

"No. Not really."

She looked at Wallace's chair. *I was so proud when Wallace
enlisted at the very beginning of the war. He's been badly
wounded* . . . but she pushed that memory as far back as she
could. *All those promotions . . . and now he's at an officer's training school in England: Lieutenant Clarke Wallace Smallwood. It
would have a nice ring to it if it didn't mean that he is always in
the thick of the fighting* . . . but then she pushed that thought
away again. *Maybe there will be a letter from him this week!*

Wallace had a girlfriend in Moncton but she hadn't heard
from him recently either. Wallace wrote letters to the two
women so they each received them at the same time with the
same news. It annoyed Hannah because, while she wanted to
hear from him, and appreciated his thoughtfulness, she did
want to hear first. *After all, Wallace is <u>my son</u>.*

"And that Jack!" Hannah knew she shouldn't be impatient
with her youngest but she couldn't help herself. "He knows
when breakfast is! He should be here on time. His food is getting cold!"

"Let his food get cold." Daniel had a mouthful that he
took the time to push over to one side so he could speak without losing some of it. "He's grown up and is responsible for his
own actions."

"Yes, but . . ."

Jack came whistling down the hall. He gave his mother a
quick kiss on the cheek, swung his leg over the back of the
chair and lowered himself into the seat without moving the
chair back. In the process, he jiggled the table.

"You jiggled the table." Daniel was almost finished but he had yet to touch his coffee. The cup had been full and now the saucer was wet with the spillage.

Hannah took the cup and saucer away to the sink where she cleaned it up. Daniel sat, waiting for the return of his coffee. "You have some holidays coming to you?"

Jack nodded his head as he chewed his bacon. He swallowed. "Yes. I can be away from the road for six glorious days! Gonna spend my time sleeping and eating."

"Not going anywhere?"

"Nope. Just laze around home."

"I'm going to Halifax any time now. The ICR is transporting army horses to Halifax for ship loading on December 5th or 6th."

"How come you're goin'? What do you know about horses?"

"Not very much, but every time we transport horses, our cars are damaged so badly we can't use them for weeks. The army pays for the repair, but the railway can't afford the luxury of having the rolling stock out of service."

"Not with a war on." Hannah brought Daniel's coffee back. "So, Inspector Daniel Smallwood to the rescue!"

Daniel grinned. He sipped his coffee. "Yikes! It's hot!"

"Sorry, Danny. I freshened up your drink."

Daniel pushed the cup aside. "I'll let it cool a bit."

"Sorry, dear."

Daniel watched his son wolf down his breakfast. "Why don't you come to Halifax with me?"

"Sure, why not?"

"Don't you want to know what you'll be doing?"

"Not really. Cousin Joe spent a couple of weeks at the Lodge on his honeymoon . . . amd now he's . . ."

Hannah smirked. "Must run in the family."

Jack asked, "What do you mean by that?"

"His father, Duke, took his bride to the Lodge, fishing."

"Oh, well. Joe didn't take his bride fishing, he took her moose hunting . . ." Jack ignored his parents' laughter, continuing, "After they got their moose, they went cruising down the Saint John River and then took the boat/train across the Bay of Fundy to Halifax. They should be home by now. I sure would like to visit them."

Danny wiped his mouth with his napkin. "Well, you can do that, as soon as we get rid of the horses," he said as he pushed his chair back. "I'll get the paperwork done; let you know the details by tonight." He patted his son's shoulder as he passed, kissed his wife on the cheek, slid into his coat, and marched off to another day on the Canadian Government Railway.

4 December 1917
Halifax
Nova Scotia

"Do you have some makin's?"

Joe Smallwood looked through the glass display case at the young fellow. The customer was dressed as if he had just come in from the country to watch the parade on Natal Day. "Large or small?"

"Just a packet will do. I don't smoke much."

"I have several kinds . . . Player's . . ."

"That will do fine, Mister."

"Anything else?"

The bell rang on the door to the shop. The mailman came jauntily through the door. "I've got a bunch of letters for you, Mister Smallwood. There's one from Newcastle but it doesn't look like your mother's handwriting."

"Probably written by her companion." Joe picked up a small envelope and turned it over. "Yep! Lottie Borland. Sometimes Mother talks to her companion, who writes it down for her."

"Whatever works, Joe. Good day." The bell on the door jingled and the postman was gone.

Joe put the letter down and asked his customer, "Anything else?"

When the customer hesitated, Joe took a closer look at him. He was young, red hair and freckles. *Doesn't look to be more than fourteen if he's a day. Nice-looking kid,* Joe thought. *Too young to smoke, though.*

The kid had obviously made up his mind about something. "Are you a Smallwood?"

"Yes, I am. Joe Smallwood is my name. Why do you ask?"

"Well, it's not a common name. I mean, you don't hear it very often. My name is Ronald Cameron. We have some Smallwoods living on our land on Prince Edward Island. You wouldn't be one of them, would you?"

"I've cousins on the Island but I've never met them. Neighbours of yours, eh? That's nice." Joe put the tobacco on the counter. "Need some papers?"

"Yes, please. I don't know the Smallwoods very well." He put a dollar on the counter.

Joe dropped the tobacco and cigarette papers in a bag. He made change and handed it to the customer along with the bag. Still the boy hesitated.

"Visiting the city?"

"Yes, sort of. I'm a deck-hand on a ship."

"Which one?"

"*S.S. Hilford.*"

"Ah, yes. She's a tug under contract to the British Admiralty. Your captain, Captain Gordon, is a regular customer when he's in port."

"Oh." Cameron picked up the bag. The boy squinted as he said, "I'm not really a deck-hand, yet. I will be, but right now I'm Cook's Boy."

Joe smiled, trying to reassure him. "I'm sure when it's time for you to become a deck-hand, it'll happen."

"Yes." The boy began backing out of the store. He blurted, "You won't see Captain Gordon tomorrow because he's going to North Sydney. We're going to spend a couple of days tied up at Pier 8. The captain will be back on Friday."

"Why, thank you for the information, Mister Cameron. I appreciate knowing because then I won't have to worry about the captain when he's missing for a bit. These are perilous times."

Ronald Cameron pushed against the door and the bell jingled. "Perhaps I could become a regular here, too."

"Then I'll look forward to seeing you again."

The door closed and the bell became silent.

December 5, 1917
Pier 9, Halifax Harbour
Nova Scotia

Daniel put his arm around Jack's shoulders. "That's a job well done!"[1]

They were standing on Pier 9 watching as the last of the horses disappeared over the side into the holds of the British ship *Calonne.*

The *Calonne* and the American ship, *Curaca,* had taken the entire trainload of horses. Both ships (the *Curaca* at Pier 8) would remain at dockside until it was their turn to join the procession of ships as the convoy left Halifax Harbour. No one was supposed to know when that was (there could be spies everywhere) but Jack felt the Navy wouldn't want the horses loaded if the convoy wasn't going to leave really soon.

Jack gazed at the beauty and grandeur of the largest natural harbour in the world. "God! It's beautiful! Look at all the ships!"

A voice, coming from behind them, said, "That's not many! We had over a hunnert ships in here t'other day."

Turning, Jack and Daniel were confronted by a tall man in a navy blue jacket and turtleneck sweater. His officer's cap was worn at a jaunty angle and he was supporting one side of a steamer trunk.

On the opposite side of the trunk, struggling somewhat against the weight of it, was a young lad with red hair and freckles.

The man with the cap indicated that the trunk could be put down and the redhead did so with an expression of relief.

He rubbed circulation into his abused hand.

Daniel spoke first. "Where the hell did you come from?" They had been working on the pier and were sure that the last of the pier personnel had left at least five minutes ago.

"I'm pleased t'meet you, too." He extended his hand. "I'm Captain Alexander Gordon of *S.S. Hilford.* This here lad is one of m'crew, Ronald Cameron. We were watchin' you as you mother-henned those horses off the rail cars. Good show!"

"This is Jack and I'm Daniel Smallwood of the Canadian Government Railway."

"Good thing you were here to oversee the unloadin'. I'm told that the last time there was a horse shipment, the handlers were only interested in the horses. The railroad equipment took a beatin'."

"Yes, we experienced a lot of damage. That's why the Railway sent us along."

"Well, as far as I c'ud see, horses and railroad did right some good, this time."

Daniel scratched his head. "But that doesn't answer my question; where did you come from, lugging that trunk?"

"Step away from *Calonne*, you should be able to see *Hilford* at the end of Pier 8. That's where we like t'be, eh, Ronald? We're right smack dab in the middle of the Narrows; Bedford Basin that-a-way and the harbour over there. Right in the centre of the action where we can watch it all happen, eh?"

Daniel stepped back a number of paces and shielded his eyes from the December sun. Sure enough, at the end of the pier, he could see the wheelhouse and black funnel of a small ship. "Oh she's a . . ." He hesitated; not knowing what a little thing like that might be doing in among such large ships.

"She's a tugboat." The captain indicated to his crewman that they should be lifting the trunk and moving on.

Jack put his hand out to stop them. "Please, sir. Would you tell us a little of what is going on . . . what these ships are?"

In the process of picking up the trunk, Gordon stood up. "If y'er not German spies, I'll tell you." He gave a hearty laugh, clapping his heavy arm across Jack's shoulders. Gordon then turned Jack's body until he was facing Bedford Basin. He pointed with his free hand. "That big square ship out there is the *Olympic*. She's full of men bound directly for France"

"How many men would a big ship like that carry?"

"Mabbe four thousand, dependin' how they stack 'em."

Gordon then turned Jack's body so he was looking down harbour.

"Y'know the *Calonne* and *Curaca*. They have horses. Further down, no, look inshore, in the dry-dock. That's the Norwegian *Hovland*. She suffered some damage on her last crossin' so she's in for some repairs." Gordon jabbed with his fingers. "Next to her, tied to the graving dock, is the *Middleham Castle*. She won't be goin' out with a convoy any time soon. Lotta pipe work bein' done on her. The British ship, *Picton*, is also in for repair. I suppose she'll go with the next convoy 'cause she's got a full cargo."

"What would she carry?"

"The British mix their cargoes. They don't load a ship fulla munitions in case somethin' goes wrong. The *Picton* is carryin' ammunition but it's beneath her load of foodstuffs." Gordon pointed again. "See! The Dockyard workers are takin' down the scaffolding. She'll probably be declared fit t'sail with the convoy."

"When would that be?"

Captain Gordon let go of Jack and stepped back. "Now I know you're a German spy!" He laughed heartily. "I don't s'pose even the captains know, yet." He waved his hand at the boy. "Take up your load, Red!"

"I have only the one question, and then I'll give you a hand with the trunk." Daniel gave the Captain a meaningful look and glanced at the boy. "It's a long way to the street where the trams are."

"Sounds good t'me. Sound good t'you, Red?"

"Yes, sir."

Daniel pointed at a long, sleek ship anchored in the Upper Harbour just short of the Narrows joining Bedford

Basin and Halifax Harbour. "You didn't mention that big ship."

"That's *H.M.S. Highflyer.* British cruiser came inta port t'other day. She'll be escortin' the next convoy. Her last time out, she sank a big German cruiser. There's goin' to be a party on 'er tonight."

"Guess they earned it."

"Earlier in the day, I saw a ship with wooden shacks built on her decks . . . sorta like permanent-looking huts. Why would they do that to a fighting ship?"

"That'll be the *Niobe.* The Canadian Navy bought 'er from the British. Officially, she's *H.M.C.S. Niobe* but she's been beached. That's where t'office of the Chief Commandin' Officer, you know, the naval command centre is. That's where they know everythin' that's goin' on in the Basin or the Harbour."

"Funny looking headquarters." Daniel bent down and hefted one end of the trunk. He put it down and motioned for Jack to take up the other end. They lifted in unison. Jack grunted from the weight.

"Yeah, bit of a surprise, son?"

The Captain laughed his laugh. "My books. I'm takin 'em home to North Sydney for my son t'study. Someday, he'll be a cap'n, too."

Walking in silence for a few moments the boy sought permission of his captain to ask a question.

Gordon was quite jovial now that he wasn't carrying the trunk. "Only way you'll learn, m'boy, is t'ask questions . . . but mind you listen real careful-like t' the answers."

"For most of my life I have lived knowing there were Smallwoods but I never met one before. Now, in two days, I have met three of them."

"Where did you meet the other one?"

Jack and Daniel put the trunk down and rubbed their hands.

"Mister Smallwood has a store at the corner of Morris and Barrington streets." Looking at his captain for approval, the boy added, "I'm one of his regulars." Gordon smiled at that.

Cameron and the captain took their place on either end of the trunk and heaved. The street was now in sight. "Ask your question, Cameron. We're almost finished with this task and you'll be goin' back to *Hilford*." They reached the horse/tram tracks. The trunk was deposited on the side of the road.

"Yes." He bit his lip before he spoke. "Are you two gentlemen from Lot 38 on Prince Edward Island?"

"No. We're from New Brunswick."

"Then there must be a lot more Smallwoods than I thought. Wait 'til I tell my Ma. She won't hardly believe there's more of you in this world."

The boy saluted his captain and walked back across the Richmond Rail yards heading for his ship.

"What was that all about?" Daniel looked at the captain. "Any idea?"

"No. But I'll ask 'im when I get back on Friday. Can I let you know?"

"Yes. Just have any Railway telegrapher send a note to Inspector Smallwood, Moncton. I'm just curious. Should have asked him, but he caught me by surprise."

When the tram arrived, the Smallwoods helped the captain board the tram with his trunk. At the train station, the trio split up: Gordon to catch his train to Cape Breton, and Daniel to walk over to the hotel for a few hours of shut-eye. Jack stayed on the tram going to Morris Street, where he hoped he would have a little visit with Joe before leaving town.

The bell on the door tinkled as Jack entered the shop. He was met by a hearty, "Jack! It's good to see you!" as he walked to the counter where an older man was being served. Joe leaned across the counter and grasped Jack's extended hand, shaking it vigorously. "Where did you come from?"

"The Railway was transporting some horses for the army."

"Being loaded on the next convoy?"

"I suppose so."

"What were you doing with horses?"

"Someone described it as being a mother hen to a herd of horses."

"If that is meant to be funny, I don't get it."

With good humour, Jack explained. "Every time we transported horses, our rolling stock got damaged. This time, with Dad and me there, it didn't."

"Where's your Dad?"

"He said he was tired and has gone to the hotel to get some shut-eye. We're going back to Moncton in a couple of hours."

"You won't have time to come see us at our new house?"

"Not really. How's married life?" Jack gave Joe a broad wink. "Is it everything it's meant to be?"

"Jack, I'd like you to meet my wife's grandfather, Warren Gray."

Jack's face reddened a little, partly, perhaps, because he recognized the name. "I remember a story when I was a kid about iron men and wooden ships. There was a tale about a Warren Gray who took a small boat into a storm off Devil's Island to save some seaman whose ship was wrecked."

The other man moved closer to accept Jack's hand. He shook it, saying, "No, that was Thomas Henneberry, a cousin of mine." He looked down modestly. "In the story, I was the man who didn't save the *Jane McLeod* and got lost at sea."[2]

Jack was impressed. "Yes! That was exciting!"

Warren Gray said, "It was just a story."

Joe wasn't letting the old man belittle himself. "Don't you believe it, Jack. Warren was a real hero!"

"What do you do now, Mister Gray?" Jack asked, politely.

"I eat Joe's jawbreakers and do some vitillin' for His Majesty's Ships."[3]

Warren lifted up the glass jar with the wide top and unscrewed the metal lid. He held the jar out to Jack, indicating the brightly coloured, sugar-coated balls. "Take one, but if you're like your cousin, maybe two. Sometimes I swear that Joe here can squeeze two in his mouth."

Jack grinned. "I sometimes think his mouth is big enough to put his foot in it."

"Both feet."

Joe hit the side of the jar with a pencil, making a ringing sound. "Time! Gentlemen! I need time to call Gladys down here and take care of you, Warren. And Jack, Warren doesn't need any help from you. He's always razzing me."

Warren Gray made his apologies, shook hands saying that he had some deliveries to make, and hurried to the door. The doorbell tinkled and the two cousins were alone.

"Imagine! I actually met Warren Gray. Wallace would have liked that, too."

"How's Wallace? Has your Mom heard from him?"

"He's learning how to be an officer. They sent him to an officer training school in England."

"That's wonderful!"

Jack shook his head from side to side. "Yesterday the newspapers were full of the heavy casualties being suffered at Passchendaele in Belgium. The Nova Scotia Highlanders received heaviest losses. As soon as Wallace graduates, he'll be sent back into that kind of thing."

Joe offered a cigarette. Jack said, "No thanks."

"He'll be all right. Wallace is smart. He knows how to stay out of trouble."

"Speaking of trouble, how's marriage?"

"Just fine, Jack."

"Is that all I'm going to get?"

Joe looked his cousin right in the eye. "It isn't like the old days, Jack. This is my wife, not some . . ."

"Sorry. I understand. I'll take that cigarette now."

Joe tried to lighten it up a bit. "You know that coffee our Aunt Mary Anne used to drink all of the time?"

"Yes. It was a special blend made here in Halifax."

"That's my wife's family. She was Gladys Schwartz."[4]

Jack had a moment of remembrance. "That was the blind gentleman Dad was talking about. The man who could do all of his sums in his head!"

"That's the one! Well, he's my father-in-law."

The cousins talked in that vein for the next hour as customers came and went, but soon it was time for Jack to go.

"Gotta pick up Dad and catch the train home."

"It was nice of you to drop by, Jack. Say hello to your Dad."

"I will." They shook hands. Jack was almost out the door when he asked, "Do you know a Ronald Cameron from Prince Edward Island?"

"Little fellow, with red hair and freckles? He's a . . . regular customer of mine."

"What's he got against Smallwoods?"

"I dunno what's bugging him, but years and years ago, the Smallwoods and the Camerons argued over some land on the Island; I don't think it's a problem today."[5]

"Oh! Seems the Camerons haven't forgotten it."

"Bad feelings live longer than the people."

"Yeah, I guess so. Well, bye, Joe."

"Best of luck, Jack."

Endnotes

1. The movements of the trains and ships are as accurate as I could make them.

2. The story of Warren Gray and the *Jane McLeod* is told in book 3 of the Abuse of Power series, *Crooked Paths.*

3. In real life Warren Gray loved hard candies; the author assumed they would be jawbreakers. Warren Gray had business contracts with the various shipping companies to supply provisions to the ships.

4. Joseph Howie Smallwood and Gladys Evelyn Schwartz were married in the Brunswick Street United Church, September 19, 1917. Cecil John Havill and Edith Florence Schwartz were married on June 12, 1918.

5. The Proprietor System of Land Ownership (established by the English in 1768 as a form of governance for Prince Edward Island) placed the Camerons and the Smallwoods on opposite sides. Their story is told in book 5, *Expulsion and Survival.*

Chapter Twenty-One
The 6th of December Dawned Crisp and Clear

December 6, 1917[1]
Halifax
Nova Scotia

The 6th of December dawned crisp and clear. There was no wind. The harbour was blanketed with mist and, as the sun rose, the mist began to dissolve. At 76 Walnut Street, Joe Smallwood stoked the furnace, catching the last embers of the night's fire.

The newlyweds had settled into a comfortable routine. Joe got up first, and now that the weather was colder, set the furnace for the day. Gladys made breakfast. Then the two of them sat in the kitchen enjoying the first glimmer of the sun peeking around the edge of the Citadel. They talked about the day and made plans for the evening.

These days, Gladys was often called upon to sing at Pier 24 to entertain the troops. This morning the newlyweds were discussing how Gladys could be at the Brunswick Street United Church for a choir practice and still make it to the pier in time for her performance for the troops. Joe had told her not to worry; he would return from work at lunchtime and take the car to the store—that way he could pick her up at six.

Joe put on his suit jacket.

"Do you think you will need an overcoat, dear?" Gladys asked as she handed him his hat. "It seems very cool."

Joe left the overcoat on the clothes tree. He looked around the front of the house. It was so . . . so perfect. They had ordered a piano from Phinney's Music Store. Last night, Joe had moved the furniture so the living room looked like it was waiting for the instrument. "If they arrive today with the piano, don't you try to help them. They are professional movers and they will do everything."

Gladys promised to step back and let it all happen. They kissed. Joe walked down the street. He turned to wave. Gladys stood on the veranda and waved back. She blew him a kiss.

Joe usually walked along Spring Garden Road to Barrington Street and then south the few blocks to the corner of Morris and Barrington streets where the new store was located. He made a practice of being there at eight o'clock to catch the early trade.

On the morning of 6th of December, Joe changed his routine and picked South Street instead of Spring Garden. As he walked down South Street, he thought he might have a better view of the harbour and part of George's Island. The closer he got to Barrington Street, the more of the harbour he could see. It was a pretty scene, with the trees' finger-like branches scratching the sky while the mists formed curious shapes as the feeble warmth of the sun lifted them off the water. The green slopes of George's Island were wet with dew, shimmering in the sunlight. The harbour waters were slate grey and looked cold. A huge black and grey shape glided along the harbour leaving swirls of mist in its wake.

That's a big ship, he thought. As he turned the corner, he could see she was British; *probably a cruiser. I might get some business out of the crew if they are allowed ashore later in the day.* He slowed as he approached the store. Looking into the front windows, Joe was unhappy with the display. He made up his mind. *First thing this morning I'm gonna change the display and spruce it up a bit.* Joe unlocked the door and went into the shop to begin his workday. He was still in the storeroom, selecting stock for his new display, when the first customer entered. *That would be Warren*, he thought. *He never misses a morning.* Joe called out, "G'morning, Warren."

"How did you know it was me?"

Let's see, yesterday I told him I could hear his squeaking shoes . . . "I can tell by the smell of your cologne; you know, that awful stuff Gladys gave you on your birthday."

Warren Gray went behind the counter and helped himself to some hard candy. He opened the till and put in two cents.

Closing the till he said, "When are you going to get some jaw-breakers, Joe?"

"For sure, later today." Joe came out of the storeroom with his arms filled with boxes and samples. He put them down at the front of the store. Looking at Warren Gray, Joe thought, *the man never changes. He's tall, strong. Just look at the muscles in those arms! That short military haircut and moustache of his are almost white . . . but I guess that's to be expected in a man of more than seventy years.*

"I got a big order for a British ship that's comin' in today."[2]

"That must have been her I saw passing about eight o'clock."

Warren tucked a hard candy in his mouth. "I'd better hurry along then." He moved toward the door. "Anything I can help you with before I go?"

"No, thanks."

"What's my darling granddaughter doing today?"

Joe held the door open for the old man as they walked out into the sunlight. "She's probably not up yet. She gets me breakfast, cleans up, and then goes back to bed for a snooze." Joe pulled out his pocket watch. "It's only eight-thirty. Gladys won't be up for another half an hour. We'll be running late tonight; she needs all of the sleep she can get."

As Joe was talking, Warren had turned to watch as another ship came up the harbour. "Now, there's a real rust bucket, eh?"

Joe nodded his head in agreement. "Funny the way she moves through the water; down at the bow and high at the stern. I wonder what's in those canisters."

"She's flying a French flag . . ."

They turned their heads in the direction of a distinctive sound. From somewhere up the harbour came the heavy rumble of a ship's anchor chains.

"That'll be my Britisher." Warren stepped over to the curb. He reached into the cab of the motor truck and turned the ignition. He set the throttle and spark, and then walked around to the front to work the crank. The engine was warm and the motor came to life immediately. "Wish she would always start that way." He walked back and climbed into the cab. Raising his voice over the sound of the motor Warren asked, "Have you seen my daughter or her husband this week?"

"Yep! Saw Emma yesterday. She said Freddie went to Montreal on Schwartz and Sons business. He won't be back until the end of the week."

"I'll drop by after lunch to see if there's anything she might want." Warren waved his hand and drove north on Barrington Street to the Dockyard.

Joe looked out at the harbour. He could still see the stern of the French ship. *Must be going to Bedford Basin to join the convoy. I'm glad I'm not a sailor.* He hummed the popular song, "All the Nice Girls Love a Sailor," as he started work on the display.

In the galley of the *S.S. Hilford*, Ronald Cameron put down his coffee mug. "That's a ship's whistle in the Narrows. Let's step out and have a look."[3]

"Yeah, Red." Foster Jenkins, in charge of *S.S. Hilford* during the absence of Captain Gordon, picked up his coffee mug and took it with him. "Tell me, Red, what did the whistle mean?"

Cameron was used to being quizzed by the crew and he appreciated it because he desperately wanted to qualify as a crewman.

"One whistle means, 'I am in my proper channel' or 'I am continuing in my proper channel.'"

"Good." Foster surveyed the Narrows. "See! That ship . . ." he lifted his coffee mug to point at a ship with "BELGIAN RELIEF" printed on her side, " . . . well, she must've just signalled the tugboat *Stella Maris* . . ."

Cameron could see where the *Stella Maris* had steamed out from the dry-dock area towing two scows, probably full of ashes to be taken to the Basin.

" . . . that she was in her proper channel. The tug should

get out of her way." Foster watched for a second and then hollered, "Jock! Bring me the captain's glasses!"

A voice from the galley said, "Aye, Foster."

Foster waved his mug in the general direction of the tugboat. "But it seems that the *Stella Maris* wants to stick in close to the shore and let that other ship pass by before she comes out further." Foster accepted the eyeglass from the third man, who leaned against the rail to watch too.

"What's goin' on?" he asked.

"That Belgian Relief Ship comes down from the Basin in her proper channel, close to the Halifax side. The *Stella*, draggin' a couple of scows, comes out of the Dockyard and gets whistled by the Belgian . . ." Foster looked in his glass, " . . . who is the *Imo* . . . to get out of the channel." Foster then explained to Cameron, "If the tug is goin' to the Basin, she should be over close to the Dartmouth shore, but see what she's doin'? She's huggin' the Halifax side and lettin' the *Imo* pass starboard to starboard." Like a patient teacher, Foster asked the boy, "and ships should pass?"

"Left side to left side, er, port side to port side."

"Right. But you remember, Red; always use port and starboard, not left and right."

"Yes, Foster."

"And you should say, 'Aye, aye.'" Foster pointed again. "See! The *Imo* had to let the tug and her barges pass starboard to starboard because the *Imo* was goin' too fast to do anything else. Now the *Imo* is in mid-stream instead of in her proper channel."

Suddenly there was a sharp whistle from another ship. The three men swung their heads around to look where the whistle had come from. "That's from somewheres down the Narrows," Foster said as he raised his glasses.

"She's the *Mont Blanc*. What does the one whistle mean, Red?"

"I am in my proper channel."

"By the looks of her, she means to stay there."

Jock sucked his teeth. "The *Imo* is a big ship. She'll need lots of room to manoeuvre."

"Hee, hee!" Foster had the glasses to his eyes and seemed to be enjoying the show. "They're both in the same channel." Talking as if he were speaking to the two captains, Foster said, "Come on boys, you have less than a mile to make up your minds. Whatcha gonna do?"

The *Imo* responded with two short blasts.

All thoughts of teaching Cameron seamanship went by the boards as Foster exclaimed, "The *Imo* has just said that she is going further out of her channel . . . moving toward Dartmouth." He switched to examine the stern of the *Mont Blanc.* "The *Mont Blanc* is going dead slow."

The two short blasts from the *Imo* were followed almost immediately by two short blasts from the *Mont Blanc.*

Cameron said, "And now the *Mont Blanc* is leaving her channel?"

Foster nodded his head in agreement as he watched the bow of the *Mont Blanc* slowly swing across the path of the oncoming *Imo.* "They are going to try to pass starboard to starboard. There's not much room between those ships but I think they'll make it!"

The men could see that the ships were now steaming parallel to each other, the *Mont Blanc* moving slowly, probably with her engines at full stop; the *Imo* slicing quickly through the almost calm waters.

Three blasts from the *Imo.*

"That's full speed astern!" Cameron whispered.

"Full speed astern?" Foster yelled. "You idiot! Captain, you're an idiot!"[4]

It was going to happen! They could see the foam and spray at the stern of the *Mont Blanc* as that captain put his ship in full astern as well.[5]

"He's trying to reduce the impact, 'cause there's going to be a collision!" Foster watched as the effects of the full astern (with her far greater speed) swung the *Imo's* bow to starboard where it struck the starboard bow of the *Mont Blanc.*[6]

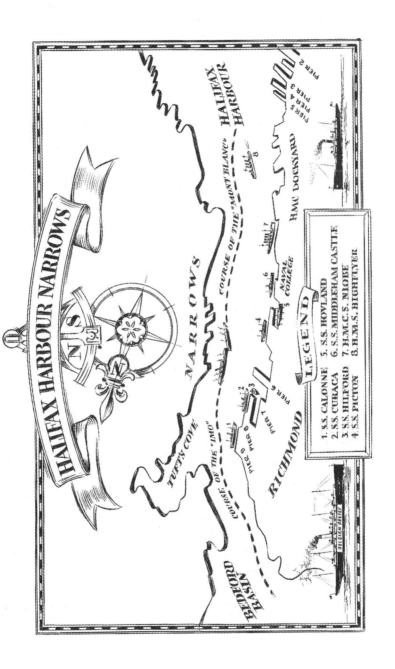

HALIFAX HARBOUR NARROWS

BEDFORD BASIN

TUFT'S COVE

NARROWS

COURSE OF THE "IMO"

COURSE OF THE "MONT BLANC"

HALIFAX HARBOUR

RICHMOND

NAVAL COLLEGE

HMC DOCKYARD

PIER 9 PIER 8

PIER 7

PIER 6

PIER 2
PIER 3
PIER 4
PIER 5

LEGEND

1. S.S. CALONNE   5. S.S. HOVLAND
2. S.S. CURACA   6. S.S. MIDDLEHAM CASTLE
3. S.S. HILFORD   7. H.M.C.S. NIOBE
4. S.S. PICTON   8. H.M.S. HIGHFLYER

BELGIAN RELIEF

Foster had his glasses glued on the two ships. From this distance, there was no noise of impact, but Foster could see sparks and, when the two ships separated, there was a large wedge-shaped hole on the starboard side of the *Mont Blanc*.

The crew of the *Imo* could be seen looking over the side trying to assess the amount of damage to their ship.

Meanwhile, on the *Mont Blanc,* there was a wisp of black smoke coming from the hole in the bow which rapidly developed into a thick, black cloud enveloping the entire ship.

Since Foster couldn't see anything on the *Mont Blanc* he moved his attention to the *Imo*. She was under way again. The captain was attempting to turn the ship and head back up to the safety of the Basin.

Cameron pointed at the *Mont Blanc*. "Look she's coming out of the smoke!"

Foster focused his glass on the stricken ship. "The ship is moving. She's coming this way." He watched for a few seconds longer. "She'll be coming in near Pier 6."

Cameron saw activity at Pier 6. The men on that pier had no doubt where the *Mont Blanc* would come ashore.

"Christ!" Foster took a deep breath. "They're abandoning ship!"

"Who is?"

"The crew of the *Mont Blanc*! They've got a boat in the water and they're rowing like hell for the Dartmouth shore!"

"Look! The crew of the *Middleham Castle* are putting fenders over the side." There was excitement in Cameron's voice.

"Good boys! With no crew on her, the *Mont Blanc* will just crunch in there, somewhere. No tellin' where. We'd better put some fenders over as well. We're pretty close."

Jock and Cameron quickly complied. Foster continued watching the activity on the harbour. He kept his two crewmen up to date as they worked. "The *Imo* has given up trying to turn around. She's heading down harbour to'ard the sea. The *Mont Blanc* is definitely going t'come ashore at Pier 6." Foster refocused the glasses on the beach where the *Mont*

Blanc's boats had gone. "The ship's boats have landed on the Dartmouth shore. Christ! The captain has lined his crew up on the beach for a roll call!"

There were several explosions on the *Mont Blanc*. Something arced through the air like a rocket and fell with a big splash a hundred feet away from *Hilford*.

Foster caught some movement out of the corner of his eye. "The *Stella Maris* has come back!" By this time, *Mont Blanc* was almost touching Pier 6. "The *Stella's* crew is using fire hoses on the *Mont Blanc!*" Foster watched for a few moments. "It's not doing much good. The pier is catching fire!"

Foster brought the glasses down from his face. He watched the spreading fire and could hear the crumps as something exploded in the holds of the *Mont Blanc*. He turned to his crew. "Let's get out of here! Jock! See how fast we can get steam up."

"But Foss! You're not a captain."

"Move it, Jock!"

"Aye, sir."

"Red, you're the deck-hand. See to your lines! Make ready to cast off as soon as I give the order!"

"Aye, aye, Captain." Cameron had the broadest, happiest smile of any man in the whole province of Nova Scotia. *I'm the deck-hand!*

Warren Gray didn't have to show any identification at the South Gate to the Dockyard; he and his truck were waved through. *I could have Kaiser Bill on this truck and they wouldn't look at me twice.* He drove past the Supply Depot. He had planned to park near the Boiler Shop and walk back. *No luck. Too much traffic. Maybe over at the rear of the Harbour Master's Office. Nope. Somethin's goin' on. There's a bunch of people on the roof of the Sail Loft. Wonder what's the excitement?* He stopped the truck. Leaving the motor running he got down and asked the nearest person, "What's all the excitement?"

"There's a fire on one of the ships."

"Where?"

The workman pointed beyond the dry-dock.

Warren decided to leave the truck running and go have a look. *It will only take a minute,* he told himself.

William Lovett, Chief Clerk of the Richmond railway yards located behind Pier 9, was a worried man. A sailor had come running through the yard telling the men there was a munitions ship on fire in the harbour. Within seconds, the men were leaving their workstations in droves. Lovett's main concern was safety: cranes were being left with a load on them, machines still running, lights left on . . . *it isn't safe!*

Lovett spoke on the telephone with Henry Dustan, the terminal agent whose office was at the foot of Cornwallis Street. Dustan didn't hesitate. "Get out of there, William. Get a move on!"

Placing the receiver carefully on the hook, William took one last look around his office. He picked up a picture of his family and tucked it under his arm. He suddenly had a sense of urgency come over him and he ran out the door, almost knocking over the train dispatcher, Vince Coleman, an old friend.

"Let's get out of here, Vince."

"What? What for?"

Not breaking his stride, William said, "There's a steamer coming into Pier 6, on fire, loaded with explosives. There's likely to be an explosion." Then he was gone.

"But what about the trains coming in? Dammit, Bill. What about the trains?" He realized he was talking to himself. Quickly he ran to the telegrapher's room and keyed; "Munitions ship on fire. Making for Pier 6." *There! The message had gone down the line.* With a sense of foreboding, he keyed one last word. "Good-bye."

On *Hilford*, Jock scrambled up the ladder to the main deck. "Foss! We'll have steam in a few minutes."

Deck-hand Cameron reported that the lines were singled up and could be slipped the moment the captain gave the order.

Foster accepted the reports and walked to the railing. He leaned against it and watched what was happening at Pier 6.

Several boats were near the *Mont Blanc*. *Looks like the Halifax Fire Department is working the blaze from the shore.* He put the captain's glass to his eyes and looked further down the harbour. He saw that on *Picton*, the other ship with munitions on board, men were scrambling over the decks battening down the hatches.

There was loud crackling and banging coming from the *Mont Blanc*. He swung his glasses back to the *Mont Blanc*. Without taking his glasses off her he said, "Jock, check if we can move, now. Quick, lad."

Cameron was standing next to him. "Foss. That doesn't sound good."

Flames were shooting skyward. There were individual shots, like cannons being fired, and the flames were spectacular. Suddenly there was a large explosion. Then another, even larger.

The *Mont Blanc* disappeared, with pieces of her going in all directions. Foster watched as a part of the superstructure separated and came away, moving directly at him. He didn't have time to blink before it took his head off.

Ronald Cameron had a moment longer to watch the sight. He held onto the railing until the main force of the blast threw him against the wheelhouse bulkhead. His body was shattered and would have left a bloody smear if given a moment in time, but then a gigantic wave came and washed away everything above the main deck. A huge boulder, possibly from the bottom of the harbour, crashed through the main deck, exposing the engine room to the darkness and swirling hell that was the immediate vicinity of the explosion. Jock might have had his last look at the sky, but probably not. The boilers were ruptured at about the same instant, adding their fury to the hellish forces that killed him.

That was a great sleep, Gladys thought. *Poor Joe; he never gets a chance to sleep in.* The chimes of the grandfather clock struck nine. Gladys got up and pulled on her housecoat. *The house is warm and cozy thanks to my Joe. My world is wonderful thanks to my Joe.* She went into the bathroom and did some necessary things. *Perhaps another sip of tea before I begin to dress.* She left the bathroom, went down the hall, and was descending the steps when she was shocked by a surge of harsh, blinding light. She stopped on the landing and looked out the window; a cloud was forming over the harbour . . .

Joe served customers and worked on the display window. At nine o'clock, he imagined that Gladys might be stirring. *I think I'll wait a little bit longer and then I'll give her a call to make sure she's up and started on her day.* He put his hands on his hips. *The display sure looks good, now.* He stepped back, almost to the window, and regarded his handiwork. There was a stunning, bright flash of light behind him, coming from the street. *I wonder what that was.* Out of the corner of his eye . . .

Emma Schwartz was lying in the exact middle of the double bed. She had her arms spread out on either side as if she were reaching for her Freddie. *I miss Freddie when he has to go away on business trips. He finds travelling difficult but he won't admit that his eyesight is a problem. Maybe I should talk to Freddie's brother. It isn't fair that Freddie is expected to do all of the business travel just because William wants to be the front office man like old W.H. . . . with the big cigars and big lunches. If I speak up, it would probably start a family row. That William Schwartz! Thinks he's the head of Schwartz and* **Son.**

Emma saw the bright, bright light behind the window blinds. A moment later, the glass from the windows shredded the blinds and drapes. She started to get up but quickly changed her mind as the whole house lurched sideways, with the floor of the bedroom rising on one side like the deck of a sailing ship. She held on tight to the sheets. Her last thought was, *something just hit me . . .*

In Moncton, Daniel Smallwood had just reported to the Manager about the success of his Halifax trip. Leaving the main building, he was passing the telegrapher's office when Vince Coleman's message was received. The telegrapher called Daniel in and handed him a copy of the message.

"Do you want to tell the Manager, Mister Smallwood?"

"Yes, I will. In the meantime, repeat that message to the Minister of Railways and Canals in Ottawa. You'd better send another to the Director of Naval Services in Ottawa. Then stay off the line. See if there is more traffic from Halifax."

"Do I put a preamble on the Halifax message?"

"Yes. Just say, following message received from Richmond Yards. Send it off as quickly as you can."

Joe Smallwood licked his lips. *Wet and salty, like seawater,* he thought. He was lying on his back and . . . *I'm soaking wet!* He sat up. There was water all over the display area. *Where did the window go!* He turned his head and could see that the street was deserted. *Puddles of water everywhere.* He couldn't see the surface of the harbour from the floor of the display-case but he wasn't in any hurry to get up. *Maybe I can't get up!* He checked himself over—*just wet and dirty. There's something clinging to my face!* He clawed at his forehead and removed a bunch of seaweed and held it in his hands as he stared outside. *Still nobody in the street. Couldn't someone see what happened and come help?* He kept running his hands over his body checking for missing or broken parts. *What the hell happened?*

He was lying at the foot of the wall that formed the backdrop to the display area. *I must have flown over here because I was over there by the window when . . .* He craned his neck in

the other direction to look behind the backdrop where dozens
of shards of plate glass were sticking in the wall like daggers
thrown by a circus performer. Joe started shivering.

Gladys coughed. *I'm in the foyer. Where's the wall . . . I can't see
the wall. No, I can't see the ceiling.* She moved her head. *Yes, I'm
lying on my back in the foyer. Why can't I see the ceiling! Smoke!*
She sat up but had to support herself with both arms behind
her. *Joe's beautiful staircase, gone! The window where I had been
standing, the wall, the staircase, all gone! The house next door
looks crooked!* She smiled at the thought of a house being
crooked . . . *oh! My face hurts so.* The smoke was now finding
its way out through the open wall at the head of the staircase,
*or where the staircase used to be. But there's a lot of smoke! That's
right! Joe stoked the fire. I had better call him to come home.*

With some difficulty, Gladys got up and walked over to
the telephone. *Of course! The wall is gone so the wall telephone
is gone too!* Without giving it much thought, Gladys went to
the cellar entrance. The hinges were there but the door wasn't.
She looked down into the basement. The stairs were at the
wrong angle. She tested them and went down. The furnace
must have shifted because, there it was, sitting in the middle
of the basement but most of the pipes were misaligned. One
of them was pouring smoke into the house. Gladys looked at
the gap between where the pipe should be and where it was;
the first thing to do is to lift the pipe.

She found the winter tire chains that Joe had put out ready
for the first sign of a storm. It wasn't hard to find a hammer and
nail. Soon she had the chain around the pipe and hitched to the
ceiling, where she drew the pipe up level with the flue.

It was then she realized that it wasn't the furnace that was
the problem. No, her new, deluxe furnace was not to blame.
Instead, she could see that the house had shifted about three
inches on its foundation.

Gladys found a piece of sheet metal that the contractor
had left when they had worked on the house. She pushed the
piece of metal against the wall of the basement until it was

shaped like a "C." After several tries, she was able to place the metal piece over the pipe and the flue. She stepped back to admire her handiwork. *Now, at least, most of the smoke is going up the chimney where it belongs.* Whether or not there was a chimney did not occur to her.

There was blood on her hands and arms, but someone was crying next door. *That would be Agnes Stewart.* She left the basement, went out the side door and around to the Stewarts'. She could see the trees were broken. There were no telephone lines. Only one house had any glass in the windows; she could look into it like a dollhouse since there were only two walls standing. "Nobody home." She giggled.

Agnes was sitting on the back step of her house, sobbing. Gladys could see she was cuddling something. "Agnes, what is wrong?"

Without looking up, Agnes whined, "He was sitting in the window; the one at the top of the landing."

Gladys looked at the cat. "He's gone, Agnes. We have other things to do. Do you have a fire in your furnace?"

Agnes, sobbing and moaning, fiercely hugged the dead animal. She looked up with desperation in her eyes. "You don't know how much I love Tiger!" For the first time, Agnes had taken her eyes off the cat. "My God, Gladys! You're bleeding to death!" She stood, dropping the body of the cat. "I'll get the first aid kit and then we must get you to a hospital!"

With the help of a passer-by, Joe covered over the windows with boards from packing cases held together with nails and wire. As they worked, Joe found out that the man, John Weston, was a British officer heading back to his ship, *H.M.S. Highflyer*, anchored in the upper harbour. He had stayed overnight with relatives in the south end.

John was well dressed, clean-shaven, and had obviously enjoyed a good night's rest. Even in his walking-out dress, the man looked every inch the British Naval Officer. "It was probably a German bomb. My cousin said he thought he saw a

Zeppelin north of the Dockyard early this morning when he was walking his dog." John had a very cultured English accent. Joe had to pay attention to get the gist of what he was saying.

Joe listened but his concern was that John might tear his suit on the rough boards. Joe smiled; *it's not in the cards. Naval Officers never get a crease or a mark on their clothes, particularly when they are committing a good deed.*

"No damage in the south end?"

"The damage was largely confined to windows and alarmed animals. I saw where a horse, pulling a milk wagon, was startled and ran down Ogilvie Street spilling bottles of milk right and left. No, nothing very much," John said.

"We're just about finished. The shop's front door is in one piece. Must have been open when the bomb fell. All I have to do is lock it now." Joe thanked the officer for his help and offered him some cigarettes for his trouble.

With a—"no, no thank, you very much" and "I was glad to have been of help," the British officer walked north toward the Dockyard.

Taking a last look at the battered shop, Joe started for home. *Gladys will be surprised when I tell her about the German bomb. Maybe she heard it and wondered what it was. I'll be able to tell her.*

With a shock, Joe realized that the further north he went, the more damage to the houses, to the trees, to everything. He ran. *My God! Gladys!*

Walnut Street was a disaster. The Stewarts' house was shoved to one side, but the Smallwood house looked fine from what Joe could see. A piano was perched on the lawn. Gladys was sitting on the step; her forearms and hands were covered in bandages. Agnes Stewart was picking at Gladys' face with tweezers. He wanted to hug his wife, but Agnes pushed him away. "I'm getting the worst of the window glass out of her face. None of it went in her eyes because I guess she had her eyeglasses on."

Gladys looked up at her Joe. "I was so worried about you." Tears started, turning red as they travelled over her cheekbones. "The Phinneys' truck was here. Look what they did to our piano. They dumped it on the lawn to make room for a load of injured going to the Victoria General."

"Why didn't you go with them?"

Agnes shook her head. "She wasn't hurt bad enough."

Joe waved his hand in the direction of the front lawn. "Don't worry about the piano." He went in the front door. "I'll get some blankets and towels."

Gladys called after him, "No, Joe. You can't get to the linen closet!"

Joe hadn't really heard her. Now he stood still in the foyer realizing for the first time the extent of the damage. Shaking his head, Joe got a ladder from next door. Soon he was back on the front porch with blankets and towels. More and more wounded were gathering at the point where they thought the truck would return. The injuries were terrible. Joe and Gladys tried to help any way they could.

Joe approached a young man sitting on the lawn with his wife and baby. The man was talking in a rambling sort of way. "The whole north end is gone. I looked back as we crossed the Citadel. There isn't a house left standing. They say two ships collided in the harbour by the Dockyard and one of them blew up. What's left up there is burning. People are being burned . . ." He was talking to no one and everyone.

His wife pulled his arm. "Paul, the baby is cold. Do something, Paul. I can't keep him warm."

Paul didn't hear her. By this time, he was talking about the tidal wave. It had caught them while they were in the garden behind the house. Now he could hear the water; taste the choking salt. He sobbed. "The house is gone. My parents are gone."

Joe thought of Warren Gray. *He was at the Dockyard this morning. Emma lives closer to the Dockyard. I will have to do something . . .* he stood with his hands on his hips and looked around . . . *but there's too much to do right here.* Joe got a big fluffy towel that had been a wedding gift and took the baby from its mother, saying that he would wrap the child warmly.

"Thank you. You're so kind." She ran her fingers through her hair. "I must look awful."

Joe saw the dagger of glass sticking out of the baby's side. He felt for a pulse. There was none. He turned away from the mother and removed the glass. Tenderly he wrapped the child and handed the little bundle back to the care of its mother.

The Phinneys' truck was back. The driver said there was no more room for the injured at the Victoria General but he had heard there was a doctor working an emergency clinic on Wellington. He would take the next load there. Again, he could only take those with life-threatening wounds. Joe helped load the truck. Gladys seemed better; she had unwrapped her hands and was giving cookies and apples to the children. Everyone stopped what he or she was doing and watched as the truck turned and drove south.

A young lad in the dark blue uniform of the Royal Canadian Naval College asked Joe if his car was working.

"How do you know I have a car?"

"My officer knows you from your shop, Mister Smallwood. He said you would make your car available. Is it working?"

Joe said he didn't know and told him that he was free to look. The car was soon running smoothly.

"With your permission, sir, I will take your vehicle to Camp Hill Hospital. A rescue centre is established there. Your car would be a great help." The cadet handed Joe a slip of paper. "I was ordered to make out a receipt."[7]

Joe took the paper. "Were you near the Dockyard this morning?"

"Yes. We watched the burning ship for a few moments . . . she flew a French flag . . .the crew abandoned her almost immediately . . . but then it was time to get ready for parade. While we were getting ready, the College building collapsed around us. We had to jump out a window ten feet off the ground to get to parade on time. At the parade, the watch officer told us to leave the area and find something useful to do."

Almost to himself Joe said, "So, people from the Dockyard survived."

The cadet smiled. "Yes, sir. I'm proof of that!"

As his car disappeared north, Joe thought, *at least the young whippersnapper can drive.* He surveyed the front of his property. Where a half an hour ago there had been fifty or sixty people, now there were none. There were some apple cores, some bloodied and soiled towels, cigarette butts, and—he looked carefully—no little body in a white, fluffy towel.

Gladys was shivering. "I think the crowd realized that the Phinneys' truck wasn't coming back. They might get some help at Wellington Street so that's where most of them went."

"We'll have to go inside. It's chilly. Where's Agnes?"

"She went to find her husband. He works on Barrington Street." Gladys lightly touched the rough edges of the skin on her face. "She was awfully good to me, Joe."

"Yes. Come on, sweetheart. In you go." He didn't know where to touch her because of all of the dried blood so he let her make her own way into the house. It was a bit warmer inside, but the cold came through the windows and the holes in what felt like a gale.

That's the first thing to do. Get some protection from the weather. Fortunately, Joe hadn't put up his storm windows; they were in the basement where the builder had stored them. The basement door had broken the first three when it was blown off. He put up all of the good ones—some of them fit, some of them he nailed onto the house.

Joe had a good-sized tarpaulin in the basement that was actually the winter cover for his boat. *That should fix the missing wall,* he thought. It didn't. There was still a sizable gap. He thought of the piano on the front lawn; *it has a tarpaulin.*

Joe had closed most of the holes in the house when darkness arrived. Gladys used her candelabra with fancy candles for light. She managed to brew some tea. She peeked out through the canvas to see if anyone was home at the Stewarts'—no sound, no light. Gladys took two cups from the china cabinet without a thought of the miracle that it had survived intact. She poured the tea. Joe raised his little pinkie in an exaggerated fashion. "Well, my dear, how was your day?" They put their cups down and held hands across the table.

"It's as if Halifax disappeared from the map!" Daniel was sitting in the telegrapher's office drinking a coffee. Since the fateful message about the burning munitions ship, there had been no traffic out of Halifax. Whatever had happened at Pier 6 had also taken in the Richmond Yards and the Main Terminal.

The telegrapher, Peter James, raised his coffee cup and took a sip, his breath showing over the rim of the cup. "You were there yesterday, Mister Smallwood?"

"Yes. We were looking after the transport of the horses." Daniel looked down into his cup and swirled it around. "All those splendid horses." He regarded the telegrapher for a minute before going on. "The ships that boarded the horses were at Pier 8 and Pier 9."

"Is that far from Pier 6?"

"Spitting distance."

The key began its chatter. Daniel watched as the telegrapher glanced at the clock and marked down the time. He began to copy the message.[8]

10:40 am   To: Navyard via North Sydney.

Radio Sable Island and Camperdown. Urgent.
Understand ship has blown up in Halifax Harbour.
Report by wireless name and if any damage done to
Dockyard.

Director of Naval Service, Ottawa

Peter gave the first copy to Daniel, retaining the second copy in his ledger. "Looks like the navy is trying to set up some alternate communications system. They're going to use the radios at Sable Island and Camperdown. I'm not biased, mind, but I bet they don't get anything out of the radios.

Those radio operators need antennae just as much as we need wires. If our wires are down, so are their antennae, I bet."

Daniel knocked on the wall behind him, which was answered, instantly, by a young man sticking his head in the side door. "You want a runner, sir?"

"Yes. Take this to the Manager's office. Tell his secretary that the navy must have received our message and are trying to set up radio contact with Halifax."

Daniel had barely finished his cup of coffee when the key began again.

10:57 am   To: Mayor F. Martin, Mayor of Halifax

Citizens of the State of Massachusetts are responding to your plight. Relief train being organized in Boston. Advise us of your requirements. Anticipate medical personnel and supplies first priority.

Samuel W. McColl, Governor of Massachusetts.

Daniel took his copy and knocked on the wall. When he had finished writing a note across the bottom of the page he read it aloud to himself. "If they get the train organized, they will be using our road and will need help from our personnel. Have advised the Division Heads." He handed the message to the runner. "Take this to the Manager." Turning to the telegrapher he said, "Peter, I will be back as soon as I can. I have some work to do with the Division Heads," and he left the office.

Daniel came back several hours later. "Peter, I hoped if there were anything happening, you would have sent a runner after me."

"Yes, sir, Mister Smallwood. I'd been sure to do that."

"Any other traffic?"

"Just the one." Peter held it with the ends of his fingers as if the paper itself were poison. "Someone in our organization thinks he's going to get information from Halifax by wireless and has given up trying by land line."

4:00 pm   To: Naval Headquarters, Ottawa, Ont..

All telegraph and train service with Halifax suspended. Shall communicate messages by wireless.

Great North Western Telegram.

"I thought you might have gone off duty by now, Peter."

"Not yet, sir. I have family living in Dartmouth. Don't think I can sleep until I find out what happened."

"Yes. I know how you feel. I have family there, too. A nephew. I feel guilty. I had the chance to drop by and see him, yesterday. I went back to the hotel for a rest, instead." He grunted. "Must be getting old."

"Don't feel bad about that, Mister Smallwood. You didn't know what was comin'."

They sat for a while, saying nothing.

Peter looked over at the older man. He cleared his throat. "It could be real bad . . . couldn't it?"

"Yes."

* * *

In the morning, the weather turned colder and it started to snow; it looked like a blizzard.

Joe and Gladys discussed the problem of finding Emma and Warren. How would they start looking for them? They knew that the military were keeping everyone except rescue personnel out of the area around the Dockyard, the hospitals were overflowing, and records of patients were scanty. Temporary morgues were set up in the schools that were still standing but little attempt at identification of victims could be made since most of the bodies were naked from the blast or badly burned. Shelters for the living were scattered all over the city. There was, as yet, no central agency set up to coordinate all the activity that was going on. Where could they start?

Joe recognized the sound of his car at the front door. They both ran out. Emma was being assisted out of Joe's car by a very attentive and polite army sergeant. They heard him say, "I was most pleased to have been of service, Mrs. Schwartz."

Emma gestured to the neat bandage on her forehead as she purred. "You couldn't have been more attentive or kind, Sergeant." She waited by the sidewalk until the car began to move away and then she turned around and, for the first time, took notice of the two people on the front lawn of her daughter's house.

Emma gave Joe a very self-satisfied smile. "Yesterday my house fell down and the framed picture hanging over the bed hit me on the head. I was trying to walk here and I recognized your car. I stepped out to wave you down and almost got run over. It was one of the Isnor boys driving your car!" She touched her forehead again. She glanced at the person standing behind Joe. The smile left her face. "Dear heavens! Is that you, Gladys? What did they do to your face?" She extended her hand to caress her daughter's mutilated face. "The Isnors told me there were a lot of people hurt by flying glass . . ." But she didn't actually touch Gladys; she was afraid she might hurt her.

Gladys took her mother's hand in hers. "It's not as bad as it looks, Mother. Most of the glass is out. Our next-door neighbour is a practical nurse. She stayed here giving me first aid before she went looking for her husband. I was lucky she was here."

Emma looked closely at her daughter. She checked Joe over. Apparently satisfied, she continued, "That Isnor boy wouldn't hear of me staying anywhere but at the Isnor Farm out the Dutch Village Road. I had a lovely visit." She walked down the path and into the house. Looking around, she selected the most comfortable chair and sat down. "How are we going to reach Freddie in Montreal to tell him we are well and living at 76 Walnut Street?"

* * *

9:15 pm   To: Senior Naval Officer, Halifax

Very Urgent.
Report immediately all casualties and damage.

CE Kingsmill, Admiral, Director of Naval Service

Daniel smiled when he saw that this imperative message was from the Director of Naval Service himself. "Isn't that typical! The big man thinks all he has to do is speak and they will answer!"

Peter smiled, sadly. "I wish they could hear him. And answer."

At ten-thirty, they learned that the Massachusetts Relief Train had left Boston.

About twenty to twelve, Peter's midnight replacement reported in to the telegrapher's office. Peter collected his things and prepared to go home to his wife and family.

The key clattered.

11:40 pm   To: DNS, Ottawa.

Regret to report French munitions ship Mont Blanc blew up at 9am after collision with Belgian Relief Ship in Narrows leading to Basin. Most yard buildings practically wrecked, certain number of service casualties and deaths but unable at present to report numbers or names. Understand Rear Admiral Chambers has already reported that no convoy work or other operations can be carried out from Halifax at present. I concur this. Damage to city very extensive and it appears that the town to the north of Dockyard is destroyed.

Navyard

"Shit! What happened to Dartmouth?"

"And the rest of the city?"

The men sat there willing the key to tell them.

Eventually it sprang to life but the message was from an irate admiral in Ottawa.

00.01 am   To: Captain Superintendent of HMC Dockyard

With reference to your telegram, it is to be reported who actually compiled this telegram and under what conditions, observing that the information contained therein is practically useless. It gives no information as to such important matters as which, if any, Dockyard buildings have collapsed, whether any HM Ships have been damaged, etc., etc.,

CE Kingsmill, Admiral, Director of the Naval Service.

The men in the telegraph office drank their coffee and smoked their cigarettes. Daniel dozed with his head on his arms. He must have slept about forty-five minutes because the next message was at 1:03 a.m.

1:03 am   To: DNS, Ottawa

Survey of Dockyard facilities under way. Extensive damage.

Following ships destroyed. Munitions ship Mont Blanc, steamer Stella Maris, tug Hilford, schooner St. Benard.

Following ships badly damaged. Norwegian steamer Hovland, Belgian Relief Imo, Curaca, Picton, Middleham Castle, Calonne and tugs Mereid, Musquash, Roebling.

Dockyard civilian workforce mostly domiciled in North End. All houses from North Street to the Narrows have been levelled and from that south all glass has been smashed, and other damage done both in shops and dwellings over pretty near the entire city. Still recovering bodies from the ruins.

Captain Hose, Acting Captain Superintendent of the Dockyard.

Daniel passed the message back to the replacement telegrapher. He pulled on his coat and opened the door to leave.

"What about the message, Mister Smallwood?"

"That should keep 'til morning. There's nothing much we can do to help Halifax from here." Daniel started out the door again but paused. "Put a note with it saying Mister Smallwood will be going home to Newcastle on the first train out in the morning. Pass it to the Manager when he comes in."

Endnotes

1. I have taken individual experiences for the 6th of December as related by the family members and fit them very carefully into details from sources such as *The Shattered City* by Janet Kitz, *Barometer Rising* by Hugh MacLennan, *Worse Than War* by Pauline Murphy Sutow, *The Town That Died"* by Michael Bird, records at the National Archives, and newspaper accounts.

2. According to Emma Schwartz, Warren Gray supplied the Canadian Navy and the Royal Navy with baking soda when they were being resupplied at Halifax. He was the only supplier who pre-packaged baking soda according to each ship's daily usage. The ships radioed ahead to the Dockyard making their requirements known. The Dockyard Naval Supply Depot would then telephone Warren Gray.

3. Details of the movement of ships, trains, and personnel were taken from the investigative reports concerning the Halifax Explosion which are on file at the National Archives.

4. The *Imo* was under charter to the Belgian Relief Commission. She was 430 ft long with a draught of 30.3 ft. She would be difficult to manoeuvre because of her length, depth and the nature of her propulsion. The steam engine was efficient and could deliver 12 knots at sea. Propulsion was from a 20 foot propeller which had its own inherent problems: when sailing forward, the vessel had a tendency to veer to the left; and when in reverse, she would veer to the right.

5. The *Mont Blanc* was a French general cargo ship; she was 320 ft long with a draught of 15.3 ft. *Mont Blanc* would be about half as fast as the *Imo*. Given her smaller size and slower speed, she would be more manoeuvrable than *Imo*. They both would have a tendency to veer to starboard when put into reverse. In the story, the ships were trying to pass starboard to starboard (right to right quite close to each other) and they would have difficulty avoiding a collision if they were in reverse.

6. The vessels on the map have been placed based upon my interpretation of naval documents at the National Archives. I could not be reasonably sure of the locations of the following vessels and so I didn't place them: S.S. *Stella Maris* (destroyed); schooner *St. Benard* (destroyed); S.S. *Mereid*, and the S.S. *Roebling* (both damaged).

7. I don't remember either Gladys or Joe mentioning that they had the use of a car during this period. If it had been destroyed, I would have remembered. So I allowed it to be commandeered.

8. Message traffic is taken from the files at the National Archives and used largely unaltered.

Chapter Twenty-two
Massachusetts Relief Train

December 7, 1917
Near Amherst, Nova Scotia

Daniel recalled his own words: *the messages should keep 'til morning,* and *Mister Smallwood will go home to Newcastle on the first train out in the morning.* Daniel shook his head at the thought of it. *Wrong, wrong, wrong on both counts!*

The Massachusetts Relief Train, loaded with building supplies, surgeons, doctors, nurses, American Red Cross officials, and a number of newspaper representatives, had come through Moncton on its way to the disaster area. The Moncton Manager of the Canadian Government Railway then chose Daniel to head up the Moncton work party to accompany the Massachusetts train with the ominous words "I expect that you will do everything necessary to get the Relief Train to Halifax in good time, Daniel." So, instead of experiencing Hannah's warm reception, a hot meal, and his own comfortable bed, Daniel was sitting in an overheated Pullman car heading into a disaster area where he was expected to be compassionate to the terrible needs of strangers; the possibility of a hot meal and a warm bed were remote.[1]

Gazing out the window at the wintry scene, he was feeling slightly sorry for himself: his cough was worse; he was hungry, tired, and irritable; and that Canadian Red Cross woman, Mrs. Sexton, was trying to organize him into a formal meeting in the dining car. On top of all that, he was sure he had read in one of the newspapers that Friday, December 7, had been forecast to be "fair and cold." What the train was rushing through was an increasingly severe winter storm. Every now and then the train would shudder as the locomotive pushed through a drift. With a growing sense of concern, he realized that the section crews were not keeping up with the rate of snowfall. Of course, it wasn't just the snowfall; it was the winds causing the snow to drift.

He let his eyes close. *By all that is right and holy, I should be in bed snuggling up to Hannah . . .* he pulled out his watch and opened it . . . *yes, just about now.* He put his watch back into his vest pocket, adjusting his chain and fob. He smiled to himself remembering that the family had given him the fob for his birthday the last year he was a fireman. He rubbed the gold Masonic Lodge emblem with his thumb. *I have such a nice family . . .. I worry about the girls being out on their own . . . and, of course I always have to worry about Wallace . . .* he sighed . . . *he'll soon be going back to France. We haven't heard anything from him in a while. I always tell Hannah that no news is good news.* With that, he pushed thoughts of home and family from his mind. Opening his eyes he watched the evergreens—his view occasionally blurred by squalls of snow—twist and bend.

Daniel saw the trainman coming through. He raised his hand to indicate that he wanted to speak with him. The man leaned over to listen to what Daniel had to say.

"Would you please have the conductor come speak to me? Ask him to come as soon as he can."

The trainman nodded his head and went back the way he had come.

Daniel leaned his head back on the seat and closed his eyes. *Maybe, tonight,* he thought, *I might get a good night's sleep without having the coughing spells. I feel so, so tired.* Then he smiled at his forgetfulness; *there probably isn't a warm hotel room to be had within a hundred miles of Halifax.* He coughed a couple of times. *I would have liked to have gone home to Hannah.*

Someone was shaking his shoulder. Respectfully, the conductor said, "You wanted to speak to me, sir."

"Yes. You are aware of my function on this train?"

"Yes, sir. You are aboard to help us in any way possible, Inspector Smallwood."

"This is going to be as bad a storm as I have ever seen. I would stop before we hit Folly Mountain and send a locomotive ahead with a plough. Talk to one of my men and get a message off to see if it can be accomplished."

"Yessir."

Daniel was just closing his eyes when he was again shaken. This time it was Mrs. Sexton of the Canadian Red Cross.

"Dear Mister Smallwood, we plan to have an organizing meeting in the dining car. Would you like to come?"

"Who will be there, Mrs. Sexton?"

She pulled out a notebook and began reading names.

"No, Mrs. Sexton, what kinds of people will be there?"

"Oh, my . . . the surgeons, doctors, nurses and American Red Cross officials. Then there'll be railroad people and, of course, the representatives of the press."

"Billy Parsons, one of my men, will be there for me. He's sitting inside the door on the left side, next car down. Tell him I said he should be there."

Mrs. Sexton might have been going to argue but the train surged and then bucked and faltered. Daniel knew the snow on the tracks was stopping the train.

"Excuse me, Mrs. Sexton." Daniel pushed himself erect and walked toward the rear of the train. "Looks like we will have to organize a team to clear some snow off the tracks."

That was the first of a dozen stops where Daniel led men into the blizzard to clear the tracks of the larger drifts. Directing his teams of shovellers, he would cast a professional eye to see if the section crews had properly placed the snow fences. Each time he concluded that the fences were doing their job; there was just too much snow. The men kept on shovelling, and as a result of this back-breaking effort, the train inched closer and closer to Folly Mountain.

At every station, Daniel would request snow-moving equipment. His first and best choice would have been to have a second locomotive made available to him. If he had two locomotives, Daniel believed the train could handle almost any amount of storm. What he found: there was no other engine within reach of the Relief Train. Therefore, a second engine was not an option. At one of the stations there was a blade plough, but it could not be fitted on the American engine. What he would have liked to use was a self-contained unit of a wedge-shaped plough on the front of an unpowered car. But Daniel knew even under normal circumstances, it was only available when arranged, ahead of time, with Halifax. Of course, there was no hope of that now. So they fought the snowdrifts by hand.

What gladdened the heart were the volunteers at every station who were willing to go to Halifax to help. Initially, preference was given to medical staff. As the storm intensified and they approached the mountain, Daniel began to choose heavy-set, strong-looking men who said they were willing to handle a shovel. With a fresh, stronger shovel team, the train made better progress on the long uphill grade to Folly Lake.

1:37 a.m., December 8, 1917
Westchester Mountain,
Nova Scotia

Daniel stepped down from the Pullman car. As soon as he was on the ground, he couldn't stop himself; he stamped his feet, really hard, and looked off into the darkness over the side of the mountain at the valley, unseen in the storm, far below. It was here, somewhere here, that the rail line had been washed away so many years ago. That boy, John Hudson, had stood here, in the freezing cold that was Westchester Mountain in winter, and flagged down the train, saving the train and the souls aboard her. He stamped his feet, again, reassuring himself that the road bed was solid, but he sincerely wished that the driver had found some other place to make an unscheduled stop.[2]

The night was pitch black, the air bitterly cold. Blowing snow went into his nostrils as he hurried along behind the conductor. At the foot of the engine ladder Daniel asked, "What kind of breakdown?"

The conductor climbed the ladder without answering. Perhaps, with the noise of the engine and the rushing wind, he hadn't heard Daniel's question. Daniel felt a cold spot in the pit of his stomach as he thought, *perhaps he doesn't know.* Unbidden, another thought surfaced: *perhaps it would have been better if this American train had been assigned an ICR crew.*

Breathing heavily, Daniel pulled himself up into the cab. The engineer was already explaining to the conductor what was wrong.

" . . . so we are not getting enough steam into the pistons. We have no power."

The conductor breathed into his hands, trying to warm them. "What are you going to do, engineer?"

"We can't fix it here. We need assistance . . ." The wind blew away the Engineer's words. "in the Roundhouse, we should be able to find . . ." Again, the wind snatched the words away.

Daniel pushed his way into the little circle. "We won't get any assistance. There won't be any Roundhouse." In the rosy light from the slot in the firebox door, he could see the protest forming on the driver's lips. Daniel went on, "Do you know what the problem is?"

"Yes, I think so. The snow has been freezing and melting on the engine. Some of the water has found its way into the valve gear. This high up, the air is colder and the water is freezing again. The valve isn't working. It's the mechanism that controls . . ."

Daniel waved his hands to stop the man. "I know what the valve gear does. What do you need to fix it?"

"We can't fix it here."

"We're going to have to fix it here. What do you need?"

"Maybe we could work the ice out of there, away from the linkage but the wind is so cold. We would never have a chance to do it."

Daniel looked at the fireman and engineer. "I know I'm asking a lot of you. I will get a shelter built so you can unfreeze the linkage. We'll start building you a shelter. All I ask is that you do your best for me." He saw them hesitate. "Do your best for the people of Halifax. They need what's on this train as soon as we can get it there."

The conductor spoke up. "You're right, Mister Small-wood. You get your men to build the shelter and we will get the valve working again."

Daniel smiled. "It's a deal." Daniel hurried down the ladder and walked the long, long distance back to the caboose.

The Moncton men opened the boxcars and removed some of the building supplies destined for Halifax. There were plenty of timbers and boards but it was some while before they could find any tools to work with. While some men worked with the scanty assortment of tools from the caboose, others kept checking the manifests until they found where the construction tools were being carried. After that, a shelter of sorts was built over the windward side of the engine. Heavy canvas was stretched over the frame so that the engineer and his fireman had reasonable protection from the deadly cold and murderous wind.

Leaving the train crew to their work, Daniel returned to the Pullman where he sat down, weary with it all.

Mrs. Sexton approached him. "Will we be delayed long?"

"I don't know, Mrs. Sexton. If the shelter holds, if the trainmen find the fault . . ."

"What is the problem?"

"Well, Mrs. Sexton, to put it very simply, the steam valves regulate the admission of steam to the cylinders. When the steam goes into the cylinders, it pushes on the pistons during their strokes giving the power to move the train. The valves also provide for the escape of the used steam from the cylinders after it's through pushing. What automatically controls the necessary movements of the valves is called the valve gear; and the workings of this are governed by the reverse lever in the cab under the control of the engineer."

"Oh! That's so interesting! So what went wrong with it all?"

"Between the reverse lever and the valve gear are some linkages. Ice formed on the linkages. We are melting the ice and, hopefully, everything will work fine."

"How long will it take?"

"We'll know any minute now."

"Will you explain all of that to the newsmen?"

Daniel ran his hand over his eyes. Wearily he said, "I think all they will want to know is there was a breakdown and, under very difficult circumstances, it was fixed." Daniel smiled the Smallwood smile. "*If* it gets fixed."

Over Mrs. Sexton's shoulder Daniel could see a happy conductor coming down the aisle.

"I believe, Mrs. Sexton, the problem has been resolved. Am I right, conductor?"

"We are ready to move along, Mister Smallwood. I have given orders for the shelter to be pushed over the side of the mountain."

"No! Have the men salvage as much of the material as they can. We will need every bit of it in Halifax."

"Right away, Mister Smallwood."

A short time later, as the train got under way, the trainmen joked that it would be "all downhill" from here. There might be more snowdrifts, but they could handle snowdrifts. Whatever happened, they couldn't be stopped. The Massachusetts Relief Train was going into Halifax!

Daniel asked for a blanket and a pillow. The conductor offered to put the bed down but Daniel thought there were too many people in the cars to allow the beds to be made. Daniel curled himself into a ball and went to sleep. His last thought was: *next stop, Halifax.*

Someone was shaking his arm. "Mister Smallwood. We can't take the train into the city. We're told there's too much destruction."

"What? What was that?" Daniel sat up—neck stiff and leg still asleep. "We can't get into the city? Why not?" He rubbed the back of his neck. When he stood up, he almost fell over. Mrs. Sexton grabbed him and supported him.

"Sorry, Mrs. Sexton. Leg's asleep." He sat down. "What's the problem?"

"We're past Bedford. Almost at Prince's Lodge. Take a look."

Daniel looked out the window and could see some destruction. It wasn't as bad as he had imagined. "Get me Mister Parsons." As he waited, he looked out the window again and saw that, as they moved along, the damages were more severe. Soon the train stopped.

Billy Parsons came down the aisle. "We have been told that the area around Richmond is flattened. There is no way we can get into the city." He sat down next to Daniel. "Debris is on the track and the boys are out clearing it away."

"Can we work from here? Can we provide help from here?"

"There's no one to help in this part of the city. There are no buildings. There are no people. If there were any left alive around here, they have gone to where there is some shelter."

"Keep moving the train toward the city. Keep clearing the tracks."

"That's what I told the boys. They're doin' it, but we'll never get past Richmond. The places where we can be of some help are in the west and south of the city."

"Where did you get that information?"

"There was a soldier on a horse. He's the only person we have seen out in this cold. He said he would ride back into the city and get us instructions."

"Well, we aren't going to wait for a guy on a horse to come to our rescue!"

Billy smiled at that.

The conductor hurried down the aisle. "Mister Smallwood! Your men say they have found a switch signal."

Daniel smacked his forehead. "Of course! The tracks to the new South End Station! Does anyone know if they were finished?"

Throwing on his coat, Daniel raced down the aisle, through the door, and down the steps, almost falling into the deep snow as he lost his footing. He ran to the front of the slowly moving train. "Stop! Stop the train." He waved his hands at the engineer. Suddenly feeling very foolish, Daniel let his arms fall to his side. He remembered. *That driver isn't going to take any orders from me. I'm not his conductor. I'll have to go back and get . . .*

The train squealed to a stop.

Daniel started running again. He got up to where his men were working and told them to go back and inspect the switch. "Will it work?"

"I don't know, sir," was the leadhand's reply.

Daniel waved his arms around. *I'm getting hysterical in my old age*, he thought. Forcing himself to be more restrained, he said, "Get some shovels and brooms. Clear out the snow and ice from the switch plates." Turning to Billy Parsons who had caught up to him, Daniel ordered him, and as many men as he had with him, to follow the tracks that led to the west, away from Richmond. "I don't know if they finished the line to the south end of the city or not, but we do know that we can't get past Richmond on the main line. Hop to it, Billy! Get us as far south on the new line as you can!"

The switch plates worked! The Relief Train left the main line and followed the new line to the west.

Billy sent back a man to tell Daniel that there were tracks for a mile or more going to the west and then turning south. There were no mile markers so he wasn't sure of the distances. Billy also reported that a man out walking his dog had told him that he had seen a motorized handcar on the rails the day before the explosion. Perhaps they could get the train right into the city!

Daniel asked the conductor to move his train more swiftly until they caught up with the men on foot, pick them up, and then take the train as far as he could. By the looks of the houses, there seemed to be much less damage in this part of the city so, to save time, they should assume that the line was clear.

Daniel went back to his blanket, curled up, and promptly fell asleep. The cheering when the Massachusetts Relief Train arrived at the south end of Halifax didn't waken him.

Endnotes

1. Neither the newspaper accounts nor the files in the archives named the man who brought the relief train into Halifax. I made him our Daniel.

2. The complete story of how John Hudson saved the ICR train from certain disaster is told in book 6 of the Abuse of Power series: *Rebels, Royalists and Railroaders.*

Chapter Twenty-Three
The Devastated Area

3:30 p.m., December 8, 1917
Halifax, Nova Scotia

A man stepped out of the shelter of a collapsed building. He was carrying a rifle.

Daniel and Billy Parsons had been walking for over an hour. The snow was waist-deep on either side of the narrow path they were following. As they travelled in single file, Billy was leading the way. When Billy saw the figure, he gave a little wave. When he saw the rifle, he stopped, short. Daniel ran into him and fell to one side in the deep snow.

"Help me up, Billy! You ass! Why did you stop?"

Billy stood very still. He raised his arms out to the side, palms up. Otherwise, he stood very still.

Daniel was thrashing in the snow, getting in deeper.

The man motioned with the rifle. "Better help your friend before he gets in there any further."

Without taking his eyes off the rifle, Billy reached down and hauled Daniel upright.

Daniel was quick to understand the situation. "I have a pass issued by Frank Hanrahan, Chief of Police."

The soldier, because now they could see that the man was wearing a uniform, slung his rifle over his shoulder. "Let's see!"

Daniel searched in his clothing for the little piece of paper. His hands were cold and he had some difficulty making them work.

The soldier was patient. "Don't hurry. I'm not doin' much here. You're the first to come this way since the snow stopped."

Daniel and Billy looked up at the sky. For the first time since they started out, they could see the sun shining, faintly, through a thin overcast. Daniel found the pass and handed it to the guard.

"What's your purpose in the devastated area?"

"I'm Inspector Smallwood and this is Foreman Parsons. We're from the Government Railways. We want to see what's left of our Richmond Yards."

"Where's the other guy?"

"How do you know there were three of us?"

The guard showed Daniel the pass. "It says party of three."

Daniel gave a short laugh of surprise. "Didn't notice that. The other man went back. He found the going hard."

The guard gave the pass back. "Keep following this path. It will take you through the Dockyard, or what's left of the Dockyard, and along the railway tracks, past the Sugar Refinery docks. When you get to where Pier 6 used to be, the path moves away from the harbour and up the hill a bit. Don't worry, though, it will come down again into the Richmond yards."

"Thanks."

"Good luck. It's a long walk."

They shuffled away from the guard post. This time, Daniel was leading. He raised his hand indicating that he wanted Billy to stop.

"What is it? What's wrong?" Billy looked into Daniel's face. Daniel was laughing.

"Just practising our stops!"

Billy laughed, too.

They stopped laughing. They had both heard it: the whistle of a train coming into a station. They hugged each other and clapped each other on the back.

"Another train got through!"

"We're back in business!"

Daniel became quite serious. "I bet the Manager is on that train. He'll want a report. We'd better get it for him."

They trudged on.

As they walked through the north end of the Dockyard, they saw a house burning. Sailors were wetting down the sides of the houses next to it but the house in the middle was being allowed to burn.

Billy regarded it as an opportunity to get warm.

Daniel thought it was a good idea and the two of them stood and watched as the little house burned and collapsed in on itself.

A naval officer spoke to them, fleetingly, telling him that it was House No. 13. They were letting it burn because they didn't have the equipment to handle all the fires. The lieutenant offered them a drink from his water bottle, which the railroad men accepted. He left them, taking his fire picket with him to some other site that needed their attention.

Billy and Daniel trudged on. Neither of them discussed how much they appreciated the warm glow from the contents of the water bottle. When they were in sight of the crater that had been Pier 6, they stopped. There was little point in going any further.

"Oh! God!" Billy said it with a catch in his throat as he scanned the snow-covered hulks that had once been a bustling rail yard.

Daniel began making mental notes so he could report to the Manager. There was no Pier 6. Where Pier 6 had been was a crater and the wreck of a ship (later identified as the *Stella Maris*.) He looked for the *Curaca*, which had been moored at Pier 8, but saw no sign of her. (The *Curaca* had taken the full blast of the explosion. She had drifted across the Narrows after the explosion and beached just inside the Basin. With most of her superstructure gone, Daniel didn't recognize her.) He saw that the *Collone*, which had been at Pier 9, was a torn and twisted hulk. Perched on top of Pier 9 was a partly blown-up hull of a small ship. He pointed at her. "That's probably the *S.S. Hilford*."

Billy didn't ask how Daniel could recognize a hulk as badly battered as this one was.

Daniel went on, telling him why. "When I first saw her, I thought she was too small to be doing anything in amongst these big ships."

Billy pointed to a vessel beached on the Dartmouth shore. She was well aground, canted to one side with her four bare masts making her look pathetically forlorn. "That's the Belgian Relief Ship." Billy had read the big letters on the side of the stricken vessel. "What's her name?"

"*Imo*."

The sun went behind the clouds. It was suddenly colder.

"We must head back." They turned to go back the way they had come.

Billy saw another ship, close to the Dockyard. "What is that ship, Mister Smallwood?"

"I'm not sure. The *Middleham Castle* was there the other day. She was expected to go out with the next convoy. She didn't look like that." (In fact, it was *Middleham Castle* with her funnels gone and her superstructure badly battered.)

It was a difficult walk out of the devastated area. The extra energy from the lieutenant's water bottle deserted them as quickly as the sun had. Fortunately, when they reached Barrington Street, a man driving a horse and sleigh gave them a lift to the South End Train Station.

Tired and cold, they found their Manager, Mister Hayes, waiting for them.

The first thing Daniel said was, "Mister Hayes, if you must go into the devastated area, wait until there is a watercraft available to take you up the shore." He grinned at Billy. "There's men with guns and you could get hurt, especially if Mister Parsons is leading the way."

"Why, Inspector, whatever do you mean?" Mister Hayes put his arm over Daniel's shoulder and led him further into the building away from the cold draughts of the door. "But you can tell me all about it after you've had some hot soup." He smiled at Billy, who followed along. "I'm sure, when you are rested a little, the first thing you will tell me is why I shouldn't go into the Devastated Area with Mister . . ."

"Parsons, sir." Billy was grinning from ear to ear. "Billy Parsons."

Report To The Minister of National Defence and The Minister of Railways and Canals December 15, 1917[1]

The first Maritime Express subsequent to the explosion arrived at Halifax Ocean Terminal at 4:00 pm, Saturday, December 8. Mr. Hayes, General Manager and Mr. C.B. Brown, Chief Engineer of the Canadian Government Railways, were on the train. They examined the damage to the Railway property on the 10th and, accompanied by Captain Hose, Acting Captain Superintendent of the Dockyard, surveyed the waterfront damage in a vessel provided by the Department of National Defence on the morning of the 15th. As a consequence, they had a good idea of the actual conditions in general before leaving Halifax on the 16th.

The Departments of National Defence and Railways and Canals decided to cooperate to form an emergency organization to handle such Government work, as might be necessary, on a common basis. A tentative proposal was drawn up dividing the repair and reconstruction work to the various Railway shops and facilities and other firms. (Still in discussions on the 15th.)

The **Richmond Railway Yards** are obliterated. Although firm numbers are not as yet known, remarkably few of the work force were killed, having received sufficient warning to have sought shelter. Vince Coleman, train dispatcher, who is believed to have sent the warning message just before the explosion, was instantly killed. William Lovett, Chief Clerk of the Richmond Railway Yards, is not expected to survive his injuries.

Canadian Government Railway Shops, while severely damaged, should function again once the workforce has been able to find shelter for their families and to trace, and hopefully recover, missing loved ones.

Halifax City, Saturday, December 8. No street cars were running and all other conveyances were engaged in relief work. As reported earlier, all houses from North Street to the Narrows were levelled. Secondary damage and loss of life from fires, extensive. Halifax Fire Department suffered great personnel and equipment losses since they responded, promptly, to the initial report of a fire at Pier 6.

As of this date (December 15th), recovery of bodies is still continuing. Continual heavy storms since the explosion have delayed recovery. December 7th was a blizzard, December 8th a terrific rainstorm and then again another snowstorm. Yesterday, December 14th, it was raining and blowing a hurricane. Many bodies are disfigured and unidentifiable. Others have had all means of identification stripped away by the horrific blast. Morgues have been established in various public buildings such as schools.

Medical facilities were generally outside the devastated area and are continuing to function although over burdened. Most common injury is facial cuts sustained from flying glass. Compression injuries from fallen buildings surprisingly few.
Emergency dressing stations were opened all over the city.
Emergency hospitals were opened at the YMCA, the Halifax Ladies College, St. Mary's College as well as the American hospital ship the *U.S.S. Old Colony*.

HMC Dockyard, Saturday, December 8. Dockyard heavily damaged, beyond repair in many instances. Some temporary shelter for all requirements erected on the Parade Ground. The Dock and Caisson were undamaged. Shops and power plant buildings were totally destroyed. Some of the machinery and boilers could be saved. The pumps for emptying the Dock were unfit as a brick wall had fallen into the pump pit and, until the debris is removed, the damage can not be ascertained.

Loss of life among the Dockyard employees is not yet known but will probably not be very heavy but many have lost families and relatives and are rendered homeless. Mister Salter of the Stores staff received severe cuts in the eyes and it is questionable whether they can be saved. Laurie, Crook, Crieghton, Morrow, and many others were pretty badly cut up. Miss Vaughan of Commander Holloway's staff was killed. Burnette and Mattison of the *Niobe* were killed. Brown, Chief Writer, lost his wife.

Most of the labour force employed in National Defence and the Government Railways had residences in the North end of the city, which were destroyed. Their time and energy are fully taken up with the rescue of their families and restoration of houses where possible. The labour force, therefore, was not available during the first few days after the explosion and nothing very much could be done to protect government stores from the elements. There were exceptions: Mister Townshend, Acting Victualling Assistant , Mister Matthews and Mister Ring (Storehousemen) directed working parties from the *Niobe* saving perishable clothing and stores worth probably over a quarter of a million dollars. This work was performed under the most arduous weather conditions.

Current situation.
Relief. Relief continues to pour into the city.
The first relief train was from Massachusetts which arrived early on the morning of December 8 bearing medical personnel and tradesmen with $750,000 of medical stores and building supplies. Canadian Government Railway employees were assigned to

bring this train through severe winter conditions that would have, in normal times, stopped the train.

December 9, Kentville relief train arrived with personnel and supplies from Aldershot.
Montreal and Toronto relief trains arrived December 11. The food supplies and clothing were immediately unloaded and distributed around the relief stations.

December 12, the *Calvin Austen* from Boston docked with $200,000 in supplies as well as glaziers and engineers.
December 13, the *Northland*, also from Boston, arrived with $100,000 worth of supplies.

Cleanup. Hulks of the wrecked vessels are to be blown up immediately. The Relief Committee feared panic may result if the public was not duly warned. Notice has been placed in the Halifax newspapers and was passed through the telephone exchanges. Blasting operations were in progress yesterday (December 14). Public reaction is minimal.

Ongoing problems. Identification of the casualties. Where there is no hope of identification, a history of the corpse has been carefully recorded, artifacts catalogued, and location of the grave numbered in case of a possible identification later on.
Where the corpse is not disfigured, embalming will be done so that the period available for possible identification can be extended.

Effect on War Effort. There are eight or ten large vessels requiring most extensive repairs in port for which the facilities are absolutely non-existent. The value of these ships at present is incalculable and no expense and effort should be spared to install the former facilities and also augment them as largely as possible in the immediate future. The loss of the time and tonnage is much more serious than the money required to install the plant to repair the vessels.

Endnotes

1. This report has been edited somewhat to reduce its length but, otherwise, is much the same as the material on file at the National Archives.

Chapter Twenty-Four
Unwelcome Guests

December 16, 1917
76 Walnut Street
Halifax, N.S.

"How long have you been away from home, Uncle Dan?"

"Well, Joe, I left Newcastle on the second of December. I was supposed to go home on the seventh, but was assigned, instead, to bring the Boston Relief Train through to Halifax." Daniel smiled ruefully. "I have been here ever since. Sorry I didn't have the time to check up on you people until today. Very nice of you to ask me over."

Daniel looked around. From where they were seated in the front room, the street looked quite normal. "How did your family fare?"

"My father-in-law was in Montreal. We were worried about my mother-in-law for a while, but it was Warren Gray, my wife's grandfather, who gave us the most concern. There was no trace of him for days."

"There must be a story there," said Daniel.

"Well, yes."

"I'd like to hear it."

"Well, we had visited the temporary morgue at the Chebucto Road School but did not see any sign of Warren or Agnes, the next-door neighbour, who was also missing. A few days later, a mortuary committee set up a system; so Gladys and I searched again. No luck. Then the committee announced that all unidentified bodies were stored on the basement floor of the Chebucto Road School. We went back a third time. Didn't find him." Joe offered cigarettes to his guest and then continued.

"The bodies were in rows with white sheets over them. There were no intact windows in the whole building, the

weather was bitterly cold, so there was little need for refriger-
ation . . ." Joe shook his head in remembrance. "It was
horrible."

"He wasn't there?"

"No, he wasn't."

But Warren Gray *had* been there, lying on a table in the
Chebucto Road Morgue.[1]

> *Cold. I'm cold. Why so cold. When
> I wake up I will be warmer . . .
> sleep for now.*
>
> *I know I am awake. Why can't I
> move? Oh God, help me get up. I
> need to get up.*

"Let's move this one over to the table."

The workmen took each end of the body and lifted it
onto the embalming table. The sheet started to slide off to one
side but they caught it and tucked it in under the body.

"The card says he was found in the Dockyard. He's an
older white male, no clothing or identification."

> *What was that? Someone touched
> me. Maybe they'll help me. Where
> am I? It's so cold. I . . .*
>
> *. . . need to get warm or I'll die!*

"Professor Stone!" The volunteer was calling the embalmer.
"We're ready for you.'" In a much quieter voice he said, "He gets
to go up by the fire between procedures. If we don't get a break
soon, we will be as stiff as these frozen bodies."

"That last one wasn't as stiff as some of them."

"Look! Here come some visitors. Stone doesn't embalm
when there are visitors searching for loved ones."

The workmen watched as three women came down the steps to the basement.

"Maybe we can sneak up by the fire while they're here."

"You're on!"

"Ladies, if you need any help, just give a little holler and we'll be here." The two volunteers went up to the heat.

The women looked around. The obvious place to start was at the table at the entrance. The first woman raised the sheet and gazed at the body. "My, he's remarkably composed. He looks like he's sleeping."

> *My God. That's a voice. There's light! I can't open my eyes. Hey! Don't cover me up! Help m . . .*

The second woman lifted the sheet, looked and passed on to inspect the bodies on the floor.

The third woman coughed as she approached the table.

> *They're right here. I must speak to them. Must speak to . . .*

She lifted the sheet. "My, he was a nice looking man." She replaced the sheet.

Warren tried to move. *I must reach them. I . . . move my arm . . . Pain! My God, the pain!*

"ARGH!" He kept moving his arm. "*Ohh, ARGH!*"

The third woman stood perfectly still, scared to death. She looked at the other two women to see if they had heard the noise. They were looking back at her and could see the hand coming out from under the sheet. Neither of the women could speak. One of the two raised a hand as if to point . . .

Warren made his supreme effort extending his arm. His hand encountered the third woman and he clutched her thigh in a firm grip.

The poor woman jumped away, screaming AIEEEEEE-EEEE, dragging Warren off the table because Warren was not letting go of life; he was holding on.

The pain was terrible and he cried ARGHHHHHH-HHH. The other women were running and jumping in several directions shouting HELLLLLP. The volunteers raced down the stairs and added to the din by shouting for Professor Stone.

Despite all of the noise, it took but a moment and Warren Gray was back in the land of the living. The woman with the bruised thigh took off her fur coat and wrapped Warren tightly. She hugged him and crooned a lullaby. Another coat went over his feet. The volunteers gave him hot tea and called for an ambulance . . .

"And that's how Warren Gray returned to us. He found his own way back." Joe went on to say, "He can recall nothing about the explosion. The first thing he really remembers is the hot tea and the woman singing a lullaby."

"Time for dinner everyone," came from the back of the house.

The men rose and entered the centre hall. For the first time, Uncle Dan could see the extent of the damage from the explosion.

Gladys Smallwood joined them. "It's nice that we can have you here for supper." She gestured toward the staircase and the eastern wall of the house. "That whole wall and the staircase were only replaced yesterday. Up until then, there was just some canvas that Joe nailed to the side of the house between us and the winter."

"And I borrowed a ladder from the house next door so we could get to the bathroom."

"And you should take it back, tomorrow."

Joe made a face. "Gladys, they're both gone! Agnes didn't come back. There's no one there to use the ladder."

"If you don't take it back, Joe, you could be accused of looting. The soldiers are allowed to shoot looters, you know."

"The ladder goes back tomorrow, Gladys."

"It's only right, Joe. The ladder is not ours."

"I will take the ladder back, Gladys."

"And the shovel you used to bury her cat."

"Yes, Gladys."

Satisfied, Gladys turned away as she said, "I'll see to the dinner, gentlemen. Perhaps you can tell Uncle Dan about Agnes, Joe." Gladys returned to the kitchen.

Daniel looked expectantly at his nephew.

"Gladys was terribly cut by glass. Agnes Stewart, the next-door neighbour, is, er, or was, a nurse. She gave Gladys immediate assistance before she went off to find her husband. Agnes didn't come back. Gladys is having some trouble coming to terms with Agnes surviving the blast but disappearing after with no trace."[2]

Daniel asked, in a low voice, "What about the cat?"

"It was Agnes Stewart's pet. Died in the explosion." Joe shrugged his shoulders. "We had an elaborate ceremony, burying the cat. Sort of like burying the Stewarts. There was only the two of them. I don't know what will happen to the property."

"Sad."

"Yes." He shrugged his shoulders again. "We were lucky. The Relief Commission has fixed our house"—Joe cast a glance at the rough wall and staircase—"sort of, and Gladys was told that her wounds would heal. There should be very little scarring."

"She was lucky she wasn't blinded."

Joe hesitated. Gladys was very sensitive about the "ugly holes in her face." Joe didn't want her to think they were discussing her, so he quickly changed the subject.

"We thought it would be nice if you could get away from the railway food."

"Nice of you to ask me."

"The tradesmen just finished today. The glazier was here this morning putting the staircase window in."

Daniel grinned. "Maybe the glass came from Boston."

"I don't know about the glass, but the glazier was from Aldershot. Army boy. You wouldn't believe it but four hours ago there were two men mixing cement on the dining room floor."

"Really!"

"They came to fix some serious cracks in the foundation. The only place where it was warm enough to mix the concrete was . . ."

"On the dining room floor? How did they ever clean it up?"

"They put tarps down. Sand was brought in to thaw. They did the mixing on another tarp and took the concrete by bucket to where it was needed. When it was time to go, they just picked up the tarps and took them along to the next house."

There was some creaking on the new stairs.

Joe stood up.

Daniel did likewise, giving his nephew a quizzical look.

Sotto voce, Joe said, "It will be my in-laws, Fredrick and Emma Schwartz."

A tall, blue-eyed man holding close to a ramrod-straight woman in a black dress came slowly into the room. They had dressed for dinner. The man nervously preened his full moustache with his free hand.

"Mister and Mrs. Schwartz, may I introduce my uncle, Inspector Daniel Smallwood."

"Pleased to meet you," said Daniel, quickly. "I have already . . ."

"Yes." Fredrick interrupted, "You were the gentleman from the Intercolonial Railway who wanted coffee samples for Mrs. Russell, who was the wife of the manager. I recognize your voice." He shook Daniel's hand vigorously. "You later arranged a contract for my father-in-law, Warren Gray, to supply his premixed biscuits for the dining cars." Fredrick let go of Daniel's hand. "You are a good man to know, Inspector Daniel Smallwood."

"And you have an excellent memory, Mister Schwartz."

Emma shook hands and said, politely, "I am pleased to meet another member of Joe's family." Emma led Fredrick to a chair and then chose one where she could sit opposite the guest. "You didn't come to the wedding. Only Joe's father, William Frederick, came."

"Joe's mother, Jean, hasn't been well."

"A continuing problem?"

Joe started to interrupt this line of conversation but Daniel continued, anyway. "Joe's mother finds it hard to share her only son with another woman."

Emma liked the answer. She smiled, but it was a small smile. "I can easily understand that; but you didn't come. It was a pretty wedding."

"We are a railroading family. It's hard for us to . . ."

Emma looked at Joe and then back at Daniel. She interrupted, "I thought the Smallwoods were master shipbuilders. Joe was telling me of the schooner *Carolyn,* named after your dear mother . . ."

It was Daniel who interrupted this time. "Yes, we had great ships."

"Then the Smallwoods must have worked to secede from Confederation, being a seafaring family like the Grays and the Schwartzes. Our future, our national strength, rests in our firm place within the British Empire as a sea-faring people."

"No, I don't think so. My father was a shipbuilder and he sailed his own vessels but . . ."

"He was willing to bow to that backwoods sapital in Upper Canada?"

"I think he saw the railroad as the instrument of nationalism. We could be British subjects but also citizens of a greater Canada . . . made great by the power of the railroad. He was a Canadian."

"P'shaw!"

Gladys came back in from the kitchen. "Mother, when you get to the 'backwoods sapital' part of your speech, it will be time to change the subject." She looked around the faces in the room. "Oh! We've reached that point already." Smiling, she changed the subject. "Joe was talking to a naval officer who thought the explosion was caused by the Germans."

"That's right. The morning of the explosion, a British officer from *H.M.S. Highflyer* told me that one of his relatives saw a Zeppelin flying over the Dockyard."

Fredrick Schwartz became quite animated. "I didn't get back from Montreal until the twelfth. By that time there was more information. People on the train believed that the *Imo* helmsman was a German. He steamed his ship out of its channel to ram the *Mont Blanc*."

Emma agreed. "He was one of the men who survived. They took him to jail. He spoke English with a German accent."

Gladys could be heard from the kitchen. "If you would proceed into the dining room, you will find place cards."

The conversation continued as the party moved into the dining room.

Emma took Fredrick's arm and led the way. "I saw a picture of the helmsman. He looked very German." She helped her husband get settled as she continued, "You know it isn't the first time German spies have been caught in this city."

Gladys came into the dining room carrying two steaming serving dishes of vegetables. "We still have my good china because the china cabinet came through the explosion unharmed. Nothing was broken." She wrinkled her nose in pretended disgust, "However, the roast didn't survive my cooking. I'm sorry, there won't be any choice in cuts; the meat is well done. Joe, dear, serve some on each plate and let everyone pick their own vegetables." She put the dishes down in the middle of the table. "Olives and celery are on the table and, Mother, I would appreciate you not telling your little spy story."

There was a moment or two as they all got comfortable around the table. There was the business of getting the servings just right, seeking God's blessing, and then the conversation resumed.

"Uncle Dan, you have been working with the big mucky-mucks. What do they think happened?"

"The facts are really quite simple." Daniel noticed a black speck on his wrist and casually rubbed it away. "The *Imo* was going in ballast to New York."

Emma, fussing with the collar of her dress, asked if Daniel minded being interrupted and would he please explain what "in ballast" meant.

"In ballast means that she didn't have a cargo. Since she was built to travel with a cargo, she doesn't ride very well when she's empty. So, the ship's crew loads extra coal or even rocks, to make the ship sit in the water properly."

"Thank you. So the *Imo* was going to New York in ballast."

"Yes, under charter between her owners and the Belgian Relief Commission." Daniel watched as Joe bent over the table, his face almost in his plate. He was reaching down under the table. It looked like he was scratching himself. "Are you all right, nephew?"

Joe sat up. "Yes, thank you, Uncle Dan. Where was the *Mont Blanc* coming from?" Joe's face was flushed, and he reached down again. This time he kept his head up, facing his uncle.

"The *Mont Blanc* was coming from New York to Halifax with a full cargo." Daniel took a slip of paper out of his pocket. "I wrote down what the cargo was because my wife would want to know all about it." He read from the paper, "She had some 2,500 tons of TNT and a deck load of monochlorobenzene." He replaced the paper in his vest pocket. "The collision took place about mid-channel. The *Imo* was steering down-channel to the sea. The other ship was steaming up-channel through the Narrows to the Basin."

Everyone else at the table was fidgeting. Daniel had a curious feeling that something was going on that he wasn't aware of. "You had a question, Fredrick?"

"What about the weather? I wasn't here, you know. I was in Montreal. Was the weather a factor?"

"There was sufficient visibility, no wind and very little tide."

Fredrick turned his wrist over and looked at it. Frowning, he continued with the conversation. "What do your naval friends think happened?"

"The *Mont Blanc* was in her proper channel up until the very last when she took some evasive action. *Imo*, on the other hand, was travelling too fast and not in her channel. When she reversed, she should have gone over into her own channel. What my friends believe is, the captains allowed the ships to get too close to each other. They should have both gone astern, reversed—the both of them."

Daniel hadn't been conscious of it, but, under the table, he had been scratching his thigh. With an involuntary movement, he began scratching the back of his neck. He restrained himself and, with his hands pressed firmly against his thighs, he sat, very still, while he smiled at the rest of the party. "You were speaking, Emma, of a spy story." The itching was intense! "I know I'm not supposed to ask, Gladys, but I have a normal man's curiosity. What about the spies?"

Emma's eyes just sparkled. She was being given the opportunity of telling one of her favourite stories! "Gladys found a nest of German spies in one of the buildings overlooking the harbour. One day, she was going to the dentist . . ." Emma stopped speaking. She undid the buttons on her sleeve and examined her arm. Daniel could see a ring of red marks on the newly exposed flesh.

Emma stood up.

Gladys, alarmed, asked, "What is wrong, Mother?"

"Gladys! I have fleas!" With the grace of the Dowager Queen, Emma pushed her chair back and left the room. Her last words were, "Gladys! Your house has fleas!"

Joe pushed back his chair, too, and lifted his pant leg. He undid the suspender. Under his stocking there were several of the little devils working on his ankles. "I've got fleas, too!" Suddenly he stood up, scratching his chest, shaking his feet, doing what looked like a jig at the end of the table.

Gladys was mortified. "Fleas! Not in my house!" Her mouth dropped open and she was speechless because, on her white tablecloth, she could see the fleas, dozens of them, jumping around. "Oh Lord! I can see them. There must be hundreds."

"I can't see them," Fredrick said, "but I can certainly feel them."

Daniel laughed.

Gladys was quick to say, "It's not funny, Uncle Dan!"[3]

"It is, really. The Relief Commission sent workmen to fix your house."

"Of course!" Fredrick had taken his coat off and was scratching around his collar. "They brought the sand in and thawed it in this room."

"The fleas were in the sand. This room must be full of them."

Leaving as much of their clothing as they modestly could, everyone left the room.

Gladys said, "I will leave you gentlemen to do what you must. I will assist my Mother upstairs." As she went up the squeaking staircase she said, in mock serious tones, "First the explosion and now fleas at my dinner party. I don't know which is the worse experience!"

Endnotes

1. Actually it was a close friend of the Smallwoods who recovered consciousness to find himself in the morgue . . . and grasped the woman's thigh. I assigned it to Warren. In real life, Warren was found, naked, in the Dockyard the same day. Warren Gray's survival was not immediately made known to his family because he was unable to recall anything about his past for almost a week.

2. One of the neighbours who survived the explosion did disappear after a day or so. I made her the neighbour next door to the Smallwoods. I did not have her name.

3. Daniel wouldn't have been at the Smallwoods' dinner party but one of Gladys' cousins was. I put Daniel at the table instead of another Schwartz. The fleas were there in real life—big time.

Chapter Twenty-Five
Wallace

March 1919
Lord Nelson Hotel
Halifax

The cloakroom attendant accepted Joe's hat, coat, and cane. "You're not one of our regulars, Mister . . . ?"

"Smallwood." He slipped off his spat rubbers and handed them to her.

"I'll be sure to remember you the next time you bring your custom to the Lord Nelson, Mister Smallwood."

"Thank you." Joe checked his reflection in the mirrored door. He frowned at what he saw. "Soon won't be able to tell who's the pregnant one in the Smallwood household, me or Gladys," he said *sotto voce*. He patted his middle and then tried to smooth his vest over his rounded belly.

"I'm sorry sir, were you speaking to me?" the young lady asked with concern in her voice.

"Harrumph! What I meant to say, I am expecting a guest in the next few minutes. Would you send him into the lounge when he arrives? He'll be a handsome young army officer with lots of medals." He smiled at her. "Just the kind of man you girls adore."

"I might not let him get past me, sir," she said with a shy smile.

"No, that will never do. I do want to see him." Joe waved as he departed but then turned. With a broad smile he lowered his voice again. "I could send him back to you when we have had our reunion, young lady."

She laughed, but then put on a straight face as the floor-walker came her way. She busied herself putting away Joe's belongings under the glare of the officious-looking older man in a hotel uniform.

Ten minutes later, when Joe was seated in the lounge, Wallace Smallwood entered accompanied by the young lady who pointed in Joe's direction. She curtsied before she departed, which surprised Joe until he saw the floorwalker lurking in the lobby.

Joe rose. *My God! Wallace has a limp!* Joe extended his hand while trying to measure the changes in his old friend. "You're lookin' great!" *Wallace is no thicker through the waist than when we were at Valcartier.* The cousins shook hands. Joe could feel the deep scars and immediately relaxed his grip. Embarrassed by his limp handshake, Joe professed that Wallace looked the same as ever while thinking, *I wonder how he got those heavy scars on his neck.* Joe looked away so as not to stare but then thought better of it. He put on a broad smile and stood back a pace, pretending to give Wallace the "once over." Wallace still had a full head of hair like most of the Smallwood cousins but patches of it were pure white. Joe's face must have revealed what he was thinking—*Wallace has been badly wounded.* "You're a sight for sore eyes."

"Yeah, it's good to see you too, Joe." He rubbed his scalp with his right hand which showed heavy, heavy scarring as he laughingly said; "I bobbed when I shoulda weaved. Got a load of shrapnel. Lucky for me my face was covered. Mother always said my face was my fortune."

Joe laughed. "Have you been home yet?"

"No, I'm just passing through now. Came off the *Empress of India* last night. You were the first person I called. Tonight I leave for Newcastle where I will be demobbed."

"Well, let's sit and get caught up. Of course, the important thing is, you won the war."

"And you married a Halifax girl. Schwartz Tea and Coffee. Wow! Talk about falling into a barrel of shit and coming up smelling roses! I thought you were interested in that Bourgeois lady. At least, that's the last word I had from you." Wallace assumed a stern look and shook his head from side to side, going *tsk, tsk.* "You promised to write."

"What made you pick the Lord Nelson?" Joe wasn't going to get involved in a discussion of who owed whom what.

Wallace seemed to agree; letting bygones be bygones was good tactics. "I don't know the city but I was told that the Lord Nelson was the best and it was close to the new train station."

"They advertise a lot." Joe took a deep breath. "I married Gladys Schwartz in 1917 and now we are expecting our first child."

"A boy, of course."

"Of course."

"I have my own business and a home on one of the new streets, Walnut Street."

"The war was good for you," Wallace said, with a small edge to his voice.

Joe didn't flinch. "The war was good for both of us; I have a business and you ended up an officer. Neither of us would have achieved that without the war."[1]

Wallace turned that over in his mind. "I had two good friends." Wallace stopped and looked down at the scars on his hand. He raised both hands and placed them on the table in full view. "I think you met both of them. Albert was French . . ."

"I didn't get to know any of the French boys."

"Ned was the one who called everyone 'jack.' You remember him?"

"Yes, I do. Nice fellow."

"You think my being an officer was an achievement . . . a sort of reward for being a good soldier." Before Joe could respond, Wallace said, "I became an officer as a way to survive."

When Joe made no comment, Wallace began telling Albert's story. When he had finished he said, "Albert died because someone else decided where he should be and what he should do. He had no chance at all."

"I see."

"You probably don't . . . but let me tell you about Ned. Ned became frightened. He thought he could pick his duty and avoid the Grim Reaper. The officers kept pushing him back into the fighting so that he could . . ." Wallace's voice was loaded with sarcasm as he listed the reasons the officers gave for returning Ned to the battle, time after time: "face his devils, be a good soldier, wipe the yellow streak off the middle of his back, not let his comrades down, go get the dirty Hun, do his duty . . ."

Joe interrupted, "I get the idea, Wallace."

It was as if Wallace didn't hear him. ". . . fight for the honour of the Empire, win the war . . ." Here he stopped. "Win the war? After a while, it was just a matter of doing what you could to stay alive one more day."

Wallace flipped the ribbons on his chest. He seemed to want to say something but didn't.

Joe didn't break the silence.

Finally, Wallace spoke. "Albert was killed by a Canadian gun. Tough luck." He sighed, "I was wounded by Canadian artillery. A mistake in fusing and I almost bought it." He paused again. "Ned was abandoning his gun position and was probably shot by one of our outriders. They did that kind of thing, you know." He flipped the ribbons again. "Albert's and Ned's families probably got medals just like these." Wallace moved his hands back into his lap. "I got to be an officer and I get to talk about it." He stopped again.

Joe thought the officer was going to cry.

"I get to dream about it, too." With despair Wallace asked, "How often do I have to live it over? It never stops! I live it over and over."

"What do the doctors say?"

"They tell me the dreams will go away if I get on with my life."

"So, what are you going to do with your life?"

Without hesitation Wallace declared, "I am going to marry Vera and move to the United States. I am going to study pharmacy and start my own business so that when the dreams come, I will know the proper drug to make the dreams go away."

Joe recognized the humour in his cousin's voice and managed a laugh.

"And do you know what I am the most thankful for, Joe?" Again, he didn't wait. "I'm thankful that you got out of the army at Valcartier. I am glad you got out right then . . . because there was only one officer position available in our battery and, being so much alike—the two of us—you would have tried for it the same as I did. One of us wouldn't be sitting here today.

Joe Smallwood looked his cousin right in the eye. "And I know which one it would have been, Wallace."

Wallace Smallwood met his cousins' stare, eyeball to eyeball. "You have no idea just how much the war changed me, Joe."

"Maybe not." Joe picked up the menu. "We should order. I can't send you back to the Miramichi without a good meal. Aunt Mary Anne isn't there any more to stuff you with great food."

"She died?"

"No one wrote you?"

"They might have, but . . ."

For the next hour, they talked about nothing but their wonderful boyhood memories of the Miramichi.

Endnotes

1. In real life, Wallace Smallwood held the rank of officer cadet when he was demobilized. He did marry Vera and ran a pharmacy business.

Chapter Twenty-Six
David

January 1920
Lord Nelson Hotel
Halifax

Joe walked through the lobby of the Lord Nelson Hotel. He remembered the cloakroom attendant from his last visit when he had met Wallace and wondered if she would remember him. He was disappointed. She wasn't there. The young man who took his outer clothing and spat rubbers was wearing a First Division button on the lapel of his hotel uniform.

"You must be a returning veteran."

"Yes. They kept my job open for me while I was in France."

"What's it like, being back?"

"This was a good job when I was a youngster but I find it hard to support my wife on what they pay here. I'm on the lookout for . . ." He busied himself with putting Joe's things away.

Joe expected to see the old floorwalker but he wasn't totally surprised to find another veteran in the floorwalker's uniform. "I'm expecting a guest in the next few minutes, a sergeant. Would you please direct him to my table? I'll be in the lounge."

The floorwalker gave Joe a slight bow. "Yes, of course, sir. I'll be pleased to look after it personally." He rocked a little, toes to heel, standing in front of Joe.

Joe recognized the stance. If ever a man was looking for a tip, this was one. Joe fished into his vest pocket and tossed the floorwalker a dime.

"Thank you, sir. And the sergeant's name is?"

"Smallwood."

"I'll see to it, sir."

Joe wandered into the lounge. The convenient table near the door he had used with Wallace was occupied so he was led to another table. He spent the next half-hour wondering why David James Smallwood had bothered to call him. When Sergeant Smallwood finally did arrive, it was the first thing Joe asked him.

"Why me, David?"

"You're the only person I called, Joe, and I wouldn't have bothered you but I wanted to pay you the money I owe." He handed Joe three five-dollar bills.

"Well, this is a surprise!"

"Shouldn't be!" He paused before he said with great sarcasm, "You know I would have to pay you back or my reputation in the Smallwood family would be ruined."

"As if you care?"

"You're right. I don't much care." David allowed the waiter to pull his chair back. David sat down. "But I won't bother you for long. I just wanted to say I appreciated your help with the books."

"You're here; why not have something to eat?"

"Fine. I'm in no rush. "

They chose from the menu and, when the waiter had gone, Joe asked, "Did you get put behind a gun?"

"No. I was transferred to the Canadian Army Pay Corps." He leaned back in his chair. "What a hell of a war! I worked at the Pay Office in London on full pay and a subsistence allowance of three dollars and thirty-five cents a month. Didn't miss a revue or a girlie show."

Joe was trying to remember the name of the lady that . . .

"Her name was Tyhurst, Mrs. Edith Tyhurst, and, before you ask, I terminated my pay assignment to that woman as soon as I could." David rubbed his chin as he remembered, "I could've kept sending her the five dollars . . . I had plenty of money as a pay accounts NCO . . . but the bitch had been out to get me so I cut her off the very first time my officer gave me a good report." David snickered. "She wrote my commanding officer a couple of times but I told him my debt to the woman was paid. I told him that all those things she said in the letters were lies. I told him it was just a bald attempt to weasel money out of a simple clerk. Anyhow, two letters and she was history."[1]

Joe couldn't find much to say. They were both hungry and devoured the tasty chowder that was the specialty of the lounge.

"Anything new in your life, Joe?" David asked as he wiped his chin with the napkin.

Joe beamed at the thought of his baby. "I have a daughter named Crystal Edith and we are expecting another baby soon."

"A boy, of course."

"We certainly hope so. What about your family? Are you going home to see them?"

"No."

The waiter cleared away the dishes. Joe was wondering whether he should take David home to meet Gladys and see the baby when David interrupted his train of thought.

"Don't concern yourself with me, Joe. I arrived last night on the *S.S. Carmania*. I leave tomorrow on the Maritime Express. I will be employed in the Ottawa Pay Office until the boys are all demobbed and the pay records are put to bed and then I'm off to Victoria where I will be demobbed, myself."

"So you won't be going home."

"I'm not going to Newfoundland, if that's what you mean." David signalled to the waiter. "I don't have many plans. I intend to pay for this meal as a gesture of thanks to Joseph Smallwood, my saviour." When Joe started to protest, David made shushing motions with his hands. "Without those books, Joe, I would be a dead man today." To the waiter he said, "So, I will pay for our little repast." When the waiter hurried off, David continued with the details of his plans. "The Dartmouth woman wrote to me all the time I was in England. I plan to go see her tonight. And, finally, when I am demobbed in Victoria, I will go to San Francisco where I will happily spend the rest of my days with nary a thought of Newfoundland."[2]

David Smallwood paid the bill. When the men reached the street, David shook Joe's hand. "Thanks again, Joe."

The two men went their separate ways.

Endnotes

1. It is recorded at the National Archives that David did, indeed, terminate the pay assignment to Mrs. Tyhurst. Details such as his living off allowance are factual.

2. David James Smallwood's last known address was in San Francisco according to his demobilization file. In *I Chose Canada* Joey Smallwood wrote that the family lost touch with David after 1915.

Chapter Twenty-Seven
Out of the Lions' Den

July 1921
Moncton

"They going to give you a gold watch?" The secretary for the Manager, Maritimes Division of the Canadian National Railway, smiled up at the grey-haired man waiting to be admitted. "I hear you're retiring."

"No, not today. Next Friday is my last day."

She butted her cigarette and indicated a chair. "Please sit down, Mister Smallwood. I'll see if the boss is ready for you."

"Thank you, Miss Milton. These days I'm in no rush."

Daniel sat down. He thought of the first time he had come to this building. *The man's name was . . . Russell. Then there was that Price fellow, and they seem to be getting younger each year. Certainly, now that the ICR is a part of the Canadian National Railway, the "big boss" is no longer in Moncton. They're always sending someone down from Upper Canada to run the show, anyway. Some Upper Canadian gets the cushy job.* Daniel sniffed. *Yes, and they always smoke the big cigars.* He got up and looked out the window. *It's time I quit; I'm getting cynical.* He corrected himself. *I'm allowed to be anything I want. I'm sixty-five and don't look a day over seventy.* He strained his eyes to see better through the window. *That might be Duke walking across the yard . . . but it couldn't be; Duke is locomotive foreman in Newcastle. He wouldn't be in Moncton.*

"You may go in now, Mister Smallwood." She gave him a nice smile. "You were right about not getting the watch today. He has a file he wants you to read."

Daniel was ever anxious when he was called upon to read something and give an opinion. It was a holdover from the old days when he couldn't read; at least, he couldn't read very much. Sure enough, as he entered the big office, the man was holding a file out for him to take.

325

Daniel grunted. *No formalities, no niceties. This one is all business. Can't wait to finish his time in the backwoods of New Brunswick and return to where the action is.* "Yes, Mister Nelson. You wanted to see me?"

"Have a seat. I want you to read this file. Tell me what you know about it."

Daniel took the file. He sat down. "How have you been, sir?"

"Just fine. You were in Halifax about the time of the explosion back in '17."

"Yes, I was. I left Halifax the day before and returned with the Boston Relief Train three days later."

"Please read the page with the tag on it."

"I'm sorry, sir. I left my glasses at my desk. I can go get them if you like." Daniel stood up to leave but the young man waved him to remain seated.

He took the file from the older man. "I can read the portions that apply. This letter is from the Justice Department."

> "The tug *Hilford* was washed by the wave caused by the explosion onto the top of Pier No. 9 the property of the Canadian Government Railways. The Officer in Charge of the work of restoration for that Department states that he endeavoured for some time to locate the owners of the vessel but was unable to do so. The hull was absolutely useless. It was then destroyed, the engines, pump and boilers were salved and are now in store and may be recovered by submitting proof of ownership."

"I remember *S.S. Hilford*." Daniel didn't like the cigar smoke. It seemed to aggravate his cough. He coughed. "I saw her moored at Pier 8 on the fifth of December."

The manager continued reading from the file, skipping along, selecting the parts that interested him.

" . . . not chartered by the Canadian Government Railways or the Department of Defence. After being used for some time in North Sydney, it was ordered to Halifax where it arrived early in July of 1917. The boat was valued at $7000.00. Reportedly, the crew was killed."

Mister Nelson stopped reading when Daniel said, "Oh!" Nelson regarded his employee, waiting to see if there would be any meaningful comment.

In his mind's eye, Daniel could see the boy with the red hair manfully hanging on to the handle of the trunk. *So, Cameron . . . what was his first name? Robert, I think. So, little Robert Cameron is dead.* Daniel raised his head. "I think the captain would have survived. His name was Gordon."

"Gordon is the gentleman who has hired the solicitors. He claims that during the salvage, the agents of the Government damaged what was left of his ship, reducing her value to $2,000. Justice has ordered the Canadian Government railways to turn over the salvaged machinery to the Captain if he can prove ownership but Gordon has refused to accept it. He says that the last time he saw his ship, she was at Pier 8 engaged in active service for the Royal Navy. The next time he sees her, she's in pieces scattered around a rail yard. He has filed suit against officers of this railway."

"There must have been marine insurance; can't Gordon make a claim for the full value of his ship?"

"In the terms of the charter, there were provisions made— an allowance in the fees charged—for the owner to arrange his own insurance."

"Let me get this straight. In chartering *Hilford*, the British allowed a sum for insurance . . .

" . . . but it is doubtful whether any ordinary insurance would have covered such a loss." Nelson checked the file. "The owner carried his own insurance on account of the high rates demanded."

"Which means, Gordon took the risk because he couldn't afford the insurance."

"Yes."

Daniel breathed a long sigh. "What does this have to do with me?"

"Ah, yes. The Justice Department demands evidence of ownership from Captain Gordon. He doesn't have much left. Most of it was on the ship."

"So, I can't help there."

"Gordon claims that he spoke of owning the ship with you the day before the explosion. He believes that you saw him act in the capacity of captain and owner and might be able to describe his relationship with the crew and the harbour authorities."

"Will that help him?"

"It will be to his advantage if you confirmed his claim . . . but . . . our Justice Department solicitors . . . doubt very much that he would have spoken to you about owning *Hilford.* They also doubt that you would have been close enough to his boat for a long enough period to gain any impression about his role with the harbour authorities."

"I suppose the difficulty is that most of the people he would have worked with are dead."

"Yes. The courts do not have much to go on in these cases. A statement such as yours has more significance than it would have had in more normal times."

"There wasn't much left of *Hilford* when I saw her on the eighth of December."

"Good! You can say that in court. It will help the Railway's case." Nelson rubbed his hands together. "There are so very few witnesses. Justice will be pleased that I found you." He continued rubbing his hands. "They will certainly be pleased." He repeated what Daniel had said with a great deal of pleasure. "Not much left! Not much left. That's good, good."

"What about the Halifax Relief Commission? They have money to help people overcome their losses."

"The Relief Commission passed the problem along to the Marine Underwriters. The Underwriters have written," Mister Nelson turned to the file and read from it, "liability for loss has been rendered invalid by the allowance made for the insurance."

"A seven thousand dollar ship becomes how much?"

"Approximately two thousand dollars' worth of ship's parts scattered about the rail yard."

Daniel took out a cigarette and lit it. He could still see the flushed face of the Cameron boy; so pleased to be part of the boat's crew, dead now. He remembered Captain Gordon, now needing more help than lifting a trunk full of books. "What does the Company want me to do?"

"Gordon has called you as a witness. Go, be his witness."

"Because?"

"Justice doesn't believe that you have any information about ownership of *Hilford* that will help the dear Captain."

"And?"

"No ownership, no lawsuit."

Daniel's cigarette tasted flat. He stubbed it out. "I would have to say that he acted with his crew and the harbour authorities as I would expect an owner to act."

Nelson stubbed his cigar.

Daniel thought, *we are certainly ruining some good smokes around here.* "If he proves ownership and then wins the case, what is the difference to the Crown?"

"Since the good captain is refusing to accept the boat's salvaged parts, if he won the case, we would have to pay him what the boat was worth, sitting on Pier 9, right after the explosion."

"And I am probably the only railroad employee who can give an opinion that a judge would appreciate. After all, I saw her, real close, on the eighth."

"The boys at Justice feel that you wouldn't have an opinion contrary to that posed by the government's solicitors."

"I don't like the government's solicitors."

Mister Nelson sat behind the desk. He pulled a note pad from the middle drawer. He scribbled a few lines. "This is my note to Justice that I recommend, based on this interview, that the government's case would be hurt by your presence at

Halifax. If Captain Gordon persists, a settlement should be made in favour of the good captain."[1]

"Is that all, sir?"

"Yes, I think it is." Nelson accompanied Daniel to the office door. He opened it for Daniel and ushered him out. "This is your last week with the road?"

"Yes, it is."

Nelson shook hands with Daniel. "I guess that's all, then. Good luck."

As he left the main building, probably for the last time, Daniel had the thought that, maybe, *S.S. Hilford* had acquired another casualty—Daniel Smallwood's gold watch.

At the end of the week, he did re-enter the main building. All of his old-time friends were there, including his brother from Newcastle and as many of the men of the Giles family as were still living. Daniel made a little speech, accepted his gold watch, and left.

Hannah was waiting in a hire cab. She pushed the door open and patted the seat beside her. Daniel hesitated, turning his head to look back at the windows of the administration building.

"What's wrong?"

"Daniel has escaped the lion's den, sweetheart. We did it. We did it together."

Endnotes

1. The details of this chapter are taken from the Archive's files, but the files don't give a conclusion to the legal dispute. I truly hope Captain Gordon won.

Chapter Twenty-Eight
All Good Things . . .

May 1924
The Lodge, Miramichi River

"It's too bad your Jean couldn't come, Duke. Hannah would have liked her company."

"Jean hasn't been here since our honeymoon; didn't expect her to want to come this time, either."

"Will we be fishin' again today?"

Duke Smallwood paused on the path they were walking. He looked back at the sun-dappled river where they had been fishing. "It's great, isn't it?"

Daniel, breathing heavily, appreciated the opportunity to take a rest. "Yeah, it sure is God's Country." They stood, listening to the sounds of the forest until Duke thought his brother had regained his breath enough to continue walking back to the Lodge.

"No, I don't think we'll come down again today, Danny. We've got some things to talk over."

"Like what?"

They were approaching the bench the boys had built for old W.F. during his last years at the Lodge. Duke pointed at the bench. Daniel nodded his head and the brothers sat down.

Duke reached in his knapsack and pulled out two bottles of beer. "They might be a trifle warm by now, but they're wet."

"Sounds good to me."

Duke produced a bottle key and released the caps, handed one bottle over, and sipped from the other.

Daniel waited for his brother to speak.

"W.F. left his share of the Lodge to his sons—the last surviving son to take title."

"Yeah, I know, little brother. However, if I have to fight you for it, you can have it, right now!"

They laughed.

"You're still too big for me, Little William."

"No one has called me that since Aunt Mary Anne died."

The laughter and good feelings faded. They both sipped their beer.

Duke finally brought up what was on his mind. "Some Americans have offered a great deal of money for the Lodge and our fishing rights on the river."

"W.F.'s old partners have agreed?"

"Yep. Max Aitken agreed with the proviso that the Smallwood boys be given the opportunity to buy the partners out."

Daniel shook his head. "I can't buy them out."

"Neither can I."

Daniel looked up the incline at the Lodge. "God! It's beautiful." He drank his beer. "I'm glad we had the morning on the river before you told me."

"I thought it would be nice."

"Just the two of us left."

Duke looked a trifle self-conscious as he admitted, "I didn't know Silas very well."

"Silas was . . ." Daniel had meant to say something but changed his mind. "Mother said that we must speak well of the dead." Squinting his eyes as if he were trying to look back in time Daniel finally said, "Lenny was always defending me against Silas."

"Mary Anne said Silas could be a bully, given half a chance."

"What about our sisters?"

"The Lodge was to pass to the last surviving son."

"But . . ."

Duke smiled at his brother. "I always liked you, Daniel. He patted Daniel's hand. "Yes, we should do something about our sisters."

"Do you know where Sophia is?"

"No, kinda lost touch. Her last name was Menzie and she was living in Manitoba."

"Dru and Aylane are gone . . ."

"There's Marcella and Kate."

"So, we split it four ways?"[1]

"I think so. But to be fair, I suggest the money goes in the bank. We can put some advertisements in the Manitoba papers. If Sophia gets in touch, we can split it five ways. If not, after say, six months, we split four ways."

Duke stood up.

Daniel, with a bit of effort, stood.

They shook hands and continued their way to the Lodge where Hannah was waiting.

"What are you going to do with your money, Duke?"

"I thought I'd buy a new car, a Chevrolet this time. Then I would give the rest of the money to Joe. He wants to start a chain of grocery stores." Glancing sideways at Daniel, Duke asked, "What will you be doin' with yours?"

"Lucy and Sade are married and doing well. Wallace came back from the war as an officer. He now owns a drug manufacturing business in Boston. None of them need the money."

"And Jack?"

"Our Jack is still a section hand on the railway."

"You'll give all that money to Jack?"

"Probably, if Hannah agrees. What about you? Will Jean agree to your plans?"

They had reached the Lodge. The men could hear Hannah bustling around in the kitchen. Duke paused at the first step to the veranda. "Jean doesn't care about things any more. She uses her possessions to buy moments of peace."

"Who sells her peace?"

"There's only Lottie Borland around. Jean doesn't see anyone but Lottie."

"Is that wise?"

"Lottie is good to her. Jean feels a sense of contentment when she rewards Lottie for the happy times." Taking the second step, Duke said, "I think it would be wise to give the money directly to Joe because, when I am gone, what Jean has, Lottie will have."

Hannah must have heard them on the steps. As they came across the veranda she called out, "How was the fishing for the Smallwood boys?"

"Aren't you worried about this . . . woman . . . Lottie?" In a louder voice, Daniel answered Hannah, "The fishing was great!"

"Lottie loves Jean. Lottie is very grasping, but she loves Jean. I am not unhappy about that." Duke threw his knapsack onto the table. "Now, who's going to prepare this fish?"

Hannah came out of the kitchen. She was still a handsome woman. Her hair was pure white and she was a little bent at the shoulders, but she was a striking woman. "Who do you think?" She handed the men a bucket with two knives in it.

Endnotes

1. I do not know how the matters of the Lodge were resolved because, by the time I was writing this part, there was no one left to ask and I found no correspondence or records.

Chapter Twenty-Nine
Joey

April 1925
Halifax

Gladys Smallwood stood in the foyer of her home at 159 Oxford Street. She had been working all day long on the cash at the Gottingen Street store so she was quick to kick off her shoes and release the stays on her corset. She pulled two large pins from her hat and carefully placed her picture hat on the calling card table near the front door. Then she stuck the pins into the ribbon at the back of the hat where she could easily find them. Gladys could hear Joe whistling as he threw the canvas dust cover over the car. *I don't understand that man's infatuation with fast cars . . . and he babies them . . .* The door to the garage slammed shut. The whistling proceeded down the sidewalk to the kitchen entrance. *I hope the maid left the back door unlocked. If Joe is as tired as I am . . .* She didn't want him to have to walk all the way around to the front door. Thinking ahead, she remembered that Mrs. Norwood had said there would be cold cuts in the icebox—*so it'll be a cold supper.* Gladys Smallwood sighed. *I hate maid's night off.*

"Nanny Jane!"

A voice from the children's bedroom responded instantly, "Yes, Mrs. Smallwood. The children are here with me."

Gladys heard the kitchen door open and then close. She knew that Joe would go right to the icebox for a drink of milk; his stomach wasn't getting any better.

The children were running down the hall. Of course Crystal, the five-year-old, reached her first.

"Mother! Nanny Jane will tell you it wasn't my fault!"

Gladys could see that Crystal had been crying. She glanced down the hall to check on the condition of the little one. Jean, at two years, always seemed fragile—perhaps

335

vulnerable was a better word. *Jean is such a beautiful and loving child.* Gladys caught herself right away: *not to say that Crystal isn't lovable—but she is always so busy and full of mischief!*

"Come here, darlings. Wipe your eyes, Crystal, no! Not with the hem of your dress! Nanny Jane will . . ."

The doorknocker squeaked and then thudded dully on the brass plate.[1]

"Joe! You'll have to go to the door! It's the maid's day off and Nanny and I are busy for the moment."

Joe Smallwood came up the hall. Fortunately, he hadn't undone his tie or removed his suit coat. Gladys stopped him and wiped the milk off his upper lip with her finger. She gave him a gentle push toward the door, patting his shoulder as he went past.

"Let's go to the playroom, ladies, while Daddy sees who's at the front door." Gladys picked up the little one. Nanny Jane took Crystal's hand. Just before they turned the corner of the hall, Gladys looked back at the front door. Joe had opened the door, wide. Standing there was a dapper little man with a beak-like nose. The stranger was extending his hand to introduce himself. *I don't recognize him from anywhere.* She put Jean down and shooed the children ahead of her into the playroom. *Did that stranger just introduce himself as Joey Smallwood?* Gladys shook her head. *No. I must have misheard him.* She smiled a sly little smile. *And Joe doesn't like being called Joey . . . not even from me. That stranger is off to a bad start.* Gladys closed the panelled sliding doors behind her.

At the door, Joe Smallwood was slow to accept the extended hand.

The stranger reached down, took Joe's hand in his, and shook it vigorously. "I'm Joey Smallwood, your cousin. Our grandfathers were brothers. I'm on my way back from New York City to Newfoundland and took the opportunity to . . ."

"I'm sorry. I guess your name took me by surprise. Please come in." Joe allowed the smaller man to enter and then glanced quickly at the street to see if there was a vehicle. There wasn't. *No luggage, either.*

Joey Smallwood kept right on talking. "They were good friends, as well as brothers. My grandfather, David, built the first steam sawmill in Newfoundland while your grandfather, William Frederick, was making a fortune in New Brunswick shipping . . . not that my part of the family did poorly."

Joey entered the front room and surveyed the furnishings. Picking the most comfortable-looking chair, he sat down. "Particularly after the Governor of Newfoundland, Captain Sir Henry Prescott, authorized a road building program. You knew that your grandmother was a Prescott?" Without waiting for a reply, he continued, "Yes, the roads were a boon for the Newfoundland Smallwoods. My grandfather sold out at Gambo where he held title to a number of wood lots. Made a tidy sum! Took the proceeds and built a boot factory right in Saint John's . . . on Water Street. You've heard of *Smallwood's Boots*?" Joey crossed his legs and settled back into the chair.

Joe Smallwood, indicating that he hadn't heard of *Smallwood's Boots*, chose a chair just off to one side of the visitor. Joe noticed that there was a hole in the sole of the visitor's lifted boot and the boot was very much down at the heel.

"Yessir! They were the best fisherman's boots that money could buy!" Joey leaned forward to make his point. "David Smallwood's boots were made of leather and, if they were properly greased, they would last a lifetime!" He stroked his chin. "My grandfather was very proud of his boots. He used to tell the story of a customer who had a complaint . . ."

Gladys Smallwood entered the room. Both men rose to their feet.

"May I introduce my wife, Gladys. Gladys, this is Mister Joseph Smallwood . . ."

"Just call me Joey, Missus. Just call me Joey."

Gladys took a chair on the same side of the room as her husband. "Well . . . Joey . . ."

"I was just saying to Cousin Joe here, that my grandfather made leather boots. Remember now, they had to be greased; if they weren't greased, they would crack and fall apart.

Granddad told the story of the customer who claimed a pair of our boots had fallen off his feet! Granddad said"—and here Joey Smallwood assumed a deeper, more resonant voice—"of course they did—you smothered them in grease and they rotted off your feet!"

Turning his head to the other side of the conversation and speaking in a higher, more colourful voice, Joey went on with the anecdote. "No, sirree! I did not put any grease on them!"

Returning to the deeper voice, Joey slapped his thigh with the flat of his hand. "Right! And that's why you had trouble with your boots!"

Joey laughed at his story. "You can't put much past David Smallwood! He has a quick wit even as old as he is." Regarding his audience, Joey smiled. "The man is a treasure, a real treasure . . . always seeing the humour in things."[2]

Joe and Gladys made polite sounds, Gladys seizing the opportunity to comment that they hadn't eaten yet and perhaps Mister Smallwood—Joey—would join them for a simple meal.

"Just sit back and relax, dearie. I came to talk, not to eat, and I'm not nearly half finished, yet."

Joe Smallwood pulled out a cigarette package and offered one to his guest, who merely signalled with his hand that he would decline as Joey continued with his monologue.

"Now, my father, Charles William, was another kind of man. He always said that if it looked like rum, and smelled like rum, then Charles William Smallwood could tell you if it had tasted like rum! He lived the life of a salesman, chartering sailing vessels and taking his father's wares to the principal ports along the coasts." At this point, Joey seemed to pause. He sucked his teeth and looked into the eyes of his cousin. "Drink ruined his life. You don't have the habit, Cousin?"

Joe Smallwood jerked upright at this opportunity to speak. "No! I mean, I like a drink at political rallies."

Gladys interrupted. "What he means to say is we have no demon rum in this house, neither near the children nor near our business." Gladys stood up. Both men rose. "Please remain seated, gentlemen. It is our servant's night off but she had left something prepared for us. I will set the table. Hungry or not, Mister Smallwood, I presume you will at least sit with us as we eat?" Gladys nodded at both men as she left for the kitchen.

Joey watched the lady of the house leave the room. "A striking woman, Cousin. Never did I see such lovely hair; not red and not brown. Auburn?" Without waiting, Joey started again.

"Your Missus mentioned *our* business as if you are the sole owners."

"Yes. I used to have a partner but I now have a grocery store at a prime location in the city." Joe leaned forward, intent on continuing. "We bought all the latest equipment." He held his arms wide. "The meat section is twelve feet wide, refrigerated and with glass . . ."

"Yes, yes. I didn't realize just how successful you are. As for me, I was a journalist for a New York daily newspaper. I decided it was time to return to Newfoundland; to go back to where the name 'Smallwood' means something. I intend to start a . . ."

Gladys appeared at the archway beckoning the two men to join her in the dining room. They rose and quietly followed her.

Gladys had been busy. The candelabra pair was flanked by a tall, ornate glass pickle jar, enclosed with a silver frame, and a long silver celery dish. An array of serving pieces, glasses, and plates made a very attractive setting for what Gladys had promised would be a simple meal. "Please be seated, Joe, on my right and . . . Joey . . . on my left in the European fashion, if you will."

Both men assisted the lady with her chair.

"It's not much," Gladys apologized as she handed the crystal bowl of potato salad to the guest. "We have the salad, some greens, ham, and cold roast beef. The bread I brought home from the store this evening. It should be fresh."

"Yes. We have fresh bread every morning." Joe smiled, his hands making an expansive gesture while he proudly proclaimed to his newly found relative, "Our clients come from blocks away to see . . ."

Gladys gave Joe "the look." "That will be enough business talk for today, Joseph."

"Yes. Excuse me, my sweet. I shouldn't bring business to the table." He cast a quick glance at the visitor but Joey seemed not to have noticed the family moment.

Joey Smallwood had a good appetite. As he ate, he asked questions about Joe's father.

"Your father, Young William Frederick, worked on the railroad?"

"Yes." Joe offered some more cold cuts to the guest. He accepted.

"I would much like to speak to him. He can be of great assistance to me in my grand campaign for Newfoundland. I need to talk to someone who knows the railroad and who cares about the best interests of the working man."

Joe looked up from his plate. "There's nobody better than my Dad, then. He complained to the railway management about the way the brakemen had to risk their lives every day— needlessly risk their lives—when a little bit of equipment would have made their work a lot safer. Why, even when he was the locomotive foreman . . ."

"Your father was the locomotive foreman?"

"Yes. There isn't anything he doesn't know about running the railroad."

"Well, a foreman wouldn't be of much help to me." Joey Smallwood put his linen napkin back into the silver ring shaped like a squirrel eating a nut. He examined the napkin holder for a moment and then went on. "You must understand that I am a social . . ."

There was a timid knock at the sliding doors to the dining room. The door moved easily some several inches and an attractive woman with a white headdress could be seen holding back two children who were intent upon entering the dining area.

"Oh yes, let them in, Nanny Jane."

The bigger child curtsied to the visitor but the younger

one threw herself into her father's arms and babbled about a big, big moose.

Gladys explained that the children had seen a big moose walk past the veranda at a friend's farmhouse in New Brunswick. "She's been excited about it ever since. Everything is moose right now." Turning to the children, Gladys told them to say hello to their Cousin Joey. The girls curtsied and were soon gone after Daddy promised to come tell bedtime stories. Little Jean wanted a moose story.

In the quiet that followed with the closing of the panelled doors, Joe asked, "You were about to say?"

Joey lifted his chin. "I was a journalist for 'The Call,' a socialist newspaper. I am a socialist."

The other two Smallwoods busied themselves with their food.

Joe, without looking up, commented, "As a businessman I am against socialism—what with all the stuff about unions and the fighting for so-called rights."

Joey Smallwood took a deep breath. "I came to you, Cousin, because I am returning to Newfoundland where I plan to have a large say in the destiny of that country. I intend to have the power to make things better for Newfoundlanders. As a start, it is my plan to organize the section men on the railroad."

"You want to organize the section men?"

"Union or non-union is of no matter. It's a business proposition I offer you plain and simple. You lend me five hundred dollars and I will get it back to you, tenfold, in no time at all." Joey waved his hand around. "You won't miss the five hundred dollars and it's a sure-fire investment."

Joe Smallwood stopped eating. "You want me to lend you five hundred dollars so you can go to Newfoundland and organize a union?"

There was silence in the room. Gladys regarded the two men: her husband: tall, dark and handsome with a smile that could warm the coldest heart, and this pip-squeak of a man, slight with flowery mannerisms that Gladys found to be oddly appealing. They were so different in appearance and yet there was a strong resemblance. She could see that they were opposites in pretty well everything else, too. She wondered what her Joe would do. She wasn't long in finding out.

"Have you finished your meal, sir?"

Joey Smallwood indicated that he had.

"This is a business matter. We should adjourn to the front room." Joe stood up. "Excuse us, Gladys."

The men went into the front room. Joe closed the doors.

Gladys could hear the voices, one deeper and more resonant than the other. Before too long, the deeper voice was raised loud enough for Gladys to hear her husband say, "In a pig's eye!"

There was more discussion and then the sliding doors were forcefully parted. Gladys could hear her husband as he opened the front door. "Take your leftist ideas to Newfoundland. Don't try any of your socialist tactics in my city!"

Joey wasn't giving up. "You're a businessman. Think of it as an investment . . . a good investment!"

"I'm not going to give it another thought. Good night, sir!"

After a pause, the front door closed.

Gladys waited for Joe to come down the hall. When he approached, she put her arms around him.

"That must have been hard, darling. After all, he is a cousin. The Smallwood family is very small. When you think . . ." Gladys stopped. She could feel her husband's shoulders shaking. Concerned that her Joe was crying, she pushed back from his embrace to gaze into his eyes. Joe Smallwood was laughing!

"What is so funny, Joe?"

Joe put his arm around her waist and continued down the hall toward the bedroom.

"I don't like socialists. They're every bit as dangerous as those communists we hear about." He put his hand under his wife's chin and gently turned her face to his. He kissed her lightly on the lips. With his other hand he stroked her gorgeous hair.

Joe smiled into her eyes. "You want to know the funny part? He almost had me talked into it!"

It was Gladys' turn to laugh. "He said he didn't come to eat; he came to talk . . . and he did talk!" Gladys snuggled her nose into her husband's neck as she whispered, "And it was exciting to listen to him."

Joe playfully spanked Gladys. "That's enough about Joey Smallwood. Forget about him! I want you to pay attention to *this* Joe Smallwood!"

"Yes, dear."

Endnotes

1. Joey Smallwood's visit to the Oxford Street home was related to the author by Joe Smallwood during the Christmas season of 1949.

2. I had little information as to the nature of the small talk that occurred at the 1925 meeting, so I patterned the conversation on information and impressions that Elaine Smallwood conveyed to me after a two-hour visit with Joey in the Chateau Laurier Hotel in Ottawa (1976). Joseph (Joey) Smallwood recounted the greasy boots story in his book *I Chose Canada*, published in 1973 by Macmillan Company of Canada Ltd.

Chapter Thirty
Danny Should Have Listened

April 1925
Newcastle
New Brunswick

"What did the doctor say?"

Hannah made a shushing movement of her fingers to her lips and spoke in a whisper. "He has his bad cough back. His chest doesn't sound good but the doctor said it wasn't consumption." She brought out the big cookie jar and put it in the middle of the kitchen table. "He's sleeping right now. He'll wake up shortly. You can talk to him then." She turned her back to her son and fussed around at the stove. "Would you like me to make some tea?"

Jack sat down and pulled the jar to him. "If you have some cold milk, Mother, that would be nice."

Hannah took a plate from the shelf and put it in front of Jack, who had selected five or six oatmeal cookies and was making a mess on the table.

"You never grow up, Jack." Hannah said, somewhat crossly.

Unconcerned, Jack replied, "Sorry, Mother."

Hannah poured the milk and put the bottle back in the icebox. She sat on the chair opposite, her elbows on the table and chin in her hands. She watched her son eat cookies. "I wrote to Wallace and the girls this week."

"You think they should come home?" Jack's face showed some alarm. "Is Dad that sick?"

Hannah put her hand on her son's arm. "He's not getting better." She got up and walked to the kitchen window where she had a good view of the garden. The soil had been well turned, Jack had seen to that, but Daniel had insisted they wait until he was well enough to put the peas in. The garden was developing a fine crop of weeds. "We'll have to put the peas in for him, soon."

"What does the doctor say?"

"I'm supposed to get him to eat light foods as often as he is awake. I can give him some brandy twice a day."

"That sounds good."

"Yes, but the trouble is, the doctor tells me that Danny has to sit up and walk around the room a couple of times a day."

"Is there a problem?"

"Well, you know how your father is. He knows he's sick and he wants to lie down. I want him to sit up. We argue; he starts to cough, and cough. I let him lie down and I can hear the stuff gurgling in his chest." A tear came down Hannah's cheek. She kept her face to the window. "He is sicker this morning." Hannah wiped the tear away with a quick brush of her hand. She came back to the table. "I wanted the doctor to take him to the hospital but the doctor says Daniel is getting the best of care here."

There were coughing sounds coming from the bedroom.

Jack made a move to go up the stairs.

Hannah put a restraining hand on his shoulder. "He will stop in a moment. He will go back to sleep."

The coughing stopped.

"I got a letter from a cousin. The letter was postmarked New York."

"Which cousin?"

"Joe Smallwood."

"What was Joe doing in New York?"

"No, no, Mother. Not our cousin Joe. We have another cousin, Joe Smallwood, who says he's going to live in Newfoundland. He wants to meet me in Halifax . . . Says he has a business proposition for me."

"Where does he come from?"

"W.F. had a brother, David. This Joe Smallwood is one of David's grandsons, just like I'm one of W.F.'s grandsons."

"Well?"

·"I wrote him that Cousin Joe was the businessman in the family and gave him Joe's address in Halifax."

"Do you think Joe will mind?"

The coughing started again.

They both looked toward the staircase but Jack went on talking. "No, Joe won't mind. He'll probably find it interesting that he has a cousin named Joe Smallwood."

The coughing got deeper. The time between breaths got longer and longer.

Jack ran for the stairs, followed by Hannah.

When Jack burst into the room, Daniel was lying flat on his back being racked by deep, hard coughs. There was phlegm on his chin and down the front of his nightshirt. Daniel's eyes were closed. His mouth was open and Jack could see more of the disgusting slime in his mouth.

Jack put his arm around his father's shoulders to help him sit up.

Another, deeper spasm of coughing started and Daniel's body stiffened, forcing his head and shoulders back on the pillow, allowing the phlegm to gather in the back of his throat.

Daniel held his father, trying, without success, to help him sit up. "He's going to choke to death!" The phlegm now filled his father's mouth—thick and green.

Hannah reached into Daniel's gaping mouth and grasped the phlegm as best she could and pulled. Most of it came away in one long trailing piece like a green rope. Daniel began breathing again.

With Jack's help, Daniel sat up. He opened his eyes. His face was red. The rasping noise he made as he breathed filled the room. He held Hannah's hand. She could see fear in his eyes— perhaps not fear, perhaps concern.

"Jack. Go as quick as you can and get the doctor. He was going to the Milne's. Said he would drop in on his way back. He'll be at the Milne's." As Jack moved out, Hannah slipped in to provide support to keep Daniel sitting up.

"Milnes'. I'll be right back, Mother."

Hannah sat holding her man in her arms.

Daniel patted Hannah's hand and then stroked it lightly. "I wish . . ."

"Sh-h-h-h, darling. Jack will have the doctor here in a few minutes."

They could hear Jack as he ran across the veranda.

"That's Jack. He'll be right back. It's not far to . . ."

The terrible coughing started.

Meanwhile, at the front of the house, Jack was running across the lawn to the car, trying to ignore the terrible retching, gasping sounds as his father fought for his every breath. As he reached the car, the noises stopped.

He opened the car door.

The screams were heart-wrenching.

"Dannie! Da-n-n-n-i-e-e-e!!"

Jack Smallwood slammed the car door and hastily started the car. He drove like the furies the short distance to the Milnes'.

At the Milne house, the doctor was in the driveway putting his bag under the seat of his carriage. He turned and watched the approaching vehicle while quieting his horse.

Jack drove up the lane at breakneck speed. "Hurry, doc! Jump in! My father needs you!"

Doctor Johnson, not a young man, was surprisingly agile as he grabbed his bag and hopped into the front seat of Jack's car.

It was merely ten minutes since Jack had left when he was back again, running up the lawn to the house with Doctor Johnson puffing behind.

"Mother! We're here!"

They burst into the house and up the stairs. Once in the bedroom, they could see where Hannah had taken the time to clean up her man. The pillow was fluffed and the sheets neatly tucked under Daniel's arms. With his eyes closed and hands folded on his chest, he looked very much at peace.

"I'm sorry, Jack." Hannah was holding back her tears. "He choked so hard, I think his heart must have stopped." She put her arms around her son. "Let's leave him for the doctor to check but I don't think there's anything can be done for him now."

They left the room.

Doctor Johnson closed the door.

Jack was trying not to cry. "It was the coal dust!"

"Yes, Jack, I think it was."

"Duke used to kid him about not using enough injector water to keep the dust from swirling around in the open cab." Jack was crying. "I don't think I told him I loved him."

"He knew, son."

The collapse of the financial markets in 1928 was not immediately felt in the Maritimes. People went on working, dreaming, and making plans, not realizing the economic death that was creeping onto the land.

Jack Smallwood returned to Moncton where he worked as a staff officer of the International Brotherhood of Electrical Workers. Well thought of and successful, he bought a car and seriously thought of driving to California where the livin' was easy. His planning for the trip was interrupted by the death of Hannah, his mother, in 1931. Grieving sorely at his loss, he thought nothing of buying a large gravestone and paying cash for the perpetual care of his parents' Miramichi Cemetery gravesite. He continued to work for the IBEW at Newcastle. Unfortunately, the union was not immune to the financial disruptions during the decade that was to be called "the dirty thirties." When it came time for lay-offs, the union rule "last in, first out" put Jack out of a job and on the dole.

Joe and Gladys Smallwood had made a success of their first grocery store and invested in a second store two doors down from Cornwallis Street on trendy Gottingen Street. They had spent a great deal of money on the shiny refrigerated display cases, telephones for delivery orders, and electric cash registers. Gladys had expressed her concern about borrowing money to equip the store so lavishly, but Joe's response was "As long as people have to eat, we'll make money."

Joey and Clara Smallwood had three children: Ramsay, William, and a daughter, Clara. When times were bad, Clara took the children to Carbonear where she could have the support of her relatives. Times were often bad. Joey was editor of a series of failed businesses: the *Labour Outlook,* the *Globe,* and the *Humber Herald.*

And who has the last word?

May 1931
Halifax
Nova Scotia

The fancy black car pulled over to the side of the street and parked under the trees. The driver, after checking an address book, got out. He was wearing a dark suit and black hat and carried a briefcase. He assumed a rather serious look on his face, adjusted his light grey tie and then crossed the street to where two young girls were playing on the front veranda of a large, bungalow-style home.

"Excuse me, young ladies. This is 159 Oxford Street? The residence of Mister Joseph Smallwood?"

One of the two girls—the one with the tanned skin, brown hair, and flashing brown eyes—said that it was. He learned later that her name was Crystal.

The man started up the steps.

"I wouldn't do that, Mister. Daddy told us to play on the veranda and to make sure he wasn't disturbed." She grinned at the second girl and asked, "Isn't that right, Jean?" Without waiting for a response from the auburn-haired girl with freckles and hazel eyes, Crystal added, "And when our Daddy says . . ."

"Perhaps that is so, little Miss, but I'm sure he will want to speak with me." He took another step.

Both girls came down the steps and blocked his way.

"Really, now, girls! I have business with Mister Smallwood, very important business." *This is not going well; I don't need any trouble.* With a pleading note entering his voice he asked, "What could your father possibly be doing that would be more important than receiving some news from England."

The girls didn't budge. The older girl, the one with the mischief in her eyes, giggled.

Jean Smallwood, sensing that her sister was getting ready to set up some scheme or other, became apprehensive. "Maybe we should tell Mother and Dad." Jean was thinking that they should give their father some sort of warning that they would be going back into the house. When Crystal did things without permission, they both got into hot water.

"Yeah!" Crystal was just bouncing with devilment. "Yeah! What could they be doing that is more important than hearing from the King?" She turned and went into the house.

The man was uneasy. "I didn't say that I had something from the King."

Jean looked at the man, almost eye to eye since he was two steps below her, "It had better be from somebody important!" She turned around as she heard the creak from the hardwood floor at the entrance to their parents' bedroom. Jean tried to look down the darkened hall as the door to the main bedroom squeaked open.

"Mommy!" Crystal's voice was very theatrical. "What is Daddy doing on top of you, Mommy?"

A male voice—Jean knew it to be Daddy's voice—said, "Oh, Christ!"

Then Mother's. "Joe. You don't have to swear in front of the child!"

"She's no goddamn child!"

"Joe! That's quite enough."

The floor creaked again as Crystal backed out into the hall. "There's a man with a message from the King."

Jean had moved to the open front door and could see Crystal's face—angelic.

Gladys Smallwood, not knowing quite what to believe but being the lady no matter what the circumstance, said, "Ask him into the front room, Crystal. Make him comfortable. Your father will be there shortly."

Crystal started down the hall.

"Please close the bedroom door, Crystal," Gladys called out.

Crystal hurried back and reached in to grasp the doorknob. She was suddenly face to face with her father. He was naked. Joe Smallwood tried to shield himself from his daughter's gaze by holding his shirt in front of his body.

The twelve-year-old dropped her eyes and closed the door. As she went up the hall, she could hear the mirth in her mother's voice. "You were wondering how much she knew . . ."

Joe entered the front room. "I'm Joe Smallwood." Always direct, he said, "You look like a lawyer."

"Yes, I am. I have been engaged by a law firm . . ."

"Excuse me." Joe raised his hand to stop the man from going any further. "Jean and Crystal. Outside to play. Don't leave the veranda."

The girls got up. They both curtsied to the stranger and went out the front door.

When the front door had closed, Joe returned his attention to the lawyer. "I can't imagine how many more lawyers are going to get involved in the closing of my stores. I gave my customer accounts ledgers to Breckenridge, Henning and Demone. What more do you want?"

Gladys entered the room dressed in a dark blue housecoat. "Please excuse my attire."

The lawyer stood up. "I am terribly sorry, Ma'am." The lawyer did have an embarrassed look about him. "I would have telephoned for an appointment but . . ."

"Yes. Our telephone is . . . out of service." Gladys raised her hand to pat her hair into place. "We had it disconnected at the beginning of the month." She indicated for the men to sit. "I could bring you some tea, if you like."

"No, thank you, Ma'am." He sat on the edge of the sofa. "Like I was telling Mister Smallwood, I have been hired by a law firm in London, England . . ."

Gladys gave him a huge smile. "So, it wasn't one of Crystal's little stories."

The lawyer returned the smile. It was hard not to smile when speaking with Gladys Smallwood; she was so gracious. "Well, it isn't from the King of England, but I do have some information that concerns you."

Gladys sat in the wingback chair facing the sofa while Joe pulled the bench away from the piano and positioned it opposite the lawyer. He sat down, leaning forward with his elbows on his thighs.

"I'm Gordon Jamieson and I have been tracing the heirs to an estate at Handsworth, which is in England, near Nottingham."[1]

Both of the Smallwoods remained silent to let the man get on with his story.

Mr. Johnson opened his briefcase and spread some papers out on the sofa next to him. "In documents dating from 1532 and again in 1671, it was agreed and directed that the property associated with the estate known as 'Oakwood' should pass to the nearest male Smallwood upon the death of the Master of Oakwood. Joseph Smallwood, nineteenth Master of Oakwood, died in January 1930 leaving no male heir. There are no male Smallwoods left in England." Looking up from his papers Mr. Jamieson asked the couple, "Would you tell me what you know about your family tree?"

Joe glanced over at Gladys. "We might be able to save the stores. Wouldn't it be great if we got some money . . . ?"

"Excuse me, Mister Smallwood. Based on the information that I have already collected, I don't think you are in line for the inheritance. My visit today is merely one of confirmation of my research. I want to make sure that I leave no stone unturned, so to speak."

"Too good to be true, then." Joe smiled at his wife. He looked back at the lawyer and began the Smallwood family story—as well as he knew it.

"I am the only child of William Frederick and Jean Smallwood of Newcastle, New Brunswick. He died three months ago. My mother continues to live in Newcastle in the care of a personal nurse."

"You have my regrets about your father."

"Thank you." Joe got up from the piano bench, saying, "I think I'll join you on the sofa." He sat next to the lawyer's papers. "At least my father died happy. He was the Tory Party organizer for the eastern counties of New Brunswick. He was electioneering when he had his heart attack. 'Those Goddamn Grits' were his last words." Joe smiled at the thought. "Yes, he died happy, in the middle of a political fight." Joe picked up one of the lawyer's charts. "You have us all here." He read it a bit. "You even have my father's date of death."

The lawyer nodded his head. "Your father was the fifth child of William Frederick and Carolyn Prescott Smallwood of Rexton, New Brunswick."

The lawyer consulted his sheet. "The Rexton William Frederick was the son of John and Violet Smallwood. John, the second son of Joseph Smallwood, Master of Oakwood, came from England to Prince Edward Island to reclaim Smallwood lands from Indian and Acadian squatters in the 1840s."

"I didn't know about some of that," Joe said.

"From there, back to 1671 we have the estate 'Oakwood' being passed from eldest son to eldest son." Mister Johnson put the papers down. "It was in 1671 that an agreement was reached to allow the then eldest son, a James Smallwood, to seek his fortune in the British Province of Maryland. The 1671 document endorsed the principle of male inheritance."

"What does all that mean?"

"The English line has no males. Therefore, the descent should be through John who came to Prince Edward Island, through the Rexton William Frederick, to Silas Smallwood."

"That's my Uncle Silas." Joe leaned back in the sofa. "But Uncle Silas is dead and he had no male heirs. So, Uncle Leonard . . . but he's gone too. He had two sons, both still living. Charlie is the eldest."

"Yes. At least, that's the way I had it plotted until last week. Unfortunately for your cousin Charles, an English Court has given validity to the 1521 document which originally specified the entailment of the property, so there is another branch of the family that must be considered. The first Maryland Smallwood, James, had an uncle who remained in England but did not participate in the estate at any time.

Descendants of this uncle migrated to Virginia in the 1890s. We have found one male descendant and, following my report, he will inherit Oakwood."

The lawyer packed up his case. He stood up and shook hands with the couple. "I'm frightfully sorry to have disturbed you," he said, "but I needed to meet with all branches of the family to avoid any error." He stopped. "Oh, I almost forgot." He dug in his case and brought out a picture. "This is your family crest. Your son can pass it along to his children."

"We don't have a son," the Smallwoods answered in unison.

Joe shook Mister Jamieson's hand and opened the door, letting him out onto the veranda. "It was nice of you to check with us and we thank you for the picture."

The lawyer walked across the veranda and down the steps. "Good day, ladies," he said to the girls in passing.

"Good day, Mister Jamieson."

It wasn't until he was at the car that Mister Jamieson realized that those children had overheard the conversation in the front room. *They don't miss much,* he thought.

"What a pair," he said out loud. *Too bad there's nothing left for them.* He had read in the newspapers that the bad economic years the country was experiencing were going to be called 'The Great Depression.' *Hard times for the businessman.* "But good for the lawyers," he said with a smile.

He pushed the starter with his foot. Surprisingly, the car didn't catch the first time. "I'll have to speak to the mechanic and tell him if he doesn't do a better job, I'll take my business elsewhere." He nodded his head as he thought, *there are a lot of good mechanics looking for work.* "Perhaps I'll take my business elsewhere anyway."

The girls waved from the front door and then went inside but they were gone before Jamieson thought to wave back. He sat there for a moment or two, giving the automobile the opportunity to change its mind about not starting, enjoying the sun streaming through the windshield. Glancing down at his briefcase, he recalled the day the senior partner had handed him the file. *"Sorry tale, that," the senior partner had said. "Yes indeed . . .*

. . . yes indeed, a sorry, sorry tale." The senior partner sighed before continuing. "A great family—well placed in English society—and now there's no one left to carry on. After generations of Joseph Smallwoods . . . each in his turn Master of Oakwood, friend of the royal family, member of the King's party, and always a stalwart supporter of imperial interests . . ." He shook his head. "But now, there's no one left. The last Joseph Smallwood was laid to rest several months back."

"The line has died out?" Jamieson had asked.

"There was a James's line, but it died out after the American Revolution. It appears there are some Canadians who might inherit the estate but . . ."

"Times change, sir," Jamieson remembered saying. "The British Empire will endure."

Yes, the British Empire is a monument to the fine English families who helped change the world. Mister Jamieson removed his hat and used a handkerchief to wipe the wet from the sweatband. He put the hat back on.

Too bad the descendants of James Smallwood were traitors to their English heritage. The American Revolution would have ended at the Battle of Brooklyn Heights if a Smallwood had maintained his proper loyalty to the English Crown—if Smallwood's Rifles hadn't been there to hold the rebel line. He adjusted his hat. As he reached for the automobile's choke button he had another thought. *If I were an American, I would probably say that the United States is a monument to such a fine English family.*

He adjusted the choke and pushed the starter, feeling a sense of satisfaction when the engine caught. He glanced at the house to see if anyone had taken notice. *No.*

On the other hand, I would have to say that John Smallwood's descendants didn't amount to much: a shipbuilder, smuggler, politician, trainmen, farmer, storekeeper . . . and what did they accomplish? Certainly they have no grand monuments, no historic achievements; well, what else could you expect from ill-educated, rustic Canadians living from pay packet to pay packet . . .

The automobile stalled.

"These are going to be hard economic times for a mechanic I know," Mister Jamieson griped as he pushed harder and harder on the starter. He looked sidewise at the house but, noting that there was no activity at the windows, continued with his thoughts. *But these Smallwoods seem to be a hardworking, well-intentioned people . . . and they do come from good English stock. No matter how tough it gets, they might be able to see it through.*

The car started.

Mister Jamieson looked over his shoulder, put the car in gear, and slipped the clutch. By the time he had pulled out into the street, his mind was already on his next case.

Endnotes

1. In real life, the meeting with the lawyer occurred later in the next decade in Dartmouth, Nova Scotia. Gladys Smallwood said he was a "lawyer-type of person through and through" so I gave him that sort of character in the story. At the meeting, the lawyer discussed dates and lineage in detail, which was of little interest to the Smallwood couple after he announced that the inheritance was going to someone in the United States.

WHAT'S IN A NAME?

It wasn't easy – growing up a Smallwood.

My father was Joe Smallwood. Everybody knew Joe Smallwood and, if they had known him long enough, they remembered that he gave up everything he owned during the "dirty thirties" to help his friends, neighbours and any unfortunates he happened to meet. He lived all his life that way. Yes, it was going to be difficult to measure up as the son of Joe Smallwood . . . particularly when they gave me the traditional family first name. I was going to be Joe Smallwood, too.

During the early years, I had three mothers: my caring, mother, Gladys: my vivacious, brilliant sister, Crystal; and my quiet, talented sister, Jean; so it didn't matter what anyone called me. Once I started going out to play on my own, I progressed from Little Joe, to Joey Junior, to Junior and Ju. Mother changed my name to Bill.

As Bill Smallwood, growing up in the town of Dartmouth, any accolade I received for track and field, music or academic achievement was met by, "Well done, Bill . . . but that's what we would expect from Joe and Gladys' boy," or "Jean and Crystal's little brother." At the time of my graduation from Dartmouth High School, I was fortunate to have several career choices. I chose the Royal Roads Military College in Victoria, British Columbia. I was going far, far away to be #3169 Cadet Bill Smallwood. The year was 1949—the year Newfoundland joined Confederation.

Some senior cadets believed that my parent sponsor, Joseph Smallwood, was the man who was destroying Newfoundland (or ruining Canada depending on their political bent). They ensured that my hazing was thorough. I wrote Premier Joey Smallwood in Newfoundland and he replied that it was nice to hear from a member of the family but making it clear that I was a cousin. I put the letter on the notice board. It stopped any undue hazing.

The next bump in my military career was from my first commanding officer in Winnipeg. He changed my name; he ordered that I was to be called Joey because he wanted to be able to say that he had a Joey Smallwood working for him. As a consequence, I was Joey Smallwood during my airforce flying career on transports and jets. One time at a crew stop in Newfoundland, we were required to use commercial accommodations. I was the only crew member who didn't have a reservation because the hotel staff knew that the Premier was away in Ottawa and wouldn't have to sleep in their lobby.

When the armed forces were integrated and my beloved Royal Canadian Airforce disappeared, I returned to Dartmouth to work as a civilian personnel officer at Dockyard. The family welcomed the happy wanderer home to Dartmouth where he became Bill again.

Now, years later I look back on it all and smile. It was fun being a Joey Smallwood. I hope my son, Joe, is having as much fun.